THE
HONEYMOON
HOTEL

Hester Browne is the author of numerous bestselling novels including *The Runaway Princess*, *The Vintage Girl* and *The Finishing Touches*. She divides her time between London and Herefordshire.

THE HONEYMOON HOTEL

Hester Browne

Quercus

First published in Great Britain in 2014 by

Quercus Editions Ltd
55 Baker Street
7th Floor, South Block
London W1U 8EW

A CIP catalogue record for this book is available
from the British Library

PB ISBN 978 1 78206 569 2
EBOOK ISBN 978 1 78206 570 8

This book is a work of fiction. Names, characters,
businesses, organizations, places and events are
either the product of the author's imagination
or are used fictitiously. Any resemblance to
actual persons, living or dead, events or
locales is entirely coincidental.

10 9 8 7 6 5 4 3 2 1

Typeset in Swift by CC Book Production
Printed and bound in Great Britain by Clays Ltd, St Ives plc

For Kathryn Taussig,
with love and thanks

PROLOGUE

I flattened myself against the marble pillar and peered round into the elegant cream-and-silver function room, making sure no one in the congregation spotted me.

They didn't, of course. They were too busy admiring the hand-tied globes of roses decorating the end chairs and reading the poems in the order of service.

I was particularly pleased about the poems, which were actually snippets of Cole Porter love songs, not the hackneyed old Winnie-the-Pooh or 'Shall I compare thee to a summer's day?' clichés. I mean, who in their right mind wants to be compared to an English summer's day? English summer days: a bit wet, famously unpredictable and prone to clouding over. Like today. It had only just stopped raining and the distinctive smell of damp morning suit and hairspray was rising mustily off the congregation.

There's nothing you can do about the weather, I reminded myself.

A few people had their heads close together, obviously chatting about something. I strained my ears to catch what they were saying, but I couldn't make anything out over the sweet bubbling of harp music – selections from *The Nutcracker Suite*

– again, unusual but classic. The smiles and quick glances of anticipation suggested that no one, so far, was making much of the fact that the wedding should have started four minutes ago.

I checked my watch, something 'borrowed' from my mum. Five minutes ago. This meant that Anthony was now at least thirty-five minutes late.

My stomach turned a slow, deliberate loop and my 'calming' breakfast of porridge and blueberries repeated on me. But what could I do now? Apart from phoning, texting, ringing the police and sending one of the bridesmaids out to check his flat . . . all of which I'd done already.

The congregation didn't seem to have noticed that there were two conspicuously empty seats at the front right-side of the church, where Anthony and Phil, the best man, should have been. To their credit, the ushers were carrying on as if nothing was amiss – but that was probably because half of them hadn't realized something *was* amiss. They weren't the most switched-on ushers I'd ever met, possibly thanks to the number of head-on tackles they'd received playing rugby with Anthony, but I was actually quite grateful for that now.

Six minutes late. A late guest scuttled in, surprised not to be late after all. Seven.

The weird thing was, although my brain was racing and popping and I could feel every one of the thirty hair pins digging into my scalp, the rest of my body felt positively sleepy. I'd been twitching randomly for the last seventy-two hours, but now my arms and legs felt as if lead weights were attached to them. I'd planned and planned and planned, but this – along with the rain – was the only eventuality I didn't have a solution for.

The harpist came to the end of the 'Dance of the Sugar Plum Fairy' and glanced across at me, her eyebrows raised.

I hesitated, then made a circling *play something else* sign.

She frowned, pushed back her long blonde hair and started again, and this time three or four of the congregation looked up, because it was now very obvious that something wasn't right.

Please let me wake up, I thought. *Or at least send on my old French teacher dressed as a walrus so I know it's a bad dream.* But at that moment Andrea, my chief bridesmaid, appeared with her mobile phone in one hand and a white handkerchief in the other. She looked as if she'd drawn the short straw. A very, very short straw.

Somewhere at the back of my mind I noted that Andrea was a trained First Aider. It was always a good idea to have one bridesmaid who could do First Aid. I'd read that somewhere.

'Rosie,' she whispered. 'I've got some bad news.'

'The caterer's broken down?' I whispered back hopefully. 'The photographer's lost the list of shots?'

'No.' She bit her lip. 'It's Ant. He's not coming.'

CHAPTER ONE

People make a lot of assumptions about wedding planners.

Either we're hopeless romantics (I'm not).

Or we're terminal singletons (I live with my boyfriend, Dominic – he's a food critic. We've been together two years).

Or we got married once ourselves and loved it so much that we decided to make an entire career out of it. (This only happens in films. Trust me, making six hundred yards of gingham bunting may be fun for your own wedding but for someone else's it's a form of prison work.)

In my professional opinion, and I've done quite a few weddings now, the secret to being the best wedding planner is this:

Never think of yourself as a wedding planner. Because that way madness lies.

My name is Rosie McDonald. I'm an Events Manager.

If you chose to get married at London's Bonneville Hotel, located down a discreet side street off Piccadilly, you'd be following in the glittering footsteps of film stars, European royals, writers, politicians and wits, all of whom had passed through the polished brass revolving doors over the years, usually in dark glasses. You could have your ceremony in our airy Palm Court, or in the pale green and gold Tea Salon, or, as most winter brides did, by a roaring fire in the oak-panelled Reading Room. But nearly all our summer weddings, however, took place in the walled garden.

I loved every elegant Art Deco inch of the Bonneville, and had done ever since I'd tucked in the hospital corners on my first bed as a temporary chambermaid during the school holidays, but the rose garden had a special magic. Even without the bridal arch of jasmine and honeysuckle set up by the marble fountain, and the rows of gold chairs arranged on the lawn, the shady green courtyard summed up the discreet glamour that infused the whole hotel like the heady scent of white flowers and beeswax polish. It was secret, unexpectedly romantic. A quiet spot in the middle of London that you felt only you knew about. Well, you, and the Aga Khan, Richard Burton and some elderly Duchesses from countries that no longer existed.

On the other side of the ivy-covered wall was the wide open space of Green Park, bustling with tourists and office workers, but on our side, beyond the French windows of the black-and-white tiled lobby, was a peaceful oasis, drifting with fat pink tea roses and banks of lavender: a perfect setting in which to sip Darjeeling tea or read a film script or, as Clementine Wright was doing at 3 p.m. today, marry the stockbroker of your dreams.

Guests in morning dress and tiny hats had already begun to wander through the hotel lobby for the biggest and most important event I'd managed in the five years I'd been in charge of weddings. Jason's mother was an MP, Clementine's father was a rear admiral, and the Wright-Atkinson table plan had taken more strategic planning than a G8 summit, given the hordes of cousins on Clementine's side. Bonneville weddings were intimate and chic, on account of the limited space, and in order to keep the numbers manageable we'd had, with regret, to restrict Clemmie's guest list to adults only. This didn't go down well in certain quarters, but as I told Clemmie, who sat nervously shredding tissues in my office while I fielded tricky phone calls from one or two parents, emotional blackmail and threats were water off a duck's back to me. For me, child-free weddings were a simple catering/logistics issue, not the Christmas-card-list-deleting family nightmare they could be for the poor bride.

Don't get me wrong. It wasn't that I didn't care about making Clemmie's wedding everything she'd dreamed of; I did. I just couldn't do my job if I cried as much as my brides tended to.

With those guest-list issues in mind, I'd added an extra check to my all-important list so I could cast a discreet eye over the arrivals. In my experience, the more posh the wedding, the more outrageous the liberties taken with invitations, dress codes and so on.

The lobby was filled with the sound of Vivaldi's *Four Seasons* and the scent of calla lilies, as I smiled a warm welcome to the guests and directed them towards the French windows. I was wearing a vintage-style green suit with a nipped-in jacket to flatter my waist, which was my best feature, and a skirt that covered my knees, which definitely weren't. This was my favourite wedding outfit; it was important to look stylish, but not to be mistaken for a guest, hence the *slightly* office-y floral blouse, plus my shoes were on the sensible side, and I wasn't wearing a hat. I couldn't wear a hat anyway. I had the kind of unstyle-able short brown hair that millinery tended to slide off, as if in an attempt to get away, but I *was* wearing a floral fascinator – which had the advantage of concealing a tiny headpiece, through which the rest of the events staff could relay any fires that needed putting out. (Not literally, of course. Although you could never be sure with best men.)

It was twenty-five minutes to wedding march, a critical moment in any wedding timetable. I stepped back into an alcove so I could check my lists. My whole life was comprised of lists; I even had a list of lists to ensure I was carrying the right ones.

Bride: Clemmie had been in the bridal suite overnight, with her two **bridesmaids** and her **mother**. *Tick.*

Ushers: I'd counted all **eight** men (mostly called Josh and Hugo), **outfits** and **buttonholes** correct. *Tick tick tick.*

Best man: **Ring** in pocket; **speech** vetted; **going-away car** outside; **keys** for going-away car safely in *my* pocket.

Groom: Most important of all, Jason was in the building. I never relaxed properly until I'd seen the groom arrive, established that he was happy, and then put him somewhere safe. Jason was currently parked in the anteroom off the Palm Court, with a glass of brandy and the best man. He couldn't leave there without at least two champagne waiters noticing.

Not that I would ever *prevent* a groom from changing his

mind at the last minute, but I wanted to know about it before it happened. Ditto the bride. Damage limitation was another major part of my role and – touch wood – so far every wedding I'd planned had actually gone ahead.

Jan, the local registrar, and her deputy were due to arrive at 2.40 p.m., and I was making my way to the reception area to meet them when I was accosted by a ball of energy surging at high speed towards me, almost bursting out of its tight pink cardigan.

It was Gemma, my assistant.

'Gemma, what have I said about running before a wedding?' I reminded her, under my breath. '*It spooks the guests.*'

'Sorry, Rosie.' Gemma's round brown eyes darted from one side to the other beneath her jet-black fringe as if she was being followed by a giant rolling rock or similar. I didn't take her behaviour as an immediate sign of disaster; Gemma tended towards the dramatic, which was why, in addition to being my events assistant and the PA to Laurence Bentley Douglas, my boss and the hotel owner, she actively enjoyed doing extra shifts on reception, where most of the gossip originated.

'Emergency upstairs,' she hissed out of the corner of her mouth.

'A real emergency?' I asked with a fixed smile, as a grey-haired man sporting a lot of naval medals sailed past. 'Or just wobbles?'

'Meltdown. Code red.'

I stopped in my tracks. I hadn't had easy-going interior decorator Clemmie down for a potential meltdown.

'I see,' I said, removing a less-than-clean glass from a tray of champagne flutes going past. 'Well, let's go and mop it up.'

Inside the bridal suite, a luxurious set of interconnected rooms decorated in delicate lilacs and creams where some riotous parties had apparently taken place during the hotel's heyday during the Blitz, final preparations should have been in full swing.

Only they weren't. Everyone was on their mobile phones, which was against my normal rules. Nothing ruined the special pre-wedding atmosphere for the bridal party like guests pestering bridesmaids for directions or texting photos of their outfits to check they weren't clashing.

Clementine was sniffing and texting frantically in front of the huge circular mirror of the dressing table while the make-up artist dabbed at her mascara and the photographer took 'reportage' shots of the bride's mother, Linda, sipping champagne and trying to look serene at the same time as holding in her stomach.

'Hello, ladies!' I said with a bright smile. 'You all look beautiful! Clemmie, I hope those are happy tears?'

Clementine's bridesmaids, Hannah and Meg, stopped their own texting and looked relieved to see me.

'I can't believe what's just happened!' Clementine wailed without taking her eyes from her phone. 'I *knew* something had to go wrong!'

'Everything's fine downstairs,' I reassured her. 'If this is about the ushers, they're all here and before you ask, yes, they've all had a shave. I sent a barber up to their rooms this morning, just in case Jason had forgotten to arrange it.' I didn't let grooms 'forget' anything as important as a proper shave.

'Did you?' Clemmie looked momentarily pleased, then the anxious crease returned to her forehead. The make-up artist tried to powder over it.

'Rosie, there's a major guest problem,' said Hannah, the more anxious of the two bridesmaids.

Meg's fixed grin widened. 'Don't say *problem*.'

'Of course it's not a problem,' I assured her. 'There's nothing I can't fix, believe me, I've seen it all before.'

'I'm not sure you can fix this.' Clemmie started to chew her lip, remembered her perfect lipstick and clenched her fists instead. 'You remember my cousin in Cirencester? Katherine?'

I did. That had been a *long* phone call. I'd had to make it because Clementine was terrified of Katherine, and after thirty minutes of haranguing I could see why. Katherine hadn't been happy about her daughter's lack of invitation, to put it mildly. But I had a variety of excellent explanations as to why the Bonneville preferred tot-less weddings, from insurance reasons right up to spiky floral arrangements; also, I didn't accept Katherine's furious insistence that not inviting Maisie was a contravention of her human rights, or that Clementine was being a selfish Bridezilla. *Bridezilla* wasn't a word in my vocabulary.

'Of course I do,' I said.

'Well, she's here.' Clementine swallowed.

'Wonderful!' I patted her on the shoulder and surreptitiously checked my watch. 'I knew all those threats about boycotting the wedding were just blackmail. That makes a full row of your cousins, and—'

'No, I mean, Maisie's here, too. Her daughter. Mum's just seen her arrive.' Clementine's forehead tightened. 'Katherine brought Maisie anyway. Even though I told her *no one's* children were coming.'

Brilliant. I rolled my eyes inwardly. There was always *one*.

'That's absolutely fine, Clementine.' I immediately began calculating contingency seating plans. Irritating, but I always allowed for three unexpected guests. 'I'll ask the catering team to set an extra place with her mother—'

'No, no, it's worse than that.' Clemmie's voice was sharpening with anxiety. '*Apparently*, Katherine's dressed Maisie in the exact same colour as the bridesmaids. That was why she was asking me all those questions about the colour scheme! It wasn't so she could coordinate her own outfit at all! It was so she could put Maisie in my bridal party even though I told her we weren't even having my godchildren as flower girls!'

I kept my expression sympathetic but inside I was karate-chopping the rhino hide of the bold Katherine. This wasn't the first time this had happened. There was often one mother who refused to believe that 'no children' could apply to *their* gorgeous cherubs and smuggled them in anyway, brazenly attaching them to the back of the bridal procession like a limpet mine, while everyone was cooing at the action taking place at the business end.

'My cousin Joss is *already* going ballistic, look!' Clemmie brandished her phone in my face. 'I've had *weeks* of people trying to get an invite for their kids, and I said, I'm sorry but it's only fair if it's no children *at all*, and now they'll all think I made a special exception for Maisie! I mean, she's the last kid I'd have had as a bridesmaid! I thought she was a *boy* until she was four!'

'Clementine!' said her mother reproachfully.

'Tilly would have loved to have been a flower girl,' said Meg, looking distinctly unimpressed. 'And I wouldn't have had to drive to Macclesfield to leave her with Jack's mother.'

'I've *said* I'm sorry, Meg . . .'

Hannah's phone pinged and everyone stared at her.

'Um, it's from Serena,' said Hannah, awkwardly. 'She says . . .'

'I think we can guess,' I said, firmly. 'No need to read it out.'

'This is meant to be the happiest day of my life!' Clemmie spun round on the dressing-table stool. Her eyes were wild and hungry in the way only those of a woman who hasn't eaten anything white for six months can be. 'And I'm going to spend it apologizing to every single parent here!'

'I promise you won't,' I said. 'Clemmie, look at me. You're going to have a wonderful wedding. The day we've been planning. Your special day.'

Then I put a calming hand on her arm and looked right into her face, a trick my old boss Caroline had taught me years ago. It also worked on dogs.

After a tremulous second, Clemmie sniffed and managed a broken smile, and I knew what I had to do. It was just a gatecrasher issue, that was all. Any events manager worth her salt could handle a gatecrasher, even one in a pistachio satin bridesmaid's dress.

I marched briskly down the carpeted corridors I'd come to know like the back of my hand over the years, and asked myself a question that went through my head at least twice a day, more often at weddings: 'What would Caroline Bentley Douglas do now?'

Caroline, Laurence's first wife, had taught me everything I knew about organizing weddings – as well as everything about the Bonneville itself, from its fabulous reception area with gilded sunbursts and polished floors to its delicate domed skylights. Laurence sometimes joked that she was more in love with his hotel than with him, but I could understand that. The Bonneville had real personality, that of an old-fashioned London debutante: elegant, well-connected, sometimes a bit naughty – but always discreet. That discretion had been its calling card in the pell-mell years between the wars; The Ritz or Claridge's might have had endless flashbulbs popping outside, but love-struck stars who *didn't* want to be photographed checked into the Bonneville's suites for their secret London trysts. Caroline had regaled me with all the stories when I was a young vacation chambermaid, and then seeing my enthusiasm for the place, she'd taken me under her wing, encouraging me to study hospitality management at college. When I graduated, I walked straight into a job as her assistant, and that was when I really started learning about the hotel trade.

Nearly ten years on, I was in charge of the super-traditional wedding packages Caroline had dreamed up as part of her mission to keep the struggling hotel afloat. She was still mentoring me, but it wasn't over black coffee in her office any more. Caroline had bought her own hotel in Oxfordshire, after she finally got tired of Laurence's charming but chaotic stewardship of his family's business, and divorced him.

These days, I had to rely on Laurence for on-the-spot advice, such as it was. I liked Laurence very much, but I couldn't blame Caroline for throwing in the towel. She was the sort of boss who got down on her knees to check under beds and ran her finger along picture rails; Laurence, on the other hand, claimed to be allergic to dust. As well as chlorine, Dettol, stress, wheat, and certain types of paper. Working for him could be frustrating, particularly now that his short-lived second wife (and former receptionist) Ellie had left too, and the wifely duties of diary management and general organization had fallen to me and Gemma. But Laurence's redeeming feature – one that was quite useful on a day like today – was a knack with the guests that was something to behold. He was a natural host. A ringmaster of his own hotel, as you'd expect from someone actually born in Room 32, during a dinner-dance for one of London's most prestigious estate agencies.

As I made my way back downstairs to the wedding party in search of the interlopers, I kept an eye out for Laurence's lanky frame amongst the morning suits and floral dresses. He loved our hotel weddings – in the sense that he liked to shimmer in once everything was organized and dispense brandies to the gentlemen and compliments to the ladies – and I was very keen for him to see me at the epicentre of a well-organized and profitable event. The last general manager, Paul, had finally succumbed to the 'pressures of the role' and had checked himself into rehab at The Priory; I wanted Laurence to consider me for the job. Okay, so I was younger than most general managers, at just thirty, but I knew this hotel inside out and, more to the point, I was absolutely passionate about restoring that gleam and glamour it had once enjoyed. I wanted to hear it talked about again in smart circles; I wanted to see the hotel bar filled with attractive couples and witty chat. I wanted to see the Bonneville sparkle again.

Laurence wasn't in reception, and neither were Katherine and Maisie. I wove my way expertly between guests until my antennae twitched – there they were, lurking near the globe-shaped box trees by the side of the garden, almost out of sight: a blonde in a tight floral sheath dress and, next to her, a miserable five-year-old in a pale pistachio satin frock that pinched her plump arms.

I had no intention of telling Clemmie, but several couples *were* giving Katherine pointed glares and muttering darkly. Still, it wouldn't take a moment to sort this out.

I went over, a friendly smile on my face. 'Excuse me, is it Katherine?'

'Yes?' She looked guilty but defiant, and pulled Maisie towards her.

'Wonderful! I wonder if I could take you and your beautiful daughter to a special seat?'

'Why?'

'Because for insurance reasons we can't allow anyone under

the age of eleven to be within twenty metres of the fountain.'
I gestured towards the tumbling water feature and started to
guide them both towards the last row of chairs. They moved
without even knowing they were being directed.

Over the years, I'd developed the art of leading people from
one place to another without them realizing they were being
shepherded; Caroline had taught me as part of my gatecrash-
er-removal arsenal. It was part stage hypnotism, part lifting.

'Maisie needs access to the bridal party.' Katherine looked
at me boldly.

I gave her my very politest *really?* smile and said nothing. We
both knew she was bluffing.

'And . . . I need to be able to see,' she faltered.

'Of course! We've arranged the chairs so everyone gets a great
view,' I assured her. 'Maisie, you look a bit hot, darling. Would
you like me to find you a glass of orange juice?'

'No! What if she spills it on her bridesm– . . . on her dress?'

'I'm sure you won't,' I said, holding out my hand to Maisie.
The poor thing looked about as thrilled to be crammed into a
green satin dress as Clementine had been to find out she was
wearing it. 'I know where there's a special gold chair for you,' I
added, conspiratorially. It was a long way back. And afterwards,
I could think of a few fun things for Maisie to do – with Gemma,
and well out of Clementine's way.

The little girl beamed up at me, and I felt a glow of satisfaction at having solved another problem, and with fifteen minutes
still to go before the wedding.

*

Having got Katherine and Maisie safely trapped at the far end of a row of chairs, with several large relatives between Maisie and the aisle, I scooted back upstairs to make sure the photographer had taken all the reportage shots Clemmie had specified on her list, and then, when Gemma confirmed from downstairs that all the other wedding participants were in position and ready to go, I gave Clemmie a hug. Carefully, so as not to dislodge the family tiara.

'You look beautiful,' I said. 'Don't cry, please, Arthur,' I added to her father, standing next to her. His stiff upper lip was already wobbling, through pure pride. 'You'll set us all off.'

'This is perfect, Rosie.' Clemmie seemed dazed with happiness. 'This is just what I imagined.'

'Quite.' Arthur's voice was gruff with emotion. 'None of that fancy stuff you get these days. Just a nice simple wedding.'

'That's what we aim for,' I said, because it was. This was the moment when I really had to concentrate to keep my events focus; Clemmie looked so radiant and so excited. I'd done my job – nearly. 'Now, let me get the lift for you.'

I was always telling brides to stop and take in one still moment in their wedding day, and I made a point of taking a moment myself to stop and see exactly what I'd just achieved.

Today I stood just inside the rose garden and watched as Clemmie and Jason made their vows by the marble fountain. It was exactly how I'd pictured it during the planning meetings when I'd outlined the ideal Bonneville wedding to Clemmie: I aimed to create the wedding finale from a classic Golden Age

Hollywood movie, with a trademark English feel. Black and white sophistication, but with pink cherry blossom, and tea roses.

My eye travelled up from the bride and her groom, gazing at each other as Jason slipped the ring on Clemmie's finger; up to the tall windows of the hotel rising five elegant stories above them, punctuated by black wrought-iron balconies on which actresses and princes had once sipped morning coffee gazing over Green Park; and finally up to the curliest, widest balcony of all, at the top: the luxurious honeymoon suite where Clemmie and Jason would be spending their first night as husband and wife.

The honeymoon suite was at the heart of every wedding I arranged. It was magical. Just smoothing down the satin coverlet on the big bed with its scalloped headboard made me feel something of the hotel's romantic past, imagining all the passion and new beginnings that the room must have seen over the decades. It sounds a bit airy-fairy, but it wasn't only the Bonneville's stylish suites and elegant spaces that I loved, but its human history: the secrets and whispers from another, more glamorous age, caught in the fabric of every room. The cocktails, the black cabs, the cash tips, the forgotten red lipsticks, the snatched moments of pleasure in a place designed to shut out real life completely, just for a night or two. The honeymoon suite, up in the penthouse like a secluded nest far above the real world, seemed to distil everything the Bonneville stood for into one room.

A ripple of applause from the congregation brought me back

to myself with a jolt; the new Mr and Mrs Atkinson were turning to walk back down the white carpet towards their reception, and I needed to shift into the next phase of precision organization.

The sun broke through the fluffy clouds, reflecting off the soft cream exterior of the hotel, bathing the guests in a fresh, flattering light as they rose and began to make their way to the afternoon tea reception. It was in the Palm Court, where black-clad waiters were already gliding around with the porcelain cake stands and silver teapots, dispensing tiny macaroons and wielding proper tea-strainers.

Oh, brilliant, I thought. Right on cue, now all the hard work was done, Laurence had appeared by the entrance to the garden, resplendent in his blazer and red trousers, kissing the bride, shaking everyone else's hand, smiling and laughing away like the consummate hotel owner. I knew what he'd be saying even though I was too far away to hear; I could see from the dazzled expressions on their faces that he was working his magic on everyone in earshot.

Laurence seemed to be getting on particularly well with Clemmie's Auntie Priscilla, I noted. I was supposed to be keeping an eye out for potential dates for him, on Caroline's instructions; she was very keen to get Laurence paired up again, and weddings were a fertile source of appropriate mid-dle-aged women, most of whom he seemed to know already through his many years of extreme sociability. Laurence wasn't a man who coped well on his own, and like me, Caroline didn't have time to deal with his constant phone calls about the washing machine.

While I was watching Priscilla flirting outrageously with Laurence, and wondering if I should ask Clemmie for her details, or just take them straight off the guest database, my fascinator buzzed, and I pushed a stray curl out of the way to answer it. 'Gemma?'

'Rosie, someone's brought their dog with them? It's in the foyer? I don't know what to – urgh! Bad dog! No! Naughty!'

'Put it in Laurence's office,' I said, setting off, shoulders already pulled back in fire-fighting readiness. 'I'll be right there.'

I swished past the guests, the waiters, the caterers, the flower arrangements, the champagne, and although the stopwatch in my head was ticking, I couldn't stop the smile spreading across my face.

On a bright May day like this one, there wasn't a more romantic place to get married in all of London than the Bonneville Hotel. In all the world, actually. It's the only place I'd ever consider getting married, if I was in the market for a wedding, which I'm not.

As I said, it's not that I don't have a boyfriend, I do. And it's not as if I'm completely anti-marriage, because obviously I enjoy a good wedding as much as the next person. Even after my Unfortunate Wedding Experience – the 'j' word isn't in my vocabulary either. It's just that . . .

Well. Let me tell you about my boyfriend, Dominic.

CHAPTER TWO

When I told people my boyfriend was Dominic Crosby, they usually laughed and said, 'Not *the* Dominic Crosby, though?' and when I assured them that, yes, I lived in West Kensington with *the* Dominic Crosby, London Food Critic of the Year two years running and campaigner for Quiet Zones in restaurants, they laughed again, but more nervously, and then changed the subject.

I didn't know Dominic was *the* Dominic when I met him, about two years ago. He was just the short, rather intense bloke sitting next to me at a university friend's birthday meal in Clerkenwell – a birthday meal I didn't really want to go to but felt I had to attend, because if I didn't, the main topic of conversation would have been Rosie and her Big Fat Non-Wedding, and its sequel conversation, now starring Anthony's 'surprise' new girlfriend, Leona from Work. (*Still*. Nine months on, my non-wedding was the conversational gift that kept on giving. Luckily for me, not long after this particular dinner, another friend's boyfriend went to prison for payroll fraud and everyone started feeling sorry for Kate instead.)

I should have had an inkling about who the bloke sitting next to was when he insisted on sending back all ten plates of lamb tagine served to our table because the lamb 'had the stringy texture of knitting wool, spiced with the piquant addition of Mr Muscle'. But I'd missed the introductions at the start of the evening as I'd been dragged into Laurence's office on my way out to provide my confrontation-phobic boss with a strategy for handling the Brazilian chambermaid who'd eaten £150-worth of pillow chocolates in less than two weeks. I merely noted, with my customer service hat on, that the posh bloke in the red shirt had managed to convey his punchy opinions on the tagine in such a charming, if opinionated, manner that the waitress didn't empty the contents of his plate over his head.

It was my best friend, Helen, who alerted me to the fact that I'd been sitting next to the most controversial food writer in London. Helen managed the restaurant at the Bonneville and had headshots of all the major food critics lined up by the service hatch in the kitchens, arranged in Fear Order. (I rarely ventured into the kitchens; to be honest, I was a bit scared of the chef.)

As I recounted the horror of the complaining, Helen's expression swung between delight and alarm. 'Why didn't you tell me you knew Dominic Crosby?' She was normally quite inscrutable – her 'look' was basically that of a Hitchcock blonde: neat grey suits, immaculate blonde French pleat, composed demeanour – but occasionally flashes of excitement broke through the Nordic cool. 'Can you get him to review us? Although—' her brow creased, 'there's always the risk we'd end up on the "Killed by Quips" list.'

'How do you mean, "Killed by Quips"?'

'When he ignores the food and just takes potshots at everything else. It's worse when Dominic Crosby decides to be funny about somewhere. That's when you might as well just shut down.' Helen seemed surprised at my blank expression. 'You haven't read his columns? In the *London Reporter*? And in the Sunday papers? He's the Man in the Red Trousers.'

'These "Sunday papers" of which you speak? What exactly are they?' I pretended to look baffled.

She blinked, then realized I was joking. 'Not everyone sleeps through Sunday mornings, you know.'

'There's a *morning* on Sundays?'

Helen and I both worked the same insane hours at the Bonneville: ours was a friendship forged from late nights and blister plasters and oversharing brought on by too much Red Bull. She was the only person who really understood why I sometimes worked eighteen-hour days. She was the only person who could make me laugh at the end of them too, with her brutal assessments of which of our co-workers she'd like to murder first. And then how she'd get rid of the evidence.

She tapped me playfully on the knee. 'But, hey. Exciting. New man. Are you going to see him again?'

'He's not a new man. I don't think he noticed me,' I said firmly. 'He was paying more attention to the bread rolls. He said the yeast died in vain. He felt sorry for it, to the point of requiring revenge.'

'That place will be closed down in three weeks,' sighed Helen. 'Mark my words.'

But she was right, and I'd been wrong. Dominic had noticed me. I got an email the following week, asking if I'd mind coming along to review a restaurant with him; he made it sound, rather sweetly, as if I'd be doing him a favour by 'eating an extra starter and anything with a sauce because I have problems around cream.' Two days later, we were sitting at the best table in Windows on the World overlooking the lights strung like glittering diamonds across the patchwork squares of Hyde Park, and Dominic made me laugh so much I forgot to eat anything. (He didn't. He cleared his plate, then mine, apart from the bits with sauce on.)

I know it seems sudden, looking back, but it felt as if Dominic was the boyfriend I'd been waiting all my life to meet. For one thing I knew exactly what he did, unlike Anthony, who had never explained his 'actuary job' in a way I fully understood, possibly because he still secretly wanted to be an asset manager. Dominic was funny, extremely knowledgeable about the food and drinks industry, a terrible gossip, and good-looking in a way I couldn't quite put my finger on until I saw *Pirates of the Caribbean*, and realized he was one of the few men in London who could genuinely be described as 'swashbuckling'. Four months and many meals later, during which he actually listened to my thoughts about food (something Ant had hated because 'you sound like you're still at work') I'd moved my electric toothbrush into Dominic's garden flat in Kensington, which he shared with his collection of unopened review-copy cookbooks and an unused exercise bike.

We'd been living together for two years now, and I'd progressed to a chest of drawers of clothes and a shelf of the bathroom cabinet not taken up by indigestion remedies. Ours wasn't a traditional relationship, given our weird working hours meant we didn't spend much 'supermarket and DIY' time together, but Dominic had put my coffee choices on his Nespresso coffee pod delivery reorder, and I'd made a list of all his family birthdays and anniversaries so he could send cards before his mother told him to. We had the same taste in Chilean wine and American comedy shows, and neither made the other feel bad about late working nights or long lie-ins. And we made each other laugh. What more could you ask? as I often said to Helen.

All in all, I felt that Dominic and I were ready to take the next step and make things official. Not by getting married – Dominic thought weddings were just an excuse for couples to go on a shopping dash round the homewares departments of John Lewis, and I wasn't in a hurry to do it again – but by buying somewhere together. Our own place, to relax and cook and have people over for dinner – something we'd never been able to do, because Dominic hadn't seen the point in renting a flat with an adequate kitchen when he ate out for every meal but breakfast. The lease on his flat was up just after Christmas, and we'd talked seriously about pooling our resources which were just enough to buy something small in roughly the same area. Dominic was all for it – it was, he said, a smart move in the current market. That, for me, was a sign that he saw an active future in our relationship, much more so than if he'd just drifted into proposing like Anthony had.

Besides, let's face it, a joint mortgage is for twenty-five years. And unlike a marriage, you can get insurance to cover yourself if one party decides to bail out.

On Wednesday night I pushed open the door to the newest gastropub laying itself open to Dom's razor-sharp assessment, with a sheaf of estate agents' details tucked into my bag. I'd downloaded the particulars of some flats that were more or less on the outskirts of the areas Dominic would consider living in, while being just about inside our budget. According to my notebook, this was the two hundredth meal out we'd eaten together, and it felt like an auspicious moment to start moving on to the next phase in our relationship.

The property details were tucked into my own food notebook, a leather-bound sketchpad with my initials on that Dominic had given me for Christmas. Well, not my initials, exactly. My nom-de-plume's initials. BC.

Like most food writers' partners, I featured in the column. I was Betty, short for Betty Confetti, Dominic's nickname for me on account of the weddings that dominated my working day. I almost recognized myself: Betty was a hearty eater who cracked the occasional dry joke, although Dominic had an annoying habit of attributing Betty's best dry jokes to himself in the editing of the column, something I forgave in return for all the free meals.

Tonight's gastropub was in Kensington, round the corner from our flat, a newly refurbished former spit-and-sawdust boozer called the Loom, which I thought was pretty appropriate since the fashionably rustic staff loomed over you within thirty seconds of arriving, even before you'd got your coat off.

'Ooh, nice. Like that,' said Dominic when I muttered this observation to him after the waiter showed me to the table. He was already drinking wine and laughing at his own Twitter feed. 'Mind if I . . . ?' He made a scribbling gesture.

'Feel free.' I reached for the bottle, an excellent claret from about two-thirds down the list. Helen marked it up for a lot more in the restaurant.

'Oh dear. That bad?' He lifted his head from his notes as I topped up my glass and drank deeply. 'What happened today? Aren't you still basking in the glory of the Atkinson nuptials? Didn't that put a big star on your chart, getting an MP in the house?'

'It did. But only for about an hour, until Laurence suddenly remembered that we had the auditors coming in next week, so I've spent all today prepping every department and trying to get hold of the accountant. . . .' I tried not to think about the undisguised panic on Dino the bar manager's face. 'They didn't take it very well in the bar. There'll have to be another gin amnesty.'

'And is Laurence paying you to be the unofficial hotel manager?'

'Of course not. He's barely paying me to be the events manager.'

'And he still hasn't advertised the post?'

'No. We're all sharing the stress for the foreseeable future.'

Dominic prodded at the dish of complimentary feta-stuffed

olives with the tip of his butter knife. 'I appreciate that Laurence likes to run that hotel like a sort of gentleman's hobby, but you don't have to put up with it. The way I see it, you've got three choices. You can stay and carry on being taken advantage of. You can get a better job somewhere else – which shouldn't be hard. Or you can go in there and make him take you seriously. Time for some tough talking, Rosie.'

Dominic was a firm believer in tough talking; he got his agent to do it for him all the time.

'Meaning what?'

'Meaning . . .' Dominic pointed his knife at me, then waved it around. 'Just *tell* that floppy-haired ageing lothario that he should give you the hotel manager's job. Why not? You're propping up the profits with all the events you run. Show him those spreadsheets you're always working on. Blind him with figures. You know what happens when you wave figures under Laurence's nose. He gets those little black dots in front of his eyes.'

'Well . . .'

'Well nothing.' Job done, Dominic examined the menu. 'Paul's been in that rehab place for months. The guy's not coming back and Laurence is hoping none of you'll notice. Put it to him in a way he can't refuse, Rosie – it's your great gift, bending people painlessly to your will. If you're not bossing brides around that hotel, you're nagging me about my cholesterol or taking the rest of the building to task for not keeping the communal areas free of pizza leaflets. Tell him what you want. Let him negotiate.'

'Laurence doesn't negotiate,' I said. 'Caroline used to do all that. Every time I try to ask Laurence for anything he pretends to have an angina attack.'

'So don't let him!'

The bread arrived in a bird's nest made from raffia, with the butter in the shape of an egg. It was pale yellow, and speckled prettily with black and white pepper. Dominic peered at a seeded roll, sliced it open like a surgeon, and jotted something down in his black notebook. On the other side of the room, a harassed manager suddenly slapped his forehead and started waving his arms around in our direction, and I tried to pretend I hadn't seen.

'I could ask Caroline if—' I began, but Dominic stopped me.

'There's your problem in a nutshell,' he said, stuffing some bread into his mouth. 'You're being done up like a kipper by the outrageous way Laurence pretends to run that place like one big happy family. And you're bloody Cinderella. And Caroline is just as bad . . .'

'Caroline is more like a mentor than a boss,' I began, but Dominic was on one of his favourite high horses and enjoying a good gallop.

'. . . she's got you running errands for her in London, not to mention getting you to take an unhealthy interest in your boss's love life, while he's laying a paternal guilt trip on you the whole time. He's not your dad. He's your employer. And I don't see any of his actual family slopping out the loos and peeling potatoes, do you?'

I wished I hadn't told Dom about the loo thing. It was only

once. When the cleaners were all sick. 'Well, no, but neither of his sons is in the business—'

'Both his wives were.' Dom raised a bushy eyebrow. 'That Ellie managed to negotiate herself a massive salary increase and fewer hours. Zero hours, in fact.'

I didn't want to get onto the topic of Ellie. That was a whole other kettle of fish. Gemma, who had started working in reception at the same time, couldn't even say Ellie's name without her face going into a sort of lemon-sucking spasm of repressed emotions.

'I don't want to *marry* Laurence,' I said, heavily. 'I just want him to consider me for the manager's job.'

'Then he can't treat you like a member of the family *and* an employee. Don't mistake his dependence on you for appreciation. He's taking you for granted, Rosie.'

I sighed and reached for the bread basket. As usual, Dom had gone straight to the heart of the problem, like a guilt-seeking missile. He'd had lots of therapy, and consequently felt no hesitation about telling people what they were really thinking.

I knew Laurence took people for granted. It was one of the reasons Caroline had finally had enough and left him. And he hadn't learned his lesson: he still took it for granted that she'd be prepared to sort his life out from a safe distance now.

'To be honest with you,' I said, 'I think both Caroline and Laurence are hurt that no one in the family *does* really care about the hotel. Neither Joe nor Alec ever shows any interest in the place, and it's been in the family for years.'

Dominic paused in his bread dissection. 'Which one's the hippie, and which one's the psycho?'

'Joe's the hippie.' I corrected myself: 'No, he's *not* a hippie. He's a traveller. He runs a boutique travel service in America.' I tried to remember exactly how Caroline had described it. 'Planning wilderness experiences in the desert and spiritual discovery retreats and that sort of thing.'

'He bums around arranging adventure holidays for rich kids on their gap years, so he can pretend his hasn't finished yet. How old is he?'

'Um . . .' I did some mental calculations. 'About twenty-eight?'

'Twenty-eight? I'd been writing a column for four years by then!'

'And I'd been working at the hotel on and off for nearly twelve,' I pointed out. I was thirty. Dominic was thirty-five, but when it suited him he liked to talk as if he was at least fifty-five.

'And where's the psycho?' he went on.

'If you mean Alec, he's living with Caroline in Oxfordshire. And—' I don't even know why I was bothering to add this, since random and enthusiastic loathing of people was one of Dominic's favourite hobbies, 'Alec isn't a psycho, he left the army because he'd had enough of the moving around.'

He made a delighted scoffing noise. 'That's what Caroline told you. You don't leave the army because you're tired of moving around. That's like someone packing in international football because he was bored of sports massages.'

I started to disagree, and realized I couldn't. To be honest, Alec was a bit volatile. Good-looking and very charming, like his parents, with a shock of red hair, but . . . *energetic* was probably the kindest way to describe him.

'I think Laurence should count himself lucky neither of those two idiots wants to get involved with the family business,' observed Dom. 'If I were him, I'd be working quite hard to keep them as far away as possible. You don't want your guests being ambushed in the bar, or subjected to shamanistic healing rituals in the foyer.'

I hadn't seen Alec or Joe for years, but going by the occasional asides from Caroline it was hard to imagine either of them behind the front desk. 'But it's been in the family for so long. And it's not just a hotel. Laurence loves the Bonneville. I love the Bonneville. It's . . .'

I was about to say, 'It's more than just a hotel – it's a piece of history,' but I stopped myself just as Dominic's eyes widened in warning. He didn't subscribe to my ideas about the Bonneville having its own personality. He thought Helen's poaching a decent chef for the restaurant was the key to turning the place around. But then he would.

'It's a unique hotel in London,' I said instead. 'And it has possibilities.'

Dom buttered his roll vigorously. 'Then even better. If neither of the sons is interested in his precious hotel, Laurence should be taking more care to encourage the one competent member of his staff who is,' he said. 'He should make you manager by the end of the year. And if he doesn't, you need to think about leaving and finding an employer who will recognize your talents.'

Yes, I thought, staring at the strange collection of matted

fleece stuck in gold frames on the wall behind Dom's head. (He always got the seat that faced out into the room.) I *could* do this. A pay rise, a better job title . . . I deserved it. I just had to make a list and it would happen.

And then I just had to organize three weddings a month for the next six months on top of all my other work, and talk seriously to Laurence about promotion. I wasn't sure which was the taller order.

'Rosie! Is there a problem with the bread?'

I looked down at my plate. My roll was crumbled into bits. I'd been shredding it without realizing, and now it lay in a sad heap of organic flax and nut flakes.

Dom grinned. I could almost hear the words clicking across the screen in his brain: *'The bread roll wasn't so much a bread roll as a collection of stale crumbs huddling together in the bread basket for warmth . . .'*

'Was it a bit dry?' he enquired.

I managed a smile. *'The bread was so dry that it could have hosted its own topical news quiz. Said Betty.'*

'Very good. You should have your own column. Do you want me to look into it?' Dominic's brown eyes twinkled above the dark softness of his new beard. Helen thought the new beard was a sackable offence, but I liked it. He was carrying it off surprisingly well, even if it was now a very short step in my imagination to buckled boots and a sword. We were a proper power couple, me and Dom, I thought with a tingle. Betty and Dom. The king and queen of the London restaurant scene.

'No, I don't think I can eat enough,' I said airily. 'And who would make up the jokes for *your* column? Although maybe Betty could write about cocktails somewhere?'

Helen and I could do a brilliant cocktail column . . .

'You know, I'm not sure I should be encouraging you to work even more hours than you already do,' he said, leaning forward. 'I don't see you enough as it is.' We both ignored the ominous creak from the table. Well, I did. Who knew what mental notes Dominic was making about the furniture.

'No, actually,' I said quickly, 'I think you're right. I should go for the promotion sooner rather than later. Because it would be very handy to have some extra money for a deposit, wouldn't it?'

Dominic wasn't listening. A wicked smile was spreading across his face. The one that made me think of pirates and cutlasses. I pressed on, because this was actually all fitting together nicely.

'I've been looking at flats . . .'

'Have you?' he murmured.

Out of the corner of my eye I noticed the waiter hovering by the table, beaming nervously and brandishing a notepad. 'Ready to order, guys?'

I stopped myself. Later. I didn't want to rush this conversation. I'd bring up the details over pudding. Dom was always happier over pudding.

'Do you know what you want?' he asked me, more for the waiter's benefit than mine, because we both knew what I'd be having. I had all the dishes Dom didn't like – squiddy things, vegetarian options, cream sauces, warm puddings – fortunately all the dishes I'd have picked anyway. We were a good team like that.

I glanced at the menu, which appeared to have been written in crayon by the chef during a power cut. There was a fine line between rustic and crusty when it came to gastropubs.

'I'll have the squid to start, followed by the artichoke and quail's egg risotto.'

'Great choice,' said the waiter with an obsequious nod.

'We'll be the judge of that,' muttered Dominic. 'And I'll have the potted shrimps, and the rabbit rillettes, followed by the steak and kidney pudding, and the skate. And can we have some, ah, spinach, please. And whatever squeezed potatoes might be. I'll just have mine affectionately cuddled, if that's all right.'

The waiter glanced over his shoulder at the manager and the chef, both of whom were standing by the door to the kitchen. They waved their arms at him, saw me looking, and pretended they were examining a light fitting.

'So,' said Dom when the waiter was gone, leaning forward again and giving me a tantalizing waft of his aftershave, 'what does Betty think about the décor? Has it all been stolen from a barn in Wiltshire, do you reckon? Or an abandoned Victorian school?'

I looked down, trying not to smile. Even after two hundred dinners, the novelty of being part of Dom's weekly column hadn't worn off. Moments like this made me almost glad things hadn't worked out with Anthony. With Dominic, I felt as if I was a proper grown-up, with an exciting social life, right in the heart of where everything was happening in London.

We discussed the décor for a bit, the food arrived, we ate it and joked about the reclaimed plates; then over coffee, I seized the moment and got the flat details out of my bag.

'I know we haven't got a proper budget yet,' I said, pushing the printouts across the table, 'but I thought it'd be a good idea to start working out what areas we could live in. I've found some that I think you might like . . .'

'Where are they? Because you know I've got to be central for work.' Dominic eyed the papers warily. 'And near somewhere that sells decent bread. And at least four Tube stops away from any hipsters wearing cardigans.'

'We can't afford to live near hipsters. You're safe there.'

'Pass me your A to Z.' I had an old-fashioned A–Z for flat-hunting purposes. Dominic took a water glass, opened the A–Z on the Kensington page, squinted, put the glass down and drew a circle round it, then passed the map back. 'There. Within that should be fine.'

I looked at it. 'Sorry, have you had a three hundred per cent pay rise and not mentioned it?'

He picked up his espresso cup. 'You want me to make a smaller circle?'

This was why I wanted to start looking early, before the lease ran out. It was going to take a few months before Dominic came to terms with what we could actually afford to buy.

'If we go for a one-bedroom rather than—'

'Got to be two,' Dominic started, but then his phone rang in his pocket. He ignored it for a few seconds, which I found flattering; then he pulled it out of his pocket, winced, and put it back.

'Who was that?' I asked.

'Oh, just Jacob.'

'Jacob . . . from the office?' I hadn't met many of Dominic's work friends. They all kept strange hours and, according to Dominic, were best left at work because 'writers are only amusing on email, not in real life when they can't edit themselves.'

'Yeah, he's at some bar down the road.' He studied a printout. 'Is this legally a flat? Are you sure it's not a cupboard?'

'If Jacob's just down the road, tell him to come here and join us for a drink,' I suggested. 'I'd like to meet Jacob. Is he the music writer?'

Dominic pulled a face. 'No. He writes about wine. Good reason not to bring him here. Anyway, didn't you want to talk about these flats?'

I gave Dominic a look, but decided not to say anything. When we had a place of our own, I was going to throw the most amazing soirées. Writers, chefs, restaurateurs, his friends, my friends . . . it would be a salon. A foodie salon. I ignored the fact that I'd be working God knows how many hours a day to pay the mortgage.

'This one's got a brilliant kitchen,' I said with a confident smile, and slid the paper over the table towards the man already wearing a velvet smoking jacket in my head.

CHAPTER THREE

For the rest of the week, when I wasn't on the phone to brides or running round the hotel setting up client meetings and cake tastings, I thought about various ways to bring up the topic of the manager's job with Laurence. It wasn't that I didn't want to ask him, but I knew I had one chance to get it right. Laurence was so adept at wriggling out of conversations he didn't want to have that he could change the subject before you'd even finished outlining it.

I thought about the best tactics all through that weekend's wedding – a small but no-expense-spared second marriage of a hedge fund manager and his childhood sweetheart, now a successful interior designer – and by the time I headed towards the conference room for the weekly Monday morning management meeting, I'd more or less decided that my best bet was just to spring it on him.

We had a quick meeting every morning in Laurence's office, but Monday was the formal one where the weekend's cock-ups were dragged out from under the carpet, if they hadn't been swept there firmly enough, and for that, everyone needed to sit down. Some of the things that could go wrong at the weekend in even a smallish London hotel would make your hair curl.

Gemma usually took the minutes, but when I pushed open the meeting room door, decorated with brass sunburst reliefs to match the exuberant Deco mirrors that lined the corridor, she was already hopping from foot to foot as if she needed to be somewhere else. Possibly the loo.

'Brilliant, you're here,' she said in a rush before I could speak. 'Laurence says can you take minutes for the meeting, because I've got to get his prescription?'

'His what?' That was typical of Laurence's management style. Zero concern for the staff meeting, yet a move bordering on genius to ask Gemma to run his errand before the weekly round-up, her favourite source of fresh gossip, thus ensuring the prescription gathering would be done at full speed, so as not to miss any juicy details.

'His magnesium and iron are at a dangerous level, he says. Won't be long. Thanks, Rosie,' said Gemma, shoving her notebook and pen at me, and dashing out.

I sat down next to the plate of Danish pastries, freshly baked by our French pâtisserie chef, Delphine, and opened the notebook to a new page. I looked round to see who was here, and started to scan her notes from last week, while jotting down today's attendees.

Taking minutes was one of the first jobs Caroline had given me when I came back to the Bonneville after college, so I could learn how all the hotel departments fitted together to make one smoothly humming machine. I'd got used to interpreting the various unvarnished comments into records-friendly management-ese, something Gemma hadn't yet mastered, going by the rather literal transcript of Dino the bar manager's face-off last week with Sam the concierge over who got room-service tips for after-hours cocktails. They were both pretty sweary, although to give Gemma her due, it made for surprisingly colourful reading. If things didn't work out for her here, she had a future in writing quite violent film scripts.

Monday Head of Dept. meeting, 12 May 2014

Present:

[I left a gap for **Laurence Bentley Douglas, executive manager**]
Rosie McDonald, events
Dino Verdi, bar
Diane Holloway, HR
Jean Hogg, housekeeping

I glanced up to see who else had walked in, and caught a snippet of conversation between Diane and Jean, the magnificently upholstered housekeeper. I heard, 'Laurence', 'stock check' and 'general manager's job', and then Diane rolled her eyes and said, 'Well, I'd be the last one to know.' Which led me to guess they were talking about Paul's as yet unappointed replacement as hotel manager. We were all wondering about it, since his duties were being shared out between us in the meantime.

My chest fluttered. What if Laurence was going to announce the appointment in this meeting? My plan might be too late. Not too late, I reminded myself. I had a strong case to make. I had to think big.

A sudden gust of Hugo Boss wafted over my head, and Sam the concierge slid into the chair next to me. 'Morning, gorgeous,' he said, right into my ear.

I added **Sam Smith, concierge services** to my notes, and said, 'Morning, gorgeous, yourself.' Across the table, Diane giggled in a very un-HR-manager way, and I knew Sam had given her his special Monday morning wink.

I didn't attach a lot of significance to Sam's *gorgeous*; Sam called everyone *gorgeous*, even the porters. It was why he got the best tips in the hotel, that and his ability to produce tables from nowhere at booked-out restaurants, and top seats for *The Lion King*.

In the interests of fairness, I should explain that Sam was very good-looking. It's a lot easier to get away with calling everyone *gorgeous* when you look like you've just stepped out of an Armani advert yourself. You with your perfectly cut hair, and your David Beckham eyes, and your wink that you shouldn't be able to get away with, but you do. Except with me. Too many tipsy best men trying it on had rendered me impervious to winkage.

'So listen, Miss Moneypenny, what do you know about Paul's replacement?' Sam muttered, leaning over to get a Danish pastry from the plate. 'Rumour has it Laurence was spending a lot of time with the Do Not Disturb sign on his office door last week.'

Across the table, Diane's ears swivelled.

'Was he?' I poured him some coffee from the jug, then topped up my own cup. 'You know what Laurence is like. He's probably found a new website that can diagnose skin conditions by holding your palm up to the screen.' I raised a finger, seeing Sam's mouth twitch mischievously. 'Don't tell him that, by the way. If I find him palming his laptop, *I will know*.'

Sam raised his eyebrows and popped a chunk of pastry in his mouth. 'Something's afoot. Mark my words. The lawyer's been in. The one who looks like an undertaker.'

'You've been listening at the door?' I turned in my chair to look at him properly, suddenly interested.

'Not listening at the door as such. Just . . . keeping my ear to the ground. If you know what I mean.'

'I don't know what you mean. Elaborate.'

Sam inclined his head so Diane couldn't hear, and muttered, 'One of the maids popped in to empty his bin and he slammed the phone down.'

I raised an eyebrow. Laurence didn't slam phones down. He usually couldn't remember how they worked, and ended up putting the baffled caller on speakerphone instead, which led to some interesting revelations.

'*And,*' Sam went on, 'he was talking to Caroline.'

I frowned. 'Caroline?'

'Morning. Is this about Laurence?' There was a whoosh of garlic-scented kitchen air and my friend Helen dumped her file on the table next to us. 'I've got a bone to pick with him.'

I added **Helen Yardley, restaurant** to the minutes.

'I thought picking bones was your job?' Sam's face lit up at the sight of Helen in her smart suit. 'Restaurant? Picking bones? No?'

'No,' said Helen. 'My job is running the restaurant, and I do not need Laurence popping up in the kitchens like he did all weekend, disrupting the highly strung team of sociopaths we have working in there. And Kevin. The last thing I need is Laurence upsetting Kevin.'

'Laurence in the *kitchens*?' I said. This really was out of character. Laurence was terrified of Helen and, to a lesser extent, of Kevin Lomax, the head chef and Helen's secret weapon in her campaign to get the hotel restaurant Michelin-starred. Both had access to huge knives and were usually cross about something, which was understandable in Helen's case, at least, given that her job involved dealing with a colossal collection of egos all heated to boiling point.

Sam leaned back in his chair and crossed his arms with a conclusive smirk. 'So that's it. Lawyer's been in. Laurence has nosed around the kitchens. Phones slammed down. Laurence asking the ex-missus for advice. I reckon he's got a new manager. Or he's interviewing someone.'

'He wants Caroline to come and interview them, more like,' snorted Helen.

I tried not to let my emotions show on my face. Ugh, was I too late? Why hadn't I been to talk to Laurence sooner about this?

Because you were run off your feet covering Paul's duties, I reminded myself.

Helen turned to me. 'Wouldn't he have told you first, Rosie? I mean, you've been doing that job, more or less, since Paul left.'

I think she said it louder than was necessary because Diane the HR manager was sitting opposite us.

'You should probably have had a pay rise for your overtime,' she added helpfully, in case Diane hadn't got it the first time. Helen was a good friend like that. 'You're never out of here before ten. And you're here most weekends with weddings, too.'

Diane maintained her bland smile. She'd trained for a long time to get her face that non-commital.

'I bet Dominic Crosby's not happy about the hours you're working.' Sam shook his head with regret, also for Diane's benefit but also because he never missed an opportunity to get in a dig about Dominic. 'I've noticed how busy Betty is in that column of his. Some weeks she doesn't even appear.'

'He's fine with it,' I said calmly. 'He's very busy himself. He's up for an award soon, at the London Eats and Drinks Awards. Best Food Writer.'

'Get you two. The Entertainment Power Couple. You're the Jolie-Pitts of the slate cheeseboard world,' said Sam with a straight face.

'Sod off,' I said, pleased.

Helen nudged me, because Laurence had finally arrived, followed by Tam, head of security, in a suit specially tailored to accommodate his massive thighs, which were genetically better-suited to a kilt, preferably a Highland battle kilt. Tam was always the last in. He stood outside the door until the final moment, on account of the meeting-room chairs which were original Art Deco ones, and somewhat fragile. Or maybe because he found the weekly politics of it all less interesting than standing outside, eyeballing potential intruders.

I squinted at Laurence. There was no immediate sign, as far as I could see, of any dangerously low magnesium and iron levels. In fact, he looked positively chipper.

'Good morning, troops!' he said, sweeping to the head of the table and sitting down with a habitual flick of his suit jacket, and the meeting began.

Depending on the sorts of problems that needed raking over, Monday morning meetings could roll on for ages, but today's drew to a close after a brisk thirty minutes. Everyone rushed out to get on with the working day, but I hung around until only Laurence, Sam and I remained.

I gave Sam a *get lost* look, and he slid away to make some lucky guest's day with a table at the Ivy.

'Rosie.' Laurence beamed. 'Just the person.'

I assumed it was about the minutes. He probably wanted me to edit the bit where Helen asked him about the budget for the kitchen upgrades, and then asked when the last renovation of the dining room had been, and he couldn't remember. 'I'll get these minutes typed up and drop them by later,' I said. 'But I wonder if I could have a quick chat with you.'

'What? A quick chat about what?' Laurence's expression froze. 'You're not going on holiday?'

'Ha! No, as if,' I reassured him.

'So what's it about?'

'About weddings. And me.'

He clapped a hand to his chest. 'Dominic's proposed?'

I tried not to take offence at the surprise in his voice. 'I'm not getting married, Laurence.'

'Thank God.' He seemed relieved and I was starting to wonder whether I should be reading anything into it, when he added, 'Because I've just had to give Jean a fortnight off in July for some cruise, and frankly we can't afford to lose the only other person who knows how to handle the chambermaids.'

I followed him into his office.

Laurence's office hadn't changed much since his grandfather had barked orders into the big black telephone nearly a century ago.

By the window, which overlooked the gardens, were a side table covered in silver-framed photos of celebrity guests from eras past and an antique cocktail cabinet in the shape of a globe. It opened at five fifteen daily for Laurence's gin and tonic: some of the sticky bottles were original 1960s liqueurs that were probably illegal in the EU now. The only concession to the twenty-first century was a computer, placed uncomfortably on the desk between a photo of Caroline (and Joe and Alec) on one side, and Ellie (with Ripley and Otto, Laurence's two very young, very blonde children with Ellie) on the other. I was often called to turn the computer on and off again when it crashed. Laurence thoughtfully draped the screen with his red spotted hanky first, but I knew what he was looking at: gruesome symptom checkers, not porn.

'Sit ye, sit ye,' he said, wafting a hand at the leather chair opposite his desk, as he lowered himself gingerly into his seat. 'Ooh, dear.'

I smiled sympathetically, but didn't ask. He groaned a lot, and I had two trendy confetti suppliers arriving at eleven to demonstrate the 'perfect flutter and easy clean-up' for their fake rose petals. (*Fauxses*, as they called them.) Asking Laurence about his twinges could easily run into, then wipe out the entire appointment.

'Now, what was it you wanted to talk to me about?' He appeared to be bracing himself against the chair, but I ignored that, too.

'I wanted to talk to you about my role in the hotel.' I took a deep breath, and prepared myself to deliver my big speech.

He stopped wincing and flinching and suddenly looked rather focused. 'Your role in the hotel?'

'Yes.' I produced some spreadsheets I'd printed out, complete with projections for the rest of the year. I'd been realistic, and ignored Dominic's suggestions to 'forecast' three royal weddings taking place in our conservatory. 'This is the breakdown of the hotel turnover on weddings, and another on the other events business I've brought in. Conferences, parties, private dinners, that sort of thing. And I've added projected figures for the weddings I've already booked in for the rest of the year.'

I passed the papers over the desk to him, and Laurence glanced down the columns. I could tell he was impressed, because he didn't say anything. Or maybe he wasn't completely sure what he was looking at. Laurence had never been one for the financial side of things. That's what Ray the accountant was for. Ray 'Two Yachts' Temple.

'So, are you . . . asking for a pay rise?' Laurence ventured, like a man in socks stepping into a darkened room full of upturned plugs.

Do it, I told myself. *It's no harder than the time you had to sack Katie Hicks's maid of honour for her. It's just words.*

'Not exactly.' I looked Laurence in the (pale blue) eye. 'I feel that these figures show that I've proved my capability in the events department, and I feel ready for a new challenge. I'd like you to consider me for the role of hotel manager.'

'Hotel manager? As in, Paul's job?'

'Yes,' I said. 'As in Paul's job. I've been doing quite a lot of it lately, as you know. Like the general stock audit next week. And I've been responsible for doing timesheets with housekeeping, and reviewing the website overhaul.'

'I know, I know. Well. That's . . . quite an ambitious proposal,' said Laurence. 'You're only thirty.'

'I realize that,' I replied, 'but look at the budgets I've been managing. And I can bring things to the role that an outsider can't. I've been working in this hotel since I was sixteen years old. I know every room inside out, and I understand the family approach, all the traditions. I totally share your vision about reviving the Bonneville's reputation but in a modern way. That's starting to happen, with the weddings. People are talking about us being one of the classic, traditional wedding venues. That's a brilliant marketing keystone. We can make the Bonneville the ultimate *honeymoon* destination again, as well as being the ultimate London wedding venue. Can't you see it? *The Bonneville . . . London's Honeymoon Hotel.*'

I realized I was two seconds away from jabbing at the desk as if I were in a film. Something about Laurence's office had that effect on me. All the black-and-white photos, probably. I sat back in my chair, feeling exhilarated. My heart was hammering in my chest; I really believed what I'd just said – it wasn't what I'd rehearsed with Dominic at all.

Laurence opened his mouth to say something, but I had another sudden persuasive brainwave.

'Think how *expensive* it would be advertising for a new manager,' I pointed out. 'And then there are the interviews, the contract negotiations, the in-house training you'd have to do . . .'

That hit home. Laurence hated anything that smacked of extra work, or more time with Diane, the inefficient but annoyingly unsackable HR manager.

'What if . . .' he said, and I knew from the way he placed his fingertips carefully together, one by one, that he was plucking ideas out of the air while pretending to deliberate in a sage fashion. 'What if . . . we set a target?'

'A target?'

'Yes.' Laurence glanced down at the spreadsheets I'd handed him. 'What if you aim to increase the revenue you're generating on your weddings by, um, twenty per cent, and get the hotel some coverage in, say, three national magazines.'

I blinked, still working out how many more weddings I'd have to book to up my revenue by twenty per cent. 'Three?'

'Why not?' Laurence shrugged as if national magazine coverage was something he sorted out all the time. 'One big-name wedding would do that, wouldn't it?'

'Well, yes, but what ...' I stopped. He'd clearly forgotten that I did have a big-name wedding lined up: the 'English rose' model Flora Thornbury, whose mother was an old friend of Caroline's. But that wasn't a done deal. That was just a breakfast interview so far.

'And then you'd promote me to general manager?' I tried to keep my expression bold but professional, despite my heart rate going through the roof.

'I don't want to rush into a decision,' said Laurence firmly. 'But, Rosie, I do see you as a strong contender for this position, and if you can meet this target, then ...'

'By?'

He looked anxious. 'Bye? You'd leave?'

'No, when do I have to meet the target by?' I repeated.

'By, um ...' Again with the thoughtful/idea-plucking finger-tips. 'By the end of next summer.'

I narrowly prevented myself from saying, 'You want us to cope without Paul for another *year*?' but instead managed, 'And you can put that in writing?'

'Er, yes.'

'And in the meantime, who's going to do the manager's job?'

He swung on his chair and did not, I noted, seem keen to meet my eye. 'We seem to be getting along all right, don't we? Splitting the duties among the departmental heads?'

'It's a lot of extra work,' I reminded him, 'for not much overtime. Gemma's already assisting you *and* me *and* doing reception shifts – I can't delegate much more to her.'

'Well, I have some ideas in hand,' said Laurence mysteriously.

'For what?'

He mumbled something that I didn't catch and then pushed himself away from the desk. 'Rosie, you struck a chord there, with what you were saying about honeymoons. Call me an old romantic, but when I was chatting with your bride and groom this weekend, it did remind me of the good old days, when I was a little boy and we had some wonderful receptions here. Bit of *glamour* again in the Palm Court, folk all dressed up in hats and morning suits . . . Did I ever tell you that there used to be a dedicated girl just to spruce up guests' sables in the coat check . . .'

He got up and started wandering around his office, picking up the framed photographs and putting them down again with a wistful huff.

I knew where this was going. Despite being only in his late fifties, Laurence was a big fan of 'the good old days,' when London was being bombed to smithereens but martinis were still being quaffed in the Bonneville's wine cellar/air raid shelter by Errol Flynn *et al*. He claimed to remember all kinds of things that he'd technically require a TARDIS to have experienced.

He gazed at a photograph of Ava Gardner sharing a glass of champagne with his grandfather, the reckless serial adulterer who, Caroline once told me, had nearly gambled the hotel away in a game of Scrabble. The Bonneville had been saved, ironically, by a lucky triple word score. 'It's very unusual, you know, for a hotel to stay in one family for so long. I often wonder what advice my dad would give to me, if he had his time again.'

'Yeeees,' I said, with a surreptitious glance at my watch. I hoped this wasn't anything to do with Ellie going off on another 'girls' holiday' and handing over Ripley and Otto to their father. Melancholy discussions about the importance of 'family' and the need for them to 'understand the hotel' frequently led to me being asked to babysit Laurence's second family, something I tried to avoid at all costs. I'd never met two under-fives with such world-weariness about Hamleys *and* Father Christmas.

Laurence blinked at Ava, put her down, and looked at me with a directness that could be disarmingly charming if you weren't prepared for it.

But I was. I looked straight back at him. 'Laurence?'

He seemed to be on the verge of telling me something; then his expression changed.

'So,' he said. 'Monday morning! Plenty to do, eh?'

'Of course.' Especially if you had to increase your wedding revenue by twenty per cent. I got to my feet, and was almost at the leather-covered door when I remembered that Laurence had initially seemed to want me for something.

'What was it you wanted me for?' I asked.

He looked blank, then a bit shifty, then turned back to his computer. 'Not to worry,' he said airily, 'nothing important.'

Which of course meant it was exactly the opposite, but irritatingly, I couldn't ask. So I just smiled, and left to start crunching numbers before the confetti people arrived. And also crunching as many of Delphine's *langues de chat* as Helen could nick out of the kitchen for me. I was going to need serious amounts of sugar to meet Laurence's targets, but I knew one thing: I was going to work out a way to meet them.

CHAPTER FOUR

Fortunately my first chance to meet my new wedding target arrived the following morning, in the shape of Sadie Hunter and her mother, Margot. I'd already spoken to Sadie on the phone, and now I just had to persuade her mother, who was stumping up the cash for the wedding, that the Bonneville was the venue of their (but mainly Margot's) dreams.

These initial client meetings were always nerve-racking, but I enjoyed them, because showing off the Bonneville and all its wedding-day potential was easy. Unlike some hotels, designed for business or efficiency, the Bonneville didn't need to wrap gauze round metal conference chairs and put up extra flower displays to hide ugly fire doors: you could see the romantic mood already in the intimate alcoves and the lovely double staircases in the foyer, curving like two elegant swans' necks to the mezzanine level where the musicians played. I loved watching the possibilities dawn on the bride as we walked around, and I told them stories about previous weddings, and also the hotel's celebrity-filled past. We offered ceremonies in the courtyard where dukes had proposed to actresses, in the ballroom where debs and officers had fallen urgently in love during the war, and in the cosy library during the winter. Each event was tailored exactly to the bride's vision, which, after an hour of anecdotes, usually coincided with the classic and sophisticated wedding I wanted to arrange for her.

My job was to combine the magical atmosphere of the hotel with the not very romantic financial specifics of our wedding package, a diplomatic business art Caroline had taught me, and which I was trying to pass on to Gemma, with less success.

I could see Gemma's attention was wandering already as we prepared my office for the Hunter meeting. I used the official events meeting room for arranging conferences or charity functions, but when I was talking to brides I preferred my own small office: a morning room next door to Laurence's office, decorated in pale fondant colours with misty watercolour paintings of London scenes on the walls. It looked out onto the garden through French windows, with the wedding fountain in full view. I liked to set the scene from the start, hence the cream and pink roses I was arranging on the desk.

'Gemma?' I said, as she dumped some wedding magazines unceremoniously in the wastepaper basket instead of fanning them out on the coffee table as instructed.

'What? Sorry . . .'

'Remember, this is about the *light touch*,' I said. 'Think dream hotel. I want this to be everything Sadie Hunter's been picturing in her mind when she's been imagining her wedding. If we get this right, ideally she'll book it today, before she sees anywhere else.'

'Is she looking at other places?'

'All brides are looking at other places, even if they say they're not.' I moved to the sofa and plumped up the round satin cushions with swift punches. 'But we're special. We're unique and personal, and we can offer Sadie the sort of wedding that'll feel as if she's starring in her own romantic film. From the moment she steps through the door this morning, I want her to feel as if the whole world's gone into black-and-white, and there's a string orchestra playing in the background.'

Gemma paused to make a note in her ever-present notebook. 'So we should put the Ella Fitzgerald CD on?'

'Yes,' I said patiently, 'put the Ella Fitzgerald CD on. We'll have morning coffee served in the lounge once we've done the tour – can you ask Delphine for the special mini pastries? The pretty ones that look like shells. I want to sell Sadie the mothers' afternoon tea package as well as the wedding.' I paused as she wrote it down. Her mouth formed the words 'afternoon' and 'tea'.

'Now. Have I forgotten anything?' I asked.

'Hen package?'

'The attendants' treat,' I corrected her. 'Hens go to Blackpool, *attendants* drink special cocktails and have massages at the Bonneville. And yes, we'll talk to her about the spa and the girls' pampering weekend, and about the stag do Sam can arrange from here, to keep it all under control.' I checked my notes. Brides liked our stag night package. And once the groom and best man had talked to Sam, they were quite keen on it too.

'Have I missed anything?'

Gemma tapped the pen against her lips. 'Keeping the hotel

clear? I'll remind Dino not to let the lads deliver the lager through the main bar till she's gone,' she said. 'Don't want two sweaty delivery men spoiling the magic.'

'Good,' I said approvingly. 'You're getting the hang of this.'

Sadie and her mother arrived bearing a thick folder each, and with a list of questions about a mile long. Sadie's were mainly about rose petals and places the hired London bus bringing her from the church could park; Margot's were more about cost per head. It didn't put me off; I liked providing quick and reassuring answers to bridal questions. I'd heard most of them.

Sadie informed me that she'd set up a wedding Pinterest board and whipped out her iPad so she could 'run through the themes and moods'. 'The theme I want is Golden Age of Hollywood,' she explained as we swiped our way through her gallery of moody brides in lace cloches and images of icy martini glasses. 'Style, elegance, satin, romance.'

'Oh, you've come to the right place for that,' I said, pouring them some tea from the silver pot in front of us on the low table. 'We could book you into the same junior suite Grace Kelly used to reserve, the one overlooking the park?'

'Really? Did she stay here?' Sadie looked starstruck.

'She did. She had a special extra-deep bath installed. The taps were flown in from France and installed overnight for her. She had a special key so she could let herself in through the kitchens, to avoid any photographers.' I loved all these vintage details – I'd spent hours poring over the yellowed documents in Laurence's archives, fascinated by the luggage lists and special-request notes.

Margot Hunter raised her eyebrows. 'I thought she stayed at the Connaught? There are all those photographs of her arriving at the front door . . .'

'Oh, she did stay there, yes.' I nodded. 'But quite a few stars used to stay at the Bonneville when they didn't want to be seen, if you know what I mean.' I smiled enigmatically. 'They wanted to be treated just like regular people, which is fine, because our ethos is to treat all our guests like Hollywood stars.'

'Ooh,' sighed Sadie, and I knew I'd just added another bride to my year's tally.

I sent Gemma ahead to sweep the corridors clear of all chambermaids and cleaning carts, and ushered the Hunters into the elevator, pointing out the polished brass stars on the ceiling as well as the hidden uplights that gave everyone a flattering candlelit glow. With that, Margot Hunter abandoned her practical questions about seating numbers and plug sockets in the rooms and joined in with Sadie's eager questions about the hotel's glamorous past.

I happily told them about how the ballroom swung to the sound of the house band with trumpeters moonlighting from Buckingham Palace, and about the secret tunnel from the Bonneville to the umbrella shop across the road that used to be an underground jazz club before the war.

'The whole third floor was designed to accommodate foreign dignitaries travelling with large retinues – the rooms can be opened out into one long area,' I explained as I led Sadie and her mother down the corridor towards the bridal suite.

'It makes it perfect for our wedding parties now, of course. The bride's room is one of our biggest on its own, but it also has folding doors at the far end, so you can open it all up and have the attendants and the bride getting ready together if you want!'

'Oh, that's a lovely idea!' Sadie actually clasped her hands together.

'And I can keep an eye on Amy if we're all together,' said her mother, darkly. 'Make sure she doesn't decide to make some alterations to her bridesmaid's dress, like she did at your cousin's wedding . . .'

'Mum! She wouldn't. Just think of the gorgeous reportage photos . . .'

I was feeling very confident now. 'There's a wonderful moment when the bride pulls back the folding doors and her family see her for the first time in her gown – really special. Even I always end up in floods of tears.'

As we turned the corner, I was surprised to see Gemma with Maricruz, the most thorough of our chambermaids, outside the white double doors of the bridal suite. They both looked confused, which was more normal for Gemma than Maricruz, who usually appeared all too aware of what was going on.

Maricruz had one hand on the glass doorknob; she removed it, then she grabbed it again, and then, when she saw me and the Hunters, she let go of it as if it were red-hot, and shoved her hand into her green apron.

'Good morning, Maricruz!' I said cheerily. 'Are we all done in there?'

'Ah, no. Not yet.' Her dark eyes were clearly warning me about something but I couldn't work out what.

'Maricruz is a perfectionist,' I explained to Sadie, reaching for the doorknob. 'It's okay, Mari, we just want a quick look.'

Maricruz grabbed my arm. 'No. Is not ready.'

'The room isn't ready?' I frowned. There was no one booked in the bridal suite, and I'd checked it myself on Monday, after it had been cleaned up following the weekend's wedding. In fact I'd checked it again before I left last night, in preparation for this visit – I'd even put some fresh flowers by the bed.

I looked at Gemma, who shrugged and mouthed, *Won't let me in.*

'Is not ready,' Maricruz repeated, with a nervous side glance at Sadie and her mother.

'Is there a problem?' enquired Margot Hunter.

Unease fluttered in the pit of my stomach. The bridal suite was the jewel in my presentation, the place where the bride really starting picturing herself, getting married in our hotel. The last thing I wanted was to lose the Hunters now.

I flashed them a reassuring smile, then steered Maricruz to one side and lowered my voice. 'Maricruz, tell me the truth. Is Beatriz sleeping in there again? Because that's not the first time I've—'

'No!' Maricruz looked indignant, then panicky. Her eyes hopped from side to side, as if she were following a tennis match behind me. 'No, is not Beatriz.'

'Estrella?'

'No!'

We had a lot of sleeping beauties on the chambermaid team. Sleeping beauties and pillow-chocoholics. The minibar raiders were usually caught by their clinking, but some of the girls working two or three jobs snuck naps where they could. I didn't blame them.

'Is there a problem?' Sadie had been away with the celebrity fairies, but now even she was intrigued.

'No!' said Maricruz at the same time as I did.

'Not at all!' I said. I had to get in there and find out exactly what it was Maricruz didn't want me to see. 'I just want to check that . . .' I racked my brains. 'That the balcony doors are open – it makes all the difference to the first impression, being able to see the wonderful view of the garden. One second! Gemma? Gemma is my very capable assistant. Why don't you tell Sadie about the wedding we had at the weekend? With the croquembouche?'

I grabbed the doorknob and opened the door, steeling my face to wake Sancha up without her screaming. Not before I could get a pillow over her face, anyway.

I slid my way around the door so the Hunters couldn't crane their necks and see what was going on, but then froze on the other side.

I wasn't prepared for the sight before me on the bed.

Sprawled facedown over the satin coverlet was the long, half-naked body of a man in boxer shorts, his blond hair tangled and his arms splayed as if trying to hug the whole mattress.

He was so still that if he hadn't been snoring very gently, I'd have considered drawing a white chalk line around him and calling the police.

I leaned against the closed door, still holding the handle behind my back, and wrinkled my nose as I tried to take in all the details as fast as possible while blocking anyone behind me from seeing what was inside. Going by the smell of stale alcohol, whoever he was, he'd made a night of it. Empty miniature bottles from the minibar were scattered across the floor, underneath discarded items of clothing and all four towels from the bathroom, trailing in tangled heaps. His blue shirt was hanging over the dressing table's huge circular mirror, and a pair of dark jeans was bunched by the television, as if he'd just dropped trou then and there.

My eyes stopped on his bare back, rising and falling with each rasping snore. It was tanned the rich gold of a sandy beach somewhere hot, with a small compass on the right shoulder blade and a dark blue star right at the bottom of his spine, just above the baggy boxer shorts, which were the regulation public-schoolboy XXXXL size, despite the lightly muscled legs beneath. His back was finely muscled too, and . . .

I pulled myself up with a jolt. Enough of the boxer-short ogling. I had about ten seconds to work out what was going on and how I could handle it so the Hunters didn't get a very wrong impression about the hotel. And then I needed to find out which of the chambermaids had left the bridal suite unlocked.

Guest wandered in from another room after midnight sleepwalk/ drunken search for the bathroom? I had no idea how he could have got in, but it was possible – chambermaids found guests in the most unlikely places. At least this one still had his pants on.

Random dinner guest wandered up after coffee in the restaurant and passed out? Also happened. Often after large corporate parties. *Note:* check bathroom for 'dining companion'.

Random bloke wandered in from street? Not unknown to happen, but much rarer, thanks to the eagle eyes of Frank the doorman. And they didn't have boxer shorts with . . . little yellow ducks on them.

I averted my eyes, which had slid back to the intruder's long tanned legs, and thought fast. Most likely to be a dinner guest. In which case Tam from security could stick him under one arm and sweep him out via the other set of doors so the Hunters wouldn't even see, and in the meantime, I'd just have to show them a different suite.

Just as I was about to quietly close the door on the man and text Tam to come and deal with the situation, the intruder groaned, muttered to himself, and reached out his left arm in search of something. The hand patted the bed, up and down, up and down, as if every movement was painful.

I was hypnotized by it. It was a broad, tanned hand, with a thin cotton friendship bracelet around the wrist. The way it was groping across the coverlet was oddly sensual, and I knew I should say something, but I couldn't think what.

The hand finally connected with the phone on the pillow, and the blond man lifted himself on one elbow. As he opened one bleary eye, he suddenly saw me standing there, staring at him with my hands on my hips.

An expression of sheer fear crossed his face, and collided with his hangover. He winced, croaked, 'Shit!' then winced again.

Something about his bleary eyes – blue and large, with purply-dark shadows underneath – seemed familiar. I didn't know a lot of honeymoon-suite crashers, but at the same time, neither did I want to stare at him long enough to work out where I knew him from. Another wedding? A best man, maybe?

'Whoa! Ummph, I can explain!' he started in a slurred, cracked voice, and finally my brain kicked in.

I leaned on the door, already paging Tam in my pocket, not wanting any of this to filter through the keyhole.

'You don't have to explain to me,' I assured him in a polite voice, scanning the room for damage. It was in a state, but nothing seemed to be broken. 'Our security team will handle this. They're on their way now, sir, so if you could please get dressed and . . . and . . .'

The yellow ducks were moving. They were very baggy boxer shorts. I stared at his shoulder instead. His tanned shoulder. I always noticed men's shoulders. Anthony had had nice shoulders, from swimming; they were one of my favourite things about him. This man's shoulders were even better, with soft golden hollows between . . .

I shifted my gaze to the pillow, appalled at myself.

'So please remain here until they arrive,' I finished, and let myself out before we could get into conversation. My face, I realized, was very hot.

Outside in the corridor, Gemma's description of the croquembouche appeared to have run short.

'. . . lots of cream,' she finished lamely, in an attempt to conceal the fact that she'd been listening to the whole thing.

I turned from locking the door swiftly with my skeleton key to find Margot's and Sadie Hunter's eyes boring into me, as were Maricruz's and Gemma's.

'Sorry about that,' I said, leaning on the door and holding the doorknob behind my back in case the half-naked stranger decided to get out of bed and attempt an escape. 'My mistake! We've got some workmen in the bridal suite today – they've started early. We're installing new . . . um, new headboards.'

'Really?' Margot looked unconvinced. 'Was there a problem with the old headboards?'

'No! They're for a celebrity client!' I added, touched with inspiration. 'A special request!'

Sadie's eyes lit up. 'Who is it?'

'Ah, I wish I could tell you,' I said, hurrying them away from the room as firmly as I could. Was that the door rattling? I thought I could hear movement inside. 'Now, what I *really* want to show you is the honeymoon suite . . .' I guided them down the thick cream carpet towards the third-floor lifts, before the mood could be shattered by a burly security man on his way to tackle an intruder.

Margot glanced back at the mysterious door. 'I thought *that* was the honeymoon suite?'

The doorknob was definitely rattling now. 'Hello?' came a muffled voice. Then a less happy, 'Oi!'

'That's the *bridal* suite.' I jabbed at the button for the penthouse. *Hurry up, hurry up.* 'This is the *honeymoon* suite. It's very special – my favourite room in the whole hotel. It's like a cosy little nest in the sky!' I could hear myself gabbling uncharacteristically and made an effort to calm my voice. *You're in control,* I told myself.

This was so unlike me. Gatecrashers were easy to handle: I'd dispatched at least one a year since I started work. It was Laurence's stupid budget challenge that had put me on edge like this, I decided. All I could think of were my new target calculations – and losing a key wedding booking like Sadie's would be a really bad start.

'Is that workman locked in?' asked Margot Hunter.

My brain scrabbled for a credible explanation. 'Not at all! He's testing the, um, doorknobs. They're very old, so we have to do routine maintenance on them.' I smiled confidently at Sadie. 'Don't want our brides getting stuck, do we?'

She smiled back, and I gave Gemma a discreet shove.

'Gemma,' I said, 'would you pop back and let that workman know the door is fine, and when Tam arrives, buzz me?'

'Tam?' She frowned. 'What's Tam—'

'He's giving them a hand with the bed.' I fixed my smile, although my palms were now quite damp. How long before the stranger decided to start banging on the door? That would look awful in about seventeen different ways.

'But he's from the security—'

'It's a very expensive headboard,' I said over the top of her. 'And heavy. Tam's very strong. Gemma? Buzz me when Tam gets here.'

Sadie and Margot were now staring openly at the noise

coming from the bridal suite, but at that moment the lift saved me from a very loud rattle, and with a silent thanks to the hotel guardian angel, I swept the Hunters into the lift and pressed the top-floor button so fast I nearly trapped Margot's cardigan in the closing doors. My mind was already racing through how I'd explain this to Laurence, not to mention what I would say to Tam when I caught up with him.

Watertight security systems technology solutions, eh? *Right*. Maricruz would be more effective on the door than he was.

I managed to show the Hunters around the romantic honeymoon suite without any interruptions, but my mind wasn't really on the lovely dusty pink colour scheme, or the glorious mother-of-pearl headboard that rose like a scallop shell over the king-size bed. Or the special rose champagne breakfast, or the picturesque double balcony overlooking Green Park, with jasmine climbing around the wrought-iron detailing.

I kept seeing the hungover guest's long golden back, sprawled over the bedspread. And the tattoo. And the familiar eyes.

And even though Delphine had excelled her chilly self with the pâtisserie served with our morning coffee downstairs, I was a bit distracted by the text from Gemma that said:

Tam taken intruder downstairs!

Well, not that one so much as the one that appeared five minutes later:

Laurence says he wants to see you as soon as you've finished.

Then another, saying:

Laurence says hurry up.

I answered Margot Hunter's questions about our catering options and our florist packages, then escorted them to the taxi rank, where I gave Sadie my card and our full details in the lovely pale blue folder embossed with the hotel's signature star motif. I never pushed too hard – hard-sell wasn't part of the wedding package, in my opinion – but I knew if I'd shown them the bridal suite it'd have been a done deal. Now it just looked as if we had something to hide. Margot was already eyeing every closed door with a suspicious glance, as if the doorknob might start rattling. And if this became the reason that Sadie decided to go with a different venue and I lost a key booking towards my target, I was going to march that intruder off the premises myself, preferably off the honeymoon suite balcony.

Gemma was hovering outside Laurence's office, wearing the sort of semi-gleeful expression that indicated that she'd already got half of a great bit of gossip and was very keen to hang around for part two.

'What's going on?' I asked. 'Have they called the police? Has reception confirmed who that intruder is?'

'Better than that,' said Gemma.

'What do you mean, better than that?'

She didn't answer. She just rounded her eyes and tapped her nose.

'Oh, for heaven's sake,' I snapped. 'It's not a spoiler,' and I knocked twice, before pushing open the heavy door and going in.

Laurence was perched on his desk, not in his Swivelling Chair O'Power behind it – already very unusual – so I didn't immediately notice that someone was in the chair to the left.

'Laurence, we need to talk to Tam about security in the hotel, I've just had the most *embarrassing* experience with. . .' I began crossly, and then my brain caught up with my eyes as the man in the chair spun round at the sound of my voice.

'Oh, fantastic,' he said ambiguously. 'You again.'

It took me a moment or two to connect the fully dressed man with the half-naked one on the bed. He'd pulled on a shirt and long khaki shorts, and had obviously been given enough time to drag himself into the shower, going by his wet hair and more fragrant aroma – that of our luxury-suites-only house shampoo, I noted. He still looked hungover, though. Very, very hungover.

Tam was not in the office and, I was disappointed to see, neither was Jean, the exacting head of housekeeping. Which meant that either Laurence was waiting for one or both of them to arrive, or he was going to deal with this himself. Either way, the intruder didn't look nearly worried enough for my liking. Margot Hunter's unimpressed face floated in front of my mind and I felt my face get hot for the second time that day, and for a very different reason than the first time.

'I hope you've apologized to our chambermaid for giving her a terrible shock,' I said, sarcastically. 'And for vandalizing our bridal suite.'

'I will,' he said, 'when you apologize for incarcerating me, against my will, in a room with borderline-antique air conditioning. And that's being generous. Which is more than you can say for the minibar provision.'

My mouth dropped open. Amazed at his coolness, I glanced at Laurence, who was doing his anxious half-smile, half-frown of confrontation fear.

I couldn't stop myself. 'I hardly think I need to apologize for anything! Aren't you going to explain what you were doing in there?'

'For crying out loud, keep it down, would you?' He clutched his head. 'And FYI, if someone puts a Do Not Disturb sign on the door, don't you generally take that to mean, like, *do not disturb* them? God help anyone getting married here if the bridal suite's knock and enter.'

I was stunned. My blood pressure was now rising to dangerous levels. Somewhere in the back of my head, it occurred to me that this was what Dominic must feel like when someone served him 'an impertinently bad burger'.

'Did Gemma tell you this . . . *gentleman* interrupted an important client meeting?' I asked Laurence, somewhat rhetorically. 'Did she describe to you what sort of state the room was in? Worse than when . . . when *that band we don't talk about* had it?'

'Ah. Yes. Gemma did say you, er, handled the incident very professionally.' Laurence smiled. He was smiling too much.

I felt as if I'd skipped the first chapter of whatever was going on here. I put my hands on my hips. 'Laurence. This man *broke into* the bridal suite and trashed it. Am I missing something?'

'Just a sense of proportion,' groaned the blond man. 'Can you get brain damage from taking too much Berocca for a hangover?'

'Rosie, you remember Joseph?' said Laurence, leaning over to pat the man's shoulder.

'For the love of God,' the man moaned, 'not so sodding loud.'

I had a reasonable memory for faces and names, but this wasn't ringing any bells.

'Joe,' said Laurence. 'My son!'

And then I did remember.

CHAPTER FIVE

Joe Bentley Douglas – because that, I now realized all too well, was who my 'intruder' was – and I stared at each other over the desk like two people who'd met and rejected each other on a speed-dating night, only to be reintroduced in a formal job interview situation.

Typically, Laurence seemed oblivious to the tension turning the air around us into a thick soup of awkwardness. It was a *broth* of embarrassment.

'Joe, I'm surprised you didn't recognize Rosie,' he said. 'She's our events manager now. She's officially indispensable.'

I went to shake his hand, but Joe raised his in an uncomfortable *so hello!* fashion, and finally turned his head towards me so I could get a proper look at him.

The last time I'd seen Joe, he was eighteen, and I'd arranged for him to be kicked off my bed-making squad for slacking. He'd just left boarding school and was suffering from a particularly cruel allergy to all known acne treatments, combined with chronic acne. He'd been miserable too, probably as a result of the acne and the boarding school, but also because he spent most of his time listening to Leonard Cohen records. Plus he had to live in Laurence and Caroline's flat upstairs in the hotel with Alec, who hadn't yet joined the army but dressed in camo gear and set fire to things all the time anyway.

I didn't blame myself for failing to recognize Joe, because he looked completely different ten years on. The spots had gone, and unexpected cheekbones had emerged from the old chip-munkiness: he was handsome, in a scruffy surfer sort of way, with Laurence's pale blue eyes, a wide mouth and a faint scuff of golden stubble over his jaw. He also wore a necklace with a shell on it.

Helen would *love* that, I thought. I didn't. It looked stinky. Men with necklaces really weren't my type. I preferred men in suits. That was one thing Anthony and Dominic did have in common: a commitment to tailoring.

I'd never really noticed before, but apart from the Bentley Douglas blue eyes and the wide mouth, Joe was the spitting image of Caroline, minus the energy and positive outlook. The miserable teenage attitude still seemed to be firmly in place, although maybe that was the result of mixing every single bottle in the minibar into a sort of hellish cocktail.

He gave me an appraising look. Some might have called it a scowl. 'You haven't changed,' he said. 'Still as bossy as ever.'

'Me? Bossy?' I felt my face go red for the third time that day, and hoped he wasn't going to bring up the housekeeping sacking in front of his dad.

'Yeah.' Joe glared at me. 'You probably don't even remember, but Mum put me on your room service team. You re-did my hospital corners because you said they were amateurish.'

'Did I?' I pretended to smile nostalgically.

He nodded. 'And when I suggested the hotel needed to get with the times and provide duvets, you went ballistic and gave me a lecture about traditional hotel standards.'

I opened and closed my mouth because I couldn't actually deny that had happened. Satin counterpanes in the honeymoon suite, yes. Anything other than crisp white linens and blankets in the main rooms, no.

Fine, well, if we were going to be *honest* . . .

'I'm surprised you can remember,' I said breezily. 'Didn't you only stay on the room service team for a week?'

I was being kind. Joe had lasted two and a half days on my team, and I'd found him asleep in the linen cupboard on the half day. On days one and two, he'd spent most of his time being cooed over by the two Spanish girls, and Caroline had decided he'd get into less trouble collecting glasses in the bar, so she'd moved him. The following Saturday he went off backpacking round Portugal and we all breathed a sigh of relief, apart from Maria and Lucia, who cried for two days.

'Still no duvets, I see,' Joe remarked.

'Because we are a traditional hotel,' I replied, equally pointedly.

'Rosie is a fine upholder of tradition,' said Laurence proudly. 'She shares my vision of the Bonneville shining like a modern beacon of old-fashioned hospitality in a bland corporate world.'

Joe muttered something that might have been 'beacon' but probably wasn't.

'I thought you were in America,' I said, trying to change the subject to something positive. 'Is this a holiday?'

Joe scowled again, and Laurence stepped in. 'Joe's going to be staying here with his old Dad awhile,' he explained. 'Aren't you?'

'I don't have much choice,' said Joe, but that didn't stop a broad smile breaking over Laurence's face.

I hadn't seen Laurence this happy since he'd discovered he had a one-in-a-million allergy to pomegranates, and for that reason alone I gave Joe my best customer-facing smile and held out a hand. This time he shook it.

'How nice to see you again,' I said, squeezing his hand. Maybe I squeezed his hand a little tightly and spoke slightly too loud. Just so he knew I wouldn't be forgetting how he'd left the towels in my beautiful bridal suite. All scrunched up and making stains on the satin throw.

Joe winced. 'Yeah, thanks.'

'Marvellous,' said Laurence, jumping off the desk, so happy he forgot to flinch. 'Now, Rosie, I called you in first because as my right-hand woman, I require your assistance. Joe needs to learn how this place works, so he'll spend a few months shadowing each departmental head to get a proper sense of how we do things. And I thought where better to start than in events?'

'Events?' I repeated, at the same time as Joe groaned.

And what did he mean, *Joe needs to learn how this place works*? A nasty suspicion was forming in the back of my mind. That 'right-hand woman' compliment was masking something else.

'Events is where it's all happening.' Laurence beamed. 'I had a look at the diary and you've got weddings booked in at least twice a month for as far as the eye can see.'

'Of course I have,' I said, meeting his eye. 'I'm *right on target*.'

He didn't rise to it, so I said, 'When you say events . . . what exactly will Joe be doing?'

'Yes, what will Joe be doing?' Joe asked. 'Because I'm not doing weddings. I'm telling you that right now.'

'The events department isn't just weddings!' I turned to him. This was one of my bugbears. 'We provide a broad range of entertainment planning for clients. Balls, parties, corporate events. It just *happens* that weddings are a growing element of the hotel's profile. It's not all cake knives and . . . and veils. There's a lot of planning and budgeting and organization and client liaison. It's hard work.'

'And weren't you saying you needed more help?' said Laurence. 'Joe can start immediately. What have you got on this afternoon?'

'No. Absolutely not. He can't come to events meetings dressed like that,' I said, horrified. 'Prospective brides don't expect to talk about their twenty-thousand-pound receptions with someone wearing . . . board shorts.'

'Well, this is me,' Joe started indignantly, but Laurence cut across him.

'Joe's got plenty of time to pop down to the King's Road and get himself something suitable,' he said, and he sounded firmer than I'd ever heard him sound before.

'Tomorrow,' I said. I needed time to arrange my diary.

'Oh, for God's sake,' said Joe, and got up and slouched out.

Laurence looked at me and smiled as if the conversation had been a sparkling success, and I was so thrown, all I could do was smile back.

As I left Laurence's office, I spotted Gemma by the portrait of Mrs Maude Bentley Douglas, Laurence's grandmother and a noted society stirrer. Gemma was clutching a pile of napkins in a way that suggested she'd just grabbed them at random, and when she saw me she began walking.

It didn't fool me for a second. I'd been a practiced eaves-dropper myself, back in the day. I still was.

'Gemma,' I said, grabbing her arm before she could scuttle past. 'Could you track Helen down and tell her I need to have a state of the nation meeting with her after lunch service?'

'What about?'

'About Antonia Devereux's wedding,' I said, off the top of my head. 'She's emailed me ahead of the meeting about some very complicated food requests. She wants an oyster table. And a lobster tank. With ice luges.'

'Really? But Antonia's a vegetarian.' Gemma looked sur-prised. 'Don't you remember?'

'It's a special ethical lobster tank,' I improvised. 'They free-range around in there ... Anyway, just tell Helen, will you? Four thirty, if she can.'

'Shouldn't I be there? If it's a wedding meeting?' Gemma persisted. 'Laurence did say, as part of my last review, that I could start taking on more managerial roles in the wedding planning.'

Laurence probably *hadn't* said that, given that Gemma tended to 'improve' everything, from people's coffee orders upwards, but my brain wasn't really engaged. I was too cross – with Laurence, with Joe, and now with myself. Visions of Joe and the havoc he'd wreaked in the bridal suite kept floating back to me, as well as the things I'd very nearly said to him in the office, when I hadn't known who he was. And now I'd have Joe sitting in on every single meeting with a face like a wet weekend, potentially affecting the targets I'd convinced Laurence I could achieve.

I groaned aloud, saw Gemma looking at me oddly, and tried to regain my composure.

I wanted to help Laurence, I really did, but this wasn't the month to have Joe hanging around scowling at clients and hating me for criticizing his hospital corners ten years ago. Plus, I had a bad feeling about that tour around the departments. A very bad feeling.

Helen would have a plan. Maybe I could persuade her to have Joe in the restaurant. Just until I'd reached my bookings target.

'Rosie?' Gemma prodded me. I was so tense I didn't even tell her off for prodding me.

'What? Fine. You can sit in on the meeting tomorrow. Just go and find Helen and tell her I need to see her this afternoon, asap. Please.'

Gemma made a *yessss!* face and wiggled off down the corridor.

Why not? I thought, heading into my own office. Gemma's

enthusiasm and Joe's distinct lack of it might cancel each other out.

'State of the nation meeting' was the code Helen and I used for our emergency vent sessions, which were usually required a couple of times a week in order to deal with the pressures created by working for Laurence and/or living with our equally-annoying-but-in-different-ways boyfriends.

We met on the external fire escape between the fourth and fifth floors of the hotel; it was directly above the kitchen, so it was warm in winter and smelled pleasantly of pâtisserie, and had a soothing view of Green Park. More than that, Laurence had no head for heights, so it was very unlikely we'd ever be overheard.

When I went up there at half past four, Helen was already sitting on the black iron steps, her long legs resting on the *Danger: No Leaning* sign, with a white kitchen mug in one hand and her smooth forehead clutched in the other. As she heard my feet clanging on the metal, she jerked to attention.

'Listen, you don't even need to tell me,' she said, seeing my dark expression. 'I felt like throwing a brick at Dominic's head myself when I read that review.'

That brought me up short. 'What review?'

I hadn't had time to catch up with Dominic's latest. He did a big ranty review for the weekend paper, and a shorter, more practical one on Wednesdays. Wednesdays were supposed to be the affordable places normal people could go. They tended to make him even crosser than the expensive places.

'The pub in Balham where Betty had a meltdown about the chips?'

'Betty had a meltdown?' I frowned. '*He* had a meltdown about the chips. He made the kitchen bring him a potato just so he could establish that they knew what one was. He blamed me for that?'

'He was very witty about it. He did a hilarious riff about "You say potato, I say reconstituted carbohydrate substitute".'

'What?' I pretended to look outraged. Well, half-pretended. 'That's what *I* said! Dominic said *he* said that?'

Dominic had been taking liberties more and more of late. He'd also taken to ascribing his more acerbic observations to Betty, 'So the restaurants will still serve me.' I know. Not very gallant.

'Sorry, I thought you knew,' said Helen. 'Look, I've got some cake from the kitchen. I take it you're okay with cake?'

Thanks to the Hunter fiasco, then Joe, I hadn't had time for lunch, and I reached hungrily for the plate she was offering. 'Have you ever known me not be okay with cake?'

'Oh. It's just that in that review, Dominic said Betty was . . .' Helen slowed awkwardly. 'On a diet? You're not on a diet.'

'Of course I'm not on a diet! If anyone's on a diet, it's Dom!'

She gave me the side-eye look that had become our shorthand for 'He's really taking the piss, you know,' and I did a mime of a furious girlfriend throttling an irritating plagiarist.

'Eat the cake, you'll feel better,' she said, and as ever, she was right. My fork hit a thick stratum of Italian meringue buttercream, and the world tilted back onto its axis. It'd be fine. We were buying a flat together in real life. He loved me in real life. Betty was just for the column. She wasn't *me*.

'Ooh. This is good,' I said, gesturing through a mouthful of sponge cake. 'Delphine's back from the dark side?'

For the last five days we'd had some very angry profiteroles and dark, dark chocolate confections leaving the chilly depths of the pastry room.

'It's the moon.' Helen sipped her coffee. 'Affects pastry chefs, I've noticed. We need to schedule the weddings to avoid full ones. So, come on, what did you need to see me about so urgently, if not Dominic's review?'

I carved off a bigger chunk of cake as the reality of the next few weeks hit me again. 'Guess who the intruder in the honeymoon suite was? You won't guess, I'll tell you – Joe Bentley Douglas.'

But Helen didn't look as surprised as I'd expected. 'I know! I heard them discussing it in the kitchen. I thought he was in California? What happened with the fire-walking and surfing and all that?'

'Dunno. Wasn't mentioned. But there's more – Laurence wants him to learn about the hotel business.'

Helen clearly hadn't had that gossip memo yet – or she hadn't given Gemma the chance to pass on the news. She lowered her coffee mug in surprise. 'What?'

'Two months shadowing each head of department. I'm first. Do you want to trade?'

'Jesus, no, not until I've checked the books and – oh.' Helen's eyes widened, then she pointed at me. 'You don't think . . .' She put her hand over her mouth.

I made an *And?* gesture.

'You don't think . . . Laurence is training him up to give him the manager's job?'

Once she said it, it confirmed the suspicions that had been multiplying in the back of my mind, and a heavy sensation settled in the pit of my stomach. 'I hope not. What does Joe know about running the hotel?'

'That's what he's here to learn?' suggested Helen, wincing apologetically.

'If that's the case,' I said, 'he's not exactly looking thrilled about it.'

'That's probably why Laurence has made him start in your department. You know everything there is to know about the hotel. And events is fun.'

'No, it's not,' I countered, out of habit. 'It might look like fun but I take it very seriously.'

She rolled her eyes. 'Come on, who doesn't like weddings?'

'Dominic?' I suggested. 'Seamus?'

Seamus was Helen's boyfriend. Like Dominic, he was in food – but on the other side of the service hatch, as head chef at the Marden Arms, a gastropub with pretensions in Fulham. No chips. Not even chips in terracotta plant pots. Not even molecular deconstructed thrice-fried chips.

'I'm not going to rise to that,' she said. 'We're talking about Joe. When's he starting?'

'Now. He's started. Laurence sent him off to get some clothes befitting wedding –' I corrected myself – '*events* planning meet-ings. He's the kind of overgrown student who still wears *shorts*. I mean, how is that supposed to fit in with the Bonneville's timeless elegance?'

'Shorts, eh?' said Helen, but she didn't look very disapproving. 'I bet he's got a great tan if he's been on the beach for the last, how long? Ten years? But then you'd know all about his tan, wouldn't you? What with you seeing him in the nip this morning.'

'He wasn't in the nip.' You can't keep a secret in a hotel. Especially when it involves partial nudity. 'Can we stop going on about that?'

'No,' she said cheerfully. 'It's already legendary in the kitchens. Is it true that you punched him? And that he was completely naked in the Jacuzzi when you and the bride's mother walked in?'

'No! No! He was on the bed and he had his boxers on and . . .' I put my head in my hands. How did they know all this? 'Is everyone in the kitchens having a good laugh about me throwing the owner's son out of his own hotel room?' I mum-bled through my fingers, cringing at the thought.

'No, of course not! They're . . .' Helen stifled a snigger without much success. 'They're talking about how it *would* be you who found the naked gatecrasher.'

'And what's that supposed to mean?' I asked, affronted. 'It *would* be me?'

'Nothing, never mind. Look, I don't know what you're getting your knickers in a twist about,' she said. 'Running a hotel's a thankless task, you know that. Joe's clearly just doing this under sufferance. Give him a fortnight and he'll be back on the plane to LA. Get him to assemble wedding favours or something. Listen, forget about all that. I need your advice about something much more important.'

I gave Helen my most 'professional ethics' look. 'If it's about Kevin and his new menu, I keep telling you – I can't make Dominic review restaurants. And it would look really dodgy for him to give Kevin five stars, even if the meal is amazing. . .'

'I wish.' She gripped her mug to her chest and suddenly looked droopy. 'No, it's about Seamus. I don't know what to do.'

'About what?' I asked warily. There was a lot Helen didn't know what to do about Seamus. Where did you start? 'About moving in together?'

'No. That's on the back burner again, after we, er, had a disagreement about, look, it doesn't matter what.'

'Tell me.'

Helen groaned. 'His glasses.'

'His glasses? Seamus wears glasses?'

'No, he doesn't. That's the point. We had a humungous fight about it over the weekend.'

'Okay,' I said slowly.

The things that Seamus could pick a Big Fight over were astonishing. He had a real talent for being offended. Over the years I'd known Seamus be plunged into filthy moods by, in no particular order, vegetarians, Hass avocados, pigeon (the version you find on menus, not the 'Feed the birds, tuppence a bag' kind) and diners who ordered soup off his menu. Or indeed anyone who tried to order anything off his menu who he didn't think would appreciate it.

Personally I thought most of Seamus's problems could be cured by Helen dumping him, but she was my best friend, so I did what I could. 'So, what brought this on?'

Helen looked uncomfortable, as if she knew what she was about to say was crazy, but, to be honest, by now nothing she could tell me about Seamus would be a surprise. 'Oh, he had another near miss with my depilatory cream at the weekend – thought it was toothpaste, you know, the usual . . . and I told him he should get an eye test, before he chopped his finger off or worse . . .' She shrugged self-consciously, then ploughed on; '. . . and he said that he couldn't possibly go to the opticians in case they did something to interfere with his palate. His senses are very finely balanced, apparently. Doesn't need to see what he's chopping, he *feels* it around him. And he doesn't want people to mistake him for Heston Blumenthal. But then he kicked over two glasses of wine on my carpet, so we ended up having an argument about that and he stormed out again,' she finished quickly.

We looked at each other, each thinking exactly the same thing ('Helen, you are dating a rageful toddler'), then she came out with the thing one of us said every time we had this conversation, and we'd had it lots.

'It's good that he has passion, though. It's what makes him the brilliant chef he is.'

It was what made him the least suitable boyfriend in the world for someone as nice as Helen, I thought, but since Dominic was also prone to irrational tantrums and equally vain about his appearance, I just said, 'Well, yes. Obviously.'

This time, Helen carried on staring at me, a helpless look in her eyes, as if this time she hoped I'd say something different.

'What?' I asked. 'I had the same thing with Dom the other weekend. He walked out of a café because the waiter said the poached eggs were organic free-range, so he asked for one from the kitchen to check and it was only free-range.' It had been quite a scene. Someone had even tweeted a photo of him yelling about it. 'But it's important to keep your standards high, isn't it?'

'Yes. Well . . . oh dear.' Helen bit her lower lip, and for the millionth time I wondered if Seamus had the faintest idea how much he'd lucked out by dating her.

Some things you need to know about Seamus Lynch:

1. He's a brilliant chef and has won all sorts of awards for doing mind-blowing things with cinnamon ketchup and so on.
2. He's a total idiot.

It's quite a short list. That's literally all you need to know. Well, actually, there's also:

3. He is a classic Sexy Chef – stubbly demi-beard, very short blond hair, rock-star mood swings, can make you an incredible omelette at three in the morning, speaks fluent French and Italian (but mainly swearwords).

Number 3 didn't cut much ice with me; I was immune to Seamus's stringy sex appeal. Dominic could be rude, but he could also be very charming, and I never trusted skinny chefs. All that energy had to go somewhere. However, Helen was besotted with Seamus and put up with the most outrageous behaviour, so he clearly had skills I wasn't aware of, and frankly didn't want to know about. They'd been dating for three years on and off (often off); it was a very intense relationship, based on the two hours per month they managed to carve out when neither of them was working late.

'If he needs an eye test, he should go for an eye test. You're not his mother, Hel. You don't have to put up with—' I started, but she raised a hand.

'I know,' she said. 'Don't tell me.'

I bit my lip. It was hard to stop myself marching into Helen's house and dumping Seamus personally. But then it's always easier to see what's wrong in other people's relationships, isn't it? Especially when they make you feel a bit less bad about your own.

I checked my watch; I had ten minutes before a conference call between a florist and a bride who now carried Farrow & Ball paint cards around to ensure everything was exactly the right shade for her dress. I had visions of her holding it up to the sky on her wedding day and demanding the clouds were more Wimborne White. The afternoon sun was warming the fire escape and the tangy smell of London summer rose up from the streets below: crushed grass, sun-baked pavements, and the roses and lavender from the courtyard gardens.

I loved this private side of the hotel no one knew about. It was like being allowed to go behind the stage curtains and see all the lifts and trapdoors, being able to watch all the passersby and pigeons and black cabs and red buses from high up in the balconies.

Helen finished her mouthful of cake and fixed me with her poised expression. She was already looking less droopy, and more Grace Kelly.

Time for our reaffirmation.

'It's better to date a complicated man than a boring one,' she said, solemnly. 'Right?'

'Right,' I said, thinking of the conversation Dominic and I had had about the flat. At least when he committed to the joint mortgage I'd know he really meant it. I'd rather he took his time to decide and was sure, rather than promising and then backing . . . I swallowed.

Dominic wasn't going to back out. He wasn't like Anthony. I always knew exactly what Dominic was thinking because he had no compunction about telling me or anyone else what was on his mind. Anthony had been a brooder. Politer than Dominic but – hang on, what was I saying? What the hell was *polite* about leaving your bride at the altar because you couldn't think of 'the right way' to tell her you didn't want to get married?

'Much better,' I said.

'Good,' she said. 'Now, make sure you make that follow-up call to the Hunters, and I'll go and invent a fabulous reception tasting menu for them.'

It hadn't escaped my notice that for two women who spent their days arranging the perfect start to other people's married lives, we weren't exactly making great progress with our own. Or maybe that was part of the problem.

CHAPTER SIX

Though my office was small, it had three perfect features: a large original French window that opened out onto the rose garden; a wall thin enough to hear loud conversations going on in Laurence's office next door (something he wasn't aware of, going the other way, because I never yelped in agony when bending over a drinks cabinet or yelled down the phone at my ex-wives); and a wall big enough to take my Bridelizer.

The Bridelizer was a modified year planner mounted on a massive pinboard, and it was the secret weapon in my meticulous wedding planning. I'd originally called it the Strategic Wedding Planner, but that had been shortened early on by Gemma to something 'a bit less policey-sounding.' It was mounted on a pinboard so it could be turned around to display an engraving of Green Park when a bride was in my office – she was, obviously, the only bride I was looking after ever in the history of weddings – but for the rest of the time it served as a visual reminder to me and the team of where we were on the merry-go-round of hypnotically similar tied bouquets and poached salmon luncheons.

Now that I was working to Laurence's revised target, the

Bridelizer was more important than ever in terms of keeping me on track. It was divided into months, with a Polaroid of the bride, and sometimes her fiancé if we'd met him, plus her theme, and an invitation so the details were engraved on our minds, as well as on the cards. Some months were more crowded than others. I already had two weddings in April and three in May for next year, and the following Valentine's Day slot was being held two years in advance for one particularly starry-eyed girl called Lauren who'd already bought her dress in a Vera Wang sample sale. I wasn't sure if her boyfriend knew, though. About the dress or the wedding booking.

For every successful wedding completed, I added a bouquet to the column running up the right-hand edge of the pinboard. Gemma and Helen assumed they were just to keep track of how many weddings we'd done, but what I didn't tell them was that each bouquet now represented the tiny steps I was taking towards Laurence's target of a twenty per cent increase. Once I got level with Alice Invarary's Roman nose in March next year, I'd have done it. Laurence had said June, but it had occurred to me that if I hit it earlier I could push to get my pay rise and promotion sooner, the better to convince the bank to approve my joint mortgage with Dominic.

So far, the bouquets had only reached Laura Southwell (December wedding, mulled wine on arrival, huge globes of mistletoe and holly, vintage fur-tipped cape for the bride). A really major society wedding – ideally Flora Thornbury's – would punt that bouquet up to Jessie Callum's *My Fair Lady*-themed reception, and I'd be home and dry.

But first I had to book in seventeen classically English weddings, arrange them, run them, wave the bride and groom off on honeymoon, settle the invoice – starting this morning with a new assistant who didn't even wear full-length trousers.

It's only for a couple of months, I told myself, and opened my day book to prepare for the day ahead. Then I closed the book, and made a very strong pot of coffee.

Joe's introductory meeting as part of the events team didn't bode well for his future contribution to our department.

He was ten minutes late, which made me fidgety, on top of my existing 'boss's son sitting in on my meeting' nervous. I didn't like lateness – it reduced the amount of time available to sort out cock-ups – and as I was always telling Gemma, you couldn't afford to be even a second over your timetable as an events planner. It could be the difference between a bride staying, and a bride flouncing off.

Gemma and Helen had both appeared in my office five minutes early; neither of them was bothering to hide her curiosity about Joe, though I was doing my best to ignore it.

'I think we should make a start,' I said, shuffling my papers in a way that made me feel like a newsreader. I didn't mean to, but I couldn't stop myself. For some reason, I'd thought it was a good idea to wear my skirt suit to reinforce the message that events was a serious business, and the waistband was cutting into me. 'It's twenty to ten already.'

'No,' said Helen, as if she were speaking to a small child. She crossed her legs and leaned back on the padded chair. 'We're not all here. Chill your boots. He's probably got lost. This hotel's like a rabbit warren if you're not familiar with it. All the carpets are the same.'

'This is the office next to his dad's,' I pointed out. 'And he lived here until he was eighteen.'

'Shall I note that?' Gemma asked, her pen poised. 'Joe is late?'

I was about to say, 'Yes, why not note that,' when the door opened and Joe appeared.

I blinked because for a moment I didn't realize it *was* Joe. This morning's Joe looked like a different person again to the one I'd met in Laurence's office, much less the one I'd encountered in the bridal suite. The board shorts had gone, and in their place was a pair of chinos topped by a blue checked shirt – albeit one that already looked as if it had spent several weeks at the bottom of a laundry basket at the same time as still having visible packet creases.

The blond hair was still long and rumpled, though, and he hadn't shaved. And he was wearing his horrible shell necklace. On this showing I could probably introduce him to a florist, but definitely nobody more important in the wedding hierarchy.

'Sorry I'm late,' he said, with a half-apologetic smile that I spotted Gemma returning at full-beam. 'Slept in. Jet lag.'

'Which?' I said, before I could stop myself.

He raised an eyebrow, as if he couldn't believe someone might question why he was late for his first-ever meeting. 'Both?'

'Probably culture shock, too,' said Helen cheerfully. 'Getting used to an English breakfast again, eh?'

Joe ran a hand through his hair. 'Yeah, actually, where are you getting your coffee from? Because it's pretty poor compared with what people expect as standard in the US now.'

Gemma's mouth dropped open.

Fresh start, I told myself, before the irritation could take hold. *Be positive. Be nice.* The coffee could be a bit . . . variable, sometimes. Laurence thought caffeine was the devil's work.

'I'll speak with our supplier!' said Helen brightly.

'Joe, do you know Helen? Helen Yardley, our restaurant manager, and Gemma Lane, Laurence's PA and my events assistant.'

'Junior events planner,' said Gemma. 'Or deputy wedding coordinator, depending on the event.'

'Again, Gemma, that remains technically under discussion,' I added, still smiling.

Helen had risen from her seat and extended her hand towards Joe; she had a very elegant way of doing that which I'd tried and failed to master since we'd been mates. My handshake was still more headmistress than cool starlet. 'Hello!' She smiled charmingly. 'How lovely to meet you at last. I've heard so much about you.'

'Really?' said Joe, casting a wary look in my direction. 'What's Rosie said? That she had to call security on me?'

'Of course not! I never said—' I blustered.

'She hasn't told us anything, apart from the exciting news that you're work-shadowing us all.' Helen carried on smiling at Joe. 'I had a brief meeting with Laurence this morning – he told me that you were working your way around the hotel. He's trying to get the heads of department together for a formal lunch so we can welcome you properly.'

Joe immediately looked pained, the same expression he'd worn when Laurence told him he'd be starting with weddings. 'Really? I told him not to do that. I don't want a big fuss made about the boss's son, you know, touring the hotel . . .'

Being handed a plum job on a plate without any experience or actual desire to do it, said a voice that sounded a bit like Dominic's in my head. I squashed it.

'Don't worry. We'll treat you exactly as we would any intern,' I said, and shuffled my papers again. 'So, ah ha! You're late! Don't be late again! Sit down and let's get on with the meeting.'

Helen looked at me a bit oddly and made a *stop shuffling the papers* gesture. I guessed it had come out less amusingly than it had sounded in my head.

'Joe?' Gemma was tilting her head. 'I'm taking minutes, but if you'd like to take minutes in the future, as part of your shadowing experience, you only have to say.'

'Thank you,' said Joe. 'But I have no idea how you'd even start doing that.'

'I can show you,' she said, getting up eagerly. 'It's very easy . . .'

I coughed. 'Gemma, if you could minute for today. Joe, have a seat, and we'll get started. Lots to get through.'

He sat down and I noticed that both Helen and Gemma started fiddling with their hair. Even Helen, whose hair was usually so neatly hair-sprayed it could withstand both kitchen flood and chef meltdown.

'Normally in these meetings we have a discussion about what's coming up in the longer-term diary, as well as the weddings booked in for the next few weeks,' I began briskly. 'It should give you an idea of the sort of workload we manage on a daily basis.'

I was hoping that mention of workload would be enough to put off Joe and his 'wilderness experience' background, but he just leaned back in his chair, crossed his long legs and started to inspect the plate of biscuits Helen had brought with her from Delphine's pastry room.

'So, first of all, the headline news is that Flora Thornbury will be coming in at the end of the week to discuss her potential wedding with us next June. This could be a milestone wedding for us, because as you know, Flora's just landed the big Marks and Spencer contract, so please can we make sure that everything is absolutely spot on and camera-ready, in case Flora's taking photos. We might end up on her Instagram feed or something.'

Gemma made an *ooh* noise as her pen flew across the page.

'We'll be treating her in exactly the same way we would any other potential bride at the Bonneville,' I went on, 'which is to say, as if she's the only bride marrying in our hotel. It's a very important part of our wedding ethos,' I added, more to Joe than to the others, who'd heard this many times before, 'that we make the bride feel as if she's stepping into her own private venue from the moment we begin to plan her big day. We don't ever refer to any other weddings taking place, or make any sort of comparisons.'

Joe's brow furrowed. 'I thought the aim of building the wedding service was to make make this into the most *popular* place in London?'

'Exactly.' I nodded.

'So presumably brides *want* to know that lots of other very fashionable people have got married here?'

'Word of mouth is our best advert, yes.'

'So why are you pretending she's the only bride you're looking after?'

I stopped. There was a certain – *male* – logic to that. 'Well, because all brides want to feel they're special. A bride chooses the Bonneville because she's heard our weddings are super-elegant and sophisticated and romantic. And she wants to know she's choosing a trusted venue. But once she's here, we want to make her feel as if she's the only bride in the world.'

Joe looked confused. Or possibly 'confused'; I couldn't imagine what was confusing about what I'd just said. 'But I don't get why you'd even pretend. Isn't it better to be really honest and upfront about it from the start?'

'There's honesty and there's wedding honesty,' I said.

'And what does that mean?'

'As in, "Pale green doesn't suit all bridesmaids",' Gemma supplied helpfully, 'as opposed to, "You look like you're being followed down the aisle by four leeks".'

I looked askance at her; Helen snorted with laughter and pretended she was clearing her throat.

'So,' I went on, because time was pressing, 'Flora will be coming in, and we'll be going through the wedding options with her—'

'Isn't it the other way round?'

Again I looked up from my notes to see Joe looking 'confused'. 'Sorry?'

'Shouldn't *she* be telling *you* what *she* wants?' He raised his palms in apparent confusion. 'Isn't that how it works? She comes in, and we give her the unique, personalized wedding of her dreams?'

I put my pen down. 'The thing is, Joe, weddings are complicated, and for everyone's sake, they need to run on a timetable and in a certain way. We've got a system we trust—'

'Then no is the answer,' said Joe. 'You give them the wedding *you* want.'

'No! Of course we *listen* to their requests and I do everything we can to accommodate them ... within reason,' I protested, 'but our job is to give them the Bonneville wedding we're known for, and that's a very traditional affair. That's why they come here. You don't go to Chanel for a onesie, do you?'

Joe slumped back in his seat. 'Okay. Fine. So what about the groom? When's he coming in?'

'I don't think he is. Is he, Gemma?'

'No,' said Gemma. 'I can't even remember what he's called.'

'His name is Milo,' I said at once. 'Milo McKnight. He's an art dealer. I doubt he'll be joining us in the planning meetings. We tend to see brides with their mothers or their bridesmaids, not their fiancés.'

'Why? Isn't it the groom's day too?'

Gemma's head was swivelling between me and Joe, her eyes

wide. She clearly hadn't anticipated him taking such an active role in the proceedings. Neither had I.

I realized I didn't have an official answer for this. 'Grooms just don't tend to be as interested. And the bride's often been thinking about her dream wedding for a long time. She has specific ideas.'

'As has her mother,' Helen added. 'Usually her mother's been thinking about the wedding *she* wanted to have, before *her* mother made her have the wedding *she* wanted.'

I nodded. We'd had a run of difficult mothers in the past few months. I'd had to deploy Laurence and his charm offensive to talk them down.

'Ooh, are you talking about that right Mumzilla we had in last week?' Gemma said, reading my mind with her usual magnificent discretion. 'Did Mr Bentley Douglas manage to talk her out of having the joint vow renewal with the bride's dad?'

I glanced at Joe, who didn't really need to know this, and said quickly, 'He did, yes. But she still wants to sing. So we'll need to come up with another strategy for that.'

'Professional performing rights,' said Helen in a flash. 'Or piano issues.'

'*Why* would you want to stop her mother singing?' Joe argued. 'Or having a vow renewal? Isn't it a nice celebration of a lasting marriage?'

'Not when Mummy wants to wear her original wedding dress too,' said Gemma. 'That's just showing off. Poor bride's already on a liquid vegan diet.'

Joe's eyes focused properly for the first time since he'd

arrived, but not in a good way. In an argumentative way. 'I'm amazed anyone's actually allowed to get married here.'

I felt tetchy. Why should I have to justify my highly regarded events planning to someone who'd never even *been* to a Bonneville wedding? 'Joe, you've clearly got some strong ideas of your own about weddings,' I said lightly. 'Have you been to many?'

'Enough. And is it a *strong* idea to think it should be all about the bride *and* groom, not just some big princess wish-fulfilment party?' he countered. 'That weddings should just be about two people and their spiritual commitment to each other in their own way, not what kind of canapés are in this week?'

'And that's what we provide,' I said hotly. 'An elegant celebration of the marriage of two people, without any tacky glitz or trendy nonsense. The perfect English hotel wedding ceremony.'

He raised an eyebrow, then sank back into his chair, crossed his arms, and looked tired again. As if he really, *really* didn't want to be here now.

I thought I was pretty good at reading people, but I couldn't work out what was going on under the messy blond hair. Was he pro-weddings? Anti-weddings? Whatever, I had no intention of letting him derail the Thornbury wedding meeting. Even if Laurence was lining Joe up to be manager, I wanted it to be clear from the start: there was no way he was going to interfere with my events.

'Right, so when Flora comes in with her mother on Friday, I thought we'd start with tea,' I said, 'then show off the rooms. Helen, you could come in and have a chat about the menu options?'

Helen uncapped her silver pen. 'Okay. What time?'

'About half ten? Just for ten minutes.'

'Fine.' She made a note. 'I'll tell Delphine to do those special almondy pastry things in the shape of hearts. Oh, hang on. Do supermodels eat pastries?'

I thought of Flora's last lingerie campaign, the one that had been projected on the side of the Tate Modern. Even magnified to that size, I hadn't been able to spot any cellulite on her racehorse legs. 'No. But her mum probably will.'

'Would you like me to come and take notes?' Gemma asked.

'No,' I said firmly, 'I think we should keep it quite low-key.'

'Aw, please? I can fill you in on all her exes. So you don't put your foot in it?'

Gemma was an avid reader of *Heat* magazine – and any other magazine that featured Circles of Shame and charts that detailed who'd dated whom and when. She was constantly revising her own spreadsheet about which celebrity couples were about to get engaged, and how she would arrange their weddings in the hotel. I thanked God most days that we didn't have a big enough turning circle in the courtyard for Gemma's favourite glass coach and two white horses.

'I'm the celebrity consultant,' Gemma informed Joe. 'I keep Rosie up to speed with all the breaking celebrity news.'

He leaned forward in his chair, fixed her with his pale blue eyes, and, just as Gemma flushed an excited deep pink, said, in the manner of a guru, 'Gemma, all that celebrity stuff is utter bollocks.' Then, to my surprise, he turned to me and said, 'Can I sit in?'

I was thrown. I couldn't say no. I didn't really want to say yes. 'Why, if it's all bollocks?'

'Because I'm supposed to be learning how weddings work?'

'Er, yes. Of course.'

I tried to work out whether there was an ulterior motive in it. Joe probably wanted to see a supermodel in the flesh, I reckoned, regardless of all that high-minded business about celebs. Anthony had always claimed to be a card-carrying socialist, but he'd still made a special detour to collect me from work when Kate Middleton had popped in for tea in the Palm Court with her sister.

Joe was regarding me with an expression that reminded me of Laurence at his most inscrutable, so I smiled back in a blandly friendly way. What harm could it do? He'd probably be bored senseless within five minutes. I'd go through the catering quote in minute detail and he'd soon make his excuses.

'Good, so that's that,' I said, turning to the rest of my agenda. 'Now, the rest of this week. Stephanie Miller's rehearsal dinner is tomorrow night, after the rehearsal in the afternoon. To recap, the wedding's on Saturday – three o'clock start, afternoon tea in the garden, black tie dinner in the evening in the ballroom, then dancing until one . . .'

I watched out of the corner of my eye as Joe's attention drifted into the garden, where pigeons were perching on the fountain.

'Big princess wish-fulfilment thing' indeed. Pretty rich coming from a man who hadn't, as far as I could see, ever come back off his gap year.

CHAPTER SEVEN

Dominic and I had a lot of meals out, but they weren't all what you'd call romantic. There were usually at least three of us round the table at any intimate dinner for two: me, him and his notebook.

This was actually an intimate lunch for nine, if you also counted the waiters, the manager, the chef, the sommelier and the 'cocktail creative' who were hovering nervously around us like shy moths at a lamp party. We were in a new seafood bar, Benny and the Nets, I was trying to whisk Dominic through the courses as quickly as possible, so we could pop into an open-house viewing in Lambeth before I had to get back to meet some florists at four, but we kept being interrupted by staff checking we were having a wonderful time.

The flat situation had moved on a few steps, in that I'd spoken to my bank, cajoled a vague promise of a deposit loan from my parents, and managed to steer Dominic's attention away from his main priority, a flat with 'a shower powerful enough to peel new potatoes', and onto how we'd actually finance our joint purchase.

'. . . and I know you'll like this place because apparently the showers are so violent that you can't let children use them unsupervised – oh, for heaven's sake,' I muttered, after yet another *amuse-bouche* was delivered to our table under two choreographed silver domes. We hadn't even finished looking at the menu. I'd only just worked out how to get it open. It came in a weird orange net that was meant to reflect the restaurant theme: organic seafood 'with a twist'.

In the two years I'd been living my twilight life as Betty, I'd learned to dread the phrase 'with a twist'. It usually just meant 'served in a plant pot'.

'Those sound like my kind of showers,' said Dominic without taking his eyes off the bizarre list of starters. 'Ooh. What do you think jellyfish in froth tastes like?'

'Angry? Excited?' I shoved the Old Vintners Development prospectus towards him. 'Sounds more like a natural disaster than a seafood special. Look, the completion date for this conversion is November, so if we put a deposit down now we could—'

'Ha! Very good. Natural disaster.' Dom reached for his notebook, and I told myself to say something. I didn't mind helping him with observations about the food but I did want proper credit for my jokes. Talking to Helen about Seamus had that effect; for a few days afterwards, it made me more determined not to let things get *that* bad.

But, to my surprise, Dominic murmured aloud as he wrote, 'Betty said she was more concerned for the frothy jellyfish than tempted to eat it.'

'Thank you,' I said, mollified somewhat.

No, Dominic was nothing like Seamus. Seamus was a liability.

Dominic was . . . the right side of unpredictable. The interesting side.

The waiter reappeared, doing that invisible hand-washing thing that gave me unwelcome mental images of hand sanitizer. I kept that to myself.

'Are you ready to order?' he enquired. 'Because chef wanted me to pass on the message that if there's anything off our menu you'd like, you only have to say. Anything at all.'

'We'll be ordering from the menu, thanks,' Dominic assured him, safe in the knowledge that *he* wouldn't have to have the frothy jellyfish.

'We can always rustle you up . . . a burger?' The waiter raised his eyebrow. When Dominic got too impatient with a restaurant's conceptual offerings, he sometimes asked for a burger. To see if the chef could really cook – or, alternatively, how fast one of the washing-up lads could sprint round to the nearest burger joint.

'No, it all looks so delicious.' I really hated the grovelling that often ensued on these meals out. I couldn't help thinking of Helen, fuming in the kitchen trying to please the critic while keeping the chef from putting a pan through the wall because the critic had asked for salt.

I glanced down, and tried to remember what I was supposed to have. For once, I felt like having what I actually wanted. 'I'll have the potted mackerel to start, then the, um, prawns on the lawn? Whatever they are?'

'A great choice. And for you, sir?'

Dominic reeled off (ha! I made a note to use that later) a selection of dishes he fancied, but, I noted, no chips. 'And can you serve the sauce on the side?' he added, with a light pat to the stomach.

'No chips?' I said before I could stop myself. In addition to last week's reference to Betty being on a diet – which I wasn't – I'd noticed Dom had omitted to put Nutella on last week's supermarket delivery, despite Nutella sandwiches being his favourite midnight snack. Four jars of Nutella were usually the only things on 'his' side of the kitchen cupboard.

He pretended to be surprised that I'd asked. 'Not unless you want some?'

'I'm on a diet. Apparently,' I said, but he didn't react, so I looked up at the waiter and handed back my menu. 'That's all, thanks.'

Was Dominic on a diet? I knew better than to bring up the sticky topic of weight – I spent my day with brides, after all – but maybe he was. I wondered why. He'd always been pleasantly solid, something I found rather attractive, actually, but maybe the constant eating was getting to him.

'So how are things going with Little Lord Fauntleroy, King of the Wild Frontier?' he asked as the bread arrived in a miniature lobster pot. No matter how crazily themed the restaurant, there was always bread. Only the receptacle changed. 'Has he had the revolving door replaced with a zip wire yet?'

'Not yet.' Helen and Gemma were both rather taken by Joe, but Dominic wasn't impressed so far with my reports. He was highly scornful of people who didn't own hard-shell luggage and talked about 'travelling' instead of 'going on holiday'. 'I don't know how long he's going to stick it in events. He told me yesterday that weddings should be individual celebrations of a couple's relationship, ideally with just the bride and groom and a humanist minister. Everything else is merely social pressure to eat tiny cakes.'

'He *said* that?'

I nodded. 'In front of Delphine, too. It's a good job she's still not great with English accents. He'd have been wearing those éclairs otherwise.'

Dominic winced. 'Well, those tiny cakes are doing pretty well for his dad's hotel, aren't they? Hasn't he seen how his inheritance is being financially stabilised by a pile of tee-ny-weeny cupcakes while he surfs his way round the world? The ungrateful slacker.'

I reached for a roll. 'I think it's the celebrity thing he doesn't have much time for. Or fashion. He's one of those "be honest all the time" types.'

Dominic looked gleefully disapproving. 'And that's what happens when you move to California. They encourage people to be brutally honest just to keep the therapy industry going.'

'Well, it bothers me. I don't think it's always *best* to be completely honest with brides. They're in a different reality as it is.' I stared at the tiny crystals of salt on the dish; it was perfect salty butter. 'If he talks to them like he talks to the rest of us, I'm going to be mopping up hysterics for the next seven weeks. Laurence is insisting he's in every meeting.'

'What? Even that big meeting with the supermodel?'

'Even that. In fact, Joe asked to be there. Specifically. God knows why.'

Dominic waved his butter knife dismissively. 'Send him out to get whatever the wedding equivalent of tartan paint is. Invisible confetti, or bride hooks, or something. Get her in, do the meeting, let him wave her off. I can't think that Pouty McLegs—'

'Flora Thornbury.'

'—is going to be impressed with some beach bum banging on about being *totally honest* about her wedding vows and how fat her bridesmaids look.' He sat back in his chair and gazed across the table at me with delight. 'Honesty at a wedding. I love it. Only a complete idiot could think that's a good idea. Can you imagine? If Jamie Hobson had been *honest* about the fact that the stag do was in Prague and not at Silverstone, like Sophie thought? Or if I'd been *totally honest* about that weird cake they tried to serve at the McLintock reception?'

Dominic and I didn't go to a lot of weddings, mainly thanks to my weekends being taken up with arranging other people's, and him professing to be very tired of poached salmon. He'd been to a few recently on his own – he had a lot of university mates, as well as work colleagues – but I was happy to let him go by himself. To be honest, even though I was *very* much over Ant, if I wasn't actively running proceedings, weddings made me a bit self-conscious. Dominic was surprisingly sensitive about it. He and I had never really talked about the Non-Wedding of the Year, apart from one night when we'd been drunk and he'd told me he'd have punched Ant, had he been his best man. I'd been quite touched by that.

I could see a waiter hovering in the background, and suddenly I wished we could be having this private conversation at home, in our flat. On our sofa, with our feet up. Not in a restaurant with waiters hovering and Dominic's notebook out. But then we were only ever at home together for about twenty minutes a day; most of those breakfast conversations were him giving me directions to some pop-up chimichanga-Korean-fusion launch.

A funny pang hit me from nowhere, and I blinked. Had I really just yearned for a boring night in with my boyfriend and a bottle of wine, rather than a glittery free dinner out in a new restaurant?

'Rosie?' Dom prompted. 'Admit it. You're thinking about that awful wonky wedding cake? The one you said looked like a badly stacked set of soup plates.'

'I didn't go to the McLintock wedding,' I reminded him. 'That must have been one of your own jokes.'

'Ah yes.' He pretended to look apologetic. 'I thought it wasn't up to your usual high standard.'

I felt his foot press against my inner calf under the table, and my funny pang changed to a more warming glow of happiness that this handsome, funny man was *my* man. I'd never met anyone whose eyes actually twinkled like Dom's. Thank God they did. They were nature's way of compensating for some of the things he came out with.

'What were you thinking about?' he asked. 'You looked miles away. Was it this flat we're going to see? The shower sounds great, by the way. I'm really looking forward to living somewhere with modern heating. I don't think I could have stood another winter wrapped in blankets like a Victorian urchin.'

I hesitated – I didn't want to say I'd been thinking about weddings, it'd come out wrong – but I was too late. Dominic pretended to look reproachful. 'You were thinking about work. Sorry, for a moment there I thought we were talking about something not related to your job.'

'No. I was thinking about the flat . . .' I started, but Dominic could read me too well.

He squinched up his face, then said, 'Look, don't worry, he can't give his son the job straight off the bat.'

'What do you mean?'

'I know that's what you're bothered about. Laurence doing the old nepotism-promotion thing. But how many departments has the prodigal son got to work his way around?' Dominic started counting on his fingers. 'Events, bar, restaurant, house-keeping, reservations . . . that's nearly a year. He's bound to get bored by then. You'll be fine. And if Laurence is daft enough to give a beach bum with no management experience the most important job in the hotel, then I will write your resignation letter myself and find you a decent position somewhere else, where your boss might actually appreciate the work you do, and maybe even let you have a life. Ah, the starters! Marvellous!'

The team of choreographed waiters arrived and started putting the usual slabs of slate down in front of us, but even though the food smelled very nice, suddenly I didn't feel very hungry.

One of the growing number of American wedding traditions that was becoming very popular for us in the hotel was the rehearsal dinner.

I didn't suggest it to clients as such – it was yet another potential seating-plan stress-out, at the exact moment that most brides didn't need more stress *or* seating plans *or* additional time with their immediate family – but if I had a bride who either was American or read a lot of American wedding sites, then we could cater the most fabulous rehearsal dinner required in the private dining room. It did bump up my profit margin, I'll be honest. And it flushed out any post-rehearsal familial simmering before the official photographer arrived on the scene.

Stephanie Miller was both of the above: a Bostonian bride who began every other sentence with the phrase, 'I saw this amazing thing online . . .' The sentences that didn't start like that started with, 'Rosie, I don't want to make a fuss but . . .' On the whole, I preferred the 'online' sentences; they usually featured something that actually existed, whereas most of Stephanie's own detail-driven suggestions would only be possible in films. I did my best, obviously.

When Stephanie wasn't detailing the exact dimensions of the petits fours she wanted placed on each coffee saucer or making paper models of her entire guest list with photo faces so she could 'visualize their conversation' at the reception tables, she was a mergers and acquisitions lawyer in an American law firm. I could see the crossover; she was very, very sure about what she wanted, which included her husband-to-be, English Richard, a handsome, bald, golf-playing businessman whose company Stephanie's firm had put into receivership three years earlier.

'As soon as I saw Richard on the other side of the table in the liquidation meeting, I knew we were destined to be together,' she'd told me in our first meeting, eighteen months ago. 'And would you believe it, he said the same thing! It was like the most amicable merger ever!'

Richard didn't say much. He was one of those strong, silent types, which was just as well, because Stephanie did the talking for both of them. But they never stopped holding hands, and on one occasion arrived to taste wedding cake in matching golf wear. Since then, I'd seen Stephanie on a regular basis, and I'd privately rated them at a solid eight-out-of-ten compatibility on my private How Long Do You Give It?-o-meter.

Today was the first time all the bridesmaids, ushers and families on both sides had met, with some having flown in just that morning. I'd suggested having the dinner, held in our private dining room, a few nights before the wedding – Stephanie's preparation timetable didn't allow for it happening any sooner anyway – just in case there were any tricky issues, but for once even I couldn't see a single cloud in the nuptial sky.

I was so confident that all arrangements were in place that once I'd welcomed Stephanie and Richard to the drinks reception, I let Laurence 'steal me away' for half an hour to explain how to make his printer work. By the time it was happily spewing out his latest medical forms (I tried not to look), the party seemed to be well under way with Gemma and the bar staff in charge.

'Is everything okay with the Millers?' I accosted Gemma as she went past with a depleted canapé tray. I had my file of final ideas with me, just in case Stephanie wanted to discuss anything, but this was meant to be a relaxing evening. The fun part of the wedding prep.

'Everything's fine.'

'Happy with their rooms? Did they get the Welcome to London packs I left for them? With the Oyster cards?'

'Loved them. Mrs Miller wants to thank you herself later.'

I beamed. 'Good. And the Hendersons?'

'Drinking like they haven't seen water in weeks. But that might be because the ushers are starting to spill the beans about the stag do.'

'I'd better get in there,' I said. 'Don't want them to think we've abandoned them!'

'No worries, Joe's in there with the drinks.'

I stopped, my hand on the door. 'Joe? I didn't know *Joe* was involved tonight?'

Gemma looked harassed. 'You'd gone off to deal with whatever you were dealing with, and I needed to get the canapés. He was passing so I just asked him—'

'I was only in Laurence's office, Gemma! Why didn't you come and get me?' My palms were going clammy.

'The door was shut! And I had to let Helen know that Stephanie's mother's on some new diet and can't eat the main we requested for her after all, and you told me not to leave the party unattended in case they needed something so . . . I asked Joe to go in there and keep an eye on things.'

I made some swift mental calculations. Joe had attended the first part of our rehearsal that afternoon – who stood where, who said what, who passed the hankies to whom, when the music started, that sort of thing – but he'd started to look sceptical when Stephanie wanted to rehearse the perfect kiss moment for the videographer, so there was no unflattering light bounce off Richard's bald head. At that point, I'd dispatched him to the kitchen to be briefed by Helen about catering rehearsal dinners. He hadn't come back, but by then it was five o'clock, so I'd assumed he'd sloped off.

'Don't worry, he knows who everyone is,' Gemma went on. 'And he's good at chit-chat.'

'Is he?'

She looked at me as if I were stupid. 'He's Laurence's son! And he's obviously had loads of practice with American mothers. When I left, Stephanie's aunt was asking him if he'd been to Downton Abbey and he was giving her some spiel about boarding school.'

'And that was all?'

'She was eating out of his hand. Not literally.' Gemma squinted at me. 'I don't know what you've got your knickers in a twist about Joe for. He's fine.'

Mollified, I pushed open the door, but the scene that greeted me wasn't the happy celebration I'd spent a week crafting.

The champagne was out in the silver ice buckets, and the Ella Fitzgerald album was filling the awkward silence, but going by the drawn faces and anxious knots of guests, it looked more like a funeral than a pre-wedding party.

Joe was nearest the door, holding forth to Zara, one of the bridesmaids, about wedding name badges, something he'd brought up at the rehearsal and refused to let go.

'. . . makes complete sense, because how else are you supposed to remember who everyone – oh, hello, Rosie.'

'Hello, Rosie.' Zara's eyes were wide. 'Have you seen Stephanie?'

Something in her tone set off alarm bells. 'Not yet,' I said, trying to keep my own voice neutral. 'Why? Is she wearing that gorgeous dress she said she was saving for this evening?'

'Er, no,' said Zara. 'She vanished about ten minutes ago, and no one knows where she is. She's not in her room. Joe here was the last person who saw her.'

We both turned accusingly to Joe, who helped himself to a passing canapé as if he were a guest, then said, 'What?' through a mouthful of puff pastry.

'Joe?' I said pleasantly, steering him away towards the door. 'Can I just borrow you for a moment to talk about . . . dinner?'

When we were out of earshot, I dropped the pleasantness. 'Where's Stephanie gone?' I hissed. 'Is she all right? Has someone said something to her?'

By 'someone' I really meant 'you'.

He shook his head. 'I don't know. One minute she was fine, the next she was all . . .'

'All what?'

'All ashen-faced. A bit sick? Kind of like she'd eaten magic mushrooms.' Light dawned in his face. 'Oh, man. Is she into that kind of thing?'

'No! Of course not!' My voice rose into a squeak; my bat sensors were detecting a code red. A proper meltdown. 'Stephanie's a corporate lawyer!'

'That means nothing.' Joe arched his eyebrows. 'You would not believe the types I took to the Burning Man festival. Some of them were senior—'

'Please don't tell me.' I raised a warning hand. 'I haven't got time to get annoyed about people I don't know.'

I scanned the room with a grin plastered to my face. I didn't think for one second that Stephanie had taken anything stronger than the cocktail of vitamins and supplements she'd been chugging for the past year, but . . . the canapés? Had there been something in the canapés? Some of the sous had been talking about some mushroom festival they were going to in France. They wouldn't be . . . Surely Kevin wouldn't . . .

Apart from the clear looks of anxiety on her family's faces, there didn't seem to be any immediate signs of vomiting or sickness among the guests.

'Although I suppose I might have . . .' Joe stopped.

I snapped my head back. 'What? Did you say something to Stephanie?'

'Nothing!'

'It can't have been nothing,' I hissed furiously. 'It must have been something.'

Joe raised his hands and dropped them as if he couldn't even remember, but I kept glaring until he sighed and admitted, 'I just asked her where she was planning on going for her honeymoon.'

'Her honeymoon,' I repeated slowly. Innocuous enough. 'Where *are* they going on honeymoon?'

'Some boring art tour of Florence. And I said, "Why? You can go to Florence any time. This is your chance to share an adventure! Why not go to one of those private beaches in Koh Samui and dance on the sand in bare feet, and swim naked in the sea at midnight, or drive across the desert, or try something neither of you have done before, make your own history. Live a little."'

'And?' I had a weird sensation in my chest: it was simultaneously sinking yet fluttery, like lead butterflies crashing away in there. Stephanie was a classicist, a traditionalist, my ideal Bonneville 'family pearls and old lace' bride. She loved old things, like Florence. 'She told you not to be such an old hippie – that there's some amazing art in Florence?'

'No. She said that she'd never swum naked anywhere, and I said, "Seriously, man, you should, it's mind-blowing," and she said that Richard wasn't a swimming-naked guy, but . . .'

'And, and?' I made furious *hurry up* gestures with my hands. Stephanie's parents, two ushers, and the maid of honour all had their phones out and were texting and frowning at the same time. Would a phone amnesty make me look a bit totalitarian, I wondered. Would it be *too* bad to demand everyone put their phones into a box I could lock in my office?

Joe gazed at me. 'Well, Stephanie said that she'd actually looked into swimming with dolphins on their honeymoon because she'd always wanted to do it, but Richard had said that was exploitative – which I kind of agree with, but anyway – so I said, "Don't *you* ever get to choose where you go on holiday?" . . .' He paused. 'And she said no. And that's when she went kind of quiet.'

We stared at each other, and I fought the temptation to throttle him.

'Brilliant. And five seconds later, she leaves the room and no one knows where she is,' I hissed. 'Are you sure that's all you said?'

'Well. I might have . . . asked her if she really wanted to spend the rest of her life with someone who thought swimming naked was unhygienic,' Joe admitted, reluctantly, but at the same time rather *smugly*.

I shoved the file into his hands and ran out of the room. I didn't even care who saw me. All I could see was a forty-thousand-pound wedding collapsing in slow motion like a four-tier cake with its props kicked out.

CHAPTER EIGHT

The ladies' powder rooms at the Bonneville were more elegant than most hotel bedrooms. Each one was decorated in period hand-printed wallpapers and scented with fresh flowers; this one, downstairs near the spa, was a delicate china blue with black-and-white floor tiles and big grey marble sinks, with fluffy hand towels and Jo Malone hand cream.

And a huge mirror decorated with scrolls, in which I could see my own panicked face. I couldn't see Stephanie's face because she was locked in one of the cubicles. I could hear her sobbing, though, so I had a fairly good idea of what it would look like.

'It's fine, Stephanie,' I kept saying. 'Honestly. Whatever it is, we can work it out. I promise.'

I'd almost given up hope and was about to text Jean to come down from housekeeping with her motherly bosom (and her secret key for all the cubicles), when the door finally opened and Stephanie appeared. Her eyes were red and puffy, and her miserable expression didn't go with her chic Diane von Fürstenberg dress and red-soled pumps. She looked guilty and scared, like a little girl.

'Is everybody talking about me?' she asked in a broken voice.

'No, of course not,' I lied. 'I said you've just gone to check on the surprise. I didn't say what the surprise was.' I paused, then added, 'Don't worry, we always have a cake for an emergency surprise.'

Stephanie's lip wobbled as if she were about to burst into tears again. I guided her towards the velvet loveseat in the corner, sat her down, and passed her the box of tissues.

'I'm really sorry if Joe said something to upset you,' I began. 'He's not used to dealing with weddings, he doesn't really understand how stressful . . .'

Stephanie shook her head. 'He didn't upset me.' She took a shuddering breath and covered her mouth, then pressed her lips together. 'Joe put something into words that I realize now I've been thinking for a long time.'

I didn't know how to respond to that: I couldn't imagine Stephanie having an unarticulated thought. She was one of the few people I knew who spoke in complete and legally binding sentences. It was hard to think what *Joe* could have unlocked in her meticulously ordered brain.

'It's Richard.' Stephanie turned her mascara-smeared eyes towards me, and I had to brace myself not to flinch at the panic in them. 'He's boring.'

'Richard? No, he's not boring,' I started, but she grabbed my hand.

'He is. He's really bloody *boring*. We're boring together. We're a boring couple! I've been trying to ignore it, but something Joe said really made me confront it. What kind of *boring* man wants to go to art galleries on his honeymoon? What kind of man doesn't want to swim naked with his girlfriend – because of hygiene issues?' Her voice was getting higher and higher.

'Well, I'm not sure my boyfriend would really want . . .' I had to stop there. I *could* imagine Dominic wanting to swim naked. As long as it was a very exclusive and private beach, I could absolutely see him roaring with glee as he charged down the beach, discarding clothes over his head like an excited bear as he hit the waves. It was *me* who didn't fancy it much.

'Well,' I amended, 'swimming naked isn't everyone's . . .'

Stephanie fixed me with a scared but exhilarated gaze, and the grip on my hand tightened. 'Rosie, I have to call off the wedding.'

The words went through me like a knife. Literally like a knife. Sharp and cold and very painful. I tried to speak despite the sensation of bones grinding in my hand. Stephanie was very nervous, and she had the bride's grip already.

'I understand why you might feel a bit . . . frazzled,' I said. 'This is a very emotional day for you. Getting the families together, going through the ceremony . . . Don't let a little wobble about the honeymoon spoil things. You and Richard are a *wonderful* couple. You're going to be *so* happy together.'

Think about Richard. Does he have any idea you're planning to humiliate him in front of everyone he knows? I bit back the words.

But Stephanie wasn't listening; her eyes were glassy. 'Are we, though? What comes after the wedding? I feel as if I've just been on an escalator towards this weekend – the flowers, the dress, the diet – and I can't get off till we're at the top. No one's ever stopped me to ask if I'm really sure, not until now.'

'But you were going to wedding classes!' I reminded her. 'You must have discussed it there?'

We'd been to wedding classes, me and Ant. We'd worked through conflict resolution, role-played family Christmas bust-ups over in-laws, been very honest about our emotional deal-breakers. Well, I had been, anyway. Anthony had been quiet on the topic. Something twisted inside me. I'd been with Anthony since the night of my nineteenth birthday at college, and yet I hadn't known him at all, not when it came down to it.

Would Ant have gone nudie swimming? I honestly didn't know.

Maybe that should be on the list of topics to discuss with the vicar.

Stephanie gave me a weary look. 'Rosie, have you ever been to a wedding class? They ask you questions about who'll put the trash out. Whether you should be getting married or not tends to be a given. Besides, they want you to finish the course, you pay by the session.' She slumped back against the arm of the loveseat. 'Joe's the first person – the only person! – who's ever asked me if I'm absolutely sure, and . . . I'm not. I'm going to have to call it off.'

As Stephanie said that, my brain divided into two halves like one of those arty split-screen films. One half was panicking about saving this wedding, getting my client calmed down and back into the wedding schedule.

The other half was wondering if Anthony had had a similar

conversation with an unknown Joe the night before *our* wedding. And if so, what had been the tipping point for him? He'd never actually told me specifically, just that it hadn't felt right.

The thoughts flashed across my mind like tiny headaches. Had it been our honeymoon? It was going to be New York. Was that boring? Was I too dull? Had the thought of a lifetime with me made him freeze with panic?

It didn't matter, I told myself, pushing the ache away. Ant was abroad now, he had a new life, and so did I. And thank God I hadn't married him. I'd never have met Dominic, for a start.

'Rosie?' Stephanie's voice dragged me back to the moment. 'What am I going to do?'

'We'll fix it,' I said, automatically, and grabbed her hand. 'It'll be fine.'

Bloody, bloody Joe, I thought, as both halves of my brain united in making a contingency plan to save Stephanie Miller's rehearsal dinner from turning into someone else's horrified anecdote.

'Well, I hope you're pleased with yourself,' I said to Joe under my breath, as Mr and Mrs Miller finally staggered out of the hotel lounge bar, discreetly holding each other up, thanks to the treble brandies Dino had been pouring down them while Richard and Stephanie 'talked' in the room I'd found. Not the bridal suite, obviously. Or the one with the view over the courtyard where they were supposed to be getting married at the weekend. I'd sent Gemma out to get the gold chairs moved, just to be on the safe side.

'I am pleased,' Joe replied, with the pained yet smug regret I recognized from the rare occasions when Laurence's midnight appointment with Dr Google had turned out to be correct. 'I've saved them both from a potential jilting, and the family from a massive nuclear fallout.'

'No, the nuclear fallout is going on now,' I informed him, gesturing tersely upwards. I *hated* the word *jilting*. 'In several rooms. Two sets of parents blaming themselves, then each other, for Stephanie's cold feet. Several best friends squabbling over whether Steph's been seeing someone else. A groom wondering what else he's done because it can't just be about Florence. And meanwhile, is the wedding going to go ahead? It's a major booking, in a peak weekend slot! Not just the wedding, but the guests' rooms, the bar takings, the extra staff . . .'

'So you'd rather she got married to someone she didn't love?' Joe looked astonished. 'For the sake of your spreadsheet?'

I blushed furiously. It was exactly what I meant . . . and it wasn't.

'No!' I took a deep breath. Joe was still my boss's son. I shouldn't project my own experiences onto this. 'We take our wedding planning very seriously here, and of course we do everything we can to make sure we fulfil the bride's and groom's dreams, but it's a *service*. It's not our job to get involved in their relationships. We're here to provide hospitality, not amateur psychotherapy. It's none of our business. Good night!' I added in a brighter tone, as a couple of Stephanie's guests stumbled out of the bar and slunk past us towards the lifts. His hand on her bottom suggested that they were oblivious to anyone else around.

The usher jumped, and the bridesmaid bumped into him. Joe and I smiled back in unison, and they waved and mumbled self-consciously.

'Sympathy and whiskey cocktails are a dangerous combination,' muttered Joe, still smiling.

'As are high heels and hotel carpet,' I muttered back.

And pre-booked rooms and attractive friends of friends in black tie, I thought. Well, if they weren't going to get the chance to have a drunken indiscretion at the wedding . . .

'Good night!' said Joe with a wave; then he turned back to me with a furrowed brow and a much less friendly tone.

'Let me get this straight. Are you really such a business robot that you care more about the takings than two people making a lifetime commitment to each other?'

'I'm not a *business robot*,' I protested. 'You're assuming I don't care about poor Richard in there, not knowing what was going on with Stephanie. And then having to tell everyone he knows that it's all off. You don't know them! I do! They're a perfectly well-matched couple.'

'Obviously not,' he retorted. 'And why poor Richard? Surely it's way better to cancel things now than have Richard end up with a wife who doesn't love him, just because she didn't have the courage to tell him he wasn't right for her? If you ask me, it should be part of the wedding planner's job – to check they really do know what they want.'

The knife was back, steely sharp under my ribs, taking my breath and my common sense away. A half-forgotten pain made me blurt out the words that leaped into my head.

'Why is it any of your business?'

'Because sometimes it's easier for a stranger to be honest,' said Joe, with an expression of humility that was a bit too Bono. 'You have to be honest in life, Rosie. Yes, it's sometimes hard, but it's better to do this now than to get divorced in a year's time.'

'How on *earth* can you know that?' I exploded. 'Lots of people have pre-marriage wobbles. All brides do! It's what happens when you spend four grand on a dress – it passes!'

'That's so English,' snorted Joe. 'Don't talk about your feelings. Bottle it up. *It'll pass.* Like love is some kind of virus.'

'Viruses are forever,' I snapped. 'You're thinking of a cold.'

I stepped back to let a waitress come through with a silver room-service tray. She ducked as she went, as if she might get punched.

'See that? That's a lovely room-service supper,' I said, pointing at it before Joe could comment. 'I asked the kitchens to send something up to Stephanie and Richard. A really nice comfort-food supper. Don't say I'm cold, because I'm not. I care a lot about this hotel, and everyone we look after here. *A lot.*'

It all burst out more emotionally than I'd meant it to. Joe gave me a look that might have been about to turn into a question about whether I'd charged it to their room, but obviously something in my expression told him that was a bad idea. And I was pleased about that. It *annoyed* me to think he could be so wrong about my priorities.

He ran a hand through his thick blond hair. 'It's been a long day,' he said instead.

'It has.'

An awkward silence spread between us. Joe seemed angry but not specifically with me. I was simmering inside, but not specifically with him.

Although, no – I *was* pretty annoyed with him. If Joe was going to start playing the armchair counsellor with every client I had, I wasn't even going to make it to August in my job, let alone meet any targets.

It's just for a few more weeks, I told myself. And then I could pass him on to Helen or Dino, and he could give them grief about the fat content of the tiramisu or whether we should only serve spritzers to people who looked like they might be alcoholics.

The only problem was that I had Flora Thornbury and her mum booked in soon. There was no way I wanted Joe being 'honest' with Flora about her previous boyfriends or how she really felt about millionaire serial-fiancé Milo.

(Yes, I'd done my research.)

I was about to tell Joe, very calmly, that he needed to keep it buttoned from now on, when he disarmed me with a very charming smile. I hadn't seen it before, and it took me by surprise.

'How about a nightcap in the bar?' he suggested. 'Wind down a bit. I think Richard's dad's still in there. Seems like he wants some company now all the bridesmaids have turned in.'

The abrupt change in mood threw me. Joe seemed relaxed enough, but blood was still pounding through my veins like turbo-charged treacle. How could he just switch off like that?

'I need to get home,' I said tightly. 'We can talk about this in the morning.'

'Haven't we talked about it already?' Joe shrugged and smiled again, more encouragingly this time. 'It's done. I hear you. Tact. Be more English. Move on. Come on, let's have a drink.'

'It's nearly midnight.'

'What happens at midnight?' He tipped his head. 'Do you turn into a pumpkin? No, wait – it'd be something hotelly, right? Do you turn into a . . . room-service trolley?'

I wanted to be friendly too, but I couldn't. The talk of jilting had scraped against an old wound, and it was impossible to get the primness out of my voice. I didn't like things going wrong like this. I struggled with myself.

'No, I need to see my boyfriend,' I said. 'I . . . I need to discuss some stuff with him. I'll see you in the morning. We've got a couple coming in to look around the hotel for their reception.' I paused, not wanting to sound as snotty as I suspected I did.

Joe regarded me wryly. 'And you want me to sit there and shut up?'

'No! Just . . . just think of it as an *event* we're pitching,' I said. 'Not a wedding. A complicated, expensive, elegant event. With two people conducting a touching legal ceremony in the middle.'

'That's all it is to you? An event? Like signing a mortgage, but in front of a bunch of friends?' Joe's eyes searched my face with a teasing sort of disbelief, but I found myself resisting the invitation to joke. I could understand now why Stephanie had had had her mental filing thrown up in the air by Joe; something about him was simultaneously provoking, challenging and a bit unsettling. It wasn't so much that he was good-looking – which

I had to admit he was – but that he was . . . genuinely curious. He was that window letting a sharp spring breeze into a room. Sort of refreshing but also, well . . .

'Yes. A really special event that means a lot to the people involved.' I lifted my chin. 'Leave the romance to the happy couple, and we'll concentrate on everything else. It makes it easier all round.'

'Really?' said Joe softly, as if he didn't believe me.

I held his gaze for a few long moments. *No,* I thought, *not really really.* But I didn't have the energy to explain myself right now. Not after a day like today. So I said nothing, a tactic that his mother had taught me for dealing with tricky management situations. Laurence found it unbearable.

Joe, too, seemed to find it quite unsettling. He blinked and ran his hand through his hair again, then coughed.

'Okay,' he said with a wry half-smile. 'Then I'll see you in the morning.'

I managed a smile. As I walked away down the corridor to get my bag from the office, I had the sense that he was watching me, and it took more concentration than normal not to scuff my heels on the thick hotel carpet.

CHAPTER NINE

I woke up the next morning with a throbbing migraine, after a series of too-vivid dreams about being deserted at the altar by a skinny-dipping Stephanie Miller. The rest of the congregation behind me was also naked, and cross about it not being mentioned on the dress code, and in my dream I felt responsible for that too. It was a relief to open my eyes to see Dominic snoring away next to me. Snoring, and smelling of last night's garlic vodka shots, but there.

I left him in bed and got up, checking my phone repeatedly as I made myself breakfast in case there was a message from either Stephanie or Richard, but there was nothing. No messages on my work voicemail either. Despite what I'd said to Joe about a wedding 'just being an event', I felt terrible about poor Stephanie and poor Richard. And I felt even more terrible that them cancelling really would really make a hole on my Bridelizer, even with our cancellation clauses.

I frowned at the boiling kettle. I couldn't get Stephanie's forlorn expression from last night out of my head. For the first time in ages – ever, maybe – I was torn between getting in to work to sort out this mess, and not wanting to go in at all, *because* of it.

When Dominic did appear, looking rakish in the Noël Coward-esque dressing gown his mum had bought him for Christmas, he rolled his sleepy eyes at my attempts to eat porridge, check my phone, shovel down some ibruprofen and do my make-up all at the same time.

'This new flat of ours,' he said, pouring himself some coffee, 'will it have a special room for you to do your early morning panic routine in? You're making me feel like I've forgotten to revise for an exam.'

'I think you're overestimating our budget again,' I said, blinking my mascara dry. 'We can only just afford three whole rooms as it is. Anyway, I only ever see you in the mornings. I relish these brief moments of intimacy.'

'So do I, darling. Why are we out of bran flakes?' Dominic was opening and shutting the kitchen cupboards. 'Oh, hang on! Have you been at my special marmalade?'

'I thought it was just marmalade.' Still no texts. Had Stephanie and Richard checked out? 'Sorry.'

Dominic made a grumbling noise. He was quite territorial about his cupboards. Upstairs, downstairs, in the bathroom. It probably came from being at boarding school. I was hoping that would change when we moved into the new place and made a fresh start, with *our* cupboards, although I couldn't completely dismiss the mental image of Dominic going round bagging the biggest cupboards for himself.

'You're very welcome to do some shopping,' I added. 'Then you can order in what you want.'

He made another noise that might have been 'But you're so much better at it.'

'Are you out this evening?' I asked as he sat down at the breakfast bar with his coffee and nicked my piece of toast.

'Um, yes. Work thing.'

'Want me to come with you? I've got an early finish.'

'What?' Dominic looked horrified. 'God, no, don't waste your night off – it's just a boring drinks thing. You enjoy some down-time. Have a bath, watch a film. Relax.'

I peered at him over my coffee. 'But I'd love to come with you. I'd like to meet some of your work colleagues.'

It was true: I rarely got the chance to meet Dominic's friends because of my stupid hours, but the ones I had met were a lot of fun. Plus, Caroline was always nudging me to make some contacts outside the hospitality network, to expand the possi-bilities for corporate entertaining at the hotel, and Dominic's office was full not only of journalists but of other trendy Hoxton types – the sorts of hipsters who owned pop-up art galleries or ran charity fundraisers – all of which could usefully be trans-lated into events.

'You really don't,' he said evasively.

'Are you ashamed of Betty?' I pretended to pout. 'Have you told them I'm six foot and a blonde lingerie model? Are you worried I won't be as funny in real life? Or—' I pushed a Scooby Doo style finger into my cheek, 'is there *more than one* Betty?'

'Don't be ridiculous,' said Dominic. 'How many meals do you think one man can eat in a week?'

I laughed, and was about to ask if he wanted any more toast when my phone finally pinged with a text and I grabbed it eagerly.

It was from Stephanie:

Checking out now. Wedding off. We need some thinking time. Will be in touch. Thank you for all you've done. Best, S

'Oh, bollocks,' I breathed. A cold hand clutched at my chest. Technically, it was for the best. And it wasn't anything to do with me, I was just their planner. But at the same time, that was a *big* wedding I'd just lost for the hotel. Not only for my department, but for the bar, the rooms – everything. Laurence would want a full explanation.

'What's the matter?' Dominic was reading my stricken face. He didn't make a joke, for which I was grateful.

'I might *need* to come out for a drink tonight,' I said. 'That couple from the rehearsal dinner I told you about? They've cancelled their wedding.'

'God, I'm sorry to hear that, Rosie,' he said. 'But it's not your fault, before you even try to tell me it is.'

'Isn't it?' I felt a bit wobbly. 'Shouldn't I have ... noticed something was up?'

'No!' exclaimed Dominic. 'It's your job to notice if the wine's corked and if the ushers are pissed. Everything else is up to them. And the customer is always right, remember?'

I smiled, but it felt tremulous. What was Joe going to say? He'd probably be pleased. Was I? I honestly didn't know.

'How's this going to make me look to Laurence?' My voice cracked. 'General managers don't lose big bookings like this at the last minute, do they?'

'Come here.' Dominic held out his arms, and I walked into them, grateful for his comforting hug that smelled of sleepy bloke and my good shower gel. 'You stay in tonight and treat yourself. Get a takeaway. And, listen, I'm seeing the managing editor's secretary at this drinks thing tonight. They haven't finalized a venue for the Christmas party yet – I'll tell them I can swing a great deal at this very chic London hotel I know.'

'Would you?' I brightened up a bit. 'That'd help.'

'No problem.' Dominic detached himself and went back to his coffee. 'You can thank me in the form of special marmalade.'

'I'll go past Fortnum's on my way home.' I shouldered my bag and grabbed my jacket. The day was looking slightly brighter.

'Love you, Dom,' I said, and kissed his head as I left.

'Don't forget the marmalade,' he replied, which wasn't quite the same thing, but I was too relieved to care.

I was determined not to let last night's drama affect the wedding meeting I had lined up for that afternoon: Polly Stewart and Dan Clayton, a lovely couple whom I'd met a few times already. Polly particularly was a dream Bonneville bride: in love with vintage dresses, classic films and proper heels. The wedding was themed around *Breakfast at Tiffany's*: a long column dress for her, bridesmaids in turquoise, and strings of sugar pearls all around the cake. If Polly could have had the wedding ceremony conducted in black-and-white, I think she would.

Joe had turned up to the meeting in a fresh shirt and with a fresher new attitude. I didn't know if Laurence had spoken to him overnight or if what I'd said about our wedding style at the Bonneville had sunk in, but he seemed determined to stay in the background, and just made notes and smiled at the couple every so often like a benevolent vicar.

The only minor hiccup was Dan's unexpected request to have 'Perfect Day' as their first dance, rather than 'Moon River,' which I knew Polly was planning to choreograph as their first dance as a surprise.

'It's my favourite song,' Dan whined when I made diplomatic *Are you sure?* noises. 'It's a classic!'

I glanced over at Polly, who clearly didn't agree. 'It's quite a . . . melancholy tune,' I said. 'Bit sad?'

'"Perfect Day"? What's melancholy about that?'

'What about a swing version?' suggested Joe, coming to life for the first time. 'Best of both worlds. Upbeat *and* classic!'

Polly looked horrified. So did Dan, come to that.

'I think we should stick to what we've agreed,' I said firmly. '"Moon River" is a beautiful choice. Maybe "Perfect Day" for the . . . follow-up dance? Okay? Brilliant. Now, did you two reach a decision about where you want to cut the cake?'

Joe opened his mouth to argue, but I gave him a swift kick under the table, and gratefully Polly moved the conversation on.

*

We waved Polly and Dan off from the sunny front steps, and I waited until their black cab had safely pulled away before turning to Joe, who was idly tossing the remaining sweets into his mouth as if they were mint imperials off the bar and not handmade petits fours.

'Before you start on all the things I shouldn't have said,' he began, seeing my expression, 'what was all that about? Can't they even choose their own first dance now?'

'For the record,' I said, in as friendly a way as I could manage, 'you might want to have a look at the list of songs we recommend for first dances.'

'We recommend them? Isn't that the kind of thing couples have picked out years in advance?'

'Well, yes, but sometimes what feels right when they were planning the wedding at home doesn't always work when you factor in the setting, the band, the moment . . .'

'Seriously?'

'Seriously.'

I pushed my way back in through the brass revolving doors, and set off down the corridor towards my office. Joe loped along beside me. His long athletic strides made me more conscious of my own mincing steps in my pencil skirt and high heels, and for some reason that annoyed me too.

'All right, so you'd prefer them to do a proper waltz, but I *like* "Perfect Day". Didn't you like my compromise? A big-band version? Although if they wanted "Firestarter" by The Prodigy, I still think you should let them have it.'

I stopped in front of an unspecific watery photographic print, chosen as part of Ellie's short-lived revamp of the hotel when she took over as Mrs Bentley Douglas II. She ended up making everywhere look like reception. I'd have junked all her horrible prints, but this one was covering a stain on the wallpaper, and Laurence refused to pay for mass redecoration until he'd had his annual Mayo Clinic all-clear.

'A jazzy version of a song about being off your face and drinking sangria out of a brown paper bag in a park – in the elegant Art Deco ballroom of this hotel?' I demanded, all in one breath. 'No. That's not what Polly wants to do her first dance to. Definitely not.'

Joe stopped too. 'But Dan *likes* that song. I bet it's the one thing he's actually chosen in this wedding. Why does it matter to you?'

'Because it's not . . . it's not a happy song.'

Joe tilted his head and gave me another of his Californian expressions: the *own your feelings* one. I felt my cheeks redden under his direct gaze. He seemed to be looking straight into my head, and I hated having to justify things I *knew* were right. 'Go on, say it,' he said easily. 'Be honest, *you* don't like it.'

'I don't tell them what kind of wedding to have,' I said, through gritted teeth. 'I just try to make sure nothing goes wrong. And that starts with guiding them towards the right choices in the early stages. Polly wants "Moon River" because she's got a vision about being swept around the floor in a waltz.'

As I said it, I knew this wasn't about Polly and Dan and Lou

Reed. It was about Stephanie and Richard and the cancelled wedding. But Joe could bring it up. I wasn't going to.

'Does Dan even know he's got waltzing lessons coming up? Or are you booking those for him too?'

I swallowed and tried to keep my voice level. 'I know you think I'm a control freak, but my job is to keep an eye on the bigger picture, as well as the details. Sometimes couples are a bit too close to emotional issues like keeping the family happy and adding up their budget so that they miss things.'

'Or maybe you're too close to the details to see the people,' said Joe. 'Details are fine, but they're only details at the end of the day. Maybe it's good to step back from that and ask what it is that the couple actually want, and give it some room to breathe.' He made an expansive gesture. 'To evolve.'

I closed my eyes. Who exactly did he think he was? Some kind of workplace examiner? 'You seem a lot more into the whole concept of weddings than you were a few days ago.'

Joe shrugged. 'Jet lag wore off? I'm feeling a bit more human. Plus I had a chat with Mum on the phone this morning. She wants me to go down to stay with her at Wragley Hall, to help out Alec with some building work she's got him doing. Something about a golf course? He's got an explosives licence now.'

'You're kidding me?' I said without thinking. 'Someone gave Alec a licence to blow things up?'

'I know. Like he normally asks first.' Joe shared my recoil of horror. 'So, as you can imagine, the prospect of being here and helping out with a few weddings suddenly took on a much less . . . potentially fatal attraction. To coin a phrase.'

I couldn't blame him for that. And it also reminded me that Caroline would be getting updates on my mentoring from Joe, and I didn't want to look bad in *her* eyes.

'And,' he went on less cockily, 'last night . . . bit awkward. I probably owe you some overtime for that. Not that I think I did the wrong thing,' he added, 'but, yeah . . .'

'They cancelled the wedding,' I said shortly.

'I know. I heard.'

We stared at each other, Joe's earnest eyes raking my face, while I tried to guard my expression as best I could. I must have been tired, because I honestly didn't know what I thought, I just felt weary. All that effort, all that planning, for nothing. And what about Stephanie and Richard? What sort of conversation were *they* having now?

'Look,' I said, trying to control the situation before Gemma or Helen saw me looking so rattled, 'I'm not saying it's up to us to decide the wedding for the bride, but it's like Polly said, it's reassuring for her to know that someone's calm enough to say yes or no. Because in my experience, none of the wedding party ever really is.'

'You're the expert,' said Joe, and offered me some of my own wedding petit fours.

After a moment's hesitation I took a couple. I never usually ate between meals.

They were actually pretty good.

Helen and Gemma were sitting in my office when I got back, scoffing green and lilac macaroons left over from another of

Grace Dewberry's wedding cake tastings. Grace and her brides-maids had already been in for two tastings. I was beginning to think Gemma might be confusing Grace deliberately, just to get yet another round of leftovers.

'Before you ask, I'm not here,' said Helen, waving a macaroon in my direction. 'I'm with the cheese supplier.'

'And before you ask, I'm *meant* to be here,' said Gemma defen-sively. 'Laurence has locked his door. A package came for him in the post. From Sweden. So I had to divert all his calls to your phone. I took some messages for you too, though.'

'Thank you, Gemma.' I started checking the pile of notes. There were a lot. Most of them were from Stephanie Miller's parents, bridesmaids and family. I groaned inwardly. This was going to take quite some unpicking.

'How were Polly and Dan?' asked Helen. 'Everything looking set for the big day?'

'Yup! Well, I hope so. First time Dan's bothered to come along, and he tried to change the first dance to "Perfect Day".'

Gemma pulled a face. 'Ooh, gloomy. Why do men always pick "Perfect Day"?'

'I have absolutely no idea, but they do. Probably because it's always used on *Match of the Day* montages.'

'Wasn't Joe helpful?' asked Helen.

'No, he suggested they get a lounge version arranged. Because Lou Reed and Frank Sinatra are natural bedfellows.'

'That's not a bad – oh dear,' said Helen, seeing my face.

I swivelled round and stared at my Bridelizer. There was now a distinct gap where Stephanie and Richard had been at the weekend, and I needed four more weddings booked in before the end of the year if I was going to beat the projection I'd given Laurence. Just four more. The Thornbury wedding would be a biggie, but every smaller one counted now I'd lost the Millers.

It's how you deal with setbacks that prove you're manager material, I reminded myself, chewing my lip. This could be a blessing in disguise. It could.

'Has Joe told you what he was doing out in California?' asked Gemma dreamily. 'He was telling me about the moonlight jeep trips he organized in Joshua Tree National Park. You drive out after sunset, under the stars, along an old gold miners' trail, and—'

I banged the desk with the flat of my hand and she jumped.

'Sorry. But don't start. I'm not in the mood for Poor Joe this morning. I had to listen to him telling Polly and Dan how rubbish our English coffee is again this morning.' I opened up Polly's file to type up the notes from our meeting. 'Even Dan suggested he get with the tea programme now he's back here.'

'Aw.' Gemma made a sad pouty face, as if Joe were some kind of tragic wartime orphan who'd fetched up on the doorstep. 'You can't blame him. It sounds like he had an amazing life out there. And now he's back in rainy old London.'

'He must miss California. Specially the weather,' Helen agreed. 'It's freezing this morning. He did a lot of surfing, didn't he?'

'Ooh, you can tell, with those shoulders. And he's so tanned.'

I didn't look up or join in. I was trying to make sense of Polly's list of photography requirements. It sounded more like she was making a documentary about herself than getting married. She wanted the photographer to come to her next dress fitting.

'Ask Rosie about his tan,' said Helen. 'She's the one who had the full inspection . . .'

I started to tune Helen and Gemma out as I finished the notes and began to rattle through the emails that had piled up in my inbox while I'd been away from my desk.

Daphne, October bride: Is it Bridezilla to ask everyone to wear black clothes so my wedding dress will stand out in the photos? No, it's fine, as long as you want to look like you've crashed a funeral party. **Polite A: Maybe give them a couple of colour choices, Daphne?**

Emilia, December bride: Can we let Mother's dog stay in hotel overnight? Why not? It could go in with Laurence. He liked dogs. **Polite A: Yes, we can arrange that, no problem!**

Catherine, September bride: Pls advise re etiquette of sacking maid of honour. I racked my brains. Was that the MoH who was in love with the groom, or the one who I suspected was in love with the bride? Maids of honour nearly always had an agenda of some kind. **Polite A: Catherine, that's quite a delicate problem; why don't I call you later so we can discuss it properly?**

So much to do. So many things to worry about. And I needed to phone someone about the mortgage later – I focused on that. All this stress was going to lead to something good: me and Dominic, in our own place . . .

'Rosie?'

I looked up. Helen was staring at me. 'Why did he come back?' she repeated.

'Why did who come back?'

'Joe!'

'I have no idea. I guess Laurence asked him to come back to help out with the hotel.' I gave them both a look. 'We are short-staffed, as you might have noticed.'

'But why would he leave his business?' Gemma persisted. 'I looked on the internet and it wasn't like there was a terrible accident with his company or anything. It was going really well. He had celebrity clients, and everything.'

'It doesn't always take a big accident to sink a business,' I said, refreshing my emails to find out if Dominic had had a look at the flat particulars I'd sent him. 'Sometimes it can be down to something as tiny as not paying tax.'

'I don't think he's a tax evader,' said Gemma decisively. 'What if it was a broken heart?'

'Ooh, yes.' Helen helped herself to another macaroon. 'I bet he either broke someone's heart with his footloose Sagittarian ways, or some ice maiden of a woman broke his.'

'How on earth do you know he's a Sagittarian?' I was trying very hard not to get sucked into this conversation, but Gemma and Helen's speculation was infectious.

'He told us. And I reckon someone broke his,' agreed Gemma. 'Definitely.'

I frowned at the computer screen. Dominic hadn't looked at the flats; instead I had a one-line email asking if I could think of something funny to say about a pop-up Cumberland sausage restaurant.

I clicked the email shut crossly. 'I agree,' I said.

'What?'

I spun round in my chair to face them. 'I'm joining in, in an attempt to bring this conversation to a close. I bet Joe irritated his last girlfriend so much that it was leave the country or risk being hurled over a balcony.'

'Ooh, touchy,' said Helen. 'Is this because he criticized your afternoon tea wedding?'

I nearly said, 'No, it's because he is the anti-Cupid,' but discretion stopped me. I wasn't going to discuss why Stephanie and Richard had decided to call things off.

'No, it's because Joe's just one of those irritating types who *feel* everything and know nothing. Anyway, I'm seeing Caroline for lunch in a few weeks,' I said. 'I'll ask her why he came back if you're so desperate to find out.'

'Will you? I'll put a cocktail on it being a girl.'

'Her dumping or him dumping?' asked Gemma, quick as a flash.

Helen joggled her head from side to side, considering. 'Um . . . *her* dumping,' she decided. 'I reckon she broke his heart and he couldn't face staying. Joe's the "this whole country is dead to me now" type.' She put the back of her hand to her brow and looked distraught. '"I have to leave it all behind if she doesn't love me." Or,' she added, 'she found him in bed with someone else and her dad's after him with a shotgun.'

I stared at them. 'We *are* talking about the same Joe? Joe with his horrible ratty plaits that he's only just cut off? And the shorts? "I'm a Sagittarian kind of guy" Joe?'

Gemma ignored me. '*Him* dumping. He's too cute to have been dumped. It's guilt, I reckon.'

Helen looked at me. 'Rosie? What's your guess?'

'I'm not betting because it's obvious why he came back,' I said haughtily. 'Laurence and Caroline told him to. Or he got bored. I know guys like Joe. They do things passionately for about eighteen months, get bored, pack it in.'

'Except he's been working out there since he left college,' Helen pointed out. 'And his business was doing all right.'

'Then he's just come back . . . to take over here.'

Urgh, that didn't make me feel any better. In fact, it made me feel even more resentful; presumably Caroline and Laurence were giving him some sort of compensation for giving up his business to work here?

'Doesn't explain why he was hungover and miserable when Rosie found him,' Gemma persisted. 'That says "drinking to forget" to me. Especially in the bridal suite.'

'For God's sake, it was jet lag. That's enough, Cagney and Lacey,' I said, reaching for my bag. 'I'm off to get something to eat. If you discover any more fascinating details about Joe, please be sure to leave me a note on my desk so I can ignore it.'

'You're no fun,' said Helen.

'I know,' I said, and left.

CHAPTER TEN

Caroline hadn't been my boss, technically, since she'd left the Bonneville five years ago to set up her own country house hotel in Oxfordshire. It was called Wragley Hall and it was basically heaven, but with fluffier towels. Everything was lilac-grey and cream, and the whole house smelled of lavender and beeswax polish, with soft lambswool blankets over the brass bed ends and comfy velvet chairs beside the huge log fire in the library. Caroline had bought it for nearly nothing as a leaking, squirrel-infested wreck; she had rolled up her sleeves and, as she put it, 'created the hotel I wished Laurence had taken me to on our honeymoon.'

I sent a lot of my engaged couples to Wragley Hall to calm down when the wedding planning got too tense and we were in danger of losing the booking to a broken engagement. The deputy manager, who she'd poached from Laurence after the divorce settlement, had created a spa in the old dairy sheds that managed to be simultaneously luxurious and brisk; instead of whale noise, you could listen to birdsong and the blissful sound of absolutely no questions about anything wedding related.

Though Wragley Hall was busy year-round, Caroline still came up to London every couple of weeks to see what was going on, and to hoover up any gossip that hadn't reached Oxfordshire yet. She always made time to see me, and though I'd graduated from college nearly ten years ago, I still learned more about hotel management and hospitality from my lunches with Caroline than I had in three years at college. Lunch tended to swish past in a blur of outrageous stories and things I probably shouldn't have let slip about Laurence's latest ailments, so today I'd made a list.

In the space of potted shrimps on toast and a salad, we'd covered how the Bonneville was preparing for Christmas (only seven months away); what had happened on the date Laurence had been on with Caroline's hairdresser's friend, Diana (nothing; she'd had to bring him back to the hotel when he'd had an allergic reaction to some pineapple, much to Caroline's disappointment – 'I need someone else to shoulder the burden of his basic running, Rosie'); and what extra staff I should be booking for the Christmas parties; and in return I told her about a new supplier of top quality bed linen Jean had sourced in Leeds.

I hadn't actually written down 'ask about Joe,' but it was on my mental list of things I wanted to talk to Caroline about anyway. Not so much the personal stuff that Helen and Gemma were itching to know, but the part that affected me: what Joe was really doing back at the hotel and, if he was staying, which department I should try to move him into. If I was going to make my projected bonus total, I couldn't have Joe putting me off my stride for too long. Even en route to lunch, I'd had an email from a potential bride we'd seen earlier in the week, politely letting me know she'd decided to go with the Ritz instead of us; I had a feeling Joe's questions about how exactly she'd met her millionaire hedge-funder fiancé might have had something to do with it.

But, on the other hand, Caroline was his mother. I didn't want to offend her by asking outright how long her son was intending to get in my way.

Luckily for me, Caroline brought up the topic herself without any prompting, shortly after she'd put away an 'adequate' strawberry cheesecake. She never pretended not to want dessert, which I liked. But then it was always nice to have a meal in which I could order whatever I wanted to eat, rather than what Dominic didn't fancy but felt he should form an opinion about.

'So, how's Joe getting on?' She replaced the fork neatly across the plate and looked at me over the top of her tortoiseshell glasses. 'Be honest. I know I'm his mother, but I'm also his *mother*, if you know what I mean.'

I sipped my mint tea and scrabbled around in my head for something positive to say first. Laurence had sent me on a management course: I knew the theory. Compliment-awkward truth-compliment.

'Well, he's really getting to know the hotel from the rooms up.'

'Which means what?' Caroline raised her eyebrows, and looked unsettlingly like Joe himself. 'Laurence claims he doesn't have space for him in the flat, so he's got Joe staying in whichever room isn't occupied that night?'

'Did he tell you that?' I felt a little nervous. What else had Joe told her?

'No,' she sighed. 'He doesn't tell me anything. It was just a lucky guess. Laurence is so territorial about that flat. I'm surprised he let that receptionist live in there.'

She meant Ellie.

'I think it's more that Laurence is keen for him to appraise the hotel,' I pointed out, before we could get on to Ellie's shortcomings. 'It's ages since anyone in management slept in any of the rooms, and Joe's already told us which ones, um, need updating.' For someone who claimed to love sleeping rough beneath the Californian stars, Joe was a delicate flower of the princess/pea variety when it came to our 'British' mattresses, 'loud' air conditioning, and 'insufficient' towels.

'I suppose it means he's always at work by nine. But what about the work experience? He's with you in events, isn't he?'

'Yes.' I paused. This was the awkward truth part.

'And?'

'Um, he's been working with me for almost four weeks now, so I suppose he'll be moving on to the next division soon.'

'That doesn't answer the question I asked, but still . . .' Caroline motioned for some mint tea for herself. 'I thought he'd be shadowing you for a bit longer. Isn't he enjoying it?'

I squirmed. This was tricky. I should have known where Joe got his directness from.

'I don't know if events is where his heart lies,' I said.

Caroline looked surprised. 'But he was managing his own events company out in California.'

'Well, fire-walking and wilderness sleeping aren't exactly the same as society weddings.' I tried to put it into diplomatic words that would somehow get Joe out of my hair, but not make me look unhelpful. 'I've been trying to build towards that classic Bonneville image we always had in mind when you set out the mission statement for the future, and . . . I'm not sure it's really Joe's style.'

Caroline tipped her head on one side, in that *go on, hang yourself* way, and it occurred to me that this might actually be a useful line. She wouldn't want all her – and my – hard work of bringing the Bonneville back into the pages of London's best glossy lifestyle mags undone by Joe running riot with his ideas about slapping name badges on guests or letting dogs bring the rings in on a little cart.

'I think he finds traditional English weddings boring,' I went on. 'He'd rather there was more dancing and quirky themes and . . . wackiness.'

'Wackiness?'

'Last week I had a meeting with a very traditional couple who wanted the full romantic hotel wedding. The most outrageous thing the bride wanted was for everyone to dress in black-and-white so her red Manolos would stand out. No problem, fine. But Joe tried to talk them into having the groom's side all in black, the bride's side all in white.'

Caroline laughed as if I were having her on, then realized I wasn't.

'Can you imagine the photos?' I added, remembering my

desperate attempts to shut him up. 'It'd look like a really bad Pet Shop Boys concept video from the eighties. The problem was the groom loved it. He said it was perfect because he was a part-time jazz pianist. Joe's reaction was, "Brilliant! We can arrange everyone into a human keyboard for the going-away photos, and the groom can play them."'

'And the bride?'

'Thought Joe was taking the mickey out of her wedding. I had to give her a lot of cake to take home.'

'Oh dear,' said Caroline. 'Maybe this isn't going to work out as I'd hoped.'

As she'd hoped? I fought back a sense of triumph mingled with dread. I knew there was something else behind Joe's appearance at the Bonneville. And if Caroline was behind it, then it was much more organized than I'd suspected.

'Caroline,' I said. 'What's going on, please?'

'Oh . . .' She flapped her hands. 'I might as well come clean. Joe called me about a week before he landed in London, completely out of the blue, to inform me that he was leaving the Land of the Free and coming home to the Land of the Free Bed and Board. So rather than have him turn up at Wragley Hall, because to be quite frank with you, Rosie, having *one* of my children at home, blowing up parts of my hotel garden, at any one time, is quite enough for me, I thought, no, Laurence can handle this, for a change.'

'Right,' I said. That wasn't what Joe had told me about Caroline's offer to have him in Oxfordshire, but still.

She leaned forwards in her chair, resting her elbow on the

arm and pinching her chin with glee. 'And then I thought, actually, this could be a *blessing in disguise*. As you know, Laurence and I would never force Joe or Alec to take on the Bonneville, just because they are family . . .'

'Oh no,' I lied. Of course not. It was only Laurence's sole aim in life.

'. . . but what a great opportunity, I thought, for Joe to get some decent experience with someone who *knows what they're doing*.'

'Laurence?'

'No! You!' Caroline leaned back and smiled conspiratorially. 'I thought it might give that dreadful ex-husband of mine a wake-up call. Stop him taking you for granted, if he had to see exactly how hard you work, through Joe's eyes. I told Laurence to move Joe round the departments so he knows what's what, but since you do more or less everything, I thought he might as well start with you.'

I sat back in my chair. Caroline's faith in my abilities was flattering – but at the same time, was she lining him up to get the manager's job too? That was *my* job he was going to walk into, just because he happened to be the son of the owners. Joe's impatient face floated in front of my mind's eye, the way he'd actually yawned when I gave him the grand tour of the special movie-star rooms, and I nearly yelped with the unfairness of it.

'So,' I said, as evenly as I could, 'you want me to teach Joe how to run the hotel so he can take over Paul's job as manager?'

Caroline nearly choked on her mint tea, and coughed in an

inelegant way that was very unlike her. 'No! God, no. I mean, Laurence might want that, but no, I want Joe to come and work for me. At Wragley Hall.'

She'd lost me there. If Joe found weddings at the Bonneville boring, then he was going to go into a coma of boredom at Wragley Hall, where guests often arrived by private helicopter, the wedding music was usually performed by harpists, and every single female guest wore nude LK Bennett Sledge court shoes like the Middleton ladies. Quite often because the guests in question were the Middleton ladies.

'That's lovely,' I started, 'but to be honest, Caroline, unless you're planning on introducing some kind of zip-wire ceremony—'

'Weddings? God, no!' she hooted. 'No, no. I don't want Joe involved in that side of things. I've got a top-secret new project on the go.' She leaned forward again, her eyes all glittery with project fever. 'I've finally done a deal with the farm behind the hotel and bought that big tract of woods they wouldn't sell for years. We're going to expand into one of those park-type places people take their families to so they can leave the kids while they have massages . . .'

'You're starting your own Center Parcs?'

'Yes! Well, just for very well-behaved children. And I want Joe to run that. I think he'd be rather good at it.' Caroline looked pleased with herself. 'But first, I want him to get some idea of what proper customer service entails, and I don't have time to train him up while I'm down a deputy manager and a chef myself, and with Alec rattling round the place as well. When

I say rattling, I mean literally. The place isn't big enough to contain him and his . . . energy.'

'Still no job?'

'Sadly not. It seems the French Foreign Legion isn't recruiting at the moment. Anyway, minor detail. I'll find something for Alec to do. He can blow up the bunkers for the golf course.'

She wasn't joking.

'So when is all this happening?' I asked, doing mental calculations. It wasn't going to take that long to bring Joe up to speed, not if I put my mind to it. If I could get him shipped out to Oxfordshire soon, he wouldn't get near the potential Flora Thornbury wedding next June. He wouldn't even be around to follow through on his stupid jazzy 'Perfect Day' for Dan and Polly in November.

'June next year,' said Caroline.

My mental soundtrack of happy strings screeched to a halt. 'June?'

'Well, I haven't quite got the paperwork sorted out yet,' she admitted. 'And it's not a two-minute job, learning the hotel trade, now, is it?'

The prospect of Joe sabotaging my Bridelizer well into the middle of next year floated before me. Caroline had no idea how much was riding on me making those figures. My promotion, my new flat, my entire relationship with Dominic, possibly even my sanity . . .

'I know what you're thinking,' Caroline said smoothly. 'You're thinking, "What's in it for me?"'

'No, I'm not, I'm happy to—'

'Rosie, this is me you're talking to. If you weren't asking what was in it for you, I'd wonder where I'd gone wrong. No, if you can get Joe's mind focused on British hospitality and get him a bit more enthused about the old family business – mine, I might add, not his father's – then I will put in a good word for you, shall we say, about the general manager job.'

'At the Bonneville?'

'At the Bonneville.'

I met Caroline's gaze. She looked straight back at me. She and Joe had the same straight nose and the same fine gold hair. Although Caroline's didn't have ratty little plaits in it. It made me wonder how deeply Caroline's business acumen was buried in Joe.

'Put in a good word,' I repeated.

'I can't make any promises,' she said, poker-faced. 'But you know that I know a *lot* of good words.'

'And does Laurence know about this? About the Center Parcs idea?'

For the first time she looked a bit shifty. 'Not yet. And please don't tell him. He'll only have one of his health-and-safety fits. You know what he's like.'

'I won't.' Sniping about Ellie aside, Laurence and Caroline were quite amicable divorcées. It was really only the small matter of Laurence taking Caroline entirely for granted that had withered her patience in the end. 'You know,' I added, because it was true, 'Laurence is very happy to have Joe back. I think he's enjoying having him in the hotel. He seems to be taking a lot more interest in it himself these days.'

Caroline sighed. 'I know. Joe's a good boy. Well, man, now. Do I look old enough to have a son of twenty-eight?'

'No,' I said truthfully.

'Good,' said Caroline. 'It's our new Soap and Flannel spa facial. Do recommend it to your lovely brides. Now, where's the waiter for the bill?'

We had our usual 'No, let me!' 'No, I insist!' conversation (she won), and we both checked our phones for messages while the waiter went off to get it.

I had four wedding-related problems, and one from Dom asking if I'd come up with a good Cumberland sausage joke yet. And Helen had texted me.

Ask Caroline about Joe. Hx

'Honestly, just because one goes to London,' said Caroline, texting furiously, 'does not mean that people can *take the morning off . . .*'

If Joe thought I was bossy and a bit of a control freak, I thought, he was in for a rude awakening if he got a job with his mother.

Have you asked yet? I have a tenner riding on this. Hx

I put my phone away.

'Out of interest,' I said casually, 'why did Joe decide to come back? There weren't any . . . problems out there?'

'No, it was all going fairly well, as far as I know,' said Caroline. 'Not a bad idea, getting paid to take other people on outdoor jaunts you'd be going on yourself anyway. Which is more than I can say about Alec's latest business proposal. You haven't come across any grooms who've been kidnapped by their stags, have you? I mean, properly kidnapped with bags over their heads and ransom notes. Is it a new thing?'

I blanched. 'Not as far as I know. Sorry, I was being nosy. It's just that Joe obviously loved the lifestyle out there. And from what he says, his business was pretty successful.'

Caroline checked the bill, frowned, and put her credit card down on it. 'Quite a specialist market, the sort of holidays he was running. He hasn't really gone into much detail about it with me, but Joe's like his father, terribly proud. Hates talking about money, doesn't like discussing private matters. I expect he'll end up telling you more about it than he will me.'

I moved my teaspoon round in my saucer, making it parallel to the cup. I wondered whether Caroline had seen Joe in the state I'd seen him the morning I found him in the bridal suite. Hungover and messy. He hadn't looked terribly proud then; he'd looked wrecked.

I don't know why I asked, but I did anyway. 'You don't think it was a girl?'

Caroline shook her head. 'No, he never mentioned one.'

I knew it wouldn't be a girl. No one who thought 'stag tea parties' with pork pies and lager were a good idea could possibly have had a girlfriend to be brokenhearted about.

'Why do you ask?' Caroline asked suddenly. 'Does he seem touchy when you have brides in? Oh dear.'

'Not exactly. Although he does seem a bit . . .' I tried to find the right words. '*Fixated* on making sure they're doing the right thing.'

'In what way?'

'He's mentioned wedding contracts more than a few times, and how both parties should know what they're signing up for. Not legal contracts,' I added, 'more, "I promise not to leave my snoring uninvestigated for more than a month, and I promise not to grow a moustache unless it's for charity."'

I'd managed to persuade Rory and Bethan that he was joking. But not before Bethan had got a couple of rather personal digs in about Rory's 'seasonal weight gain'.

Caroline sighed. 'He always was a very honest child.'

'Honest is fine, but he does take it a bit far,' I said. 'We had one bride call off her wedding after a chat with Joe at the rehearsal dinner about the honeymoon. I really don't want to risk the same thing happening again. We've potentially got a big wedding coming up next year, and it could lead to a lot of exposure. If it all goes ahead.' I paused significantly. 'If we get it.'

Caroline raised her eyebrows, excited. 'The Thornburys, I heard. Now if you could effect some cosy chat between Mrs. Thornbury and dear Laurence then it'd be three good words I'd be putting in.' She smiled conspiratorially. 'She'd be perfect for him. Rich and bossy and, if I remember correctly, somewhat deaf. We really have to find someone for Laurence, Rosie. I had four phone messages last week, asking me if I could remember if he'd had rubella. And when I woke up there were two absolutely traumatizing photos he'd taken of his own ... I won't tell you what ... asking me if I thought it had changed colour since I last saw it.'

'Blimey.'

'I can't imagine he bothers that Ellie woman with this sort of thing?'

'No,' I said truthfully. 'He can't. Not since the court order. It was part of their divorce agreement. No phone calls other than to discuss Otto and Ripley.'

'Otto and Ripley,' muttered Caroline. 'Dear God. Anyway, my goodness, is that the time? I need to see a man about some underfloor heating. Can I give you a lift anywhere?'

'I'll get the bus,' I said, and we made our way back out into the busy London street.

Caroline waved as her driver pulled away into the traffic, but I didn't mind hopping on the number nineteen. I needed some time to process what I'd just learned, before I had to face all the parties involved back at the hotel.

CHAPTER ELEVEN

I'd kept Flora Thornbury's wedding meeting quiet, but on Friday morning there were definitely more cleaners polishing the tables in the Palm Court than usual. Under normal circumstances, the Bonneville was so tightly staffed that you rarely saw three cleaners on the same floor, let alone five in one function room.

I reckoned Laurence must have let something slip. He was a bit of a shameless star-spotter himself, though he pretended modern stars weren't a patch on the gold-plated ones who'd frequented the Bonneville in the Good Old Days. I made a bet with myself that he'd be 'passing' the Palm Court at about, ooh, ten past ten, in a new shirt and fifty per cent more Eau Savage than normal.

Looking on the bright side – literally – the room was spotless. Every surface gleamed – the black grand piano, the glass table-tops, the silver tea services. I ran a quick critical eye over the furniture for any out-of-line chairs or used teacups, and tweaked a couple of round cushions. Sunshine streamed through the long French windows overlooking the rose gardens and creating a neat yellow column over the polished parquet. It really did feel like the sort of room in which an off-duty film star would flick through the morning's papers, while sipping a coffee poured from a silver cafetière.

Even on grey wintry days, I loved this room. Flora was a model – she'd appreciate the soft light and cleverly positioned mirrors. We could do beautiful thirties-style pre-wedding photos, I thought, she and her bridesmaids draped languidly over the Deco armchairs like Cecil Beaton models . . .

My usual secret list of photographers and make-up artists probably wouldn't be necessary, but I'd brought it with me anyway, just to show we had one. And also to show that I was the sort of wedding planner who liked to keep everything well under control.

'When's she coming in?' whispered one of the cleaners, and was shushed by her friend.

I pretended to look blank. 'When's who coming in?'

'Flora Thornbury!'

'Can you finish fiddling with that, please?' I made *hurry up* motions at the girls lingering around the white sunburst flower arrangement on the piano. They seemed to be taking it in turns to move one rose an inch to the left, then back again, while casting casual-yet-nosy glances at the door.

Reluctantly they started to slope off.

'I don't mind volunteering for extra hours,' said one as she passed. 'If there are, er, any big weddings coming up?'

'It'll be next summer,' I said, flapping them away. 'Now, if you don't mind . . .'

Flora and Julia Thornbury were due at ten o'clock, but as

per Dom's cunning suggestion, I'd told Joe to meet me in the ballroom at half past ten. It wasn't a completely mean thing to do; after all, what was he going to contribute to the discussion about supermodel dresses and celebrity guests? He hated all that 'celebrity shit', as he insisted on calling it, despite having lived virtually next door to LA for years.

Gemma dashed in, her eyes shining. She was wearing her favourite bride-interview outfit, a pale-blue cashmere cardigan over a tweedy miniskirt, powder blue Mary Janes, and a cream silk corsage. She looked about ready to pop with excitement.

Actually, I might have thought that because she was making agitated little up-and-down gestures with her hands, as if she were trying to dry her nail varnish in a rush.

'She's *here*!' she whispered. 'Flora! She's in reception! Oh my God, she is *so* beautiful! I couldn't stop looking at her. And she's wearing *jeans*.'

I glanced at my watch. 'But it's only quarter to. She's a model. They're never early. They're usually about four hours late.'

'I know. But there was a lot of noise outside, and some flashing, and we thought there was another to-do with the police, but it was just a photographer, and now she's in reception, talking to Laurence.' Gemma starfished her fingers and opened her eyes very wide. 'Well, her *mother's* talking to Laurence. Do they know each other?'

'Yes, they're old friends.'

'I thought so,' said Gemma. 'He was patting her arm.' She demonstrated. 'Like she was a horse.'

Good, I thought, I could pass that on to Caroline as a positive sign. Mrs Thornbury, according to the swift internet research I'd done, was divorced from Flora's father, a wealthy property developer. She had two houses, one of which was in Switzerland, very close to one of Laurence's favourite clinics. Only a Echinacea farm could make her more perfect.

'Shall I send her in here?' Gemma asked.

'Of course not, no, I'll come through to reception,' I said, gathering my files and notebooks together. 'Have you seen Joe this morning?'

It was more a safety check than a genuine question, since if Joe was doing what I'd specifically asked him to do by email last night, he'd be in Berry Brothers wine merchants, but there was always the chance that he hadn't actually read his emails yet.

Gemma hesitated, as if she was worried about dropping him in it, then seemed to change her mind and said, 'No.'

'Good. I mean, oh. Oh dear.'

'Should I go and see where he is? Or . . .' She put on her innocent face. 'Maybe there should just be two of us in the meeting? Don't want to crowd Flora. And it's not as if Joe's going to be able to explain what the hotel has to offer, whereas I can take notes while you talk and maybe suggest ideas . . .'

Gemma had tactics, I'd give her that.

'That's a good point,' I said. 'But just make sure he's not lurking around, will you? And then if you could get back onto the florist for the Montpelier wedding – they still haven't called to say when they're dropping off the table decorations. Go round there if you have to, they're only in Mount Street.'

'Mount Street? What about the meeting? I won't be able to get there and back in time.'

'I'm sure you will,' I said, pushing her firmly towards the foyer. To be honest, I didn't want Gemma or Joe in this meeting, not until I'd worked out what it was that Flora Thornbury wanted, and how best I could persuade her that the Bonneville Hotel, and only the Bonneville Hotel, could provide the wedding of her wildest – but still tasteful – dreams.

I met plenty of beautiful brides in the course of my job, but Flora Thornbury was an entire league of beautiful above the norm.

Even in skinny jeans and a white T-shirt, she looked as if she were made from the same translucent fine bone china as the special Georgian family tea service I only offered to brides I adjudged to have very careful relatives. Her skin glowed without make-up, her lovely long blonde hair fell in a soft fringe over her small nose, and when she smiled as I approached, it was with the whitest, most even teeth I'd ever seen.

Many brides looked almost as lovely as this, but only after about eighteen months of a really intensive improvement programme. I wondered, hopefully, if Flora had been one of those gawky, brace-faced teenagers who'd suddenly blossomed into a gorgeous swan at seventeen, but the way she was standing – half-warding off attention, half-expecting it – made me suspect that she'd probably always been like this.

'Hello, Flora, Julia, I'm Rosie,' I said, holding out my hand to her, and then her mother.

'Hey, Rosie, it's lovely to meet you.' Flora had a feathery handshake and smelled of gardenias. Julia Thornbury had a much firmer handshake and smelled of Chanel No. 5 and spaniels. If Flora was fine bone china, Julia was more your rounded Denby-ware; Flora's face was like hers – pretty nose, blue eyes, pink cheeks – but set in a much longer, finer framework.

'I thought we could have a quick tour of the rooms, then sit down for a proper chat in the Palm Court,' I said, gesturing towards the double doors with the looping arcs of stained glass. 'It's one of our smaller function rooms – we use it for more intimate wedding receptions. And of course for our famous afternoon tea.'

'Why is it famous?' asked Mrs Thornbury.

'Because it's an exact replica of the tea that the hotel was famous for in the thirties. Our pâtisserie chef makes the same beautiful tiny cakes that our original French chef created for the Bonneville, and we serve it on the same tableware, with champagne or cocktails or tea. It's like stepping back in time.' I smiled. 'Pop in one afternoon – quite a few of our brides are planning tea-party weddings. We can mix a unique cocktail, just for your event.'

''Mazing,' said Flora.

After a sweep of the main function rooms, and a peek into the dining room, where Helen gave them a mouthwatering overview of the catering options, I settled Flora and Julia into the sofa by the windows and tucked myself into the chair opposite; they had a view of the gardens, and I had a very good view of the double doors and, more importantly, the foyer, where various staff were lurking. I signalled one of them to come and deal with the tea, and a fight nearly broke out before Luisa, of the very sharp elbows, broke free.

While I sorted out the Thornburys' refreshment requirements (one herbal tea, one English breakfast; I could have guessed), I spotted that Julia was carrying a very thick, old school leather Filofax with a pen stuck in it, while Flora just had a simple notebook. As far as I could see, she didn't seem to have the standard bridal accessory of a gigantic file of 'ideas'. From experience, this might be a good thing or a bad thing. Either Flora had no idea what she wanted but was open to my suggestions (good), or she had no idea what she wanted but needed me to run through every possible permutation until I hit on something she liked by process of elimination (bad). Or she had a whole website of ideas on a laptop she hadn't even brought out yet (very bad).

It turned out to be somewhere in between, although it took us two cups of tea and a lot of roundabout discussion of flowers and vague ''Mazing!'s from Flora to get there. If it hadn't been for the enormous sugar-cube-sized diamond on her finger, I'd have wondered if Flora wasn't just one of those girls who booked wedding meetings for the sheer pleasure of discussing where to get lilacs in December. I'd had more than one of those over the past year.

'So, tell me about your dress,' I said eventually in desperation, and Flora abruptly focused as if I'd just turned on a light.

'My dress, okay, well, I'm talking to a couple of designers – I'm thinking about lace, and a sort of vintage feel.' She made a few gestures around her skinny shoulders. 'Satin, definitely. I want to look like one of those amazing film stars with marcel waves and diamonds.'

'But you're not cutting your hair,' Julia reminded her.

Flora rolled her eyes. 'No, Mummy, I'm not cutting my hair. I just want that feel.'

'Well, vintage glamour is very us.' I smiled. 'As you can see.' I gestured at the Art Deco lounge, resplendent with palms and stars, and picked up my fountain pen. 'And is that your starting point for the whole wedding?'

'Yah, I want something quite traditional,' Flora sighed in her soft King's Road drawl. 'My fiancé, Milo—'

'Milo McKnight,' added Julia. 'He's one of the shipping McKnights.'

'Mmm?' I nodded. I knew Milo – not personally, of course, but through the stacks of society magazines Gemma and I read on a monthly basis to keep up-to-date with who was who and where and with whom, and who might turn up after hours in our discreet hotel bar. The Honourable Milo didn't actually do any shipping himself, but his great-grandfather's efforts had provided enough family money for Milo to have his own art gallery in Mayfair. I'd walked by it a couple of times, but it was quite hard to work out what was art and what was wall. Also who was a customer and who was staff.

'Milo's quite a traditional person. And so am I.' Flora opened her big hazel eyes wide at me, and I tried not to feel starstruck. 'We came here for drinks one night after an opening, and I just felt as if we were stepping into a film. I can totally imagine myself getting married here.'

'I can too,' I said fervently. The exposure would be transformational not the splashy *Hello!* magazine spread sort, Flora was too classy for that, but the discreet word-of-mouth recommendations that gave priceless cachet to a venue. A real film-star wedding. Laurence would pass out with joy. My three national magazine feature spreads would be in the bag. And if I persuaded Flora to arrange the whole thing here, including a spa weekend for her attendants, most of whom would also be models, I'd guess, and a chic rehearsal dinner in Helen's restaurant, it would more than make up for the Stephanie Miller cancellation.

I can do this, I told myself. *Think like a manager, and you will become a manager.*

I smiled across the table at the Thornburys. I'd assumed supermodels would be the worst Bridezillas going, but Flora seemed very content to be led through this process. Julia might not be quite so easy – I could detect a tiny trace of 'Wedding I Never Had' – but I'd dealt with much, much worse.

'So . . .' I opened my notebook to a new page. 'How big a wedding are we talking about? Do you have a rough idea of numbers?'

'A hundred,' said Flora at the same time as Julia said, 'Two hundred and fifty.'

'Somewhere between the two, then,' I said easily, as they scowled at each other. 'Bigger numbers aren't a problem – we simply create different areas for the main meal, so you get the best of both worlds. Some guests find that a bonus, actually – you can subtly keep various factions apart!'

'Good,' said Julia a bit too emphatically.

'Oh, Mummy . . .'

I made a coded note of that. Caroline might have some insider goss on exactly who Julia wanted to park in the orangery.

'And did you have a particular date in mind? We are getting booked up already for next spring – June is looking very busy for us, but then it always is. . . .'

'We want to get married on the third weekend in June.' Flora smiled shyly. 'It's our anniversary.'

'Oh, that's very sweet,' I said, with growing pleasure. A traditional romantic supermodel – who knew? I could already see the classic shapes of this whole event. A big-budget, totally traditional wedding – my dream assignment.

And then I spotted Joe appearing in the foyer, and my stomach lurched. No. *Really no.* This wasn't a good time for him to come in; the last thing I wanted was him dropping another bouncing bomb on my plans: the innocuous comment that got bigger and bigger and finally exploded, destroying everything.

'And have you thought about photographers?' I asked quickly. 'We like to liaise with them well in advance . . .'

'I do have one,' said Julia. 'No, really, Flora, we *have* to ask Warren, he's a very old family friend, he'll be hurt . . .'

While Flora and Julia were passive-aggressively disagreeing about Warren's abilities to photograph a society fashion wedding, I shot a quick but deadly glare at Joe, who was lurking in the foyer asking a chambermaid something. I was good at precision-aimed glares: deadly enough to stun a lecherous usher, quick enough for the bride to miss.

Generally that look could cause an unsuspecting usher to leave the field in shock, but Joe just acknowledged me with a wave and slouched on in. As per my instructions, he was wearing a jacket over his blue shirt and jeans, but in a way that made it look as if an invisible doorman had forced it over his shoulders before he was allowed inside.

'I think black-and-white photography would be an interesting route to take,' I said, trying to divert him with my eyes, to no avail.

'Yes! That would be amazing,' Flora sipped her herbal tea. 'It's like you already know the kind of wedding I want.' Then she caught the death-ray flicker in my expression, flinched, and turned around to see who on earth I was looking at with such venom.

Joe was looming over them, and I had no choice.

I got up, and directed him to the chair next to mine. 'I'm so sorry, this is my temporary assistant, Joe. Joe, may I introduce Flora and Julia Thornbury?'

I prayed that he wouldn't make any cheesy remarks about which one of them was getting married.

'Hey, ladies.' Joe raised a laid-back hand.

Flora started to say hi, then leaned forward. 'Oh my *God*,' she said. 'Joe Bentley?'

Mrs Thornbury put her teacup down with a rattle. 'Joseph?'

Oh God. Please no. I prayed again that Alec hadn't accidentally set fire to any part of their house during a party, or that Joe hadn't dumped Flora as a teenager.

'Hello, Mrs Thornbury, hello, Flora.' Joe directed a polite

smile at the pair of them, shook their hands politely, offered a (single) social kiss to each cheek, and sat down with a thump.

'So, Joe.' Mrs Thornbury gave him a firm look and he sat up a bit straighter. 'How's your mother? How are Winston and Horatio?'

'She's very well, thank you. Winston's a bit creaky but still doing the rounds.'

(Winston and Horatio were Labradors. Caroline's friends always asked about dogs before children.)

'And Alec?' Mrs Thornbury tilted her head a fraction to the right. 'Any . . . news?'

'No. He's left the army now.'

'Good,' she said emphatically.

Joe slapped his knees and looked at me. 'So, um, sorry I seem to be late. I was visiting a wine merchant for another of our clients – sorting out some rather special gifts for the ushers!' He glanced over at me. 'Perhaps the meeting started a little earlier than advertised?'

Flora's pretty nose crinkled with amusement. 'You're not organizing my wedding, are you, Joe?'

'No,' said Joe at the same time as I did.

'No, Joe's just . . . taking notes,' I said smoothly. 'He's sitting in on some events meetings.'

I could tell he was looking at me, but I refused to react.

'So, where had we got to?' I wanted to get the meeting wrapped up while the Thornburys were still sounding as if they were about to book it. We'd seen the rooms, we'd talked briefly to Helen, I'd have to skip the bar tour and cocktail chat, but needs must. 'Would you like to make a date to sample some of our wedding menus? As Helen mentioned earlier, our chef likes to create tailored menus for each couple, but if you had some special favourite dishes or requests . . . ?'

'Yes,' said Julia, getting her Filofax out again, but Flora coughed.

'One idea I did have,' she said, quite vaguely, 'was a bridesmaid catwalk?'

'A bridesmaid catwalk?' I felt a tiny, ominous frisson.

Joe leaned forward on his chair, suddenly interested, and that made my frisson even more ominous.

'Yah, my friend Lily did one. It's where you send the bridesmaids down the aisle before the bride, like a fashion show? It was amazing. The bridesmaids all had, like, different styles of dresses on, and they were so good at walking that the guests all clapped. And then when Lily finally came down the aisle it was just . . . really impactful.'

Flora paused and waited for me to react. When I didn't, she added, 'You know Lily Maddox? The fashion designer?'

'Yes! Of course. Of course I do. She was the . . . bride?'

'No, she was the wedding dress designer.' Flora stared at me. 'The *bride* was Olympia Harvill. No, um . . .' She frowned. 'No, wait, it was Jasmine Russell. She came down just after Lily. But I mean, fair dos, Lily deserved a round of applause for the dress. It was just immense.'

Flora flopped back onto the chair, as if depleted of energy. 'So I thought that could be quite cool?'

'Um . . .' I wasn't sure what to say. I didn't think catwalking your bridesmaids would be 'quite cool'. I thought it would be quite tacky. And I definitely didn't think letting the dress designer upstage the bride was a good idea – not that it'd be easy to upstage Flora.

I glanced across at Julia Thornbury to see if I'd get any support there. Luckily, I did.

'Don't be silly, Flora,' she said, briskly. 'It's a solemn occasion, not a circus. You're there to make a commitment—'

'What about the guys?' Joe piped up. 'Do the ushers get to do a catwalk too? Do they all get different outfits?'

'Ha ha! Of course not,' I began, but Flora was fully engaged for the first time, and no one heard me.

'Yah!' she exclaimed. 'Why not? Actually, that could be really cool, too. We could make a feature of the ushers. I mean, they don't *have* to wear morning suits, do they?'

'They usually do.' I tried not to make my voice sound prim, and again glanced at Julia, who was now looking impatient.

'I rather think they do, darling,' she said. 'Your father will want to wear a morning suit.'

'I didn't know we'd even decided Dad was invited?' Flora turned back to Joe. 'What about ushers in the same suit but in different colours? To match the bridesmaids? Or are green suits for boys a bit much? Guess it depends on their colouring, right?'

I looked back and forth between the two of them, bewildered by the sudden change of direction. Where had this come from? Where was the traditional 1930s Cecil Beaton wedding that Flora had been so keen on ten minutes ago?

'Ushers wear anything these days,' said Joe, as if he was now a wedding fashion expert. 'I was at a wedding last year where the ushers all wore the football strip of the team the bride and groom supported. I think it was Aston Villa. They made the bridesmaids' dresses the same colours too.' He grinned. 'And the cupcakes, and all the table décor. Really broke the ice.'

Aston Villa. Aston Villa played in maroon and blue. Maroon and blue in the delicate function rooms. I felt faint.

'Oh my God, that's *amaaaaazing*,' breathed Flora. 'I don't know what team Milo supports – what's that one near us, Mum?'

'Chelsea?' Joe suggested. 'Fulham?'

'I don't think *football* is—' I started, but Julia Thornbury cut in with a swift, 'No, Flora. Absolutely not.'

'Rosie's right. Rugby would be much more appropriate,' Joe went on helpfully. 'What team does Milo support? Harlequins? What about ushers in rugby kit?'

I narrowed my eyes at Joe to get him to shut up, but to no avail.

'You could make rugby your theme?' he suggested. 'Create your own personalized strip. Have the bridesmaids doing a line-out throw for the bouquet. Arrange all the tables into Six Nations groups, and do play-off party games after the reception. And there's room for a bouncy castle in the courtyard . . .'

Could I punch him? I looked around for inspiration. A stray vase, or a flower display. Was there a way of subtly knocking him out with a blow to the head disguised as a simple swatting away of a wasp?

Delighted, Flora pointed her silver pencil at him. 'I'm so writing that down, Joe Bentley. Who knew you'd be a brilliant wedding planner? You are full of amazing ideas.'

I watched her bee-stung lips move as she wrote down 'Ushers – rugby kit' on her notebook. Just underneath where she'd written down 'String quartets playing Cole Porter medleys' after I'd suggested it.

'And the other thing I saw at a wedding that was really wow,' she went on without looking up, 'was a sort of dance back down the aisle?'

'Oh, cool,' said Joe before I could stop him. 'Like the one on YouTube?'

'Yah! It *was* that one on YouTube.' Flora beamed. 'The bride and groom were already at the, like, vicar end or whatever, and he started doing a kind of breakdance routine there, and they joined in, then came breakdancing down the aisle like it was a kind of . . . electrical current thing? And everyone was clapping and cheering? It was super emotional.'

'Really?' I said, with my teeth clamped together. It sounded awful. I kept the smile on my face as bright as I could. 'How quirky. But I suppose they were married somewhere quite informal, like Babington House or one of the London clubs?'

'Not really . . .' said Flora. 'St Luke and St Peter's church in Little Ripley.'

'And the vicar didn't mind?' Julia gasped.

Flora shook her head, and the tawny gold hair fell into her face. She pushed it back with her long hand, and the glare off her sugar-lump diamond nearly blinded us. 'They let the church keep all the Wi-Fi equipment they had installed for the videographer. He was totally cool about it.'

'Amazing,' said Joe, in exactly the same irritating beach-bum drawl as Flora. I could quite happily have throttled him.

I pulled myself together. *I am an events manager*, I told myself. I could steer Flora back towards the elegant and traditional affair the Bonneville needed to be seen to be hosting for her. I visualized the photographs in my head. What had Laurence wanted? Three major national magazines? They'd be queuing up for fashion shoots in the honeymoon suite if the world had seen Flora Thornbury exiting a vintage Rolls-Royce outside our black and gold entrance.

'Well, it's always fun when the bride has her own unique ideas to work with,' I said calmly.

Julia flashed me a look that – in my experience of mothers of the brides – said, *Nu-uh, no unique ideas here, thank you very much.* Julia, I knew from her phone calls to me, wanted morning coats and poached salmon, definitely not ushers in hot pants and jazz hands across the aisle. And since she was paying for the wedding, she wanted to make sure she got the wedding she wanted.

Our eyes locked and I tried to convey my concrete support. I couldn't say, 'Please ignore the idiot son of the owner,' when they were old family friends, but I *needed* this wedding. I opened my mouth to say something reassuring but before I could speak, Joe leaned forward.

'Have you thought about setting up a Twitter hashtag so guests can live-tweet the wedding?' he asked.

'Well, that was a delicious cup of tea,' said Julia, in an interview-ending tone.

'Did we talk about our traditional toast master?' I asked desperately but she was already getting her Filofax together, squeezing it shut like an overstuffed corset. There were thirty years' worth of contacts in there, and she was taking them all to a different hotel.

My throat went all tight and panicky. 'Or the honeymoon suite? It's the most romantic in London – and we like to create somewhere magical for the whole bridal party in our third-floor suite, not just the bride—'

'I'm so sorry, Rosie, but we need to get across town to another appointment, and my driver is hopeless.' Julia smoothed her skirt and rose, and I followed her. After a pause, Flora unfolded her endless legs from the sofa, but Joe only got up when I glared at him.

Flora let out a very pretty sigh as she gazed round the airy hotel lounge once more, as if she was sorry to be leaving so soon, but Julia was already sweeping out, taking my ambitions for the society wedding of the year with her.

Joe looked at me and gave me a quick, optimistic grin and a covert thumbs-up, as if he'd just personally secured the wedding of the century for the hotel.

I stared at him, my mouth dropping open in horror. It wasn't just that he had no idea what he'd done – he was actually taking pride in it.

That was it. I was going to have to talk to Caroline. He had to go. Before he ruined everything I'd worked for, or I strangled him, or both.

CHAPTER TWELVE

The moment that Julia and Flora had been ushered into their chauffeur-driven black Mercedes by Frank, the doorman, I let the smile drop from my face. My cheek muscles were aching with the effort of keeping it there when I actually wanted to flip my entire head back and roar with frustration like a demented Pez dispenser.

'Joe,' I said, without turning to look at him, 'Please come with me.'

Joe had been waving them off as if he were hailing someone across a festival site. 'Where? To the bar? I thought that went well, didn't you?'

'No. No, it didn't go well. We're going to Laurence's office.' I turned on my heel and stalked past the reception desk so hard my heels made indents in the thick carpet. I didn't even care that it made me look as if I was waddling.

Joe followed, but without the same urgency. 'Why?'

'So we can get in a good explanation, early, as to why we've failed to lock down the Thornbury wedding. And also the Thornbury rehearsal dinner, the Thornbury attendants' spa indulgence weekend, and all the other glamorous and very profitable Thornbury-based celebrations I had planned.'

With each item my voice got shriller and I stomped harder down the corridor. I knew I sounded hysterical, but I couldn't stop myself. I'd wanted to book this wedding *so* badly. Wasn't he listening to anything I was trying to tell him?

Joe was nearly breaking into a run keeping up with me. 'Slow down. What's the big problem?'

I stopped so abruptly that he bumped into me, and when I spun round, my nose was only inches from his.

(To be strictly accurate, my nose was about level with his chin. Joe was lanky, and I wasn't wearing my highest heels. But you get the picture. I got a faceful of deodorant and a close-up of the stupid necklace he was still wearing, the one with the whole seashell in the middle.)

Two of the waitresses from the hotel bar were heading in our direction with trays, but when they saw my face they executed a perfect spin and diverted via the lounge.

'You don't have a sense of how that could have gone better?' I asked, as calmly as I could.

'No,' said Joe. 'I made some suggestions, I listened to what the bride wanted, I agreed with her. Everything you told me to. Thought both ladies looked pretty happy by the end.'

I had a flashback to Julia Thornbury's tight-lipped expression as she left. The face of a woman who'd been promised an éclair and handed a jam doughnut, and no napkin.

'You're not supposed to agree with *everything* the bride suggests,' I said, holding on to my calm.

Joe looked 'confused'. 'But I made a point of *not* asking her the questions I wanted to ask. Like, doesn't this Milo guy get a say in what kind of wedding he has? And whether Flora's dad's coming to the wedding or not. I mean, that's bad manners, right there.'

'Their guest list is nothing to do with us! My problem is that that meeting was going *perfectly* until you arrived,' I said slowly, to stop myself screeching. 'I had it all under control. Flora's mother, who, let's face it, is *paying* for this, wanted to hear we could provide a sophisticated, traditional civil wedding ceremony. That's what she wanted when I discussed it with her on the phone. That's what she was going to get – and that was what Flora was really keen to have too, until you arrived! And started . . . started . . . *encouraging* Flora with those mad suggestions about breakdancing bridesmaids, and offering stuff that you know we don't do—'

'Stuff that you don't do *at the moment*,' Joe corrected me. 'Doesn't mean you can't in the future. Aren't you always telling me you're there to make the client's dreams come true?'

Why did he keep taking my own words and using them against me?

'That's not the point! Brides have insane dreams at this stage! Do you *really* think what the Bonneville's lacking is a themed bouncy castle?'

'But she loved the idea of dancing down the aisle.'

'Well, I didn't. It's not the sort of thing we do here.'

'But, Rosie,' said Joe, with an irritating holier-than-thou look. 'It's. Not. Your. Wedding.'

'In a sense it is! It's our *hotel* that appears in the papers.' I took deep breaths through my nose. I sounded like a bull. 'And brides are like sheep in big skirts. If Flora Thornbury has bridesmaids voguing round the garden, then everyone's going to want them, and let me tell you, for every voguing bride, you lose ten perfectly normal ones.'

The St Mary's Hotel had lost half its bookings overnight after some style blogger posted photos of the bride arriving on a donkey, and the donkey plopping its way down the aisle. And it was a really nice donkey.

'Really? Are you sure?' Joe frowned. 'Surely all publicity's good publicity?'

I rubbed my face and reminded myself that Joe was just thinking in fire-walking terms, not deliberately trying to wind me up. But hadn't Laurence or Caroline told him *anything* about their visions for the Bonneville? Couldn't he *see* the old girl's faded personality in every flirty window seat and curved porcelain coffee cup?

'Not always, no. We're trying to rebuild the hotel's reputation for elegance, for discretion – the "Hollywood's best-kept secret" it used to be. It's a *romantic* hotel, a classic honeymoon destination. The Bonneville's about champagne and flowers and long white dresses, string quartets playing Cole Porter . . . not brides twerking up against ushers in Aston Villa shirts.'

Joe said nothing, and I thought maybe I'd got through to him, but then he rolled his eyes. 'Seriously, you are a control freak. You need to relax a bit.'

That did it. That showed that (a) he hadn't been listening to a word I'd said, and (b) he didn't understand the first thing about running events. And (c) he really didn't get how annoyed Laurence would be about losing the Thornbury wedding, when I'd all but promised I had it in the bag.

'That's what brides pay me for!' I exploded. 'Flora's mother *wants* an event planner who'll keep the whole thing on track and on budget, and not let Flora start going crazy. Do you have any concept of the possible permutations of even a basic wedding?'

'What? No. I seriously don't, no. Two people turn up, promise to love each other forever, eat some cake, have a drink, go on holiday. That's it.'

I stared at him. 'Have you ever had a girlfriend, Joe?'

'What? I don't see what that's go to do with anything.' He looked properly annoyed, which only served to make *me* more annoyed, because frankly, what did *he* have to be annoyed about?

'I only meant that if you'd ever—'

'Sod that. The customer is always right, aren't they? Or is that too American for you? If she wants a bouncy castle, get the lady a bouncy castle. It's her day. Jeez.' He threw his hands in the air. 'Why are you getting so stressed out about it? It's like you said, just a big party.'

I ignored the fact that I had said that. It hadn't been quite what I meant, though. Joe was very hard to argue with.

'If that's what you think,' I said icily, 'maybe you should ask Laurence to move you on to housekeeping. You can tell Jean it's "just sheets".'

He folded his arms. 'Fine with me. And it *is* just sheets, isn't it? I don't have a problem telling Jean that.'

'Ha!' I said. 'Good luck. You'll love the laundry chute.'

'Hey, hey, hey! What's going on here?' Helen came striding round the corner from the direction of the secret side entrance. She looked flushed and guilty and slightly disgusted with herself, which made me suspect she'd been speaking to Seamus.

'Nothing,' I said.

She looked between us. 'Doesn't look like nothing.'

'I was getting a lecture in nuptial service provision from the Romance Robot here,' Joe sniffed. 'Apparently if you don't fit into the wedding template she's offering, you can't get married in this hotel.'

'Oh, don't be ridiculous. That's not what I said at all,' I began.

'Well,' Helen started, but I stopped her with a glare. She raised her hands. 'You *do* have a template. I was just going to say, fair enough. Nothing wrong with having a system. It's how we run the restaurant.'

'Exactly my point.' I turned back to Joe. 'If everyone ordered off-menu at dinner, where would that leave the kitchen?'

'Giving people what they want?' he suggested piously. 'She only wanted to dance down the aisle. It's not like she wanted the entire congregation to be naked during the ceremony.'

I closed my eyes. Dominic's face floated up in front of me, wryly amused and already constructing the anecdote. I knew how he'd play this: let Joe have enough rope to hang himself. If he found hospitality such a chore, he wouldn't stick around for very long, would he?

'Rosie, I need your thoughts about some cake,' said Helen briskly, and I felt her take my arm. 'And I need them before the lunch rush starts. Would you excuse us, Joe? Sorry . . .'

'I was going out anyway,' said Joe, and marched off towards the revolving main door.

'Hey! No!' I protested. 'We were going to—'

Helen nudged me, hard. 'Leave it till you've calmed down. I need to talk to you.'

'I really don't know if I can face cake,' I protested as she dragged me towards my office. 'Something about having tea with twenty-three-year-old lingerie models takes the shine off it.'

'It's not cake.' Helen pushed me in and closed the door behind us. Her eyes were glittering and there were pink spots on her cheekbones. She had been on the phone to Seamus. I *knew* it. She might as well have had spaghetti in her hair.

'I just wanted to check we were still on for the awards dinner next Friday,' she said.

'Of course we're still on for it,' I said. The post had arrived on my desk while I'd been out, and I started sorting through the press releases for hot-air balloons and edible flowers. 'Dominic's had his outfit picked out for weeks. He's been testing his heckler put-downs on me since the weekend. I don't know if I've mentioned it, but he's nominated for an award?'

'You have mentioned it. Every day. I thought maybe the four of us could go for a drink beforehand. And . . . a chat.'

I looked up from my pile of post at Helen. She and I had been out together plenty of times after work (and on very bad days, during work), but we'd never managed to go out as a foursome. Office hours, on all sides, made it about as easy to organize as a G8 summit, although that was probably a good thing, given the nuclear personality clash between Seamus and Dominic.

'Really? There'll be enough booze there to flood central London. And Seamus is, er, very talented in many ways, but conversation isn't exactly his strong point.' I tried a smile. 'I've had more chat out of his steak pie.'

Helen fiddled with the bowl of sugared almonds on my desk. 'I've been reading this self-help book about modelling the relationship you want, and I thought if Seamus saw how you and Dominic interact in public, you know, it'd give him some idea of . . . well, what you're meant to do. It's difficult for him, because he spends so much time at work. He doesn't know how he's supposed to *be* a boyfriend.'

Sometimes I wondered if Helen could hear the things that came out of her mouth. 'And Dominic and I are the kind of couple you want Seamus to model himself on?'

'Yes!' Helen nodded hard. 'Come on! It could be a regular date! We all work in the industry – we're supposed to go out to pop-up diners and soft openings.'

Neither of those things are as much fun as they sound, by the way, believe me.

'Hels, it's very flattering that you think Dominic and I are role models, but you do know that we're as likely to have a big row about the size of the wineglasses as we are to look all lovey-dovey?' I pointed out. 'In fact, probably more so?'

'Well, even that would be all right. Even the way you

squabble is funny. Like you're really comfortable with each other. Anyway, aren't things loads better with you and Dom now?' She offered me a sugared almond. 'Have you found a flat you both like yet?'

'Not yet.' I softened. 'But Dom's really into it, far more than I expected he'd be. That's why I really need to speed up this promotion business, so I can put my half of the money down on the flat . . .' As I said it, I saw Julia Thornbury's face again, already writing off the Bonneville as a possible venue. 'Although it looks as though Joe's put a spanner in those works.'

I turned to my Bridelizer, and the prize June spot I'd been about to stick Flora Thornbury into. I'd got my silver stars out and everything. 'Oh, *God*, how am I going to tell Laurence? He'll have one of his blood sugar collapses when he hears we haven't got that wedding. So will Caroline – she's already virtually married Laurence off to Julia."

'What?'

'She wants me to find him wife three. Get him off her hands. Again.'

Helen's eyes boggled. 'Rosie, don't you sometimes wonder if you're a bit too involved with this family?'

Luckily I didn't have to answer that, because Gemma popped her head around the door.

'Can Laurence have a word? In his office?'

It wasn't going to be a word. It was going to be one long protracted howl.

Brilliant.

In the thirty seconds between leaving my own office and knocking on Laurence's office door, I'd argued back and forth with myself several different ways about whether to drop Joe in it, and I'd more or less decided not to. Unless he'd got in there first. In which case, all was fair in love and weddings.

So when I saw Joe sitting on the Other Chair opposite Laurence's, my brain went into an abrupt reverse. How had even got there that fast? Had he done a sneaky double-back and gone straight there, to drop me in it?

'Ah, Rosie! Sit ye, sit ye.' Laurence waved at the chair with a jovial expression on his hangdog face, and I cast a quick look at Joe before I sat down. I hadn't been expecting a 'sit ye'.

Meanwhile Joe seemed his usual blandly happy self. *He still thinks he's done something really clever,* I thought. *He has no idea.*

'Drink?' Laurence offered. 'Pomegranate juice? Spirulina? Green tea?'

'I'm fine, thank you,' I said.

'Joe?' He made a face. 'Wheatgrass?'

Bloody California health bollocks, I thought testily.

'So . . . ?' I said lightly. I'd taken the pink emergency mobile in with me, in order to look busy and indispensable. Helen was going to ring it after fifteen minutes, if I hadn't got out of there.

'So, yes, well, I wanted to talk to both of you.' Laurence poured himself a martini glass of something green and healthy. 'I've had Julia Thornbury on the telephone.'

Joe and I exchanged swift glances, and he pulled a rather childish *And?* face. Which I'm sorry to say I returned.

But I was the professional here, so I took a deep breath and said, 'I can explain about that . . .' at exactly the same moment that Joe said, 'The thing about that is . . .'

Laurence waved a dismissive hand. 'No need to give away your secrets of negotiation to me, Rosie. Whatever you did hit the spot perfectly. I'm delighted to say that Flora Thornbury and her very famous legs will be getting married in our little hotel next June.'

'What?' said Joe, at the same time that I said, 'Really?'

'Yes, indeed.' I'd never seen Laurence look more pleased with himself, and believe me, I'd seen a lot of it over the years. 'Apparently you are a very competent young lady, and Joe is a natural wedding planner! Very fresh. Very . . . innovative. Flora is terribly keen for Joe to help coordinate her wedding. She feels he "gets her", whatever that means, and I hope it's not rude,' he added jovially.

'Flora wants Joe working on her wedding?' My heart, which had soared with elation to the top of my mental Bridelizer at the realization that the Thornbury thousands were now heading our way again, plummeted like a bouquet made from lead, with lead ribbons, at the prospect of being stuck with Joe – for months.

'Working under your supervision, naturally. Julia specifically said she wanted you, Rosie, to oversee the wedding, but that Flora was insistent about Joe's input on the details. I said that we didn't normally assign more than one wedding coordinator to a client, but in the case of such a very special wedding, I'd be happy to make an exception, and that both of you would be at their disposal, in addition to our support team. That's fine, isn't it? I've passed on your mobile numbers, anyway.'

'Oh,' I said weakly.

'Brilliant,' said Joe. 'So I'm on weddings indefinitely now, am I?'

'No, no. I'll be moving you around the departments as planned, but you'll be working on this wedding with Rosie until June,' Laurence informed him. 'I take it Flora's not planning a function that can be dashed off in a weekend?'

'Not exactly,' I said, already seeing the endless meetings about security, Pantone-coordinated flowers, cake tastings and so on, all with Joe in the foreground, asking stupid questions and making ludicrous suggestions, while I tried to keep Julia Thornbury and Flora on speaking terms.

'Marvellous! Well, finally something to celebrate. Cheers! To the Thornburys!' Laurence rubbed his hands together, and took a big slurp of his health drink.

The strangulated face he pulled as it went down was not entirely dissimilar to the one I was pulling inside my own head.

CHAPTER THIRTEEN

As he might have mentioned once or twice – or possibly three hundred times since the email had arrived – Dominic had been nominated for the London Eats and Drinks Food Writer of the Year, but he wasn't expecting to win. Not because he didn't think he was the best – he *did* think he was the best food writer in London, by quite some margin – but because he'd won the previous two years running, 'And it starts to look like you've got something on the committee if you win more than twice.'

'And,' as he pointed out to me in the taxi on the way there, 'it depends whether they're giving Chef of the Year to Eddie Hopkirk. That would be awkward, considering the review I gave him.'

'Don't remind me about that review,' I said darkly. The colourful death threat, scrawled on the back of a menu that Dominic had described as 'the solution for dieters who don't want to be tempted to eat on their fast days' was framed and hung in the place of honour in the loo, where it would look self-deprecating yet allow everyone who visited the flat to see it.

'And Karyn Chan's nominated,' I reminded him. 'The chef whose tempura tasted like deep-fried kitchen roll.'

He didn't look up from his laptop; he was filing some very late copy to the paper's website. 'Scouring pads! I said it was like eating beer-battered scouring pads.' He gave me a playful nudge, which didn't help my last-minute make-up application; Laurence had given me the night off, but, like Cinderella, I'd had chores to do first. 'Don't you read my reviews?'

'Not the online ones. The comments underneath are too scary. And they were from the chefs.' I paused long enough to give him a firm look over my compact. 'Please don't upset anyone tonight, will you? I don't want a scene.'

'Oh, no one really cares. It's all part of the game,' said Dominic easily. 'They'd rather I wrote something about them than nothing at all. As long as it's true. It makes it all the sweeter when I love a place.'

I opened my eyes wide to check that my concealer was hiding my eye bags. It wasn't, but then after the week I'd had, not even industrial grout would have covered them. You could probably have seen them through Ray-Bans.

'Betty, darling, you look ravishing,' he said, before I could even ask. Dominic was very good at compliments when it mattered. He shut his laptop and slid an arm across the back of the taxi seat, round my shoulders. 'I don't know why you're worrying about me being rude, when we've got Seamus the Shouty Chef on our table. Makes me look like Desmond Tutu. Does the fact that he's nominated for something make it more or less likely that he'll get very drunk and go into meltdown?'

'I don't know. I don't want to find out. Please don't wind

Seamus up,' I said automatically. 'For Helen's sake, if nothing else.'

'What? It's impossible *not* to wind him up! He's permanently wound up. He's like a giant, angry alarm clock, with a big knife. I have no idea what Helen sees in the stroppy little butcher. Apart from his beef Wellington. Which is a solid eight out of ten.'

I opened my mouth to protest, and Dominic gave me a cheeky wink.

'All right, eight and a half. But his puddings are into minus figures.'

'Helen loves him, so he can't be that bad underneath.' I pressed some powder onto my shiny nose and wondered if it was too late to Botox my whole face. 'She overlooks his ... mercurial personality, because he's a genius chef and will have another Michelin star by the end of the year.'

'He's more likely to have a court order. Or a bankruptcy notice,' said Dominic happily, and the taxi pulled up outside the venue, so I was spared the dubious honour of defending Seamus Lynch's reputation.

The London Eats and Drinks Awards were being held in an old London Underground building – a tactfully neutral move, considering most of the big hotels were nominated for various awards.

Helen was waiting for us in the foyer. As always at these events, she stood half a head above the sea of black dinner jackets, her ice-blonde hair shining under the chandeliers like she was starring in a shampoo ad. When she saw us and waved, five men turned round in the hope that she might be waving at them.

Over here! she mouthed, and we shouldered through the throng to where she'd positioned herself by the bar table. I led the way, since I knew from experience that the number of people grabbing Dominic to congratulate him on his latest column – or, more likely, to want to pick a fight about it – could slow us down considerably. And I needed a glass of champagne.

'Here you go,' said Helen, pressing one into my hand the second I was within reaching distance, like a relay runner slamming over a baton. 'I thought you weren't going to make it. What was the big drama Gemma wanted you to deal with?'

'Labels on Tabitha's favours.' I let out a grateful sigh as the bubbles went straight into my system. 'She's marrying Matt, not Mike. Mike's the best man. Could have been awkward. Joe was supposed to be changing them all over, but he's gone AWOL again. Did you see him before you left?'

Helen shook her head. 'He's probably keeping out of your way after the Stag Incident. Did you smooth that over?'

'Sort of. Well, no.' Joe had livened up yesterday's first Project Thornbury meeting with Flora and Julia by offering to organize Milo's stag weekend as part of the package. And Flora's hen. I let him run with it at first: I'd been thinking along the lines of whiskey tasting for Milo and cupcake decorating for Flora, but without warning Joe had launched into wild suggestions about fire-walking and burlesque stripping – for both parties, which would include the bride's parents. I could almost see Julia's blood pressure rising as Flora and Joe discussed whether a pole could be erected in the private Clarendon room.

'I can't decide whether I mind him skiving off or not,' I said darkly. 'It's probably a good thing, on balance. Every time he opens his mouth in a meeting, I can feel my Bridelizer going backwards.'

'Forget about Joe. This is going to be a fabulous evening. Oh, look, you've finished your drink already,' said Helen. 'Have another. Is my dress okay, by the way?'

'You look amazing,' I said, because she did.

Helen was tall enough, willowy enough, and most importantly stylish enough to carry off long backless jersey numbers without looking as if she'd got them on back to front. Her hair was dressed in a messy fishtail plait over one shoulder, instead of the smooth up-do she wore for work, and every time she sipped from her wineglass, the silver statement bracelets on her wrists jangled.

I was wearing my reliable green cocktail dress, which I hoped, in certain lights, made me look a bit like Joan from *Mad Men*. It had a very powerful invisible Spanx-y type lining that made it hard to eat, but the main thing was that it was smart without being too attention-seeking, and it had a pocket for business cards.

'Thanks! You look amazing too.' Helen leaned in and whispered, 'I'm hoping tonight's the night!'

I crossed the fingers of the hand that wasn't holding my glass, and grinned. 'It will be! I've got a fiver on Seamus winning Chef of the Year. I read he's second favourite after Karyn Chan.'

'Not that,' said Helen. 'Well, that too, but no, I hope tonight's the night Seamus agrees to move in with me!'

I smiled, but deep down a voice was screeching, 'Whaaaaaaaat?' I didn't want Helen to let surly, unreliable Seamus into her tiny, beautiful flat. Or even within a mile of it. But it was complicated; I'd agreed with so many of Helen's crazy justifications for his behaviour over the years, usually in return for her reassurances that Dominic was merely eccentric, that it'd look unreasonable to do a complete U-turn now. It didn't stop me feeling very uneasy, though.

And then Seamus himself sloped into view, and Helen began to glow in the shivery way she did whenever she was with him. Seamus also had a quivery glow, but of a rather different kind. It was the kind of quivery glow you keep an eye on, in case it decides to start throwing punches.

'Rosie,' he grunted, seeing me. 'Howya?'

'I'm well, Seamus, thanks,' I said, and after an awkward moment, leaned forward and deposited a kiss on his stubbly cheek. He smelled of whiskey, soap and smoke, with a piquant top note of garlic.

Helen had talked him into a dinner jacket, but she hadn't managed to get him to shave or comb his hair, although that might have been deliberate, because it added to his general rock-star air. Or maybe he was looking more rock-star than usual because Dominic had appeared behind him like the Ghost of Awards Ceremonies Past.

In contrast to Seamus's sexy dishevelment, Dominic's rather old-fashioned features made sense when he was wearing a bow tie, and his broad shoulders were made for eveningwear, which he loved. He'd have worn an opera cape if I'd let him, but with his current beard there was a real risk he'd be mistaken for a passing music-hall magician.

'Good evening, Seamus!' he said. 'I see they let you out of the kitchen?'

'Hey, Dominic. 'S good to seeya. Been a while,' Seamus grunted back. 'Fun times.'

A pause descended between us. As I might have said, Seamus wasn't one for the unnecessary chat.

'Shall we go to our table?' Dominic suggested. 'By which I mean, can we? I can't avoid the canapés much longer, and every time they go past I feel sorry for them. They're curling up in embarrassment all on their own.'

'Did you feed him that line?' Helen murmured as we made our way to the table, but I just smiled serenely.

(Yes. I did.)

Our table – thanks to Laurence's open-handed attitude to being seen at events like these – was in a 'good' part of the room: not too far from the stage and not too close to the loos. We were entertaining two of my key events contacts – Shirin, a florist, and Charlie Nevin, a wedding photographer – plus a posh wine merchant called Josh, whom Helen wanted to get some better deals from, and Mimi, the travel journalist who'd written the lovely feature about dream bridal suites, starring the Bonneville. She was also a 'huge fan' of Dominic, so that made two of them.

Dominic was brilliant at events like these. He had endless funny stories and a lot of gossip, but he was generous at drawing the other guests into conversation, and soon we were all chatting away merrily, apart from Seamus, who'd put on shades halfway through the first course and only came to life when Dominic began deconstructing the 'tower of aubergine three ways'.

'Two ways would have been plenty,' he said, lifting it on the tip of his knife. 'Three ways is just making a point.'

'There's only one way to cook aubergine,' Seamus growled. 'Bin the slimy feckers.'

'Well said, my friend.'

I risked a side glance at Helen. She was smiling at Posh Josh the wine merchant, but her eyes kept sliding to Seamus and Dominic, and when she saw me looking, we exchanged a secret glimmer of relief.

This was what all those late nights and gluey-eyed early mornings were for, I thought, beaming at Helen and Dominic. Me and my best mate, at our table at an awards dinner, with our handsome, successful boyfriends who were both nominated for awards . . .

I felt a sharp pain in my shin; Helen was kicking me under the table. I'd slipped my high heels off, but Helen never did, and she always wore pointy ones.

'It's Seamus's category!'

'And now to one of the most important categories of the night – Young Chef of the Year . . .'

'Is that someone's phone?' asked Shirin anxiously. 'I think I can hear a phone.'

'No, I'm sure everyone's got their phones turned off,' said Dominic sanctimoniously. 'Out of respect. To the company.'

Obviously, it was my phone. To be fair, I had it on vibrate, but it was vibrating against the metal tape measure I always carried in my handbag.

Everyone pretended to look appalled, even though I refused to believe for one second that they'd turned theirs off, and I pretended it wasn't mine for a couple of loud buzzes, but then I had to cave in. It was part of our promise to Bonneville brides: that, like the AA, someone would be on call 24/7 for any breakdowns.

'Our five nominees in a very strong field this year are . . .'

'Sorry, sorry,' I apologized, scrabbling in my bag, as the names of the other chefs were read out. 'Probably Laurence. He's in charge tonight.'

'If he wants me, I'm busy.' Helen was gripping Seamus's hand so tightly both their knuckles were white. 'Tell him it can wait until Seamus has won.'

'I hope he does win,' muttered Dominic. 'If that's happy, I don't want to see disappointed.'

'From the Marden Arms, Seamus Lynch . . .'

I answered the phone under the sound of loud applause and cheering from our table. 'Hello, Rosie McDonald?'

'Hi, Rosie, it's Flora. I need to talk to you about something.'

Oh, God. Not Flora. Not now.

'Hello, Flora!' I tried to sound calm, which wasn't easy, given that I had to stage-whisper over the sound of Dominic wolf-whistling. 'This isn't a brilliant time. Can I call you back in about . . . ten minutes?'

I could hear the pout down the phone. 'It's urgent. You said I could call you any time. And I can't get hold of Joe, his phone's off.'

Helen made a *who is it?* face. I mouthed *Flora* and she mimed dropping the phone into the carafe of water, but I shook my head. This was my chance to get a toehold in Flora's favours, and emergencies were my specialty.

The spotlight was swinging around the tables. I smiled fakely as the spotlight landed on our table, specifically on Seamus's scowling mug, then leaned backwards out of the spotlight until my back screamed in protest.

'Smile, Shay!' Helen hissed under her breath, and he surprised everyone with an absolutely angelic smile that stopped us all in our tracks.

I blinked and focused on dealing with Flora as fast as I could. 'What can I help you with?' I pretended to be leaning on my hand while hiding the phone in my palm.

'Can we get snow for the wedding? I've always wanted a winter wedding.'

What?

'But you're getting married in June.'

'I know. But can we get snow? I did this amazing photo shoot last week where it was totally snowy but warm? It wasn't, like, real snow, I don't think.' She sounded a bit doubtful. 'Anyway, could we do that? Cover the courtyard in snow and I could arrive on a sledge and have a fur-lined cape? Like Narnia? Or Switzerland?'

'Won't you be too hot? If you moved the wedding to December, we could arrange some—'

'But it might rain in December! And I don't want my guests to be cold,' she argued with impeccable logic. 'Isn't it better to have snow when it's warm?'

Dominic glared at me, but Flora was still rabbiting on in my ear.

'Flora, I'll send you some details about snow over the weekend,' I promised in an urgent whisper. 'Okay? But I've got to go. Yes, I'll email them tonight. Tonight. When I've got back from – when I've got a better line.' I realized I was leaning lower and lower towards the table until now my cheek was almost resting on it. 'Bye, Flora. Bye! Bye. Bye, Flora.'

Finally, she hung up, just as the gold envelope was handed to the co-presenter.

'Was that Flora?' Dominic asked innocently.

'Yes.' I rubbed my ear. 'I blame Joe. I bet he said something to her about fake snow. It sounds like one of his ideas.'

'Shh!' Helen waved her hands at me.

We all sat back, holding our breath. Seamus looked like he couldn't care less.

Please. Please, God, let Seamus win, I prayed. *For Helen. I will deal with Flora* and *Joe without complaining if you let Seamus win.*

The pause lengthened.

And I'll even persuade Laurence to promote Gemma, I added, as a final gamble.

'And the winner is . . . Seamus Lynch.'

'Yes!' roared Seamus and punched the air, and also the table decoration, which fortunately Shirin caught before it went crashing to the ground.

Helen looked ecstatic, and managed to land a kiss on his stubbly cheek before he brushed her off and strode towards the stage to collect his award – a big golden fork with the London Eye speared on it.

Only I spotted Helen's tiny wince, but Josh and Nevin and the others round the table congratulated her, as did a few people we knew nearby, and she glowed with pride.

He'll say something nice in his speech, though, I thought, still clapping. Seamus certainly had enough to thank Helen for, what with the endless hangover cures and laundry and loans and calls to his boss making up excuses for his AWOLness.

But, obviously, he didn't. What Seamus actually said was, 'Cheers, you bastards, I should have had this three years ago.' Then he brandished it at the crowd in a half-appreciative, half-threatening manner, and walked off, to tumultuous applause.

'That guy is such a rock star,' said someone at the table behind me. 'Bet he gets his own television series.'

But my mouth hung open as I saw Helen's expression freeze; it was one of pure hurt. I couldn't believe it. Nothing? Not *one word of thanks* for everything Helen had done? It was bad enough that he hadn't thanked his boss, or his kitchen brigade, but not making a nice gesture to Helen . . .

'What a total arse,' Dominic marvelled, and I didn't even care that he'd said it aloud. I was just glad he had.

Helen's lip wobbled, and I wished I was closer, to hug her.

'Hels.' I reached across the table, but she'd put on her shiny restaurant manager face.

'I think champagne's in order!' she said brightly. 'Laurence is picking up the tab for the table, isn't he? Let's get some champagne before Seamus gets back.'

We waited ten minutes after the champagne arrived for Seamus to return, but when he didn't, I made the decision to open the bottle anyway. It was starting to look like the uninvited guest at the table.

'It's a shame Joe isn't here to see Seamus win,' I said, taking a nerve-steadying swig. 'After everything he's heard about Seamus from you. Mind you, if he had come tonight, he'd probably have slunk off somewhere else by now. As usual. I wonder what he got up to this afternoon, when he should have been tying labels onto two hundred pots of bloody strawberry jam?'

'You can ask him yourself,' said Helen, and nodded over my shoulder.

I spun round to see Joe standing right behind our table. My face went red.

'How long have you been there?' I blurted out.

'Long enough. Hello, all. Thought I should come and say hello.'

He raised a Joe-ish hand in greeting, but he looked very different: he was almost in eveningwear, in that he'd put on a dark jacket but drawn the line at a bow tie, and the scraggly ends of his long hair had been chopped into a neater style. He'd also shaved, and there were no signs of his shell-based jewellery.

To be honest, Joe scrubbed up a lot better than I'd expected him to, but still he looked as if he'd rather be at home sorting out the recycling.

'Joe!' cried Helen. She was definitely in a professional mood now. 'Let me introduce you to everyone!'

'I didn't know you were coming,' I said, once she'd done the rounds of the table. 'Didn't think these events were your kind of thing.'

He grimaced. 'I had an offer I couldn't refuse. Mum had a last-minute invitation to some old friend's table and needed a plus-one. She made the arrangements,' he added, hooking his fingers in the air. 'Up to and including dressing me, and getting my hair cut at the same place she used to drag me to when I was twelve.'

'So that's where you were this afternoon?'

'Yeah. Sorry.' He looked faintly apologetic. 'Mum frogmarched me out of the hotel while you were in a meeting. I tried to leave a message with Gemma, but—'

'It's fine,' I said airily. 'Everything was under control. We only realized you weren't there at six or so.'

Helen gave me a look.

'Where are you sitting?' I asked, angling my neck to see if I could spot Caroline's mane of bouffant hair. 'I'd love to come over and have a chat.'

'We're with some caviar importers. Interesting guys, had some good debate about ethics. Mum's coming to find you, don't worry. She's got something she wants to discuss.' Joe's mouth twisted in what might have been a self-deprecating way. 'I hope it's not me.'

'I'm sure it won't be,' I said. It came out a bit tarter than I'd meant it to and Helen gave me another *stop it!* look.

'Whatever she says,' he replied, 'take it with a pinch of salt.'

I didn't have time to probe this gnomic statement further, because there was a buzz from the front of the room and the MC tried unsuccessfully to quell several hundred coffee-fuelled conversations.

'Who is that guy?' Joe asked into an unfortunate hush. 'Should I know who he is?'

'Er, yes?' Mimi, the journalist, spoke for the first time. 'It's Michael McIntyre.'

'Who?'

'Michael McIntyre?' she repeated, in the same tone you'd use to say, 'Prince Charles'.

'Joe's been abroad,' I explained.

'How far abroad?' Mimi looked stunned. 'Mars?'

'Sit down.' Dominic gestured at the empty chair next to me: the one Seamus had been in, until quite recently. I realized he'd been gone about twenty minutes. 'People will think you're going up for the award. And this is my category. Not that I'm going to win,' he added loudly. 'Again. I shouldn't think.'

A faint look of distaste crossed Joe's face, but he smiled politely enough. 'Well, good luck, but I should get back.' But as he turned, we realized his route back to Caroline's table was now blocked by the television cameras covering the event for some digital channel.

'Stay here in Seamus's seat until they change shots,' suggested Helen. 'He's probably talking to some reporters or being congratulated by friends. Or something.'

A flipbook of all the other things Seamus was more likely to be doing ran through my head and, going by his raised eyebrows, also through Dominic's.

'And now we come to the category that no one wants to read out the introduction for! Food Writer of the Year.'

'*For which* no one wants to read out the introduction,' said Dominic, just loud enough to be heard at the tables around us. He was famous for his impeccable grammar.

'Joe, just sit down,' I hissed, smiling for the benefit of everyone looking round at us.

'It's an impressive line-up this year,' the host went on. 'The nominees are Marina O'Loughlin, Giles Coren, Dominic Crosby, Steve Morris, and Zoe Williams. And now, to give us a taste – ho-ho! – of each nominee's work, we have some guest readers!'

My heart sank as various chefs and restaurant owners gamely trailed out onto the stage, including Karyn Chan of the tempura scouring pads. As she stepped up to the podium, she shot a particularly poisonous look over at our table, and I knew which nominee's clippings she'd have on her golden clipboard.

'All an act,' Dominic reassured Mimi, who flinched at Karyn's death-ray eyes. 'Chefs love it. Banter.'

I kept my smile up through the readings, although my heart was pounding in my chest. Dominic had said he knew he wasn't going to win, but I couldn't stop myself willing them to read out his name. He deserved to win.

I glanced at Joe, hoping he'd be a bit impressed. I was pleased Caroline was here – I wanted her to see me out there, networking and making industry connections like a future general manager of the Bonneville. As Karyn read out a particularly cutting sentence, Joe looked up, met my eye, and pretended to wince at Dominic's rapier wit.

I think he pretended to wince, anyway. I wasn't sure he was really getting the very bantery nature of the evening.

'And the winner is . . .'

'It won't be me, by the way,' Dominic reminded the table. 'Which is fine.'

'. . . Steve Morris from the *Balham Post*.'

My heart sank with disappointment, and Dominic's expression flickered; then he got up and started applauding generously. Maybe a little bit too loudly? No, it just looked hearty. It was fine. Fine.

Joe leaned across to me and muttered, 'He seems very pleased for that guy.'

'He is,' I said, clapping. 'He's a big supporter of the journalistic craft.'

Then Mimi joined in, and Shirin, and we were all clapping and commiserating with Dominic, who was being very gracious, when suddenly there was a bit of a commotion behind him.

For a moment I thought it was Steve Morris making his way to the podium – the *Balham Post* hadn't stumped up for a table near the front – but then I realized the crowds were parting to make way for Seamus, who was weaving his way unsteadily towards us.

'He took his time!' I said to Helen, but the *oh, you!* expression on her face froze when Seamus pushed past and squared up to Dominic.

'You two-faced, fat bastard!' he bellowed and took an actual swing at him.

'I have no idea what you're talking about. And I'm not fat.' Dominic took a nimble step back and turned his palms up with a shrug. 'Literally. You're slurring. Can't make out a thing. Something about . . . a basket?'

'Come here and I'll punch it into your head in Morse fecking code.' Seamus lurched for Dominic, who raised his hands in a *come on, come on* pose, not easy in the limited amount of space available between the tables.

'Can you two knock it off?' My face was already scarlet with mortification; heads were turning our way. 'You're about three feet from a television camera!'

I turned round. Several tables back, Steve Morris, beaming modestly and unaware of the punch-up brewing ahead of him, was weaving his way through the chairs, straight towards us.

'There is nothing *pedestrian* about my shepherd's pie,' Seamus spat at Dominic. 'You lisping fat ponce, with your stupid fecking . . . *beard*. How you've got the fecking *nerve* to post that online and then sit down to dinner with me—'

'Come on, Shay,' Helen pleaded, at the same time that I snapped, 'For Christ's sake, be quiet!'

Seamus turned to Helen and curled his lip. 'Give it a rest, willya, Helen. You're not the boss of me.'

'Listen, guys, guys . . .' Joe, clearly unimpressed, made ineffectual soothing noises that wouldn't even have calmed Gemma down from a disappointing sandwich. 'Can't we cool it . . .'

Seamus turned to Joe, and that's when I could see that wherever he'd been in the last twenty minutes or so had had generous refreshment facilities. His eyes were bright red, with pinprick pupils. My heart sank even further. This was going to be a scene. There was no way back now.

Seamus jabbed his finger in Joe's face. 'And you can shut your hole, you—'

We never found out what Seamus was going to call Joe, because Joe had Seamus's right hand up against his shoulder blades in the time it took Dominic to start removing his jacket (he claimed later he'd got his cuff link caught in the lining and didn't want to rip it). I actually saw Seamus's eyes widen in surprise, then roll back in his head, as Joe did something to the back of his neck with a thumb.

Joe then slipped Seamus's limp form back onto his chair like a chef sliding an omelette onto a plate, keeping his grip on Seamus's collar to stop him from slipping embarrassingly under the table.

Dominic, Helen and I stared in awe. So did Steve Morris, who'd come within an inch of getting lamped. And so did everyone else in the room who'd been watching Steve Morris's progress to the stage on the big screen, which was now focused *on our table*.

I have never wanted to sink into the ground more than at that moment. I actually had to shove my nails into my palm to convince myself it wasn't a hideous dream.

'Where did you learn to do that?' Dominic asked, which was only what we were all thinking. 'Harrow?'

'You don't fight with a brother in the cadet corps without learning a few things,' muttered Joe.

Seamus made a low groan, which suggested he was coming round again.

'You know what,' said Helen brightly, 'I think it might be time to call it a night.'

'I think so,' said a familiar voice.

We turned round. Just to put the tin lid on it, Caroline was standing by the table. Like Joe, she was looking very, very unimpressed, and my shame intensified by another factor of ten.

It wasn't the most mortifying moment of my life involving public humiliation by a thoughtless bloke, but it was a very, *very* close second. And this time, I didn't have a car standing by to whisk me away from the scene, or my dad to tell me no one had really noticed.

CHAPTER FOURTEEN

I don't know whether it was a good thing or a bad thing that I had to go in to work the morning after the awards fiasco, but I did: I had to supervise a wedding reception for a couple of accountants from Stoke Newington.

Bad, because I'd got no sleep at all. I'd lain awake most of the night, staring at the ceiling and wondering whether a true best mate would just get in a taxi, track Helen down, and bring her home to detox her of that useless, selfish waste of oxygen. But she wasn't answering her phone, and I couldn't get hold of her. I gave up at about 2 a.m., and turned instead to thinking about what kind of socially maladjusted idiot slagged off his girlfriend's best friend's boyfriend's restaurant the same night that he had dinner with him – and didn't even look remorseful about it. In fact, I'd heard Dominic laughing about it with two journalists.

Seamus had behaved inexcusably, but Dominic hadn't exactly come out of the evening smelling of roses either. I couldn't ignore it: he thought more about his stupid column than he did about me. The whole evening had been mortifying and, worst of all, had taken place in front of the exact roomful who could turn it into a hilarious anecdote for months to come. Every time I thought about everyone's eyes turning to our chaotic table, I felt hot and cold with embarrassment.

Dominic had told me I was being stupid. He refused to discuss it, then fell into a drunken slumber and snored like a pig straight away. I was revolted *and* furious *and* exhausted, and in the end, I was so cross I slept on the sofa.

Fortunately – or not – I wasn't the only one who'd crawled in to work under a cloud.

'I know what you're going to say, and please don't say it,' Helen warned me when she let herself into the honeymoon suite at half past eleven. I was giving it my final inspection before Matt carried the lovely Tabitha over the threshold later, but I was doing it quite slowly. My head throbbed, and I had to fight a strong urge to curl up on the soft bedspread.

'I wasn't going to say that,' I replied.

'Good.' She handed me the plastic box of handmade chocolates and fresh mint fondants for the glass bonbon dishes. Helen looked as if she'd had about as much sleep as I had.

'But I have to say it at some stage,' I pointed out. 'I wouldn't be much of a best mate if I didn't, would I?'

'You can't say anything to me that I haven't said a billion times already to myself all night.' Helen sank onto the chaise longue and gripped the pleated cushion to her chest. 'I can't ignore it any more. The man is a complete hole. He didn't even have the guts to admit that Joe knocked him out. He claims he must have had anaphylactic shock from the olives. And then he disappeared all night while I rang his phone over and over. I still don't know where he is. Oh, God.' She buried her face in the cushion.

I pulled out the chair from the dressing table and sat down opposite her. 'Have a champagne truffle,' I said, offering her the Tupperware. 'I can always send down for more.'

Helen's hand reached out and took three tiny gold-leafed truffle balls without looking, and shoved them all in her mouth at once. That was a bad sign. Her self-control when it came to the hotel's plentiful free chocolates was normally steelier than the Forth Bridge.

I pulled the cushion away from her face. Her eyes were red, and her up-do had lost its confident swoop. It was wilty, like her mood.

'Helen,' I said gently. 'Are you all right?'

'No, not really.' She braced herself. 'Tell me what I need to hear.'

I took a deep breath. I knew she wanted to hear Seamus was a maverick genius, unbound by society's bourgeois rules, but I couldn't do it. Not this time. Not even if it meant getting a faceful of 'Dominic is an arrogant prick' in retaliation.

'Seamus does *not* deserve you,' I said. 'He should be *proud* to be your boyfriend, but he treats you with no respect at all. I mean, if he wants to look like an irresponsible prat, that's fine, but to show you up like that, in front of everyone you work with . . . ?' I spread my hands out. 'He's too old to carry on like that, anyway. There's a time limit on leather trousers.'

'I know,' Helen groaned. 'But I can't control his behaviour, can I? I'm not his mum. And he was under a lot of pressure, what with the award, and work, and—'

'Helen, listen to yourself! Forget him, it's about *you*,' I said. 'Is this really making you happy? In any way at all? Is that how a man's supposed to treat his partner? Don't you think you deserve better? Because I do.'

What I didn't say was that it had been Joe's reaction that had made me realize just how bad things had got. It kept coming back to me, when I was lying on the sofa: Joe's contempt. The polite way he'd apologized to Helen for having to knock out her boyfriend. The curt nod to Dominic, when Dominic had been joking even before Seamus came round. In fact, seeing the whole night through Joe's eyes had been sobering. I wished Joe hadn't first met Dominic when Dom was being . . . well, a bit of an arse himself.

I didn't like the Dominic Joe had seen. It was hard to persuade myself that that Dominic was someone I wanted to move in with.

'And you can say it back to me,' I went on crossly. 'I have no idea what Dominic was thinking, posting that review. It's like he's got some sort of psychological problem, that he needs to do these stupid things to get attention.' I helped myself to a truffle, and wiped a few specks of dust from the dressing-table surface. 'I sometimes wonder if his mother left him on his own a lot as a baby. I wouldn't blame her if she had.'

'That sounds like an excuse to me, too.' Helen raised an eyebrow. 'And did *he* apologize for showing you up?'

'Sort of.' He'd *looked* sorry. 'Well, no. He sort of . . .' My voice trailed off. I couldn't lie to Helen, not when she'd been honest with me about Seamus. 'No, he didn't.'

She looked at me, and we both knew. This had to stop.

'We deserve so much better.' Helen got up and stepped towards the French windows overlooking Green Park. That was another of our catchphrases. If our two-woman Bad Boyfriends Club had a motto, it would be that, in Latin. Over a pair of crossed kitchen knives, rampant.

'We do,' I said, but this time, I actually meant it. 'Helen, Seamus isn't worth your time. There are much, much better men out there for you. Dump him. Please.'

There was a long pause, in which I knew she was thinking, *Ditto, dump Dominic. He's just as bad.*

She stood there, holding the heavy gold curtain tieback, and staring out at the park like a woman in a painting.

Then she turned, and her eyes were sad but determined.

'I know,' she said. 'That's what Joe said.'

'Joe?'

'Mmm.' Helen set her lips flat. 'And he was right. You're right. I'm going to do it. I'm going to take anything he's left at my flat round to his tonight while he's doing the dinner service, and leave him a note.'

'Tonight? Even though we've—' I stopped myself just in time.

Helen glared at me. 'Were you going to say, "Even though we've got a wedding tonight?"'

I was. Busted.

'Um, no? I was going to say . . . um, what about your things?'

'He can keep them. I still haven't got the smell out of that spare duvet I lent him. Anyway, I've got the world's smallest studio flat. I need to dejunk.' Helen dumped the truffles into the Lalique dish on the dressing table and the mints into the bowl by the bed without her usual care for Delphine's confectionary work. 'It'll take me half an hour to get his stinky Converse out of my hall and into a bag. And don't worry about the wedding – I'll only be out an hour and I've got cover.'

'I wasn't worrying about the wedding,' I insisted. 'I wasn't, honestly. Who cares about the wedding? You're way more important than any wedding.'

Helen tossed her head, and I knew she was fighting back tears. She never cried in public. She'd told me it was one of the promises she'd made to herself when she decided at fifteen to model herself on Grace Kelly.

'It's just . . . it's just a bit ironic, isn't it?' she said, biting her lip hard. 'That we always seem to be making these fairy-tale weddings for everyone else, while we get stuck with complete losers.'

'But that's going to change,' I said, and I meant it. 'That's changing as of now.'

Helen gave me a long, questioning look, and then went downstairs to yell at some kitchen porters.

Tabitha and Matt were getting married in a church in Chelsea and coming to us (in a red London bus with a white ribbon on the front) for their afternoon tea reception, followed by dancing in the ballroom, and then the first night of their honeymoon upstairs in the suite.

I enjoyed arranging weddings in the hotel – there was something really satisfying about hitting the various timings in the ceremony spot-on – but an evening party, with a live band and candlelight and guests in black tie, brought an old-fashioned glamour to the whole place. The corridors seemed to come to life in mood lighting, beckoning guests down to the main event. Tabitha and Matt had met at a salsa dancing class, so they'd booked an excellent band for the evening, and asked all their guests to wear clothes 'to let their hair down in'.

I checked that everything was on track in the ballroom, then went back to the Palm Court where the wedding party would be arriving for the afternoon tea reception in about an hour. Delphine had surpassed herself with the pastries today and made about five hundred mini scones, which were to be eaten with the little pots of jam I'd spent hours relabelling the previous evening. There were four types of loose-leaf tea in battered old solid silver pots, two champagne cocktails named after the bride and groom, one non-alcoholic sparkler, and a wide variety of tiny, crustless sandwiches and fondant fancies arranged on tiered silver stands.

Four catering staff were busy laying the tables with the meticulous afternoon-tea settings, and I was pleased to see Joe hovering around them, asking them questions.

'Hey, Rosie,' he said when he saw me walk in. 'Maybe you can tell me – why do these guys have to use a ruler to do the table settings?'

'So the cutlery and the plates are in the right place,' I replied, surprised that he had to ask. 'It makes everything look symmetrical.'

'But it takes ages, right?'

Joe sauntered over and helped himself to one of the shell-pink fondants on the top tier of a cake stand, and I smacked his hand.

'I've touched it now,' he pointed out through a mouthful of cake. 'Don't worry, we can juggle the others round . . . there. You can't tell.'

I frowned. I didn't have the energy for this today. 'Karen? Did Delphine send up any spare cakes? If you could . . . thanks. Joe, leave the cake alone and come and check the seating plan with me.'

'How's Helen today?' asked Joe as I handed him Tabitha's printed list and examined the board of elegant hand-calligraphed cards.

'Helen?' I wasn't sure whether I was supposed to discuss Helen's private life with Joe. It wasn't as if he really knew the long and complicated background . . .

'Yes,' he went on, 'after that drunken fool Seamus made a show of you all last night.'

I blanched. Although that *was* the size of it. 'She's fine. Thank you for asking.'

'Stop being so English. *I* wouldn't be fine. Did she give that prick his marching orders, or what?'

I stopped running my pen down the neat list, and turned to him.

Joe was looking at me, and he seemed genuinely ticked off. 'I don't mean to sound rude . . . You know what? I *do* mean to sound rude. What on earth is a woman like Helen doing with an idiot like that? I couldn't believe the way he treated her.'

'Well, you only saw a tiny snapshot,' I began, but Joe shook his head.

'That's all I needed to see. The body language was enough. Helen *stoops* when she's with him – have you noticed?'

Body language. He'd be telling me their star signs were wrong next.

I wasn't sure why I felt so defensive. *Maybe because you haven't noticed how she stoops?* asked a voice in my head. *Because you should have said something before now?*

And because I wondered what was going through Joe's mind when he'd been looking at me and Dominic?

'He is a bit shorter than she is,' I said, and I really didn't know why I said that, because now he'd pointed it out, I realized I was furious that Helen stooped when she was with Seamus. *And* she wore awful flat shoes and pretended they were better for her feet when I'd seen her run the length of Piccadilly in heels.

Joe made a dismissive noise. 'I don't get how she's so in control of that kitchen, and yet puts up with such crap from someone like him. Why do women do that? She's so far out of his league it's painful. You're her best friend. Surely you've said something before now?'

'Of course I have. But I'll pass on your feedback,' I said, crossing off items on my list a bit too hard. 'But apart from that, did you enjoy your evening?'

'Don't be snarky. I'm just trying to understand here because I really like Helen and I hate to see her upset like that.' He sounded exasperated. 'I don't go in for physical violence, but jeez, the guy's a hard one not to punch. Why *isn't* she with a nicer man? Talk to me, Rosie.' Joe pulled my clipboard towards him, and made me meet his eye. 'You're the couples expert. Am I missing something?'

His expression was genuinely baffled, and I felt flattered – sort of – that he thought I'd have any insight into the mystery of Seamus' appeal. 'You tell me. I'm not a couples expert. Far from it.'

'Apart from the weddings you organize all day, every day.'

'Look, Joe,' I said, with a sigh, 'for what it's worth, I agree with you. Seamus is an arse, Helen deserves better, and personally, yes, I hope this is the final straw. But kitchens are a high-pressure environment. Tensions run high. You make allowances. Maybe she's made a few allowances too many.'

He gazed at me as if he was considering whether to say something or not.

'Go on.' I folded my arms. 'Say it. You're going to anyway.'

'Again, I don't mean to be rude, but is *your* boyfriend always like that?'

'Like what?'

'Like ... he has to explain everything to everyone else because they don't understand things quite as well as he does?'

Joe had only spent about fifteen minutes in Dominic's company, yet he'd unerringly zeroed in on one of Dominic's worst habits, one that always set my teeth on edge. I felt the part of me that had softened towards Joe ice up again defensively.

'Not always.' I moved a spare flower arrangement off the table and marched away to replace it in the florist's box. 'Only when he's with people who need to have things explained. Can we stick to the task at hand? Guests are going to be arriving soon. Oh, God, what *now*?'

I'd put my phone on the table, and it was making the text-alert noise and sidling its way dangerously towards a clingfilmed platter of blinis, like a fish out of water.

'I'll get it,' said Joe, and he'd grabbed it before I could stop him. I hoped it was Dominic texting something nice, ideally that he'd called in at the estate agents and picked up the details I'd asked him to find, but of course it wasn't.

'Oh, God,' said Joe, looking at the message.

'Don't tell me. It's Flora, and this time she wants a thunderstorm, but only in the Palm Court.'

'No, it's from Mum.' Joe thrust the phone at me. 'For you.'

The text was from Caroline:

Thanks for guest list: introduce Laurence to Sally Markham! Ex-matron boarding school, probably very handy with cod liver oil, etc. C

I bit my lip and blushed. 'Um, yes, pretend you didn't see that.'

'Rosie! Is it *ethical* to supply guest lists to outside parties?' Joe enquired. 'Especially when that party has a record of enforced blind dating on her male family members?'

'You know about that?' It slipped out before I could stop myself.

'Not officially. But yes. Mum's another one who can't stop micro-managing other people's lives.' He wagged a finger at me. 'Don't you start dancing to her tune.'

My cheeks went pink. 'It's called taking an interest. And I'm not – oh, why am I even discussing this with you?'

Joe raised his palms in a gesture of despair. 'Because that's what living in a hotel does for your boundaries. It completely messes with them. Watch out for that.'

'Rosie!' Gemma dashed in, waving the special pink phone reserved for really, really demanding brides. The ring tone was set to 'Crazy' by Gnarls Barkley; Gemma tried to change it to 'I Do, I Do, I Do, I Do, I Do' by Abba every so often, but Helen always changed it back.

'It's her!' she whispered, looking simultaneously thrilled and terrified. 'Ohmigod, ohmigod, ohmigod!'

'Calm down, Gemma,' I said automatically. 'Who is it?'

'Flora Thornbury,' she squeaked. '*Actual* Flora Thornbury!'

'Is there a pretend Flora Thornbury?' asked Joe.

I made a *don't wind her up* face, but he held out his hand. 'Give it here,' he said. 'I bet I know what she's calling about.'

'No, I should take it.' I reached out my hand towards Gemma. 'I'm her wedding co-ordinator.'

Gemma looked uncertainly between us. The phone went into another burst of 'craa-aaa-aazy'. I made a mental note to change it. It probably wasn't very professional.

Joe gave me a quizzical look. 'Do *you* want to hear about how Flora can't decide between Borneo or Kenya or Necker Island for her honeymoon? Because that's what the last hour-long conversation was about.'

'Wow,' breathed Gemma.

'Just don't get her back on the stag weekend,' I warned him. '*No poles.*'

'No poles,' agreed Joe, and took the phone from Gemma's hot

hand. 'I had a better idea, anyway – a bush survival weekend in Dartmoor, where Alec tracks them with his laser-sighted . . . Joking. I'm joking! Hi, Flora! How are you?'

'Is that really Flora Thornbury?' Gemma whispered as Joe strolled off towards the grand piano, dappled in the sunlight falling through the blinds.

Yes,' I said. I watched him, chatting away with a charming smile on his handsome face, helping himself to unguarded cakes during the long gaps where Flora was talking.

Part of me was very irritated by the easy way he'd commandeered the biggest-budget and potentially most useful contact I'd ever landed; part of me was relieved that I didn't have to listen to Flora agonizing over her luxury honeymoon when I hadn't had a holiday in years; and the tiniest part of me was secretly envious of the ease with which he did it all. Now that his initial grumpiness had worn off, Joe's real personality was starting to emerge. I'd grudgingly come to realize that he said what he thought, not because he was an arrogant sod, but because he didn't see any point in being anything other than himself.

That's what you got when you inherited charm from both sides of your family, as well as a hotel and two sets of blond genes.

I snapped back to the task at hand. I didn't have the luxury of charm, hotels, or genes. I'd have to work for all my breaks, and in a way, that was better, wasn't it?

'Right, Gemma,' I said briskly. 'I need to find the place card for Mrs Sally Markham . . .'

CHAPTER FIFTEEN

Summer always passed in a whirl of confetti and honeymoon-suite white linens for me, and this year was no different. A warm July and a sultry August saw the hotel full of sighing wedding guests nearly every weekend: the old cool room downstairs was constantly filled with white lilies and roses for the tables and arrangements, clanking crates of champagne were wheeled in and empty bottles wheeled out, and Fiona, the harpist, was here so often she was dating one of the barmen by the end of August.

My Bridelizer was making steady progress towards the target, and I was dropping regular hints to Laurence about how much of the general manager's job I was now doing in the hope that he might get bored and just offer me the job early. Meanwhile, in the events office, Joe was fielding most of Flora's more whimsical calls about butterflies and whether it was okay to cull guests on grounds of weight gain, while I dealt with Julia Thornbury and the nitty-gritty details, like how many people she would be inviting. Life was good. But I couldn't enjoy it as much as usual, because in the space of one painful evening, my beautiful friend Helen had gone from a poised and confident restaurant manager to a lovelorn zombie.

True to her word, the day after the awards dinner, Helen gave Seamus his marching orders, and he was happy enough to march, the rat. One of the kitchen porters let slip to me that he'd moved straight in with one of the wine buyers for a big West End restaurant chain – not that I told Helen.

Instead, I took her out for dinner – usually to McDonald's, since most London restaurants had bad associations now – and tried to keep her busy in as much social life as Laurence let us have, but the fact remained that the pair of us were condemned to celebrate other people's happy relationships at least once a week, and smile constantly while we did it. I tried to relieve the grisly irony by reintroducing our old favourite, Wedding Bingo – three guests in identical Coast dresses; Hungover Ushers; Fake Tan Lines; Spot the Exes – but Helen didn't want to play any more.

'Why is the moral high ground so boring?' she moaned to me through gritted teeth and waterproof mascara. 'Why is it so lonely? Why is doing the right thing so – so unbelievably painful?'

'You'll find someone else,' I assured her, as I did about four times a day, more on wedding weekends. 'You'll never meet Mr Right if you're shacked up with Mr Wrong.'

'But how am I going to meet Mr Right?' She rolled her eyes towards the Paris-themed wedding reception of childhood sweethearts Callum and Eithne Riley. 'Even if I found a single bloke under the age of fifty here, I'd have to fight off the three single friends of the bride who were invited specifically to scrap it out over him. I never realized how like *The Hunger Games* weddings are.'

I took the croquembouche discreetly out of her hands. She'd started to pick viciously at the spun sugar. 'The right man will come along,' I said, 'when you least expect it. What's meant for you won't go by you.'

Seriously, I should have been painting these thoughts onto pebbles and selling them to brides as wedding favours.

Over by the champagne table, two women in strapless prom dresses started having a very obvious standoff, next to a sheepish-looking bloke.

'Leave them to it,' I said. 'He's the best man's boyfriend.'

'Ha!' said Helen, and stalked back to the kitchen.

The Indian summer of Post-Seamus Gloom rolled on in London until the last week in September, and then suddenly one morning I woke up and autumn had arrived. The air changed – there was a crispness about everything, and people started to walk a little faster down Piccadilly in the mornings.

Something had changed in the hotel, too.

We'd had a weekly wedding meeting, in which Joe had brought us up to date with Flora's latest ideas for a wedding dress made entirely from rose petals and Love Hearts sweeties (she'd actually found someone mad enough to make it, too), and he and Gemma had gone off, under protest, to remove all the red Smarties from Catriona Hale's fifteen pounds of sweets for her ice cream bar. That left me and Helen to run through Delphine's cake schedule for the rest of the year.

Down in her pâtisserie cave, Delphine created beautiful bespoke wedding cakes, but lately she'd started modelling very 'realistic' toppers of the bride and groom, some of which had actually upset the brides, who'd been under the impression that their efforts on the 5:2 diet had been more successful than Delphine apparently thought.

'Helen.' I nudged her. 'You were going to talk to Delphine about being a bit less Parisian and a bit more generous in her sugar paste.'

'What?' She jumped and frowned, then smiled in a spacey way. 'Sorry, I was miles away.'

I eyed her. This was a different kind of distracted from the usual heartbroken zombie face. 'Are you all right?'

She nodded, but only stayed focused for about two nanoseconds before drifting back into her private daydream. Her eyes weren't smiling at me. They were smiling at a non-specific point about two yards to the right of my head.

I clicked my fingers in front of Helen's face to try to get her to concentrate. 'Helen? You haven't been eating anything out of the commis chef's biscuit tin again?'

She shook her head and smiled. Again, not at me.

'Don't make me throw this glass of water over you,' I warned her.

Helen pulled herself together. 'Guess what?'

'What?' I narrowed my eyes. 'Please don't tell me Seamus has come back? Whatever he's done, Helen, think about those bunny rabbits that you thought were for pets but were really—'

'No, it's not Seamus.' Helen looked scornful. 'That loser? Forget *him*. No, I've met someone else.' She glanced down, as if having a private thought of her own, and her usual poise was suddenly, and rather beautifully, disrupted by a very goofy grin.

'Really?' An odd sensation rippled through me. 'That's . . . that's brilliant! When?'

'Last week.'

Last week? I felt a bit hurt. 'When were you going to tell me?'

For the first time, she looked a little shifty. 'Um, soon. I wanted to make sure I wasn't having one of those weird rebound-goggles episodes.'

'So, who is he?' I nudged her. 'How did you meet? Come on, I want to know *everything*!'

Helen blushed. 'It's really corny, but it was in the restaurant. He came in at ten to, reservation for two people at one o'clock, so I seated him, did all the usual stuff, didn't take much notice because we were busy. He was on his iPhone, so I thought, fine . . . then I realized at ten past one that he was still on his own. And no one had come by quarter past, so I sent Rita to ask if there was a problem, he said no, but he'd finished the bread—'

'Yadda yadda,' I prompted, rolling my hands, because much as I wanted to know all the details, my schedule wasn't going to allow for a real-time re-enactment.

'Anyway, a little after half past Rita took a call from someone called Lou, to let Wynn Davies at table three know she wasn't going to make it. Could we pass on the message?' The pink flush on Helen's cheek deepened. 'I always pass on phone messages like that myself, in case it's something personal, so I went over to tell him, and he looked crushed, poor guy, and it turned out . . .'

Finally.

'. . . that he'd been set up on a blind date, and he'd been stood up. I didn't ask, he just blurted it out. I don't think he meant to tell me, but he'd been sitting there for over half an hour, eating bread.'

'Awkward,' I agreed. 'So, what did you do? Offer him the specials menu, and tell him to hurry up?'

Helen tutted. 'Of *course* not. I gave him a glass of champagne on the house. He'd made an effort too, I could tell. Nice suit, new haircut. And we're not a cheap first-date restaurant, either. I thought that said a lot about him.'

'And . . . ?'

'And then we sort of got chatting, and he, um . . .' Helen shyly curled a strand of hair round her finger. 'He asked if he could take me out for dinner, or if that was the worst thing you could ask a restaurant manager? And I said, no, it wasn't, actually, and that I'd been dying to try that place Dom reviewed last week.'

'The Fulham Rigger?'

'No, the other one.' She frowned. 'The Coach and Horsemen.'

'I don't think I've been there.'

'You have. In Canonbury? Betty was there – she had some tart comments to make about the butter.'

I hadn't been to Canonbury in over a year. 'Nope, haven't been. You'll have to tell me what it's like.'

'It's very nice, actually. We've actually, um, had the date.' Helen hugged her knees.

'What? Why didn't you tell me?'

'I thought you might think I was moving on a bit fast. From Seamus.'

Privately, I didn't think Helen *could* move on too fast from Seamus, not even if she was speeding away from him with a jetpack, but I just made a *wow!* face. 'Of course not! So tell me all about him! What does he do? Where's he from?'

'He's called Wynn, he's thirty, he's from Swansea, he's ...' Helen's sunny expression wavered a little. 'He's ...'

'He's what? A sous-chef?' Helen rarely dated anyone beneath chef status, but she'd sometimes settle for a talented sommelier. 'Another restaurant manager?'

'Don't laugh,' she warned me. 'It's not the most exciting job.'

I racked my brains. 'He's not a ... baker?'

'No, he's a dentist.'

I did a double take. 'A dentist?'

'I know it's not a very sexy profession, but I thought it could be a good idea to get away from the food industry for a bit.'

'Well, I suppose dentists deal with the ... aftermath of the food industry.'

'You're pleased?' She looked at me anxiously. 'It's not just rebound insanity?'

Helen looked like a new woman. Well, not a new woman. Her old self. Her old, glowy, confident, Scandinavian goddess self.

'No,' I said. 'Truthfully, it's the best news I've had all year.'

'I think so too.' She beamed sunnily, and opened her diary. 'So, when are you and Dominic free for a double date?'

*

As usual, Dominic insisted on taking Helen and Wynn out on a reviewing mission for our double date.

'It kills two birds with one stone,' he protested when I found he'd booked us into Jocques, 'Fulham's exciting new ground-breaking Scottish-French fusion concept'. 'And this new bloke of Helen's is bound to have some good insider gossip.'

He'd rung me up to tell me, but I could hear the eagerness in his voice; there was nothing Dominic loved more than access to foodie gossip. One of his main complaints about Seamus was that he was too high-minded – or high – to pass on kitchen scandal.

'I hate to disappoint you, but I doubt it. Not unless their salted caramel is causing root-canal traumas all round Chelsea.'

'What?'

'Wynn's a dentist.' I tucked the phone under my ear and stuck the Post-it note with Bride's Babysitter onto the new seating plan in the one remaining place it could go, between Groom Uni Friend and Mrs Bride's Boss. There. Done. Issy Livingstone's feud-riven, multi-married, half-mad family, all seated.

I stood back and surveyed the plan with some pride.

'So that's settled,' said Dom, clearly not listening to me. 'I'll see you both there at half past seven.'

'But, hang on, what sort of place is this? I don't know if he eats meat or—'

'What kind of weirdo doesn't eat meat?'

'Plenty. I don't eat a lot myself.' Lately I'd been picking Dominic up on some of his casual rudeness. Ever since the awards fiasco, it had stopped being charming and started to, well, sound plain rude.

'You know something, Rosie, you're beginning to sound like someone's mother,' said Dominic tetchily. 'Not mine. She didn't nag me quite so much.'

'This isn't nagging,' I pointed out. 'This is just manners. You could at least—'

But the line had gone dead. He'd hung up on me. I stared in mute fury at the phone. That was the third time he'd hung up on me this month. Our theoretical mortgage had finally come through from the bank, but the prospect of taking another step towards our own flat wasn't filling me with the unbridled joy I'd expected it to.

'I hate it when you hang up on me, you charmless nerk!' I yelled into the receiver, just as Joe walked in.

'Was that Issy?' he asked. 'Bit brisk?'

'No, it was bloody Dominic,' I said, then frowned at myself. I hadn't meant to tell Joe that. 'Could you knock, by the way? Before you come in?'

Joe leaned against the doorframe. 'Why? Would I have over-heard something that might have shocked me? More covert matchmaking for my mother? Date reports about my dad?'

'No, I . . .' Urgh. My mind went blank. 'But I often have brides on the phone. And they don't appreciate doors opening and shutting, and interruptions.'

As I spoke, the Chief Bridesmaid Post-It peeled slowly off the plan and fluttered to the ground, closely followed by Groom's Stepmother.

'Oh, you're kidding me,' I groaned. The groom's stepmother had been stuck to the back of the chief bridesmaid all along.

'What?'

I showed him the offending Post-its. 'Seating plan. My least favourite part of a wedding.'

'Oh,' said Joe, as if it had jogged his memory. 'Issy was trying to get hold of you. She left a message to say that her stepmother thinks she will come after all, so can we fit her in? Top table, ideally, otherwise she'll have one of her dos, whatever that means.'

I stared at the top table, already overloaded with the bride's father's three previous wives, all at very carefully spaced distances from one another. I'd worked it out with a ruler and sightlines so none of them had to look at each other directly. In the end, I'd had a brainwave and asked the florist to make an extra, very thick, freestanding arrangement to block one out.

'There's no room for another Mrs Livingstone,' I said. 'Not unless we put a hammock over the top table and stick her in that.'

Joe wrinkled up his nose as if I were just making a big fuss about nothing. 'Oh, it can't be that bad.'

'Hello?' I waved in defeat at the plan.

'Let me see.' He pushed himself off the doorframe and sloped inside.

I folded my arms and watched him as he squinted at the various Post-Its. 'Blue for groom, pink for bride, red stars one to five for "difficult behaviour",' I explained. 'Gold star for single.'

He went to tug a ratty plait, remembered they'd all been cut off, stuck a hand into his hair instead, and frowned. 'Does it have to be this complicated? Can't you just run a buffet and let them sit where they want?'

I didn't dignify that with a response.

'What if . . . ?' Joe went to move a Post-it, then stopped. 'No. Hmm.'

'See?' I said, feeling vindicated. 'Not so easy, is it?'

'Hang on. I haven't finished. What if . . . you moved this person?' He peeled a Post-it off the plan.

'What? No! That's the groom. You can't move him.'

'And *this* person.'

I folded my arms. 'Again, the bride. Not really movable.'

'Why not?' said Joe. 'I reckon they're the *most* movable. If you stick the bride and groom here at their own special top top-table . . .' He picked up a pen from my desk, drew a small square by the French windows on the plan, and restuck Issy and Adam on it. 'There. Frees up two whole places. One for the stepmother and another just in case Issy's dad ditches his current wife and trades up again before the wedding. You did say Issy didn't really get on with half the people at the top table.'

I stared at the plan. It was totally wrong, but at the same time, genius. I couldn't believe I hadn't seen it before. An unexpected calm spread through my chest.

'You want to say, "That's brilliant, Joe",' Joe prompted me.

'It's very unconventional.'

He made an outraged choking noise. 'What's the point of convention if it doesn't work? Lighten up.'

I half-smiled at him. It turned into a full smile, despite

myself: Joe looked so pleased with his solution. I couldn't help myself. 'You keep saying that.'

'And I'll keep saying it until you do,' he replied with an even cheesier smile. 'Without me having to remind you the whole time.'

Helen's new man Wynn was so far from what I was expecting that when Dominic and I met at Jocques fifteen minutes late, as usual, I was relieved that we seemed to have got there before them.

It was only when I scanned the nearly empty restaurant and spotted Helen, leaning in very close to a man I'd have taken for Prince Harry if I hadn't had my contact lenses in, that I realized Helen and Wynn had arrived. They'd probably been there for ages, but they wouldn't have noticed if we'd been another hour. Or two. Or not arrived at all.

Everything about the way they were sitting screamed 'honeymoon dating period'. The menus lay unread next to them, and their fingers were entwined as they gazed into each other's eyes with that greedy, giddy eagerness that you get when you think you've chanced upon the one person in the entire world you were supposed to meet all along. My heart fizzed with a funny cocktail of emotions at how happy Helen looked. I was happy for her, but at the same time, I wished someone would look at me like that. I wasn't sure anyone ever had.

Wynn said something to her and smiled shyly. Helen laughed, and as she looked up, she spotted us, and waved.

'Dominic.' I nudged him. He was already disputing some

spelling error in the signage outside with the bewildered girl at the door. 'Dominic!'

'. . . should have the apostrophe *after* the *s*. Is it the bar of Jocques? Or is it a collection of Jocques? What? Are they here?' He frowned and I pointed. 'Whoa. Are you sure that's him?'

'Yes.'

'Blimey,' said Dominic.

I tried not to stare as we made our way over, but I knew what Dominic meant. Wynn was the exact reverse of every single boyfriend I'd ever known Helen to have. He was gingery, chunky in a rugby-playing fashion, and had with him what looked like a zip-up cardigan. It might have been a jumper with a half-zip. Weirdly, whichever it was, he didn't look terrible in it. He looked . . . reassuring. Not malnourished, wired, angry, tormented or dangerous in any form.

He also got up with a polite smile as we got nearer, and offered his hand to shake, which was a definite improvement on Seamus.

Helen leaped up as well, and introduced us with the sort of enthusiasm normally reserved for celebrity diners. 'Guys, this is Wynn!'

'*Guys*?' muttered Dominic. 'What? Are we in *Friends* now?' but I rushed to shake Wynn's hand.

'Hello! I'm Rosie, and this is Dominic.'

'Ah, the famous Dominic,' said Wynn affably. He had a gentle Welsh accent, all daffodils and Guide Me O Thou Great Redeemer. 'I read your column every week. Very funny.'

Dominic could never resist a reader. 'Thanks.'

'Bit worried we'll end up in it this evening!' Wynn glanced at Helen. 'Helen did warn me that you write everything down.'

'Wynn!' Helen pretended to look cross, and nudged him. This time I boggled. Helen never pretended to look cross. She was either fine, or very cross, nothing in between.

'You're perfectly safe. Dominic only writes down the stuff I say,' I said.

'And only then if it's funny,' added Dominic.

'In which case he passes it off as his own.'

Helen raised her eyebrows.

'Ha-ha!' I added, to make it clear that this was just light-hearted banter and not the aftermath of a tense conversation we'd had over breakfast about 'Betty's' disdain for the wine list at a restaurant I actually went to quite regularly and liked, and which now refused to serve me 'anything with a screw top.'

'So, are you reviewing this place?' Wynn asked as we settled into our booth. It was covered with tartan, with black leather trim.

'I'm afraid so,' said Dominic, studying the menu, also tartan/leather-trimmed. 'I'm going to have to make you two eat anything with a sauce, and a pudding each.'

'Brilliant.' Wynn flapped his (tartan) napkin over his knee. 'I love a pudding.'

'Wow! So do I!' exclaimed Helen, as if they'd discovered their mothers grew up on the same street, had the same birthday, *and* had stood next to each other at a Wings gig in 1978. 'What kind?'

'Chocolate ones? And meringue-y ones.'

'Me too! That's amazing!'

'Is it going to be like this all evening?' Dominic muttered, while they did a 'you, no you, no you' routine over the warm rolls that arrived at the usual breakneck speed, with extra butter in a thistle-shaped pot. 'In which case, can they bring me a tartan-trimmed bucket?'

'Stop it,' I whispered, already seeing how this might play out in the column. 'And it's lovely, so don't spoil it.'

'How can I spoil anything? It's like we're not here.'

'Don't be mean. I'm sure we were like this once.'

But even as I said it, I wasn't sure that Dominic and I ever had been. Our early days had been above the table, all sparky repartee and spontaneous jokes, whereas Helen and Wynn were actually holding hands. Touching each other.

I reminded myself that at least the hands were where we could see them, unlike all of the double dates we'd suffered with Seamus and his ilk. Most of those might as well have been single dates for all the time Dominic and I spent twiddling our thumbs alone while Helen and the *chef du jour* 'went for a cigarette' outside. Helen didn't even smoke.

'Everything okay?' Wynn enquired. 'What have you put about the place so far? Because this bread's great. Very tasty.'

'I love the *fleur de sel* on the butter,' added Helen. 'And the imprint. I might nick that for ours.'

'I'm going to order some wine,' I said, making the executive decision that Dominic and I would get a cab home tonight. I loved Helen, but I'd need a drink to get through three courses of this.

I looked up to see where our waiter had got to, but he seemed to be heading our way already.

'Hi,' he said. 'Sorry to bother you, but do any of you own a black Smart car?'

'I should hope not,' snorted Dominic. 'Do we look like the kind of people who drive around in oversize trainers with a steering wheel?'

'Yes,' said Helen. 'It's mine.'

Dominic stared at her, ignored my kick under the table, and said, 'Oh, okay. That makes sense.'

'Is there a problem? Someone hasn't crashed into it, have they?' Helen groaned. 'I've only just got it back from the body shop. I'm not brilliant at parking,' she explained to Wynn, who just smiled.

Dominic spluttered on his wine. 'You can't park a Smart car? Doesn't parking a Smart car mean just stopping somewhere and turning the thing off?'

'Ha-ha,' I said as if he was joking, then narrowed my eyes quickly. *Not tonight.*

The waiter pointed towards the door. 'Sorry, but you might want to get out there – it's being towed.'

'Where did you park it?' asked Wynn.

'Round the corner . . . by the skip?'

Dominic let out a groan, and I could sense his Parking Warden Fury monologue rising up in his head. It was one of his favourites and ended in a freestyle rant about parking fines being used to fund CCTV to generate more parking fines. I felt a flicker of irritation. I didn't want to hear it tonight.

I wanted this evening to be about Helen and Wynn, not Dominic.

'They're quite fierce round here,' explained the waiter. 'We had one customer throw himself on the bonnet of his car to stop them ticketing it, but the parking warden just ticketed the customer.'

'But we only arrived half an hour ago!' wailed Helen, scrabbling under the table for her bag. 'How can they have ticketed it and got it towed already?'

'Did you park it *in* the skip?' Dominic inquired.

'No need to panic, I'm sure we can sort it out.' Wynn pushed his chair back and pulled his cardi-jumper back on. 'Let's go and have a word with the tow company. Calm down, lovely. Nothing to get het up about.'

'Good luck with that,' Dominic honked, but Wynn just smiled pleasantly.

'I'm used to dealing with anxious individuals at work,' he said. 'You learn to calm people down when you're holding a drill.'

I watched in amazement as he escorted Helen out of the restaurant, his hand on the small of her back as she shoved her hands into her blonde hair and flapped her hands in panic. By the time Wynn was opening the door for her (he was opening the door for her!), the flapping had calmed down to a light flutter.

Dominic and I stared after them, but sadly the frosted glass in the door prevented any amusing visions of Smart cars being hoisted into the air.

'Well,' said Dominic, once the waiter had brought us another complimentary basket of tiny rolls. 'I think you've made a mistake.'

'Sorry?'

'You told me we were coming out for dinner with Helen and her new boyfriend, but we seem to have come out for dinner with Helen and her accountant.'

'No,' I said in equally pretend patient tones, 'Wynn's definitely her boyfriend.'

'No. Helen's boyfriend is a melodramatic speed-freak chef.'

'Dominic! Don't you listen to a thing I tell you? Helen *dumped* Seamus after that business at the awards ceremony. Wynn is—'

'No, no, no.' He held up a finger to stop me. 'No, no, no. Not just Seamus. *All* Helen's boyfriends are (a) melodramatic, (b) off their tiny chumps on something or other, and (c), because of the above, usually chefs.' He made a sweeping gesture towards the door. '*This* man is normal and quiet.'

'I know,' I said. 'And that's a good thing.'

He sat back in his chair, giving it his full '*pantomime despair*'. 'Well, I give it two weeks.'

'I don't,' I said stubbornly. 'Why do you have to be so negative? Helen says she didn't realize how exhausting it was to be with someone as high-maintenance as Seamus until she met Wynn. Wynn looks after her.'

'Yes, but the novelty of that'll wear off. Women like Helen thrive on drama.'

'Seriously, Dominic, stop being negative for the sake of it. No woman *likes* drama. They just put up with it. It's an annoying by-product of going out with certain kinds of men.' I evil-eyed Dominic him, and this time I wasn't pretending. *Women like Helen.* That sounded kind of . . . sexist to me.

'What are you saying?' he asked, playfully popping another roll into his mouth, and for a weird, wavering moment, it almost broke out of me: *Why can't you be more like Wynn?*

I stuffed it back in. I loved Dominic because he was spiky and acerbic and a writer. That's what I'd fallen for. You couldn't have all that *and* gentle hands on the small of your back.

Could you?

'Can you imagine what Seamus would be doing now if his car got towed?' Dominic asked with relish. 'If he'd managed to get his licence back, of course. Ha! That was quite a night. You have to hand it to Seamus, there was never a dull moment. Happy days.'

'No, Dom, not happy days. Stressful days.' I could feel something turning inside me. I wasn't enjoying the way Dominic was deliberately not listening to anything I was saying.

'Oh, come on,' he went on with a cackle. 'Who wants to tell their kids about the time Mummy's friend filed his VAT return on time? Eh? Like that friend of my mother's who tells us about the drunk vicar at her daughter's wedding every single time we see her. That's not an anecdote! That's a *non*ecdote.'

I stared at the door, straining my neck to catch a glimpse of what was going on. 'There's a happy medium, Dom. Helen works long hours; she needs someone to cosset her, appreciate her—'

'She'll get bored with nice,' insisted Dominic. 'Girls always say they want back rubs, but that's what sports masseurs are for.'

'No, they don't,' I said, staring straight at him. 'Sometimes they like men who bring them flowers and tell them they love them.'

He stared back at me. 'Is that what you want?'

I felt as if I were falling down a deep well. Down and down and down. Of course it was. 'Do I even have to answer that?'

He didn't have time to respond because Helen and Wynn were weaving their way through the tables. Wynn looked relaxed; Helen seemed bewildered, but in a good way.

'So?' Dominic slapped the table. 'What happened? Where are they taking your tiny little car? Did they just pop it into the boot of their own?'

'They're not taking it anywhere,' Helen marvelled. 'Wynn talked them out of it.'

'What?' said Dominic and I at the same time. Dom sounded more disappointed than I did.

Helen shook her head, amazed. 'They're . . . they're not even going to fine me. Apparently the notice wasn't hanging in the right space, so it's not a valid ticket . . .'

'Very basic error,' said Wynn, settling back into his seat and ruffling his hair modestly. 'Quite a reasonable chap in the end. Anyway, now we've got that out of the way . . . Have you two had a look at the specials? Can you guide me? I can't say I've ever eaten . . .' He checked the back of the menu. 'Um, French-Scottish fusion. But first time for everything, eh?'

He glanced up to see three pairs of eyes staring in astonishment at him.

Well, two pairs astonished; one pair adoring.

This weekend, I thought, staring with fresh determination at the list of crêpes stuffed with deep-fried things, *Dominic and I are going to find a flat we both want to buy, and he is going to make me an omelette. Or wire a plug, or something. Something that'll give me that baffled but proud glow that Helen's wearing right now.*

Then I looked over at Dominic, making Wynn laugh with some witty observations about the menu and knew for absolutely certain that whatever else he brought to our relationship, the omelette-making and plug-wiring were always going to fall to me. And so would the reminders about flowers and I-love-yous.

CHAPTER SIXTEEN

In the kitchen in Dominic's flat, above the toaster, was a *Star Wars* calendar, marked up with our personal and joint comings and goings: my weddings in red, Dominic's meals out in blue, hotel events in green, our personal joint commitments in black. There weren't many black dates. We never seemed to have time at the *same* time. In fact, it was only down to the benevolent secretarial help of Darth Vader that we each knew where the other was, half the time.

Tonight, though, even Darth had let us down, and I was annoyed, because it was one event that I really hadn't wanted to miss: Dominic's *London Reporter* Quiz Night.

I'd only remembered over breakfast, when I found Dominic revising last year's Michelin-star winners for the food round.

'I'm *really* sorry, Dom,' I said for the third time, checking my work bag and my emails at the same time. 'I'll try to get away by ten. Half past ten, possibly. The groom wants to get the bride out of there by nine thirty so they can catch their flight to Dubai.'

'Don't bother,' said Dominic. 'And I mean that in a very

non-passive-aggressive way. Seriously, there is *no need* to bother. It's fine.'

'But I *want* to bother,' I insisted. 'I want to be there for you. And I'm very good on the pop music round,' I added with a smile. 'I really want to meet your friends, too.'

We'd both been making more of an effort lately – and it wasn't just me. I'd been leaving work by six, and we'd actually been to look around a couple of flats, neither of which, sadly, met Dominic's very specific requirements. But it was a start, as I'd told everyone at work. In fact, if anyone had been working late, it had been Dominic. He'd booked a couple of review meals lately with colleagues from work – 'It's an easy way to pay back favours,' he'd explained. 'And you don't like Thai food.'

'No, no. It's *my* fault, I should have checked the calendar.' He buttered himself a third slice of toast and started digging around in the marmalade jar with his buttery knife. 'Don't know why I didn't write it down. Anyway, you'll see people at the Christmas party,' he went on. 'You'll see them all, since you're organizing the party. For which, many thanks.'

'No, many thanks to you. I'll be working,' I reminded him. 'Just because you're my boyfriend doesn't mean that I can skive off to sip champagne and mingle with the stars. Anyway, I want that evening to be the best ever. I want all the star columnists talking about what an amazing night they had.' I grabbed a piece of toast for myself. 'And I want you to be proud of me,' I added.

Dominic looked up.

I wasn't sure why I'd said that. Maybe it was my nerves over today's wedding. Maybe I'd just got used to seeing the way Wynn looked at Helen, and wished Dominic would do the same.

'I'm always proud of you.' He gave me an uncertain smile. 'Are you feeling okay? You were doing your sleep muttering again.'

'I'm just . . . a bit tense. This wedding's been a bit on and off, Helen's still in her Welsh love trance, and I can't rely on Joe not to have one of his attacks of honesty. And Laurence is on some new liver diet.' I stuck my hands in my hair. 'And I said we'd get back to that estate agent about the flat in Paddington, which is bad because I should be prioritizing *us*—'

'Rosie, I keep saying – it's fine. I don't mind about tonight. You just go and make that wedding amazing for . . . whoever it is.'

'Natalie and Peter,' I said automatically. Teacher and stock-broker, afternoon tea wedding, buffet reception, swing band. Don't let the bride's mother near the punch.

'For Natalie and Peter,' Dominic repeated. 'You are a miracle worker. I appreciate that. Now, aren't you going to be late?'

'No, I'm – oh, nuts.' I glanced at the kitchen clock. It was already ten past eight, and the florists needed to start dressing the reception room at half past. I shouldered my bag. 'I'll see you later, then?'

'You just concentrate on making their day,' said Dominic, and stuck the now-crumby knife back into the marmalade.

I knew something was up when the first person I saw in recep-tion was Laurence. He had a jacket and scarf on, but something about them wasn't convincing. They weren't his usual floppy scarf and fedora – he looked like someone pretending to be about to go out with the first things that came to hand.

'Rosie! I'm so pleased to see you,' he said, with so much emphasis tiny bits of spittle flew out. 'There's been a surprise development.'

'Really?' I said, heading towards my office. I didn't need a surprise development, not today, not even for Laurence.

He followed me, keeping one eye on the foyer, as if he wanted to stay within sight of the big revolving door. 'It's Ellie. She's had to go to Dublin on some urgent business, and she's, um . . .'

We were halfway down the corridor, but I clearly heard a distant thud come from my office, followed by a high-pitched howl, followed by another thud, and then the screech of a personal attack alarm.

I stopped and spun on my kitten heel. 'Laurence,' I said, 'you're not going to tell me that she's left Otto and Ripley here again, are you?'

He winced. 'There was a crisis this morning, apparently . . .'

Another crash and some giggling. My heart sank. It was the kind of giggling that said 'cake for breakfast'.

'You're not going to tell me that they're in my office . . . and you're about to go out?'

'Gemma's with them,' he added. 'And she's told them not to touch anything.'

'But Natalie's wedding flowers are in there!' I yelped. 'And all her favours!'

'Gemma said she needed to get going with something, and

I have to get weighed,' he said apologetically, inching back towards the foyer. 'If I don't get weighed before lunch, Dr Harris can't tell if the serum's working.'

It wasn't even half past eight. I blocked his way. 'They're your children,' I protested. There had to be health and safety regulations about this. 'Ellie specified that only you should take care of them.'

'Don't I know it? That woman can be surprisingly vindictive.'

I went to run a hand through my hair and stopped myself; already my fringe was standing up. 'Laurence, I can't look after them. I've got a wedding today, and there's loads still to do. And I need Gemma, before you ask. Ah!'

It dawned on me with all the comforting shoulder-squeeze of a truly perfect idea.

'Joe!' I nearly punched the air. 'He's their half-brother. He can babysit.'

'What?'

'Joe. Has he met them?'

'Um, I think he was at their christening – it's a bit of a blur . . .'

'Good. He can get to know them now. Where is he?'

'I haven't seen him this morning,' said Laurence, just as a messy-haired Joe came yawning round the corner from the direction of the restaurant, half a croissant in one hand and his phone in the other.

I ignored my irritation that he clearly hadn't got my email about being ready for an early start, supervizing the final arrangements for the 2 p.m. ceremony, and fixed my brightest smile.

'Good morning,' said Joe, then saw my smile. 'Oh, God. What have I done?'

'Laurence has a job for you,' I said. 'And if you get stuck for ideas, Sam, our concierge, can get you tickets for *The Lion King*. Now, if you'll excuse me, I need to go and have a word with the kitchens about the buffet.'

And I went off to find Helen.

The rest of the morning passed in a hustle: checking the hairdresser and make-up artist into the bridal suite; making sure the chief bridesmaid, Lucy, didn't hog said hairdresser and make-up artist; checking the rooms; liaising with the registrars; and all the other million and one tiny details I worried about so the bride didn't have to.

My bad feeling was about the best man, Steven.

I'd been outside by the service entrance, making a discreet call to my friend in the lounge at Heathrow to see if we could swing an upgrade for the honeymooners, when I bumped into him, also on the phone. He was laughing in that smirky, lads-together way that set off my Best Man Alarm Bells.

'. . . seriously, you lot are going to piss yourselves when you see what I've got lined up for Pete's speech . . . Yeah . . . Yeah, I hope Nat's got a sense of humour . . .'

When he saw me, he hung up swiftly, and his guilty look only confirmed my suspicions. But even though I told Gemma and Helen to keep their eyes and ears open, we were so busy that none of us had time to hang around in the hope of overhearing something else.

'You could send Joe to get the goss from the ushers,' Helen suggested as we helped the temp staff finish off the airy ballroom, which had been given a warm autumnal glow with orange and cream roses, speckled ivy, and tiny pumpkins with tea lights ready to be lit when dusk fell.

'Joe's busy with his half siblings.' I straightened a heavy silver knife so it was perfectly parallel with the gold-rimmed plate. 'And will be until well after this wedding's over.'

'Are you sure you're not missing a trick there?' suggested Helen. 'He's your man for infiltrating lads. They'd tell him anything. Give him a call, send him undercover in the bar.'

'What? So he can upgrade the prank to a disaster? No way. While the wedding's happening, I prefer Joe where I can't see him,' I said. 'Babysitting.'

Helen looked me straight in the eye. Now Seamus, and the post-split gloom, was ancient history, she'd gone back to her usual precision operating. 'Aren't you just cutting off your nose to spite your face there? I'm telling you, ask Joe to find out what's happening, because you need to nix the surprise for the groom, whatever it is. I'll get one of the girls to babysit the kids while they're napping. This is something he's *good* at.'

'Fine,' I said. I hated it when Helen was right about Joe. 'But when this descends into a total farce, I will be blaming you.'

I didn't even have time to think about it, because at that point, Joe himself strolled in. On his own, not a blond-haired wrecking ball in sight.

'Chill,' he said, raising an annoying hand before I could speak. 'They're having a nap. I popped them in that big room, with the big bed . . . the honeymoon suite? Ripley's been eating the chocolates on the pillow.'

My mouth dropped open, and he laughed. 'You are too easy,' he said, doing unspeakable double finger-gun jabby-jabby movements. 'They're in Dad's flat. With Dad. They're all asleep.'

For someone who'd had London's demon children for several hours, I thought Joe looked surprisingly unruffled. I was even more amazed he'd wrangled Laurence back to look after them.

'Sounds like you've got the knack,' said Helen, impressed.

'They're no bother. Well, Ripley's going through a song and dance phase – she won't take her tap shoes off.'

'Tap shoes are an improvement,' I said. 'Last time they were here, Ripley refused to get off her tricycle. She rode it through the restaurant like the kid from *The Shining*, then rammed the kedgeree cart until they filled up her breakfast bucket. Otto didn't even ram the cart. He just stood in front of it, freaking out the server.'

Joe laughed. I wasn't joking.

'Listen, Rosie needs a favour,' said Helen, glancing at me.

I glared at her, then said, 'Um, I think something's going to happen with the best man. I need you to keep an eye on him.'

Joe folded his arms and looked 'patient'. It was an improvement on 'confused' but only just. 'Do you actually know that?' he asked. 'Or is this just you extending the iron fist of bridal control again?'

'No, she knows. Rosie's like one of those dogs who can tell when a tornado's coming,' Helen explained. 'Or one of those horses who can predict earthquakes.'

'Nice image. Does she tap out warnings with her hooves? One tap for, "He's lost the rings"? Two taps for, "He's shagging the bridesmaid"?'

'Can we be serious for a moment?' I demanded. 'I overheard the best man talking to someone on his mobile, and he's definitely planning a surprise at the speeches. And Natalie *really* doesn't like surprises. She bought her own engagement ring, and made me brief Peter about what to say in his speech.'

'We're run off our feet here,' said Helen, 'so we need you to keep an eye on him.'

Joe looked more interested. 'What? Like, track him? Or do you want me to try to talk him out of whatever he's doing?' His expression turned questioning – the annoying kind of questioning. 'Maybe it's just banter, though? Should we really be interrupting the last man-to-man moments for the groom and his mate? What if there's something Peter needs to know?'

'No!' I surprised myself with how forcefully it came out.

Helen and Joe both looked shocked.

'No,' I repeated, nettled by Joe's lack of concern for the rest of the wedding party. 'That's what the stag night's for. This is Natalie's day, and she's really not going to appreciate some embarrassing slideshow of . . . of the groom's bits, or whatever he's got lined up. Never underestimate what a sense-of-humour failure some people can have at weddings. Oh, God.' I clutched my head. 'I *knew* I should have checked Steven's speech . . .'

'Nothing's perfect, Rosie,' said Joe, with a rather patronizing head tilt.

'My weddings are as close to perfect as the Met Office will allow,' I said through gritted teeth.

'No one remembers perfect,' said Joe. 'But they do remember fun. And little things that go wrong. It makes it personal,'

I gave Helen a look which I hoped said, *Thanks, Helen. Great idea.*

'Just keep an eye on this guy.' Helen remained unruffled by the potential additional chaos now being unleashed. 'Find out what he's planning if you can. Offer to help. And then nip it in the bud.'

'Quietly,' I added. 'And tell me what's going on. And don't let Natalie know.'

He grinned. 'I appreciate your trust, ladies. Leave it with me.' Then Joe managed to pull out an irritating gesture beyond anything he'd done so far: he did a mock salute, spun on his heel, and left.

I turned to Helen and opened my mouth. No words would come out.

'Don't start,' she said, and pointed at the napkins. 'Get folding.'

I watched all the ushers – and Joe – like a hawk for the next couple of hours. Joe kept making *it's all fine!* secret gestures to me, which worried me more than the skulking best man, to be honest, but there was nothing I could do; and by two o'clock, to my relief, the wedding of Natalie Thompson and Peter Lloyd was finally under way in the courtyard.

The hotel looked breathtakingly romantic in the soft autumn

sunshine, I thought, as I made some final glass checks on the champagne reception in the foyer. A few bronze leaves were circling lazily down from the tall trees and the long windows reflected the fluffy clouds drifting across the blue sky. I just couldn't quite shake the horrible feeling that I'd given Joe permission to destroy an entire reception.

The unnatural smooth atmosphere went on until twenty past two, when the drama arrived, in the form of Gemma, the eagerest bearer of bad news in the business.

'Rosie! Rosie! I've been looking for you for ages!' Gemma darted around the corner so fast she nearly skidded into a tower of white roses. 'Oh, my God,' she said, making her hands into claws of panic. 'I heard something. That best man. Steven?'

My heart flipped. 'What? What did you hear? When?'

'He was on the phone, outside. I don't know who he was talking to, but he told them what time the reception started, and when his speech would be, and said something like . . . "burst in and wave it around".'

'Wave what around?' I stared at her. 'A gun? A marriage licence? What else would you wave around? No, actually, don't answer that.'

There was a ripple of applause from the courtyard, indicating that Natalie was now the newest Mrs Lloyd, and that the guests were raring to get started on the champagne reception in the foyer.

'Oh, no, they're coming!' Gemma looked aghast. The string quartet started up in the little alcove between the courtyard and the foyer where the waiters were standing with their silver trays of flutes. 'It Had To Be You' floated down the corridor.

'Where's Helen?'

'Kitchens.'

'Joe?'

'I don't know.'

Great. Great.

'Tell Tam to keep an eye on the doors,' I said. 'And then find Joe and tell him to stick to the best man like glue.'

'Okay,' said Gemma.

'If worse comes to worst,' I said, 'I'll just deploy Laurence's FCT again.'

'FCT?'

'Free champagne tactic. Father of the bride, speeches, got a bit personal about the mother of the bride, nasty divorce,' I explained rapidly, my attention now on the first guests streaming into the foyer in search of canapés. 'Couldn't stop him, so Laurence sent waiters in with free champagne for a toast – everyone stopped listening, he lost his thread, I got the best man to do an impromptu toast, all sorted.'

'Rosie, you are amazing,' said Gemma admiringly.

'I do my best,' I said, my eyes scanning the horizon for mis-behaving best men.

Natalie and Peter had now sailed into the foyer, bathed in the light falling from the cupola above them. Natalie looked radiant. Peter looked stunned but happy. Steven, the best man, looked smug, in that rugby-club prankster way that made me even more determined to nip his antics in the bud.

There was no sign of Joe. I'd just have to deal with this myself, as usual. I couldn't help feeling . . . a little disappointed?

I adjusted the hidden headset in my fascinator, and clicked it on. 'Okay, Gemma,' I said. 'Let's do this.'

In the main reception room, all two hundred guests were taking their seats, a genteel selection of elderly relatives, respectable university friends and other teachers, none of whom were talking above a polite murmur as the musicians carried on playing in the foyer and the chink of glass and cutlery began as the meal was served.

Somehow the calm only made me more nervous. That and the fact that Joe was evading Gemma's best efforts to track him down, and wasn't answering his phone.

The meal went off without a hitch, and by quarter past four, right on schedule, I gave the prearranged sign to Graeme, the father of the bride, that his moment had come. (The prearranged sign was a small tot of brandy, served discreetly by one of the waitresses.)

I watched as he stared at the glass for three seconds, then knocked the shot back and stood up, and I turned on the hidden microphone in his table display.

'Ladies and gentlemen, friends and family . . .' he began, and the speeches were under way.

I pressed my headset. 'Anything?' I whispered to Gemma, who was outside doing a final check on the loos to make sure no guests were missing the speeches.

'Nothing.'

The best man, Steven, caught me looking at him, and smirked.

'. . . *Burst in and wave it around* . . .' rang in my head.

Since there was nothing I could do, I forced myself to think damage limitation. Maybe Joe was right, I thought. Maybe I *was* being a bit controlling? How bad could it be? Probably just some photo of Peter in a dress at another stag do. All rugby players had at least three of those. And they were family here. They'd just laugh.

My eye fell on the guests nearest the top table. A whole table of white-haired aunts and uncles of the bride, smiling benignly up at Graeme. Two were wearing clerical collars. One looked like he might be a High Court judge.

On the other hand . . .

I swallowed.

Natalie's dad's speech was sweet and heartfelt, about what a gift Natalie had always been to him and Kathryn, his lovely wife of thirty-four years ('as of this weekend!'). Then Peter got up, to some more raucous applause. The champagne was taking hold. He kicked off with the usual, 'My wife and I . . .' line, and this time the cheering was a bit beerier.

My headset crackled. 'Red alert,' said Gemma's voice. 'I've just spoken to one of the chambermaids, and she says she thinks there might be someone in the honeymoon suite?'

I froze, torn between dashing up to sort it out, and staying put to make sure nothing happened.

It'd take me two minutes to get upstairs, if I took my shoes off and ran. Two minutes to get back. A minute to deal if there was nothing, ten if there was a problem.

Over at the top table, Steven the best man gave me a knowing eyebrow raise. One that said, *I know something you don't, love.*

'Go and check, and report back,' I said into my headset. 'I'm staying here with the best man.'

'Roger that,' said Gemma, and crackled off.

She didn't buzz me again. Peter finished his speech to generous applause, and then the best man got to his feet. My stomach muscles tightened. I could tell from the way he kept glancing at me, at the door, at the groom, then back at the door, that something was definitely up.

'When Pete asked me to be his best man, I was honoured,' Steven began, with a leer at the bride. 'I asked him why he'd chosen me for this esteemed position, and he said, "Steven, you're the man I want by my side on the most important day of my life. And also because you know a lot of good lawyers to deal with the aftermath of the stag. Wa-hey."'

'Heeeeuuuurrrrrgggggghhh!' roared the assembled members of Steven and Peter's rugby club.

The two vicars and the High Court judge nearest the top table stiffened in their seats.

Natalie's smile turned rigid, and a red flush appeared across her cheekbones.

'Now, when I say that Peter and his stags had a good time in Prague, I mean we all had a bloody good time. Mentioning no names! But when I say we *had* a good time, maybe I should be a little more specific. I mean, you're safe now, Pete, she's said yes!'

Natalie glanced over at me anxiously. I smiled back, but

kicked myself for not 'dropping in' on the groom's breakfast to head this off at the pass.

I pressed my headset. 'Anything?' I whispered. 'Gemma?'

There was no reply. 'Gemma? Where's Joe?'

The words froze on my lips. I saw her before anyone else did, through the long glass double doors, approaching from the foyer like a tidal wave of inappropriateness.

A woman – or at least, I thought so; she could have been a slightly underambitious transvestite – in a leather miniskirt and bustier top, and the sort of waist-length blond extensions designed for twirling around at the same time as the wearer's nipple tassels. She had a determined expression on her face, but that might have been on account of our slippery carpet and the very high Perspex shoes she was wearing.

I held my breath, paralyzed with indecision. If I made a move, it would attract attention; if I didn't . . .

I could *not* let this happen. But what to do? Head her off? Stop Steven? A few people near the door had also noticed her now, and a general ripple was spreading among the tables, like a sort of communal embarrassment at where this speech could be headed. They had no idea how much worse the destination could yet be.

My head flicked back and forth between the advancing stripper and Steven's red face, like a tomato above his tight morning dress. I didn't know what to do. The powerlessness gripped me.

What was it she was carrying? She was clutching something in her hand.

Something white and plastic.

Small, white, and plastic.

Was that a . . . pregnancy test?

No. I'd heard of some bad-taste best men's speeches before, but this was by far the worst.

Then, just as I thought I'd have to scream myself and pretend I'd had a vision of the Virgin Mary in the wedding cake, the stripper suddenly looked shocked and disappeared from view through the glass in the doors, sideways, like a tree being felled.

'. . . Peter was, of course, a complete gentleman and insisted on offering Svetlana his jacket to cover her . . . embarrassment, shall we say.'

'Wooooooaaaarrrrrggggh!' went the ushers, looking door-wards in anticipation of the big surprise.

I can't describe to you the relief that was rushing through my veins when the doors remained firmly closed. It was divine intervention. Thank God for slippery carpets, I thought, grate-fully, and edged towards the door to get rid of the problem before it started howling in agony.

Steven glanced at the door. I made a decision and turned off the microphone on the table. His loud voice carried on for a few words before he frowned, confused; and then, all at once, what sounded like machine-gun fire filled the air, and the doors burst open.

Oh, God, what fresh hell was this?

I should have guessed. It was Ripley. Ripley in her tap shoes, tapping out whatever the Morse code for *save me from this colossal cock-up* was, on the original parquet floor of the restaurant.

Everyone's heads spun.

'Happy feet!' yelled a shrill voice. 'I've got those happy feet!'
Tap tap tap tap tappitty-tappitty-TAP.

The blood that had drained from my head now returned with
a vengeance as Ripley, her blonde curls bobbing, jazz-handed
her way right up to the top table. From the outside, she looked
angelic – white frock, pink cheeks, blue eyes. Inside, I knew
from experience, she was more Tinie Tempah than Shirley
Temple.

But on the positive side, I thought, everyone had forgotten
about Steven's X-rated best-man speech. The two vicars were
actively cooing.

The doors burst open again, and Joe rushed in. He'd changed
into a suit, I noticed, and his hair was ruffled in the style so
beloved of male models posing with children.

'There you are, you naughty . . . oh no! It's a wedding!' He
looked round with charming, Hugh Grant-ish mortification.

Ripley, annoyed that the limelight had shifted, did a burst of
manic tapping that caused two guests to clutch at their hearing
aids, and finished with a ta-da move. I noticed that she was
carrying one of the pretty orange nosegays from the row-ends
of the seating outside.

'I'm so sorry,' Joe explained. 'Ripley saw the bride, and
thought she was so beautiful that she just had to come and
give her some flowers. You naughty girl,' he added. 'Interrupting
is extremely bad manners.'

'Aww,' chorused about a third of the female guests in unison.
Although I think they were actually fawning over Joe, not Ripley.

Out of the corner of my eye, I saw Tam's broad shoulders appear behind the glass door, stoop down, then reappear with a white sheet-covered lump over his shoulder. A pair of Perspex platforms dangled from under the sheet. I would never ever question Laurence's habit of recruiting security staff from the Special Services again.

Steven watched in horror as his surprise vanished over Tam's shoulder, and his thread of his speech evaporated, all at the same time. While all attention was on Ripley and Joe, I caught Steven's eye and did that two-finger-prong, *my eyes, your eyes* gesture. Something else that Tam had taught me. He shrank back.

'I'm so sorry we interrupted your speeches,' said Joe, turning so Ripley could hand over the makeshift bouquet and tap her way out. 'Can we send in some champagne as an apology?' He signalled to the waiters, who immediately began refilling glasses.

At that moment, I could have hugged him. Actually hugged him and his ridiculous, overly dramatic, irresponsible gestures.

'To the bridesmaids,' I said loudly, and everyone automatically stood up and raised their glasses.

'To the bridesmaids!'

Steven looked confused, and the two bridesmaids looked slightly peeved that they hadn't got their full compliments, but I motioned for the waiting staff to come out again with more champagne and fresh glasses, as well as coffee and tea, and in all the confusion, no one seemed to have noticed that the wedding had fast-forwarded by twenty minutes. Or at least, if they did, they were all too polite and relieved to comment.

Joe and Ripley were detained by the table of elderly relatives, all of whom wanted to chat to the angelic blonde child and her delightful male nanny, but after about five minutes of freestyle charm, Joe swung Ripley up onto his shoulders, to keep her happy feet off the floor and our eardrums intact.

As he turned to leave, he gave me a quick wink and mouthed, *okay?*

I was abruptly struck by how different he seemed. Not the scruffy, over-earnest beach bum Joe I was used to; he looked like a confident, tanned adult. A dad, even. For the first time I understood why Helen gave him that dopey smile whenever he walked in. And Gemma. And Delphine, come to think of it.

He scrubbed up surprisingly well. And that had been quick thinking. A bit crazy, but ... it had worked. A faint glow of something warmed me. Gratitude. And a bit of admiration. Joe had just saved me from a really, really embarrassing wedding moment.

I smiled back, and nodded. *Thanks,* I mouthed, and I really meant it.

Joe winked again, Ripley stuck her tongue out at me, and they left me to finish off Natalie and Peter Lloyd's reception – and to check that Steven hadn't done anything to the going-away car.

(He had. But I managed to get Sam the concierge to wash it off in time.)

CHAPTER SEVENTEEN

Christmas officially started at the Bonneville when the ten-foot fir tree arrived in the foyer on December 1, followed almost immediately by Laurence's annual warnings about the dangers of pine allergies and needle drop.

Traditionally, all the staff decorated the tree overnight; the branches were hung with the hotel's original silver-glass baubles and gold stars, and smoked salmon sandwiches and champagne were brought out at 2 a.m., with an official 'switch on' performed by Laurence as soon as we'd got all the lights working. But this year Christmas had been at the forefront of my mind since the summer, mainly because I was in sole charge of organizing the biggest corporate event I'd booked so far – Dominic's paper's Christmas party. More to the point, if this went well, it was almost bound to lead to a lot more work for me, since the paper ran two awards of its own, and the guests for the Christmas party included loads of corporate sponsors, all of whom regularly needed venues for parties, conferences, and sundry other entertaining requirements.

This year's theme of the *London Reporter*'s Christmas bash was heroes and villains, a choice that Dominic informed me had been made in order to allow the editor, Sally Jackson, to fulfil her childhood fantasy of dressing up as Wonder Woman and strutting about in a cape.

'She's been sending out bloody dress-code memos since October,' he told me over one of our quick shared breakfasts. 'Dictators and religious figures are banned, as are any costumes that might constitute sexual harassment or health and safety infringements. And that's just the first page of the party rules.'

'Look, she can do what she likes.' I sipped my coffee; I was skipping toast – I had a breakfast cupcake-tasting at half past eight. 'I'm excited to be organizing an event with a decent budget, a buffet, and no one ending up in tears because someone's wearing the same dress as them.'

'You say that now,' said Dominic darkly. 'There are going to be awards. If I don't get best costume, I'll make sure someone's crying.'

Like most of the smart-arses on the editorial team, Dominic had chosen the ironic option for his costume, and was going as Man Who Invented the Chorleywood Bread Process, i.e., the system that had mechanized mass-production of bread, which Dominic held personally responsible for 'all those boring bastards who claim to be gluten-intolerant and bore on about bloating until you want to punch the trapped gas out of them.'

'Is it a costume, though? I still think you should go as Blackbeard or something more in the spirit of things,' I said. Armed with the paper's generous budget, I'd already spent hours sourcing actual Hollywood props for the ballroom. I'd got hold of spiderwebs, dry ice machines, a TARDIS . . . Most of it was locked in Laurence's flat to stop any of the staff finding it and staging their own superhero battle scene.

'First rule of fancy dress: always wear black tie and add one witty extra,' he reminded me. 'In this case, a butter knife in my top pocket and some Rennie's antacid tablets.'

'But your beard's such a great starting point. Rasputin? Bluebeard? I mean,' I added selfishly, thinking I might be able to fulfil a private fantasy here, 'you'd look great in a pirate costume . . .'

'Rosie, you've got to remember there'll be *photographers* there.' Dominic helped himself to more toast, and the last of the butter. 'The last thing you want is some photo of you doing the rounds dressed as Robert Mugabe. Those are the ones that always resurface just when you don't want them to. Ask Prince Harry.'

'I very much hope there *will* be photographers,' I said. That was why I'd secretly splurged my emergency money on a flattering new dress for myself, and intended to make sure the photographers snapped evidence of me in it.

For once, I wasn't going to fade into the background: I wanted everyone to see me there. First, as the super-professional event organizer in control of every detail. This was a brilliant chance for me to step out of the shadows and really be noticed – by Laurence, as much as the clients.

But I also wanted to meet people as Dominic's other half. We'd been living together for two years, I'd been in his column for just as long, yet I'd barely met any of his colleagues, thanks to our work schedules. If I wanted to make a name for myself as an entertainment consultant, I had to be out there during an event like this, meeting people, drumming up business for the new year, networking in a good way. And one thing you could guarantee about Dominic was that wherever the epicentre of the party was, he'd be in it.

In that sense, I thought, as I put another couple of slices of bread into the toaster for Dominic and gathered my own things together, this party was ticking quite a few of my to-do list boxes at once. And the best bit of all was that if I organized it properly, I'd be at work *and* spending time with Dominic. I'd doubled the temp staff to make sure of that.

'Are you looking forward to it, darling?' I asked him, as the toast popped up and I put it on his plate.

'Absolutely.' Dominic frowned at the empty butter dish, and applied double Nutella instead. 'It'll be a night to remember.'

Up until the afternoon of the *Reporter* party, things were going so smoothly that I even had time to book myself in for an emergency blow-dry in the hotel spa. But then, at half past three, it started to unravel.

Joe and Gemma arrived in my office together, like two plucky marathon runners crossing the line holding hands so neither of them had to finish last.

'Don't go mad,' Gemma began, 'but there's been a miscommunication.'

'It's *my* fault,' said Joe gallantly.

'No,' said Gemma. 'It's probably my fault.' But she spoiled the effect by rolling her eyes sideways to indicate that, yes, it was Joe's fault.

'Just tell me,' I said.

'The extra waiting staff you wanted for tonight's party? Um, the good news is they're booked,' said Gemma.

'And?' I glanced between the pair of them.

'Bad news is they're booked for tomorrow night,' said Joe. 'I've rung round to try to get some extra bodies, but it's Christmas. Everyone's working.'

I suppressed a screech of panic. 'But we're already short-staffed!'

'I know.' Gemma looked noble. 'So I've volunteered to come in. On overtime, obviously.'

'And I'll work too,' said Joe. 'Because I live upstairs and you'll only come and get me anyway.'

'Brilliant,' I said, doing frantic mental calculations. My visions of floating around making conversation slipped away; we now had six staff in total for the whole event – including me – to hand out canapés and drinks to a party of two hundred. Seven, if Dino had a quiet night in the bar and lent me his trainee bartender.

Joe flashed his best Boy Scout grin. 'It'll be fun! It's a party – they won't mind.'

'Want to bet? Never come between a journalist and the drinks,' I said through gritted teeth. I was definitely having that blow-dry now. My hair was going to need to be sprayed to within an inch of its life with Helen's magic hairspray if I was going to withstand a party shift and still give the impression I was an unruffled organizing supremo.

As Joe and Gemma went to leave, I suddenly realized what

Joe was wearing: in honour of the Christmas period, he had taken to sporting festive Hawaiian shirts whenever he could get away with it. Today's had skiing Santas on them. It was like something a Beach Boy might wear for a joke.

'Joe?' I said. 'You do have a dinner jacket you can wear tonight, don't you?'

'No, of course I – oh. Um, I think Dad's got one, I'll ask,' he said, seeing my expression. 'Don't worry, Rosie. It'll be fine. Just go with it. Cock-ups are life's way of making things interesting.'

'Do you have an infinite number of variations on that?' I asked.

'It's because it's true,' he said calmly. 'And one day you'll come to realize that.'

Fortunately, at that moment my phone rang again, so I didn't have to think of a polite reply.

As it turned out, apart from the staff crisis, and a minor Underground problem that made half the junior partygoers using public transport late, my meticulous advance planning meant the first hour of the party went off without a hitch.

The guests arrived – including Dominic, looking brooding and magnificent and very un-bread-scientist-like in his black tie – and Dino's bar team soon had the champagne cocktails flowing. I circulated with platters of tiny hamburgers and sausages and marvelled, not for the first time, how invisible a tray suddenly makes you at a party. Not one person made eye contact with me, so busy were they staring at the delicious nibbles and wondering what they should do with the cocktail sticks they were still holding from the teriyaki prawns.

Most of the guests didn't even stop talking as I passed, which was fine: my plan was to go back and re-meet everyone once I'd ditched the tray, reapplied my lipstick, and found Dominic to introduce me properly to his colleagues. Catching juicy snippets of gossip as I hovered within grazing distance put some faces to names that I knew well.

What was particularly gratifying, I thought, was how many of them seemed to be talking about Dominic. He was obviously a bit of a star in the office and, unusually, everyone seemed to read his columns.

'Have you read Dom's latest review?' said one rosy-cheeked bloke in a Superman cape over his navy suit to his companion as I hovered politely with my tray of honey-glazed cocktail sausages. 'Bloody funny.'

'Oh, totally bloody funny,' his Batman friend agreed, dunking a chipolata into the hot sauce. 'Have you read it, Angus?'

'Which one?' Angus was wearing a dinner jacket; I wasn't sure what he'd come as. James Bond, probably. There were a lot of James Bonds. There always were at fancy dress parties. 'The one about the oyster bar? Bloody funny.'

The oyster bar! I beamed to myself. That review featured my best Betty line yet – and Dominic had actually given me full credit for it, for once. I held my breath, hoping they'd repeat it.

'No, the one for that Swedish place in Pimlico. The one Dom said should be renamed Snores-ga-bored. Hilarious. Guy's a genius.'

They guffawed appreciatively. I made a note to tell Dominic, and started to move away to share the sausages with the next clutch of guests (two Catwomen and a Smurf), but Angus/James Bond put his meaty paw on my arm to stop me.

'Lurk here for a moment, would you, darling?' he mumbled through a mouthful of prime organic pork. 'Missed lunch. Need to line the stomach a bit.'

'No problem!' I chirruped, but I needn't have bothered; as far as they were concerned, I was just an extension of the tray. Which was how it was supposed to be, I reminded myself. Unobtrusive staff. Plus, they might carry on talking about Dom, and maybe one of them might mention the hilarious witticisms of Betty Confetti and how she should really have her own column.

'Was that Swedish place the one down by Ebury Street?' Superman asked, and Batman wrinkled his forehead to think.

I almost chimed in with the information that it was closer to Ecclestone Place, but stopped myself. I hadn't actually been to the restaurant in question, but I'd seen it on Dominic's fridge list and had hoped we'd try it together: I liked meatballs. He'd gone one night when I'd been working late on a rehearsal dinner. After Joe's intervention with Stephanie, I didn't dare leave the bride unattended at a rehearsal dinner.

Batman nodded. 'Yup. Good place for him to take Siri. She'd fit right in there.'

'What, Siri from media sales?'

'Oh, my God,' groaned Angus. 'Don't tell me Dominic's finally got his hands on Siri the Swedish stunner? The jammy bastard.'

'More than just his hands, from what I hear,' said Batman with a wink. 'And there's plenty to get hold of.'

I kept smiling because it didn't register at first, but then suddenly it did. A cold chill spread over my skin.

Siri? Who the hell is Siri?

'I don't know how Dom gets away with it,' Superman went on. 'Well, I do. He's so rude to them. They *love* it. And then there's the free meals. No wonder girls are queuing up.'

'You know what's really outrageously clever?' said Batman. 'The way he puts Betty in the column. Covers a multitude of sins, if you know what I mean.' And he winked again.

'I do know what you mean,' guffawed another.

'Ha-ha! Sorry, Angus, not following. What do you mean?'

'He means,' Superman explained patiently, 'that there are any number of Bettys. Mainly Siri at the moment but . . . well. Lots of meals, only one Dominic Crosby.'

The blood rushed up to my head, and I felt sick. I wanted them to stop talking, but at the same time, I couldn't stop myself listening.

'He's a naughty boy, is Dom,' said Batman, with that horrible blokeish approval. 'Hasn't he got a girlfriend?'

'I think so.' There was a comedy pause. 'Poor thing.'

And the men laughed. At me. Even though they had no idea I was standing there.

Suddenly I heard a strange, strangled noise and realized it had come from my own mouth. The men jumped, and Batman managed to knock the big tray out of my trembling hands, sending burgers, mini sausages and tomato ketchup up into a high arc. We all watched, frozen, as they rose and fell as if in slow motion, before falling in a shower of tiny buns, tiny burgers, and gobbets of sauce.

Superman looked so horrified at the waste of food that for a surreal second I thought he was going to try to catch some in his mouth like a dog.

'What the hell are you doing?' one of them yelped, swiping at his ketchupy cape. 'It's gone all over my cape!'

I wanted to speak but nothing was coming out of my mouth. All the voices seemed really far away.

Poor thing. Girls queuing up. Siri. Who was Siri? I'd never even heard of Siri. I swayed on my sensible heels.

'Sorry, guys,' said a voice behind me. 'She's new. Here, let me sort that out. Gemma? Can we get some napkins over here? We'll get your cape dry-cleaned, sir. No problem. Gemma, if you could just mop up, and I'll take, er . . . Poppy to the kitchens, get her a new tray. You silly girl,' he added to me. 'What were you thinking? Excuse me, sorry, can I just push through . . .'

Joe. I was so stunned that I didn't even care. I let him steer me away from the grumbling party guests, out of the ballroom towards the kitchen. It was much cooler outside the throng of the party but my ears were still ringing.

He shoved through the swinging doors to the clattering, white-tiled cacophony of the hotel kitchen, and gave me a little shake to wake me up.

'What happened?' He shook me again, gently. 'Are you all right? You look like you've had a stroke. Oh, God! Are you allergic to something? There were peanuts in that satay dip . . .'

Joe sounded so much like Laurence then that I nearly

laughed, in that detached way you do when you've had a total bolt from the blue and your brain is determined to think about anything at all other than the thing that caused the shock.

'Rosie? Speak to me.' The concern in his face snapped me back to reality.

'I'm fine,' I said. I couldn't tell anyone. Not till I knew if it was true or not. 'That guy just knocked my arm. I'll be right back out. Once I've cleaned up. I just . . . I just need to check something.'

I rushed to my office on legs that felt like someone else's. I had to think consciously about each step to stop myself running, and my knees wobbled with too much energy.

Siri . . . Doesn't he have a girlfriend . . .

I shut the door behind me, and jabbed at my computer, searching for Dominic's column, hunting through the results for the one about this Swedish place. Part of me was desperate to find they'd made a mistake, that it had been someone else's review. Dominic wasn't the only food writer on the paper.

But there it was. 'Dominic Crosby visits Stockholm on Ecclestone Place.' Eight days ago. He'd given it two stars out of five; mediocre was Dominic's worst insult, because it hadn't even been bad enough to inspire him to creative sarcasm.

My eye skittered over the text, searching for the word *Betty, Betty, Betty.*

Right there, in his column, for everyone in London to read.

'*. . . my dining companion, the lovely Betty, chose oysters with dill dressing, which I hoped boded well for our evening to come. Fortunately, they were as succulent as a fresh Swedish milkmaid . . .*'

I stared at the screen, my face burning, though inside I felt icy cold. I'd noticed now and again that another Betty cropped up at restaurants I hadn't been to, but I'd always assumed it was so Dominic could use up the jokes of mine that he hadn't had room for in other columns. I knew he'd been taking other colleagues out for meals, but it hadn't even dawned on me that there could be another Betty – off-page, as well as on it.

Succulent. Was that an in-joke? The way *pleasant* – my ultimate non-comment – was with us?

Something inside me curled up and died. Hot tears blurred my vision. How could I not have noticed? How?

I stood for a moment, willing time to stand still so I could work out what to do, but my brain wouldn't function. It felt as if it was covered in treacle.

The walkie-talkie in my pocket buzzed; it would be Gemma, wondering where I'd gone. The next lot of canapés needed to go out, then more drinks, then the speeches and the Big Surprise.

The Big Surprise. Sally the editor was – at her request – going to be flown onto the ballroom floor from a cunning place of concealment in the fake Gotham skyline to present the paper's awards. I'd had proper theatre flying-harness fitters setting it up in the ballroom all yesterday. It was going to make the best photo opportunity ever.

Suddenly, it really didn't matter. Nothing did.

My eye fell on my Bridelizer and its collage of happy couples. The stupid irony of it. The whole point of my insane work schedule had been to get my promotion so Dominic and I could start *our* happily ever after. I'd been working hard, sure, but it had been for *us*. Our flat. Our future.

I've got to find him, I thought, desperately wanting to have got it wrong. *I've got to give him the chance to tell me it's all just gossip. Journalists gossip all the time. It's what they do.*

I hurried out of the office, and back towards the sound of the party in the ballroom, sidestepping another couple of Supermen and a Barack Obama, and dodging round clumps of guests until I saw Dominic holding forth in a corner with two girls dressed as policewomen. Neither of them looked Swedish, but they were gazing up at Dominic with flirty Christmas-party eyes. An hour ago I'd have been pleased my man was so popular; now I just felt sick.

He smiled when he saw me and made a *more drinks!* gesture over their heads.

I marched over anyway.

'Hey there, waitress, we need some more champagne over here!' He winked, wickedly, and they giggled. 'Katie, Heather, this is Rosie, the organizer of this wonderful party.'

'And also his girlfriend, Betty,' I said, with a too-bright smile. 'In the column!'

Did they smirk? Every face seemed to be smirking at me. My hands clenched involuntarily into fists.

'Dominic, can I have a word?' I tried to keep my voice light.

'I thought you didn't like being introduced as my girlfriend,' he muttered as I pulled him to one side.

'No,' I said. 'You didn't like introducing me as your girlfriend.' And now I knew why. 'There's something I need to talk to you about.'

'What? Now?' He glanced around.

'Yes, now. It's – what?'

Gemma had popped up at my side. 'Where've you been?' she demanded. 'You need to tell Dino to bring up more champagne. We're running out. This lot are drinking like water's been rationed.'

'Can't Joe do it?'

She looked surprised. 'You're the one with the final say.'

'Well, I'm telling you to tell him to . . . to just do it. I'll be with you in a minute.'

'Rosie, it's okay, you go and—' Dominic started, but I pulled him back.

'This is important,' I insisted, but Gemma was still waiting. 'Not you, him! Champagne, go on!' I flapped her away.

Dominic drained his flute without a care in the world. 'Is it about that business earlier?'

My stomach lurched. 'What business?'

'One of your temps threw a tray of hamburgers over the managing director and the sports editor. Dashed off, didn't apologize. I thought you should know about her, so you can sack her, then give her a pat on the back from the rest of us.'

I stared at him, and suddenly a wave of recklessness crashed through the numbness. 'Who's Siri?'

Dominic's brown eyes moved from side to side. *Exactly the way the books claim cheating eyes move,* I thought, as my heart broke. 'What, on the iPhone?'

'No,' I said. 'Siri on the media sales team.'

'Oh, Siri.' His reaction said it all: too measured, too careful. 'That Siri. She's, um, just someone I know from work . . .'

'Hi, Rosie, sorry to interrupt, but can I have a word?'

'Oh, God, what now?' I groaned.

Joe was hovering awkwardly at Dominic's shoulder. 'Hi, er, Dominic.' He raised a hand in greeting, then turned to me. 'Rosie, Gemma says you've given her permission to get more champagne out of the cellar. Is that right? I don't want to get—'

'Yes!' I squeaked. 'Yes, it's fine. Just do it! Go!'

He looked at me, jiggling his eyebrows in that *Are you okay?* face semaphore. I semaphored *Please sod off right now* as politely as I could, then turned back to Dominic.

I gave up on subtlety. 'What's going on with you and Siri?'

'What?' Dominic tried to laugh.

'You took her for dinner at Stockholm.'

'She's Swedish!' he protested. 'I wanted to get her professional opinion on the meatballs! Why? Who's said something?'

It was bluster. I knew he was bluffing from the evasive look in his eyes. Anger and humiliation rushed through me.

'Stop trying to be funny,' I snapped. 'I'm not one of your readers. I'm your *girlfriend*. Supposedly.'

And then Dominic's shoulders dropped, and he shrugged as if resigning himself to saying something he didn't want to. 'Rosie,' he began, and I had to fight the temptation to put my hand over his mouth to stop him going any further.

Oh, my God, this is it, I thought, teetering on the brink of everything changing. *This is me, getting dumped, at someone else's Christmas party. By a man in ironic fancy-dress.*

'So I took another girl out for dinner.' He spread his hands as if it was too obvious to explain, and had to raise his voice above the sound of Madonna on the sound system. 'You're always working. I can't go to these places on my own, it looks far too obvious. Professionally, I mean. As a critic.'

My heart cracked inside my chest. The worst thing was, I knew he was right. I did work unsociable hours. But so did he. And he said he didn't mind.

'So you were just doing it for the sake of your career?' I said incredulously.

'Look, it's not like you and I were—' Dominic stopped.

He and I were what? Going to get married? Were serious? Were going anywhere?

'What about the flat?' We were planning on making an offer on a flat. We'd even been to John Lewis to look at curtains!

Dominic's eyes shifted again. 'It's a flat, isn't it? Somewhere to live. It's not . . . marriage.'

I felt as if he'd punched me. For me it had been *more* than that. I stared at him. No words would form in my brain.

'Hi, guys! Can I get a photo? Say cheese, Dom! Ha-ha-ha!'

I spun round. There, right at the worst possible time, was the photographer. The one I'd imagined would take glowing photos of me and Dominic hobnobbing with the paper's star columnists, propelling me and him into London's media galaxy, and ensuring my bookings diary would be full for next year.

Instead of which it was crumbling in front of me.

'Sod off,' growled Dominic. 'Before I make you eat that camera.'

'Yeah, they said you'd be grumpy, mate! Just one shot!' The

photographer took a quick snap – me looking stunned and red-eyed, Dominic snarling like an escaped armed robber, and, I later discovered when I saw it on the *Reporter*'s website, two random women, one staring gleefully at Dominic and the other gesturing towards me with her thumb as she filled her mate in on the goss.

It was Helen's idea, to be honest. A voice at the back of my head said it was very unprofessional, but it was drowned out by the other voices in my head, most of which were wailing incoherently.

'I can't believe it,' Helen kept saying as we stood at the back of the ballroom, watching Sally Jackson swoop down from the ceiling in her gold boots, to drunken whoops from the crowd. 'I can't believe he'd be such a *complete bastard*.'

I hadn't said anything for an hour now. I couldn't. I'd just smiled and cleared glasses and poured wine and generally gone on autopilot to such a scary extent that Joe and Gemma had summoned Helen from her night off at home to check that I hadn't overdosed on some sort of drug that made you very, very normal. I was scared that if I opened my mouth, I'd start crying or yelling – I genuinely didn't know which.

I hadn't even noticed the envelopes; it had been Helen and Gemma who'd found them when they'd sat me down in the office to make me explain what had happened. Joe had suggested it, as a joke. Unfortunately, none of us was really in a joking mood, and Helen had made an executive decision to go through with it.

'You can blame me, if you want,' she'd said. 'I only wish I could tell him in person.'

'. . . award for Superhero of the Year goes to Kelly Hutchinson in the accounts department, for getting everyone's bonus payments through on that Inland Revenue code before the loophole closed!'

Tumultuous applause.

Splitting up with Dominic wasn't just going to break my heart, I thought dully, it was going to wreck any chance I had of taking on the *Reporter*'s entertainment portfolio. We could have hosted the *Reporter*'s Heart of London Awards. That alone could have put the hotel – and me – on the map, and led to who knows what other opportunities?

But you can't forgive this, just for the sake of work, I told myself. *What would that make you?*

'Dominic never deserved you,' Helen went on. 'Everything you said to me about Seamus is true about Dom, too. You'll find someone way better than him.'

I closed my eyes and felt someone squeeze my shoulder sympathetically. I had a horrible feeling it was Joe. I didn't want Joe feeling sorry for me. Up on the stage, Sally was still going. 'And . . . the last award of the night! No, no, quiet, everyone. Shut up! I'm still doing the budget for next year, don't forget!'

Instant silence.

'For a middle-aged woman in blue Spanx, she's got great crowd control,' observed Gemma.

'You can come and stay with me,' Helen went on. 'I've got a sofa bed. Just till you get sorted out.'

My eyes snapped open. The flat! The lease ran out in a few weeks. Where was I going to live now? I felt sick.

'. . . this one's for Villain in Superhero Clothing! And the nominees are . . . Marc Lucas, for the Couch to 5K Sports Desk Challenge, Karen Moore for the cat-hair birthday cake that gave the production department food poisoning . . .'

The guests went 'OooOOoooOOOoohh!' and I envied their happiness.

'Actually, I'm not sure we should have done this,' I said, suddenly gripped by common sense. 'It's not going to look very professional.'

'Too late.' Helen crossed her arms. 'And he had it coming.'

I held my breath. This wasn't going to burn bridges with Dominic and his media connections. It was going to blow them up.

'. . . and the winner is . . . Dominic Crosby, for stealing all his best jokes from his girlfriend, and wearing the same underpants three days in a row when he can't be bothered to put a wash in, and not actually knowing the difference between merlot and malbec.'

The room went wild. I should have felt triumphant, but I didn't.

I was *definitely* single now. The most single wedding planner ever, at Christmas, at an office party, about to sleep on her best mate's uncomfortable futon because she couldn't face going back to a flat that had never really felt like hers. That had to be some kind of new tragedy record.

Somewhere, a country and western singer was writing a whole album about me.

CHAPTER EIGHTEEN

It took a depressingly short time to move out of Dominic's flat, just two days after the Worst Christmas Party of All Time. I packed up all my stuff in four hours, while he was 'out' for the evening reviewing some South African barbecue pit in Covent Garden, and that included picking my unwashed laundry out of the basket.

Helen was spurring me on by reminding me just how angry I should be with him for humiliating me like that. I was quite angry now, since the initial shock had worn off, although flashes of misery were also putting in appearances, just to keep me on my toes.

'Think of all the disgusting stuff Dom made you eat,' Helen kept urging me, as she yanked open cupboards and stuffed clothes into bin liners. 'You will *never* have to choke down another yak sweetbread and think of three amusing things to say about it.'

'I didn't mind sweetbread, it was the squid that used to make me gag.' I held up a photo of the two of us on holiday in Scotland, and my heart ached at how happy we looked. Dom hated having his photo taken; I only had four nice photos of us together, whereas Helen had been dating Wynn for a matter of weeks, and she was already the screensaver on his phone.

That should have told you something, said a sad voice in my head.

'He used you for your squid eating!' Helen cried. 'And for the fact that you'd stump up half the cash for a bigger flat, the slimy little git!'

Rage returned, with a vengeance.

'That's what it was for him,' I seethed. 'He just wanted a better bathroom.'

'He was lucky to have you,' Helen agreed. 'We all thought he was punching *way* above his weight from the start. I mean, that ridiculous beard, for Christ's sake. It was like something you'd grow for charity! He only did it to hide his double chin – you do realize that, don't you?'

I wobbled. 'I quite liked the beard,' I confessed. 'I thought it made him look—'

Helen leaped in to stop the misery taking hold. 'Like Captain Haddock? Like a mass murderer? As if he might be hiding food in it for later?'

'No!' I winced. 'Is that what you all thought? I mean, fine if you did, but if you could just keep it to yourself till I'm a bit less . . . a bit less *humiliated*?'

Helen looked apologetic. 'Sorry, Rosie. But honestly, just like you said to me, you're going to wake up one morning and realize that this is the best thing that could have happened to you.'

'It feels like someone's kicked me in the stomach.' I picked up a guide to northern France, for a champagne touring holiday we were going to go on but never managed to book time off to take.

'That's normal,' insisted Helen. 'But don't forget what a pig he is. Let the rage energy through. It's cleansing. I had to keep eye masks in the kitchen fridge for a month because every time I thought about not being with Seamus any more, I cried so much I got conjunctivitis. Whereas you need to be *angry*. Because you deserve more than he was ever going to give you.'

How could I have misread it so badly? I wondered. How had I managed to ignore the fact that Dominic was more excited about a new flat than he was about sharing it with me? Had I just seen the bits of our relationship that I'd wanted to? The thoughts were sharp, and I didn't want to examine them too closely.

'But now look!' Helen pressed on. 'No sooner do I get rid of all that toxic energy from my life than I meet a really lovely man who makes me happy! It's all for the best, Rosie. Honest. Relationships don't have to be one constant headache. Love should be fun. And, let's be honest, neither of us was having any fun in our relationships, were we? We were *miserable*.'

'Mmm.' I still wasn't convinced that Seamus and Dominic fell into the same category of boyfriend. They were like parking tickets and death by dangerous driving: technically both car offences, but on separate scales.

'Is this the toaster you bought that chubby bastard for Christmas last year?' She held up the lovely blue Dualit toaster. 'I think you should take it. It's nice.'

'Toast's the only thing Dominic eats at home,' I said miserably. That's why I'd given it to him. He'd given me a . . . I frowned. What *had* he given me, actually?

'Then he's going to have to learn to eat something else.' Helen dumped the Dualit into the box of my mugs, along with two phone chargers and my expensive iron, which Dominic had broken trying to iron bread when the toaster wasn't working. 'Wynn? Could you be a love and take this for me?'

'No problem.' Wynn had been waiting patiently by the door. Helen had volunteered his Volvo to do my emergency moving: it was a mobile version of Wynn himself – a big, sensible car with a boot in which I'd spotted some walking boots, a tennis racket and a tatty 2009 road map. A normal person's car, in other words. There was a pair of floral wellies in there too, which I assumed were new ones belonging to the previously outdoor-phobic Helen.

Wynn wasn't saying much, out of respect for my wet, red face, but every so often, out of the corner of my eye, I'd catch him and Helen giving each other private, adoring half-smiles when they thought I wasn't looking, and my heart crumpled up like a used napkin. Then I felt mad again, that I'd wasted two years of my life being strung along by someone who didn't even have the courtesy to use my real name in his column, when I could have been finding a nice man like Wynn.

This rage/misery combination was really, *really* exhausting.

We'd just crammed the last box into the Volvo when I spotted movement at the end of the street, where the iron railings turned the corner into Hebden Terrace.

I knew it was Dominic. I could tell from the glint of brass buttons on the coat that he thought made him look like a U-boat commander but that Helen told me everyone else thought made him look like a fiddle player in a third-rate folk band.

I felt a flash of anger. How long had he been lurking there, waiting for me to go, so he wouldn't have to face me? *Me*, the woman he'd shared his life and his flat and his column with for two whole years. Didn't he even care enough about me to say goodbye properly?

I stopped myself, as a voice in my head pointed out that he'd barely shared his flat. Or his life. Our stuff had been so easy to separate: his drawers, my drawers; his shelves, my shelves; virtually nothing bought together in two years, because neither of us was ever home. It was his flat; I'd been like a lodger with benefits. He'd been so slippery about us buying somewhere together – why hadn't I seen it?

Because I hadn't wanted to. I'd wanted the *idea* of me and Dominic so badly that I'd ignored every tiny clue that everyone else had seen. I felt hot with shame and rage, more with myself than him. And I'd thought *Helen* had been delusional. I'd been much worse.

'Rosie, are you ready?' Helen called from the car.

The brass buttons twinkled in the light as if the coat they were attached to was ducking farther into the shadows, rather than face me. What a coward.

I didn't want to talk to him. I didn't know what I wanted to say to him. Swedish Betty was welcome to him.

'Yes,' I said loudly, towards the darkness. 'I'm ready.'

And I chucked my house keys over the wall into the recycling bins.

In all the years I'd been attending the weekly staff meetings at the Bonneville, I'd never managed to say anything that had made every single person stop talking and stare at me, not even when I announced who I'd found in the circular bath in the penthouse, and with whom (plural – and, no, I really can't say, sorry).

This time, though, I managed to make the entire meeting fall silent with one simple sentence.

The combined amazement directed towards me could have powered the ballroom chandelier, with some left over to do the wall sconces, but I didn't care. I was all out of caring. Despite the festive spirit filling the hotel, from the enormous oversize holly wreaths on the outside to *Christmas with the Rat Pack* playing inside, I could only make myself care about anything in the ten-minute windows when the caffeine wore off at the same time that the chocolate rush dropped. I carried a thermal travel coffee mug and a Twix to make sure it didn't happen often.

Helen mouthed *Are you okay?* over the table at me, and I forced on a wonky smile, at which point Laurence looked startled. He put his glasses back on to look at me properly.

'Say that again?' Sam the concierge stuck his little finger in his ear and wiggled it. 'I think my hearing's going.'

'Quick! Quick! Write it down,' hissed Dino, gesticulating at Gemma, who was doing the minutes. 'Before she changes her mind!'

'I *said*, I don't mind being on the rota for Christmas Day and New Year's Eve,' I repeated. 'In fact, count me in for the whole week. I'll do it all.'

'But, Rosie!' Jean the housekeeper looked aghast. 'Your parents! Aren't they expecting you home for Christmas?' She leaned over the table, giving me the benefit of her full Northern motherliness. Most of it was resting on the plate of Danish pastries, which I was glad Delphine wasn't here to see. 'Won't your mam need some help with the lunch?'

'No,' I said truthfully. 'They're going on a cruise with my brother and his family. Round the Scandinavian isles. All you can eat. They always do. It's their annual challenge. My dad's been looking forward to it since Lent.'

Jean looked sad, which was rich, considering she usually volunteered to work New Year's to limit her time in Keighley to the bare minimum.

'What?' I protested. 'What is so weird about parents going away for Christmas? If everyone stayed at home, this hotel would make no money at all on Christmas dinner, and it's one of the busiest days of the year!'

'So, you're volunteering to work on Christmas Day, *as well as* doing the Farewell to the Year on New Year's Eve?' Laurence repeated. 'Because you know I've booked Christmas Day off. We're having Ripley and Otto for Christmas lunch here. Ellie's joining us.'

He beamed around the table, but I saw Helen, Tam, Sam, Jean, and Dino all flinch in their seats at the same time. For individual reasons, relating to silver domes, the alarmed security doors behind the kitchens, tickets to *The Lion King*, the laundry chute, and maraschino cherries, respectively. Ripley and Otto's recent surprise visit had taken a while to get over. And, to be honest, Ellie's return wasn't exactly on a par with a royal visit. (Although ironically, in Ellie's head, it was much the same thing.)

'Yes,' I said. Then said, 'Yes,' again to Gemma, for the minutes.

'I can give Rosie a hand,' Joe piped up. 'I'll be here.'

'Not on Christmas Day,' Laurence reminded him. 'You'll be enjoying some quality time with your brother and sister.'

Joe didn't blanch at that, which was manful of him, but just said, 'Of course,' then mouthed, *I'll help you* when Laurence went back to the agenda.

I smiled tightly. I didn't want Joe's help. I didn't want anyone's help. I wanted my to-do list to pile up into a blizzard of chores and deadlines and room-servicing, if it came to that, which would propel me into the New Year – and the New Me – with the minimum time allowed for thinking about anything related to food, food writers, or writers.

I know. In a hotel. It was like something the malignant wing of Satan's Hell Committee would have chortled themselves bright red over. And I'd come up with it all by myself.

Laurence asked me to pop into his office as soon as everyone barged their way out at the end of the meeting. Guests were very generous at this time of year, and no one wanted to be invisible when it came to appreciative gestures, even heads of department.

I hoped it wouldn't take long, whatever it was. I had a potential October bride coming in at eleven, and I wanted to get her in and out before lunch, while the sun was still shining crisply over the courtyard and the Palm Court hadn't filled up with wild-eyed Christmas shoppers streaming in from Piccadilly to take the weight off their aching feet.

'Ah, Rosie. Sit ye, sit ye,' he said, but less jovially than usual.

When I was settled in the chair opposite his, Laurence steepled his fingers (minor wince for arthritis) and adopted his concerned expression, not the anxious 'my computer seems to be frozen' one I'd been expecting.

I felt slightly nervous. We hadn't actually discussed the events of the *London Reporter* Christmas party, as they related to me personally. Dominic wasn't stupid enough to complain about the blatant envelope tampering, and the hacks had spent double what we'd expected on booze, but I knew it didn't reflect well on me in a managerial capacity that I'd let it happen. Laurence might be too gallant to mention it, but I was pretty sure he knew. And Caroline would definitely find out. She found out everything eventually.

'Rosie,' he said, like someone choking down their sprouts to get them out of the way first, 'this may be none of my business, but . . . things aren't going very well at the moment, are they?'

I blinked. How did he know that? I wondered if Joe had said something about his work experience with me. We'd been getting on a bit better lately, since he'd been moved on to catering and wasn't hanging around my office asking annoying questions about *why* brides had bridal favours/three types of attendants/

fruitcake; but thanks to Flora's constant demands, he still seemed to drop into my office most days with an irritating observation about my management style.

'Has Joe said something?' I asked carefully. 'Because Flora's very happy with—'

'What? No. No, I mean, things clearly aren't quite right with you. Volunteering to work over Christmas and New Year. Letting Sam get away with comments about the brides-maids. And you look as if you haven't slept in a week. I don't mean to be rude, but you're looking a little . . . well, not as coiffed as usual? Would you like me to book you in for a health check?'

I lifted my (stress-spotty) chin, and tried to tell myself that it was a compliment to my usual high standards of appearance.

'I'm fine,' I said. 'It's just that I'm staying at Helen's at the moment. She doesn't have a lot of room.'

'Why are you staying at Helen's?' Laurence looked shocked. 'Don't tell me your flat's having to be fumigated again. Dominic hasn't been hanging pheasants in the airing cupboard?'

I sighed. I'd forgotten about that. How we'd laughed (even-tually). 'No, it's not that.'

I had to tell Laurence. He – and the rest of London, probably – would find out soon enough when bloody Dominic announced in his column that Betty was dead, long live New Betty. Swedish Betty was probably packing her Scandi-culottes for a fabulous New Year eating venison and bonfire-roasted marshmallows with Dominic's friends. My old friends. Well, acquaintances.

'Dominic and I have split up,' I said, and the invisible fist punched me in the chest this time. 'Helen's letting me sleep on her sofa till I find somewhere else.'

'Oh, Rosie. I'm sorry to hear that. I really am.'

I didn't dare look up. Laurence's sympathetic face would finish me off. As it was I was biting my lower lip so hard it was starting to go numb.

I don't know what I was expecting him to say – some too-much-information comment about the time Ellie kicked him out of his own hotel, probably – but instead he said, 'Well, this is rather fortuitous because I was going to suggest it anyway, but if you're set on working over the Christmas period, then you really ought to move in here.'

'Into the hotel?' I looked up, surprised. 'But we're fully booked.'

'No, into the staff apartment. I'm going away for a few days . . .'

'Are you?'

'I'm *detoxing*,' he said piously. 'It's not huge, as you know, and Joe's back in his old room, but it's cosy enough, and you're very welcome.' Then he spoiled it by adding, 'Anyway, you'll be downstairs most of the time if you're duty manager.'

I was intrigued, quite apart from the generosity of the offer. I'd only been into the Bentley Douglas apartment a few times. It wasn't anything like the rest of the hotel. I remembered it as being like stepping back into 1964, all jazzy sunflower wallpaper and battered yellow Formica, since any spare money the family had went on the public areas, not their own living quarters. I'd always assumed Ellie had overhauled it, just like she'd attempted to turn the rest of the hotel neutral, and that now it would look as if someone had stapled four miles of beige linen to every flat surface.

Still, it was central, it was part of the hotel I'd never had a chance to explore, and I needed every penny I could lay my hands on, if I wanted to buy a flat of my own.

Flat. I'd be lucky. On my salary, even finding a tiny studio like Helen's within the M25 would be a miracle.

'Thank you,' I said. 'That's really kind.'

'Excellent.' Laurence rubbed his hands together. 'Bring your stuff round whenever you like. We have Wi-Fi –' he said it with air hooks, as if he didn't quite believe in it – 'but only a very basic package. Joe's on at me to upgrade it.'

I smiled, touched by his thoughtfulness. It *was* like a family here. Dominic had been wrong. I hesitated. 'Laurence, um, you won't tell anyone why I'm moving in, will you? I don't really want everyone to know just yet.'

I could deal with Laurence feeling a bit sorry for me. Sam, not so much. Or Dino. Or any of the other heads of department who might either gossip about me or try to get me to join their after-hours poker circle for terminally single hotel employees.

'Of course not,' he said. 'It's none of anyone's business but yours. As my divorce lawyer liked to tell me.'

I was nearly out of the door, my head held high, when Laurence added, 'But if you don't mind me saying, Rosie, I hope your next boyfriend appreciates you a little bit more than that pretentious berk,' and I had to walk out very quickly before he saw my wobbly lip.

If even Laurence thought Dominic had taken me for granted, things must have been very bad indeed.

When I let myself into the staff flat the following evening, with most of my life in three bags, Laurence was out having a Christmas drink with 'an old friend' I'd reintroduced him to at a wedding the previous weekend, after a discreet tip-off from Caroline. Joe, though, was at home to welcome me.

Or rather, he was sitting at the yellow Formica kitchen table, eating mince pies with a casual disregard for either calories or crumbs, and going through a list with a pen. I recognized Flora Thornbury's scrawling hand – the list was titled: *Bridesmaids, Long List*, and was divided into *Blondes, Brunettes, Redheads* and *Children*. A copy of *Tatler*'s eligibles list was open next to it, with many Post-it notes.

'Don't tell me Flora's choosing bridesmaids according to hair colour now?' I asked, before I could stop myself.

Joe spun round. 'Actually, she is. Part of the bridesmaid questionnaire she sent out was, "Would you object to having your hair dyed?"'

'No.' I put my handbag down on the table and looked closer. 'You're winding me up.'

'I'm not. I had to talk her out of making them give her their weights and measurements, too. So I *am* getting more tactful, see?' He grinned. 'Flora's almost as bad as you when it comes to detail. I can see *you* asking your bridesmaids to dye their hair to—'

He stopped, suddenly remembering why I was moving in.

Because I was at the exact furthest point from requiring bridesmaids.

'Tactful,' I said. 'But for the record, I will not require my imaginary bridesmaids to dye their hair. I will have their heads shaved so I will be the prettiest woman there. I believe that's the Bridezilla principle you're always going on about?'

'Hey, let me get your bags,' he said, getting up. 'Welcome to Casa Bentley Douglas. You can pick a room, there are two spare . . .'

I followed him out into the narrow hall/landing where, as I'd guessed, Ellie had made a stab at redecorating by painting the walls 'biscuit'. She hadn't been able to do anything about the loud carpet, which had a jolly 1960s swirling pattern, or the chunky furniture, which had been out of fashion for so long it was coming back in. After the clean lines and muted thirties colours of the main hotel, it felt like going through the wardrobe to Narnia.

'I thought you might prefer the spare room rather than Ripley and Otto's,' said Joe, swinging open the door to a cosy bedroom with a terracotta carpet, pale orange walls and curtains that looked as if they'd been made from the ties of Carnaby Street hipsters. 'You think this is bad, but Ripley's going through a pink phase. The other room's like sleeping inside Peppa Pig.'

'It's great.' I eyed the décor. Thankfully I'd be asleep most of the time. If I could sleep, with those curtains.

'Bathroom's down here, shower's a bit temperamental, been on at Dad to replace it for ages, but you know what he's like

– you might be better breaking into Room 219 which is the nearest . . .'

It only took a few minutes for Joe to show me round the flat; then we were back in the kitchen, where we stood about awkwardly, as it dawned on the pair of us that we were now flatmates and privy to each other's off-duty routines, such as they were.

'So,' said Joe. He glanced at his 'off-duty' sweatpants, and I realized his feet were bare. Tanned, still, with a small star tattooed on the bone by his big toe. It reminded me that I knew where his other tattoos were. The less accessible ones.

I swallowed, and scrabbled for a neutral subject.

'So, er,' I said, gesturing towards the table, 'what's the gossip with Flora's bridesmaids? Anyone famous?'

My involvement with Flora's wedding was now largely catering-based. Joe was the one dealing with the favours, the favoured personnel, Flora's expectation that Photoshop could be performed in real time on actual people, and so on.

'Oh, she's running auditions, essentially,' he said. 'Let me show you the long list . . .'

An hour flew past discussing Flora's wedding madness, and I was surprised by how confident Joe sounded about the plans. Maybe I'd been a bit harsh on his organizational skills. Anyone who could talk Flora out of releasing ten thousand butterflies at the moment of her marriage had to have hidden steel.

At eight, he asked me if I fancied anything to eat, and when I said yes, he called down to the kitchens and persuaded them to stick a pizza in the oven for us. Then he said, conversationally,

'Listen, I meant it about helping out over the holidays. I'll be here anyway.'

'Aren't you going skiing? Or snowboarding?' I couldn't stop glancing around the kitchen; one big window looked out over the hidden rooftops of Piccadilly, and underneath it along one wall there were appliances I hadn't seen since 1970s episodes of *Fawlty Towers*. Was that a Teasmade?

'No, I've either got to work here, or work at Wragley Hall with Mum. She says I have to work Christmas week, so I can hold my head up with the staff. If I stay in London, at least I can go out into town, whereas if I go to Wragley, there's no escape from Alec. He's a complete nightmare over Christmas. He still booby-traps the chimney in case Santa drops in. I'm not even joking.'

'I know you're not,' I said. 'I heard about the reindeer.'

'Anyway, London's pretty cool at Christmas,' he went on, stretching out his long legs under the table with a yawn. 'I've never been to that skating rink at Somerset House.'

'It gets pretty busy,' I said. 'But yeah, it's nice.'

I had a sudden flashback to last year: Dominic had reviewed the café next door. We hadn't actually skated – I didn't want to make a fool of myself; he didn't want to risk his writing hand – but it had been Christmassy. A London moment we'd shared.

I didn't want to think about Dominic and the life I'd just lost, but my caffeine levels were dropping along with my energy levels, and miserable thoughts were breaking through like splinters.

'Do you want to go?' Joe suggested with an encouraging

smile. 'We do get an afternoon off between now and New Year's, don't we? I'll take you – my treat.'

Would Dominic be going this year, with New Betty? I'd bought a special skating hat, a furry Russian one from Topshop. I'd wanted it to feel like New York. It *had* felt a bit like New York. (Disclaimer: I've never been to New York.) Dominic had grumbled about the lukewarm hot chocolate, but in a funny way . . .

'Rosie?' I felt Joe touch my arm, and when I looked up, he was gazing at me as if he was worried. His unexpectedly kind expression made me feel warm inside, then sad.

'Sorry?' I blinked my tears away, and smiled manically. Work. That solved most of my problems. Lots of work. 'So!' I pulled the list towards me. 'What has Flora got in mind for her hen night?'

'Uh-uh. I called down for supper. Work's finished for today.' Joe's blue eyes were still fixed on mine, concerned. 'Look, if you—'

'If we want her wedding to be a headline feature, I don't mind putting the hours in,' I carried on. Something had changed in the atmosphere between us. It was work, but it wasn't work. I felt as if he was seeing a different me now. If he asked me how I felt about Dominic now, I wasn't sure I'd be able to stop talking.

Joe gave me a funny look. 'Okay. But only till the pizza comes.'

And so the days leading up to Christmas slipped past in a blur of tinsel, carols, mistletoe, tipsy guests, champagne and 2 a.m. finishes, until I found myself – surreally – in the Bonneville's restaurant on Christmas Day, volunteering to help dish out sprouts to a roomful of people rather than sit in my boss's empty flat watching repeats of *Christmas Top of the Pops* from 1978. In a room that was, still, to all intents and purposes, in 1978, too.

Downstairs, the restaurant was, for one day, a riot of tasteless gold and red jollity. At the beginning of December, Helen's team had added a few festive touches to the restaurant's usual eau-de-nil and seashell colour scheme, but for Christmas Day, they'd abandoned good taste and thrown all the remaining tinsel at it.

Gold garlands mingled with real pine along the banquettes and red Chinese lanterns hung from the ceiling as I shimmied round the tables dishing up sprouts and sherry trifle with the other waiting staff. I had to admit, it was fun. A sort of communal madness had got us through the early prep, and now we were openly speculating at the serving pass about the families who'd decided to have dinner in a hotel instead of at home.

The oddest family group of all was the one in the corner banquette: the Bentley Douglases.

Joe, Laurence and solemn little Otto had crammed paper hats from the crackers over their luxuriant blond hair (clearly a family trait, now I could see them all lined up), but Ripley was stubbornly wearing a pink riding helmet, while Ellie was refusing to wear anything that might spoil her immaculate Kate Middleton blow-dry. What with the fur-trimmed beige sweater, Chanel miniskirt and lace-up boots, Ellie looked as if she'd dropped in on her way to a matinee performance of *The Nutcracker on Ice*.

Three silver-service staff members were lined up behind the table, and Ripley was pointing at things with a magic wand, again pink. Otto was glaring at the four boiled eggs on the plate in front of him. Ellie had been grilling the waiter about every dish since she'd arrived, and Laurence's glassy smile told me he'd taken a lot of St John's Wort.

Only Joe seemed to be having a good time, reading out jokes from the crackers, persuading Otto to eat his eggs, acting the fool a bit, the way I'd noticed him doing with some of the youngest bridesmaids, something the photographers loved him for. Grumpy attendants were a real pain to photograph, and Joe's lack of self-consciousness – which was a bit annoying with adults – worked brilliantly on tantrumming tots.

I tried to picture the Joe I'd first met: sulky, hungover, unshaven, sprawled over the bridal suite bed like a used towel. It was hard to match the man in front of me now with that version. Something had definitely changed, but I still didn't have the first idea what had happened to put him in that state to begin with. That hadn't just been jet lag. I felt like I knew Joe much better now, yet I felt less able to ask him what exactly it was that had put his sunny nature under such a cloud.

Someone nudged me in my ribs. 'I wouldn't be serving on that table if you paid me triple,' muttered one of the waitresses as she squeezed past with an empty platter. 'Mrs BD's watching everyone – have you noticed?'

I'd noticed Ellie eyeing me a couple of times, but then I'd known her when she was a receptionist, not an ex-wife.

'You'd think her and Joe were the parents, wouldn't you?' the waitress went on. 'Poor Laurence. Looks like he's getting an earful.'

Joe was drawing faces on Otto's eggs and making hats for them out of napkins, while Laurence seemed to be listening to Ellie's list of complaints. It was funny: in all my years of working for the family, for the hotel, I'd never really pictured what their Christmas Day must look like. The human side of the magnificent machine for entertaining.

I had a sudden sense that they'd all be having a better time upstairs in the time-warp kitchen, with Christmas crackers and familiar old crockery. Well, Laurence and the kids would. If Caroline was there, dishing up her big Sunday roast.

Joe looked up and grinned in faux-despair. I half-smiled back.

'I'll be glad to get off shift and get home,' sighed the waitress. 'You havin' your dinner later?'

'Yup,' I said, and thought of the double portion of Christmas pudding waiting for me in the restaurant fridge, which I intended to eat in bed. Relaxing in my pyjamas.

Laurence left that night for his stay at the Mayo Clinic detox program.

'Now, the Farewell to the Year – please follow the instructions I left on the—'

'I know,' I said, giving his bag to the taxi driver taking him to the airport. 'I've run the New Year's Eve party for three years now. It'll be fine.'

He looked at me. 'And have a few evenings off,' he added. 'You need a rest.'

'I will.'

Laurence looked as if he was about to say something else, but I nodded at the driver to go go go! and he did.

Upstairs, Joe was settling into the comfy leather sofa in the sitting room with a giant salad bowl of crisps and a bottle of Diet Coke.

'I thought you'd be going out?' I said, surprised.

He shook his head. 'Where would I be going?'

I didn't know the answer to that. 'To friends?'

'Nope. Anyway, I couldn't leave you on your own on Christmas night, could I? Wouldn't be very chivalrous. I've got chef's ice cream and some of Ripley's DVDs. I'm afraid they're mostly tap-dancing. You might recall she's into that.'

'Only in front of a captive audience.' We shared a sardonic grin, remembering.

'I know. Look, it's sweet of you but . . .' I'd planned to have a long bath with a new book, and an earlyish night. On the other hand, ice cream did sound good.

'Don't make me sit alone watching *Singin' in the Rain* and eating ice cream on Christmas Day,' he added. 'I'm not Bridget Jones.'

'Neither am I,' I said defensively.

'Well, I'm glad we've established that,' said Joe. 'Now, there's a trough of cocktail sausages in the fridge. You and I are in charge of eating up the leftovers, apparently. And if that doesn't make you feel Christmassy, I don't know what will.'

'Done,' I said, and gave in.

The year before, I'd spent Christmas forcing down a seven-course gourmet meal with Dominic's parents and playing one fiercely competitive game of charades, before dashing back to the hotel (nursing chronic indigestion) to work an overtime shift. Dominic had promised to give me a spa day that had never materialized, and I'd maxed out my credit card on his expensive toaster.

This year, I watched *Singin' in the Rain*. Then *42nd Street*. Joe gave me some miracle repair cream for tired feet, and I gave him a Green Guide to London. We ate our combined bodyweight in sausages, ice cream and Quality Street, and didn't make a single comment about why the other wasn't somewhere more fun. Then, at some point on Christmas night, we both nodded off in front of the antiquated four-bar electric fire.

It was one of the best Christmases I'd ever spent.

CHAPTER NINETEEN

My very favourite night of the year at the hotel was, by a long, long way, New Year's Eve. And I say that as someone who generally hates the whole New Year thing.

The Bonneville Farewell to the Year was different. It was a tradition that Laurence's grandmother, Maude, had started in 1923, officially 'to give people something to look forward to after being trapped with their families over Christmas.' Laurence had told me that she'd cooked the whole thing up after the war for the benefit of her single girlfriends who weren't sufficiently top-drawer to get onto the snobby debutante circuit where all the few remaining eligible men were to be found. I liked the game old dame even more for that.

The Farewell to the Year had been a hit from the start, thanks to its glamorous guests. In 1927 the Prince of Wales was rumoured to have been spotted dancing on the conductor's podium with two divorced women. Before long, it was *the* place to go at New Year if you weren't skiing, shooting, or making appointments with the family solicitor. Even when the hotel languished in the doldrums during the seventies and eighties, the Farewell had still drawn colourful revellers from all walks of life. Aristos, actors, singers, chefs, the odd bishop – anyone who had to be in town for work over Christmas wound up under the majestic crystal chandelier as midnight struck and hundreds of balloons filled with glitter floated down from the nets above.

I never minded working at the Farewell because, for me, the hotel cast a special spell on those nights and all the ghosts of parties past walked, or rather danced, at midnight. A different kind of sparkle seemed to fall over the Bonneville on New Year's Eve – a pearlier, more moonlit sort of glamour than the cheerful glitter of Christmas. When Laurence handed the organization of it over to me after Caroline left, I'd spent hours poring over old photographs from the thirties for inspiration: the sweeping staircase decked in silver stars, wide-eyed socialites draped in long beads gazing up into the hooded eyes of their black-tied dates, champagne in ice buckets everywhere. Then, as now, the big jazz band in immaculate dinner jackets started in the ball-room at nine and played on until the last person couldn't dance another step, which was usually late, on account of the copious booze and the bacon sandwiches that appeared on heaped silver platters at two in the morning to sustain the revellers.

This year, from the moment the first cork popped, the party swung like its most riotous 1920s predecessor, and I threw myself into keeping everything running seamlessly towards midnight. I couldn't wait to say farewell to this year – I hadn't exactly covered myself in glory at another Christmas party, that one for a medium-size City law firm. My eye had been off the ball at the end, which had led to a scuffle and some unfortunate breakages and a bit of a black mark from Laurence – and I wanted to restart my promotion campaign properly.

Midnight came, the silvery balloons tumbled down, everyone cheered and hugged and kissed as Big Ben's chimes boomed out. I stood by the drinks table, alone, and felt a brief, sad pang that there was no one reaching for me to kiss. Which was ridiculous, I told myself; I'd worked this event for years, and no one had *ever* been there. This year, though, I suddenly felt the lack.

I busied myself with the glasses until the chimes finished, and when I turned round, I was hit by a full-on hug from Gemma.

'Happy New Year!' she yelled over the sound of poppers popping. Euphoria, like a good crisis, went straight to her head.

Across the room, I caught Joe's eye over her smooth dark hair. He smiled but didn't say anything, and I thought he mouthed *Happy New Year* at me. I smiled back, and the sourness inside me retreated. I'd never be completely alone, not in a hotel.

At half past four in the morning, Tam steered the final pair of revellers out of the ballroom and towards the taxi rank, where a lone black cab sat waiting. He could be surprisingly gentle for an eighteen-stone ex-international rugby player. Once he'd clocked off for the night, Gemma, Joe and I were left to start clearing the main debris of the party before the crack squad of housekeeping staff arrived at six. They were amazing to watch, like a furious army of ants, clearing mess and leaving only clean space behind, but I couldn't leave the ballroom in this state overnight.

It seemed too quiet, without the music and laughter that

had filled it an hour ago, and with the lights up, the mess was a bit depressing.

I steeled myself; Caroline had drilled it into me that, when it came to parties, it was better to get the worst done before bed, plus I needed to count the bottles back in, so I could work out how much champagne had mysteriously vanished with the temp staff.

'Just get the bottles in the crates, and put the glasses on that table,' I said, making a start on the nearest table with its sticky tangle of streamers, napkins and flutes.

'Where you do want lost property?' Gemma held up a silver shoe in one hand and a pair of black lace knickers in another. 'Shall I make a pile?'

'Tweet photos,' said Joe. '"Do you recognize these knickers? Lost at the Bonneville Farewell to the Year." Hashtag FunTimes. Brilliant publicity!'

'Again, *exactly* the classic image we're trying to promote,' I said, but my heart wasn't in sarcasm tonight.

'Seriously, shall I get a box?' Gemma had found more underwear and an umbrella. 'And labels? And the lost-property book?'

Maybe it was the evidence of everyone else's fun, but suddenly the past months caught up with me. I didn't want to dictate a list of lost knickers and mobile phones to Gemma. There was the rest of the year for that.

'Just put everything you can find in that crate, then go home,' I said. 'I'll deal with it in the morning.'

Gemma looked as though there was some sort of catch. 'Are you sure?'

'Yes, I'm sure. Go home. Get a taxi,' I said, then added, out of habit, 'Don't forget to give me the receipt in the morning.'

'A receipt? Jeez.' Joe reached into his back pocket and got out his wallet. 'Have you any cash, Gem? No? Look, here's thirty quid. How far away from here do you live?'

'On New Year's Day?' Gemma raised an eyebrow. 'About sixty quid away.'

'Oi! Don't take advantage of the fact that Joe's clearly forgotten where everything is in London,' I warned her. 'You live in Clapham, not Cheltenham.'

Joe laughed and added another tenner.

'Are you sure?' She looked between us. 'This isn't some kind of management test? Am I supposed to say, "No, Rosie, I'll stay here till the place is spotless"?'

I was shocked. 'Of course not! What kind of insane slave driver do you think I am?'

'Don't answer that.' Joe gave me a funny look, then turned back to her. 'It's a thank-you,' he said. 'You've done a great job tonight. Great teamwork.'

Gemma stifled a yawn. 'It was fun, wasn't it? Way more fun than weddings.'

'But you love weddings,' I said.

'Yeah, but *you're* less stressed-out at events like this,' she said, then looked a bit embarrassed. 'I mean, not that you're – I mean, you just seemed to be enjoying – that's not the right word either, um . . .'

'She knows what you mean,' said Joe, before I could summon up a response. 'Now, get on home.'

Gemma waved and dashed out. She had glitter all over the seat of her skirt and what looked like a tinsel tail. I decided not to say anything.

I walked across the empty ballroom, trying not to notice how shabby it was under the bright lights. A few chipped gold chairs would have to go back for a respray, and the curtains weren't quite as plush as they'd seemed from a distance. That was the best bit about being a guest, I thought: you left with the illusion of the night intact.

'I'd love to come to this as a guest,' I said.

'Why?'

'Why?' I waved a hand towards the glitter ball. 'So I could enjoy it properly. See it as it's meant to be seen.'

Something about the atmosphere tonight had fizzed with romance. I'd noticed one couple at the table nearest the ice feature who'd nearly melted it with their obvious chemistry. He hadn't taken his eyes off her all evening. She'd glowed with that fluttery delight of knowing something was starting, new possibilities and promises flickering into life. They'd flirted from the first champagne cocktail, never moving from their seats, gazing into each other's eyes; then when I looked over at midnight, their chairs were empty. They'd left.

I wondered if I'd meet them again, booking their wedding in the same ballroom where they'd met. My heart ached with envy.

Stop it, Rosie.

'Come on – sit down for ten minutes.' Joe waved a bottle of champagne at me, dripping chilly beads of water from the ice bucket. 'Have a glass of this. Someone's opened it – shame for it to go to waste.'

I started to argue, then gave up. I was tired. I needed the lift a glass of champagne would give me. 'Go on.'

Joe wandered over to the stage where the band had been playing Sinatra classics all night, and pulled himself up on it with a groan. 'Ah, that's better. Now, finally. A drink.'

He wiped the champagne bottle with a linen napkin, and I realized he was about to swig straight from the neck.

'What? No, wait.' I hunted around until I found half a tray of unused champagne coupes tucked away under the grand piano. Someone had shoved them too far to reach easily, so I had to half-crawl under it to get them, and when I looked up, Joe was watching me with his half-amused expression.

'Do you always have to do things the most difficult way?' He waved the bottle. 'I don't have anything you can catch, you know.'

'It's not that.' I held the coupes out so he could pour the champagne, which he did with a deft turn of the wrist – as you'd expect from someone who'd grown up in a hotel. 'It's doing things properly. I want to start this year as I mean to go on. With a bit of style.'

Joe raised his eyebrows but said nothing as he took the glass I was offering, and I sat myself down on the stage next to him. We stared out at the dance floor, and I wished I'd turned the lights down. They were chasing away the ghostly magic.

Good, I reminded myself. *It'll make you tidy up quicker.*

'So what are your New Year's resolutions?' Joe asked.

'Oh, you know. The usual. Work harder. Lose weight. Buy a flat. Get Dino to give me his martini recipe. How about you?'

'All the above. Plus run a marathon.'

I laughed awkwardly, not sure if he meant it.

'Hang on, I'm sorry to do this,' said Joe, slipping off the stage. 'But I'm going to have to turn these lights down. Just for ten minutes.' I was surprised at how romantic he was being; then he added, 'They're making my contact lenses dry out.'

'Just for ten minutes,' I agreed, trying not to let him see how relieved I was. 'I don't want to fall asleep.'

After a moment or two, the harsh halogen light dimmed until only the soft light of the chandelier remained, turning the room from yellow to a gentle grey.

The glitter ball was still spinning lazily and I watched it cast a shimmering net of lights over the room, now draped in a more flattering velvety shadow. Opaque diamonds tumbled over the white-clothed tables, over the huge angel wings made from hundreds of calla lilies, and across the empty dance floor.

'That's better,' said Joe, undoing his bow tie as he made his way back across the floor. Even he looked better now, dishevelled rather than tired, black-and-white, not colour. I sipped my champagne and felt the welcome bubbles trickle into my bloodstream.

'So,' he said, hoisting himself easily back up. 'Your New Year's resolutions. What are they really?'

'I just told you.'

'Yeah, sure you did. What do you really want to achieve by this time next year?'

'You've been back in the UK for months now. Have you still not worked out that direct questions are considered a bit rude over here?' I said, not entirely joking.

Joe smiled and topped up his glass. I covered mine with a hand. 'How else do you get to know people if you don't ask questions? I mean, you don't have to answer, not if it's something like *take over the hotel and start a cult in the laundry rooms*. Come on. What do you see happening this year, for you?'

The new year. It stretched out in front of me like a mountain path, winding upwards in a series of weddings and Monday morning meetings and direct debits. Not a mountain path with handrails, or steps either. One with a misty summit, and I had no map and the wrong shoes. I wobbled at the thought of climbing it alone. No Dominic. No flat to hunt for together. No parties, no newspaper column, no chance to make a name for myself with a huge *Reporter* party . . .

I blinked, hard, and the words burst out of me into the darkened room, directed more to myself than to Joe. I'd based my life round Dominic more than I'd realized. From now on, I was doing it *myself*.

'I'm going to make my target,' I said, 'and I'm going to get the promotion, and I'm going to use the raise as a deposit on a flat of my own.'

'Whoa, wind back there,' said Joe. 'Your target? And what promotion?'

I took another long sip of champagne. It was very good champagne. It was nice to drink it in this glamorous, quiet place. 'I did a deal with Laurence this summer, before you arrived. If I achieve certain goals in the events department by the end of June, he'll consider me for the general manager's job.'

'Will he now?'

'Yes.' I wasn't sure from Joe's tone whether he'd assumed he'd be in line for it. I wondered whether he knew Caroline had told me about her plans for him.

'And how near are you?' he asked. He paused. 'Guess that business with Stephanie Miller cancelling can't have helped. Sorry.'

'No, it didn't. Thanks for that.' Should I tell him the details? I wasn't sure I should. The only people who knew about my deal with Laurence were me, Caroline and Laurence, and I didn't know how the other heads of department would take it if they found out.

'Come on, I won't tell anyone,' said Joe. 'You must be doing all right. Dino was telling me he had to double the bar stock orders, because of all the weddings you've booked in this quarter.'

'We're ahead of target,' I admitted. 'Flora's wedding makes up for Stephanie cancelling, because of the extras she's booking, but it's really more about generating publicity, as much as the money. I've been getting dozens of calls from people who've heard she's having her wedding here. Our private dinner bookings are way up, and the afternoon tea's really taking off.'

'Wait till the dress gets out,' said Joe. 'There are three designers in the frame. One of them will be a big surprise, apparently.' He wiggled his eyebrows in mock excitement, then laughed. 'She thinks I'm joking when I have *no idea* who she's talking about.'

I felt a surge of gratitude. I was very tired, but dealing with Flora would be a whole other tiredness on top. 'To be honest, Joe, you're the one making that happen, not me. You're so patient.'

'Hey, I don't mind. Flora's quite sweet once you remember that six years ago she was a foot taller than everyone she knew at Downe House and was called Roadrunner.'

'Was she?' I turned to him, and he nodded. 'She told you that?'

Joe shrugged. 'It's like I said – if you don't ask people stuff, how can you make the day what they want? It's inevitable that you get to know them. You're feeling your way round their dreams. Or you should be, if you want to help them experience what they really want.'

I felt he was making a bit of a point there, so I pressed my lips together and gazed out at the elegant room in front of us.

'Isn't this a magical place?' I said. 'A ballroom after midnight. All the ghosts, the secrets.'

'I take it you've never seen *The Shining* then?' he said.

'Ha,' I said. 'Funny. You're so lucky to have grown up somewhere like this.' I watched the mirror ball spinning. 'It must have been amazing as a kid – the corridors, the smells, the mechanics of it all behind the scenes. You're a real-life Eloise.'

'It was cool having a pool in the basement, and you could always get a milkshake, but other than that . . .' He took a sip from his glass. 'I was away at school for most of it. And I don't know it did my parents' marriage much good.'

'But they both loved this place.'

'They did, you're right. But it meant there were always three people in the relationship, Mum, Dad—'

'And the hotel.' I knew Laurence had taken Caroline for granted. I'd never really thought about it from the boys' point of view, though.

'She's a very demanding mistress, Lady Bonneville,' said Joe ironically.

'A special one, though?' I waved a hand towards the dance floor, caught like an old photograph in luxurious grey and lilac shadows, with flashes of white from the flowers. 'It's more than just a hotel. It's like . . . living in a bubble of history. Your family history.'

'I guess one good thing you can say is that they both worked too hard to have affairs. I'm amazed Mum and Dad found time to have me and Alec.' He topped up my coupe. We were getting through the bottle very quickly. 'I know Dad would love me to take over, but . . .' He shrugged. 'I never want to let anything take over my life that much. It's not healthy.'

Doh. Of course that was why Joe didn't want to work here, I thought, with the clutch of embarrassment that really obvious realizations often bring. Was that why he'd left the country, rather than be guilt-tripped into working in a hotel that he associated with his parents' marriage collapsing?

We said nothing for a moment or two; then Joe said, 'Was that a factor, with you and Dominic? This place taking up too much time?'

The directness of the question didn't surprise me by now. It might have been the fact that we weren't looking at each other, and the room was dark, or that the past few days watching mindless telly with Joe at the end of our shift were all combining to blur the boundaries between on and off-duty, here in the half-light.

'Probably,' I admitted, with a shiver at hearing myself say something aloud that I'd only thought before. 'But Dominic had weird hours, too, when he was on a deadline. It wasn't like he clocked off at five. He liked the fact that we were both night owls, you know, that we understood the same industry.'

'But he was more important than work, surely? You loved each other.'

I stared at my feet, swinging against the edge of the stage. Sensible mid-heel almond pumps. Not the sort of shoes a woman of my age should be wearing on New Year's Eve. I should be wearing sky-high platforms. Sparkly stilettos. Golden sandals. Sexy, flirty shoes. I pried the left one off with my right toe, then did the same on the right, and they clattered to the floor.

That was better. I could see my scarlet pedicure glinting through my tights. Sensible tights. Helen had given me the pedicure for Christmas, 'to cheer me up'. And it had, sort of.

The silence between me and Joe was growing but it wasn't uncomfortable. I could feel him sipping his champagne next to me, his lips on the delicate glass. I wondered if he was looking at my toes and seeing a glimpse of the scarlet pedicure under the sensible tights.

I realized I wanted him to see that. To see I wasn't always To-Do List Rosie. I wondered if he'd noticed my red toenails around the flat, the way I knew about the little tattoo on his shoulder.

'Was Dominic Mr Right, though?' asked Joe. 'Really?'

'No,' I said, and there it was, out there. 'No. He wasn't Mr Right.'

I had to face it: Dominic's reluctance to share his social life should have told me something. And the way he got so uncomfortable around weddings, and the way he . . . I flinched inside. The way he never told me he loved me unless he was hammered. I was a flatmate. With benefits. And I was lucky to have got out before we signed the mortgage.

'Well, then you're a step nearer finding the right Mr Right.'

I snorted. 'Aren't we a bit old for believing in Mr and Ms Right?'

Joe went to refill his glass but the bottle was empty. He shook it, then put it down on the stage.

'You don't think there's one perfect person out there for you?' he asked, without looking round.

'No. I think there are lots of people out there who could make you happy. But not one single perfect person. You'd drive yourself mad, like all the crazy girls I see every day who think if they don't get the exact shade of lilac for their colour scheme, their marriage is doomed.'

'You're very unromantic for a wedding planner.'

'*Events* planner.'

'Events planner, whatever. Have you never imagined getting married yourself?'

The room was so intimate, the light was so low, the champagne was so comforting and Joe's voice was so gentle, that I nearly said yes. *Yes, I have been engaged. I was very nearly married. I got as far as the big pillar behind the vestry, within five minutes of 'The Arrival of the Queen of Sheba' starting up. I had the blue garter, the bouquet ready to throw, the table plan, the list of presents at John Lewis that all had to go back.*

All that rose up in my head like a conga line of rowdy guests. I hadn't thought about my non-wedding in ages. I'd managed to stack up lots of other stuff in front of it.

I wondered, in horror, whether Laurence or Caroline had said something about it to Joe. He'd have mentioned it, wouldn't he?

I mentally restacked all the other stuff in front of that embarrassing tableau: work, hotel, bouquets, deadlines, Dominic.

Dominic. I stacked more stuff in front of him: Flora Thornbury, Laurence's target, Caroline's projects. I was failing badly on that front.

I liked Joe. I didn't want him to know about that Rosie.

'No,' I said. 'What about you?'

I assumed Joe would say no, too, but he didn't reply, and when I turned my head to see what his face was doing, he was staring out across the empty dance floor. He looked lost, and there was a flash of vulnerability that took me by surprise.

'Sorry,' I started, at the same moment that he said, 'I think if you meet that perfect person . . .'

We both stopped talking, awkwardly.

'And have you?' I prompted, struck by an equally unexpected pang of . . . something.

Joe didn't reply. The glitter ball carried on turning, and I wondered if I'd touched on something too personal. Maybe it was too close to his parents' marriage. I'd never thought what it must have been like for Joe and Alec in the middle of it all. Living in the flat with Joe had tipped my perceptions of the hotel on their side; I was starting to see an off-duty side not just to Joe but also to the Bonneville. I was seeing a home, not just my place of work.

Then he jumped off the stage, and I was jerked back to reality.

My head swam as the manic activity of the last few days caught up with me all at once. 'Shouldn't have had that last glass of champagne,' I said thickly.

He held out a hand. 'Come on, Cinderella.'

'Are you asking me to dance?' I joked.

I didn't know how to dance, but I would have, in that moment. Joe in his dinner jacket, his bow tie undone, his hair rumpled, standing there in black-and-white, like a partygoer from the 1979 Farewell come back for one last turn round the dance floor.

He gazed up at me, and my stomach did a slow, drunken loop. In a nice way.

'No, you idiot, I was giving you a hand off the stage, since you seem a bit tipsy,' he said. 'Did you want to dance? We could . . .' He made twisting actions – joking, ungainly. Not romantic waltzing ones. The moment burst and vanished like a soap bubble.

Romantic waltzing ones? I could feel my face turning red. Why had I thought that?

'No need, I'm fine.' I lowered myself to the floor and felt around, rather too carefully, for my shoes. My boring shoes.

'You know what your New Year's resolution should be?' said Joe.

Suddenly I really wanted to go to bed. To fall into the spare bed upstairs and not think about any of the unwelcome wedding-guest thoughts now barging around my subconscious.

'To cut down on my drinking?'

'No, to loosen up.' Joe's voice echoed in the cavernous room. He didn't sound as drunk as I felt, but then he'd probably been stuffing himself with canapés all night. 'Let your hair down. See what the universe brings.' He paused. 'Stop making lists, and start living in the moment.'

Target, promotion, flat. That was what I needed to focus on. Not living in the moment. And definitely not love.

I frowned. Love? Where had *that* come from?

'Rosie?'

I found my shoes, shoved them on, and began walking towards the door. They were pinching me but I wasn't going to let it show.

'I'm going to start this year as I mean to go on,' I said. 'With three hours' sleep. I've got work in the morning.'

CHAPTER TWENTY

You get to know people quickly when you're sharing a fridge. Even if you barely see them, thanks to your ridiculous working hours, one shelf can tell its own story. In Laurence's case, it was an entire shelf devoted to four different probiotics. In Joe's, it was a secret stash of Cadbury's Creme Eggs.

Joe wasn't, it turned out, the complete health nut I'd assumed he was when I first met him. That, or he'd fallen off the wagon spectacularly on rediscovering British chocolate. I also discovered, through the bedroom wall adjoining mine, that we shared the same taste in sixties singer-songwriters; that he did seventy-five press-ups before getting in the shower (I honestly wasn't listening, he counted aloud and the walls were *thin*); and that like me he was weirdly specific about loading the dishwasher.

'It's in the rinsing,' he insisted. 'You're the first girl I've met who really gets the *pre-rinsing*.'

(I should add that he left the bathroom looking like a bomb had hit it, and never replaced a loo roll. The dishwasher was an isolated non-slobby instance.)

It wasn't what I'd imagined for my new year, new start, but somehow it did feel like a fresh start. I'd dreamed about settling into a flat with Dominic, planning out our new life. Instead, I was back to sharing fridge space and arguing about how to squeeze out a tea bag properly. But, oddly enough, even though I was flat-sharing with my boss and a colleague, I didn't feel half as awkward as I'd assumed I would.

I *think* Laurence and Joe felt the same. At least, they were too polite to say anything.

The good news was, as I inspected it on the first proper Monday morning of the new year, that the Bridelizer was already ahead of schedule, mainly thanks to Flora Thornbury. I had deposits banked for weddings right up until October, and my appointments book was so full I was having to turn away prospective brides. Just after Christmas, one of Flora's potential blonde bridesmaids turned up in a background role in a live (well, live-ish) reality show called *The Queens of Knightsbridge*, and spent most of her January airtime banging on about her supermodel mate's amazing bridal suite, and how she was down to 'the last three' for the role of hen night planner.

Joe claimed never to have heard of *The Queens of Knightsbridge*, of course. He also claimed to be disgusted at the torrent of freebies that began to arrive in my office after New Year, although that didn't stop him working his way through the chocolates.

'Do they think we don't *have* pink champagne?' he said, inspecting a box with silk rose petals glued all over it. It had been hand-delivered by a runner from the PR agency, along with a gushing invitation for me to meet them and 'chat with us about the brand, which Flora is a big fan of.' 'I mean, we are a hotel. With an entry in *Secret Hotel Bars of the World*.'

Laurence (or rather, Dino) had moved Joe from catering to the lovely old oak-panelled bar, and Joe had been spending some time learning the arcane ways of the cocktail. He could now mix a very passable Bonneville Martini, following some after-hours tuition. One advantage of living above the shop was that I was now invited to these 'tasting sessions'. Detoxing wasn't on my list of resolutions, fortunately.

'Oh, so Dino's been telling you about that, has he? Did he give you the Dean Martin story?'

'Yup. And the Duke of Edinburgh story, and the secret tunnel to Fortnum and Mason story, and the gold hidden in the ice-maker during the Blitz story. He still won't give me the full recipe to the Honeymoon Night cocktail, though.'

'I don't know that, and I've been here *years*.'

'I think it's bubble bath,' he said. 'Or possibly Night Nurse. So are we supposed to give this champagne to Flora?'

'No! You can have it,' I said, without turning round. 'You're the one who has to deal with her twice a week.'

I was trying to find room to pin Cressida Connor's details into the second weekend in October on the Bridelizer. She wanted a hundred and fifty guests, a fairground theme, and 'whatever wedding cake Flora Thornbury's having!'

'You must be way past your total now,' Joe observed. 'Are you aiming for a wedding every weekend?'

'No, three a month, max. I don't want us to look *too* available.' I stood back, running my eyes over the variety of brides and colour swatches. Grey was a big theme this year. Grey attendants, bone-white macaroons and picture frames made of flowers were in; tans, crafts and pastel cupcakes were out. It was already looking a bit Miss Havisham around May/June, with four brides in vintage lace. I made a mental note to steer Jessie Callum back towards rose pink.

'You should double your stakes.' Joe leaned back in his chair and put his feet on my desk. He was wearing green Converse, which were not my idea of office-appropriate footwear for planners handling wedding budgets equivalent to the cost of a Zone 4 flat.

I frowned, but he ignored me. 'Meaning? And get your feet off my desk. And get some more appropriate shoes.'

'Oh, so it'd be fine to have my feet up here if they were brogues?'

'Yes. I mean it. This hotel merits proper shoes and a decent suit.'

Joe left his feet where they were. 'I think you should ask for an additional bonus, plus a guaranteed job offer, if you hit the target early. It looks confident.' He put his hands behind his head: the image of confidence. 'If you want him to take you seriously for the role of manager, you need to look confident.'

I pressed my lips together, thinking. It *would* look confident. And I needed a bonus to boost my deposit on a studio flat, maybe even to upgrade to a nasty one-bedder. Much as living upstairs was convenient (and cheap), I knew I couldn't stay forever. 'What if it doesn't come off? What if someone cancels?'

Joe shrugged. 'Give yourself the challenge, then you'll make sure it does. Works for me. I went to LA with nothing, and I had a business within six months.'

'That's you, though.' I stared at him over the desk. I found myself confiding in Joe more lately, sometimes without meaning to. 'I'm more of a planner than a gambler.'

He rolled his eyes. 'I told you what your resolution should be for this year. Go with the flow more. Let the universe do its thing. It'll help you do yours.'

I did need something. There'd been a couple of moments lately when things hadn't quite gone to plan: I'd double-booked a rehearsal dinner, and accidentally misquoted for a wedding reception, which annoyingly we were now legally bound to honour. The whole Dominic thing had dented my confidence; I hadn't realized how much I'd come to rely on his 'they're all idiots!' support.

'You can do it, Rosie,' said Joe earnestly. 'You've got to believe.'

'Thanks for that, Oprah,' I said. I'd developed a tolerance for Joe's mess in the bathroom but not for his irritating platitudes. 'Now, if you'll excuse me, the universe doesn't seem to have done its thing about the chairs for Laura Southwell's reception. And get your feet off my desk,' I added in a 'confident' voice.

Joe put his feet back down.

It was a start. And it obviously worked, because when I put the proposal to Laurence, he said yes, pretty much straight away. Which made me wonder if he thought I was up to the challenge – or more likely, that I wasn't.

*

In the great division of Flora Thornbury labour, Joe had the madness but I had the maths. And believe me, there's more maths in a wedding than you'd think. Guests divided by tables, multiplied by canapés, all over one and a half bottles of wine ... it's endless. Especially when you have a bride who keeps remembering friends she owes invites to, or – in the case of my worst wedding last year – a bride who sends out two hundred save-the-dates, but only a hundred and fifty invitations, leading to a embarrassed knot of extra guests arriving on our doorstep, clutching presents like the additional Wise Men Mary wasn't that keen on and only gave an evening invite to.

Luckily, I enjoyed spreadsheets; I found their lack of hysterics about ribbon width soothing. And the Thornbury spreadsheet was already a thing of epic complexity. Julia Thornbury hadn't ended up with diamond earrings the size of ice cubes without keeping her eye on the maths, and she'd asked me to supply her with running totals of where her substantial budget was going. With the wedding now five months away, deposits had been taken for the flowers, catering, the two floors of rooms booked in the hotel for guests, the unbelievably elaborate stationery, the band ... My spreadsheet totals were already way over what most brides spent on their entire event, and we hadn't even got to the rehearsal dinner.

It was now the beginning of the second week in January, and I was deep in boring data entry about Flora's table linens when the door to my office burst open and Helen waltzed in.

'Good afternoon!' she sang. 'And a very Happy New Year to you!'

I hadn't seen Helen since before Christmas. She'd taken her remaining days off and allowed Wynn to sweep her off on a romantic holiday to a mystery destination, which he'd refused to let her pay for or plan.

'Happy New Year to you too!' I said, putting my pen down. 'And where did your romantic mystery tour take you? We were trying to work it out when you texted on New Year's Eve. I thought New York?'

Helen had always wanted to see the ball drop in Times Square. She'd tried to persuade Seamus to go for years, but he'd always ducked out, probably because he'd never have got past the sniffer dogs at Heathrow.

'No!' she said, as if I'd suggested something insane. 'Why spend all the time on a plane? No, we had a lovely time in Wales.'

'In Wales?' I blinked. It had rained for most of the holiday. All over the UK, but especially in Wales. I'd seen news footage of sheep being rescued in kayaks.

'Mmm. Cosy hotel, log fires, amazing food.' Helen looked very dreamy for someone who'd probably contracted trench foot by New Year's Eve. But that was love, I reasoned. It kept you very warm. And dry.

'Brilliant. So did Wynn give you something nice for Christmas?' I asked.

'You could say that.' She perched on the edge of my desk with a serene smile, and then it broke down into a broad schoolgirl grin. 'I've got gossip. Guess what?'

'You found Delphine hanging upside down in the cold walk-in again?'

'No.'

'Laurence has discovered he's got the plague? No, wait – I think he's had that. What hasn't he had? Foot-and-mouth?'

'No! Rosie, it's much better than that.'

'I give up.'

Helen was wafting her hands around her face like someone trying to mime a very complicated film, jiggling her eyebrows meaningfully.

'You've had eyelash extensions?' I hazarded.

'No! Are you doing this on purpose?' she demanded, and slammed both her hands down on either side of my keyboard. 'Oh, hang on, it's slipped round. It does that.'

She fiddled with something, and the resulting sparkle from the diamonds on her left hand almost blinded me. It looked like three sugar lumps stuck together. It was even bigger than Flora's, and hers was half a carat short of needing its own bodyguard.

'Whoa!' I blinked. 'Is Wynn a secret millionaire dentist?'

'What? Oh, it's not real. It's just a fake one he got to propose with. The real one's a family heirloom. He was waiting to make sure I said yes.' She smiled down at the ring, then looked up at me. Her face was shining brighter than the fake sparklers.

I felt a tug of envy in the middle of my happiness for her, but pushed it away. 'Congratulations!' I said, getting up to hug her. 'So come on, how did he do it?'

'Oh, Rosie, it was so romantic. We were staying in this beautiful hotel in Abergavenny, and it stopped raining one day for, like, half an hour, so we went for a walk. Seriously, who knew walking was fun? Anyway,' Helen went on, seeing my *don't push it* expression, 'we'd got to the top of the hill, and the sun was setting over the mountains, and I said, "Oh, Wynn, I'm so happy right now," meaning, "Thank God I'm not running a dinner service with a bunch of psychos," and Wynn turned to me and said, "I'm so happy right now too. Would you consider making me this happy forever?"'

She blushed. 'And he went down on one knee, and he had the ring in his pocket all ready! He said he'd had it for weeks, but he wanted to pick a perfect moment, so we'd always remember it. Just us. Privately.'

It took a lot to impress me where proposals were concerned – I'd heard everything from flashmobs to rings in trifles to flower beds planted six months in advance to spell out Will You Marry Me in tulips – but this one sent a proper lump to my throat. I put my hands to my face. It was sweet, and genuine, and I could hear Wynn saying the simple words in his gentle Welsh accent, gazing up at Helen with that unexpectedly passionate look he gave her when he thought no one else could see, the one that said, *You. Just you. Nothing else.*

'And you said?'

Helen's voice was an emotional squeak. 'I said yes.'

'That's wonderful!' I really meant it. 'I'm *so* happy for you.'

Helen grabbed my hands. 'I wanted to tell you first. I mean, because you're my best friend, but also . . . I know it's not a great time for you.'

'It's a brilliant time for me,' I insisted. 'Because you've found a good honest man who makes you happy. And that makes me happy too.'

'I know what you're thinking,' she said. 'That it's very quick. And it is quick. But Wynn's the man I've been waiting for all my life. I don't have to try to make things right with him, I just feel like the best possible version of me, all the time. We fit together, not in some big dramatic way, but in little, practical ways. And I'd never have found him if I'd carried on looking in all the places I thought I *should* be looking – it's like love found us.' She paused, and squeezed my hands. 'I just – I want you to be as happy as we are. I'm sorry I encouraged you to waste time on Dominic, like I wasted time with Seamus, because it doesn't have to be like that. Something amazing is out there for you, I just know it.'

I tried to say something, but my eyes had filled up with tears.

'Come here!' Helen's eyes were full of tears too. We had a big hug, during which her ring slipped round again and the enormous cubic zirconias dug into my back, but I didn't care.

I was so happy for her. I was. I just wasn't sure there was enough luck like that for both of us.

Helen and Wynn's engagement drinks weren't taking place in the hotel, as I'd assumed they would, but in the newly refurbished pub at the end of Wynn's street in Clapham.

Joe and I headed over there after work on Friday night after promising Laurence we wouldn't be back late, and it was at the door that I got the first nasty surprise of the evening.

'You didn't tell me it was a karaoke bar,' I said accusingly to Helen.

Over in the corner by an old-fashioned piano, a woman in a suit and trendy black-framed glasses was already working her way through 'Crazy in Love'. Or stamping out a small fire. One or the other.

'It is,' said Helen. 'It's a lovely local pub that does karaoke on a Friday night.'

'Is that meant to be a sales pitch? That's like saying it's a tea shop *and* a waterboarding facility.'

Helen rolled her eyes, and blocked my line of sight. 'Come on, Rosie, it's fun. The burgers here are the best I've ever had in London, and you know how many burgers I've had.'

'But how can we relax when there are people singing as if they've got something trapped in their throats and doing that awful *X Factor* jerky hand thing? I know it's your local pub, and I really want to eat here, but can't we just go somewhere else until—'

'No,' said Helen firmly. 'We can't. Wynn and I have booked the snug. Have a drink, and in five minutes I promise you will not care.'

'Problem?' Joe strolled up behind us and knuckled my head playfully. 'Is Rosie micromanaging you?'

I rearranged my face into a forced smile. *Get a grip, Rosie.* I didn't want to look like a killjoy, but karaoke brought me out in hives of anxiety.

'There's no problem,' I said. 'And I don't micromanage—'

'Hi, Joe!' said Helen, right over me. 'Thanks for rearranging your shift – it's great you could come.'

'Wouldn't miss it for anything. Oh, wow.' His face lit up in a broad grin, and I did a brief double take, thinking he was smiling at me, but no – he was staring right over my shoulder.

I turned to see what he was smiling at, but incredibly, he was smiling at the office Beyoncé, now hunched over the microphone and clumping about as if her left leg had gone to sleep and she was trying to get the blood flowing again.

'Karaoke, amazing!' he said. 'I love it! There was this incredible karaoke bar back in Santa Cruz that we used to go to all the time. I do a brilliant Lenny Kravitz . . .'

'Excellent!' said Helen. 'You can go first.'

'We're not—' I started.

'Look, go through and meet everyone – Wynn's already in there with some of his friends. He'll introduce you, they're all lovely.'

As she spoke, Joe pushed me helpfully in the direction of the snug, and before I knew it, I was in the middle of a fierce discussion about who the greatest Bond of all time was with two of Wynn's school friends. It was quite heated, but on the positive side, it drowned out the sound of the singing in the main bar.

Soon Helen and Wynn shyly announced that they might just have a go on the karaoke now they'd worked up some Dutch courage.

'I really hope this is a short song,' I muttered to Joe. 'Karaoke's bad enough, but couples karaoke should be illegal outside the home.'

'Don't be such a buzzkill.' Joe started edging his way out from the table. 'Come on, stir yourself, she's your best mate. And they might need backing singers.'

Wynn and Helen were already clutching microphones on the stage in the corner, and gazing at each other with mischievous expressions.

I'd never seen Helen look mischievous before.

I found myself rammed up against the broad shoulders of Wynn's mate Geraint. He was also very Welsh. I already knew he'd known Wynn since school, he was an IT consultant living in Shoreditch, he'd once had a dog called Hammond, and he thought Maltesers were the ultimate individual chocolate treat. None of Wynn's friends had any trouble starting conversations, and they didn't give a toss about ethical bread production.

'Ah, it's you! Now, this should be good, look,' he said into my ear.

'Why?' I asked, at the same time that the introduction to 'You're the One That I Want' boomed out of the speakers.

No. Surely not *Grease*? Helen was too cool for—

Then Wynn started singing. Out of the mild-mannered dentist in the zip-up cardigan flowed the most amazing voice. And he was singing the goofy lyrics with a big smile on his face, right into Helen's eyes, and making them sound fresh and genuine; and when she pouted and finger-pointed back, somehow she sounded pretty tuneful too. It obviously wasn't their first time on the karaoke – a thought that shocked me even more than the idea of Helen hill-walking in the rain.

Most people in the pub had stopped drinking to watch, and some were even joining in with the 'ooh-ooh-ooooh' bits and clapping. Joe was whooping *and* clapping, slightly off the beat.

Geraint leaned over and yelled, 'He's in the choir!'

'Helen isn't!' I yelled back. 'I had no idea she could do this!'

'She's in love, isn't she?' He finished off his pint and put the glass on the bar. 'Love makes everyone sing better. Now, how about it? You and me? What duets do you know?'

'I don't do karaoke.'

'Come on, love, you can't turn me down for a song.' Geraint pretended to look sad. He wasn't bad-looking, with thick dark hair and a cheeky smile, but he could have been Ryan Gosling and I still wouldn't have got up there to sing.

'I don't do singing. And someone has to keep an eye on the bags,' I pointed out. 'Oh, look. They're finishing!' And I did lots of over-the-top clapping until Geraint and his mates were 'persuaded' to go up and sing 'Flying Without Wings'.

To prevent further song pressure, I asked the barman for a menu and started examining it hungrily.

'Those lads are good, aren't they?' Joe observed while I weighed up the burgers. 'They're almost making it look . . . "fun". Do you think you might be persuaded to have some . . . "fun"?'

'Nope, not a chance,' I said without looking up. 'I'm happy to listen, but that's as far as it goes.'

'Well, listening's an improvement on earlier.' He paused, and after a second or two, I glanced up to see why he'd stopped. It was a trick that always worked on me. Joe was looking at me with a glint in his eyes.

'What?' I asked, annoyed that he'd got me to do exactly what he wanted.

'I was just wondering where that birthmark on your forehead's gone.'

I touched my forehead self-consciously. 'I don't have a birthmark on my forehead.'

'No, you don't, I realize that now.' He was gazing at my forehead so intensely that he might as well have been touching it, and I felt myself blush. 'It's just that normally there's a crease there.'

And then Joe did touch me, very softly, between the eyebrows. It made my face tingle, and I jerked backwards.

Living together was very odd. I was much more aware of my personal space around Joe than I had been before December. I'd always noticed that he was a bit touchy-feely, but now every casual touchy-feely touch seemed more obvious.

'And it's not there now,' he announced.

'Is that a roundabout and rather patronizing way of telling me I'm relaxed?'

'Ah, no, it's back. Up till then, you were definitely looking more relaxed. You need to relax more.'

I hated being told to relax. It was the most unrelaxing thing anyone could tell you, right up there with 'Calm down' and 'Cheer up'.

'I'm very relaxed,' I said tightly.

Joe nodded. 'Maybe it's because you haven't mentioned any-thing to do with the hotel or weddings for over two hours now.'

'I don't always talk about—' I started, but he was already shaking his head.

'This is the longest I've seen you go without talking about the hotel. I wish I'd known all it would take to stop you talking about the bloody hotel was to ask you about James Bond films. Who *knew* you had so many opinions about Pierce Brosnan?' He carried on looking at me in an amused way that made me feel, well, not uncomfortable exactly, but a bit unsettled.

'He's unfairly overlooked,' I said, turning back to the menu. My cheeks felt hot, but then the pub was quite crowded now. 'He had Moore's sense of self-deprecation but Connery's under-lying mean streak. And he had the best hair.'

'I never realized,' Joe mused. 'I must have missed the ones he was good in. I only saw the ones where Brosnan looks like he's wandered in from an episode of *Murder, She Wrote*.'

The way he said it made it impossible not to laugh, even though I didn't want to. '*GoldenEye* is very underrated.'

'This weekend then,' said Joe, reaching for the menu. 'I'll download it. Actually, I think Dad's got a complete set, probably on original video. You can talk me through it. Are you having something to eat? I think I saw a review of this place in a paper recently; food's supposed to be good.'

I flinched; I knew it wasn't Dominic's review because I was still tormenting myself by reading them, skimming for men-tions of New Betty. There weren't any so far, which kept me in a state of guilty hot mess. He hadn't been in touch. But every morning, despite myself, I woke up and checked my phone hoping there'd be a 'come back!' message; luckily, by lunch Helen had normally reminded me why that would be the Worst Thing Ever.

I pushed Dominic from my mind. I still hadn't lost enough weight to stage a triumphant 'Look at me now!' chance meeting. Or got my promotion. 'I'll have a burger,' I said.

'Good choice. Still haven't found a burger in London as good as—'

'—the ones I had in the States. We know.'

'Touché.' Joe grinned, then caught the barman's eye and gave our food order. As he was adding some 'fries' and 'rings', Helen shimmied up and clapped us both on the shoulders.

'Do you want to order some food?' I asked, although Helen looked so euphoric I wasn't sure she'd ever need to eat again.

'No, I'm fine, I was coming to say, it's your turn!' she said. 'I bagged you a spot on the list! What do you want to sing?'

'What? No, Helen—'

'Oh, go on.' She squeezed both our shoulders; clearly she was having the best time ever. 'Don't knock it till you've tried it! I can't believe I let you put me off karaoke for so long!'

'It's great if you can sing, or you have no fear of public humiliation.' The pub was busy, and my innards were shrivelling at the thought of people looking at me.

'No one's watching,' she lied. 'Go on. I'll do it with you?'

'Go on,' said Joe, but I couldn't, not even for Helen.

'Let some other people have a turn,' I suggested. 'We have kind of been dominating it a bit.'

We all looked over to Karaoke Corner, where a trio of mums were daring each other to have a go. People weren't exactly queuing up, but then the Welsh Westlife was a hard act to follow.

'Twenty minutes,' said Joe. 'We've just ordered some food, but after that?'

Helen looked disappointed. 'I'll hold you to that. Order me a cheeseburger, would you? I'm going to see if Wynn's okay.'

'Wynn's fine,' Joe murmured as her blonde head bobbed back through the crowd. 'Wynn looks like the happiest man in London.'

'I know. He's lucky. She's lucky. I never thought I'd see her so happy. Kind of gives us all hope, eh?'

Joe didn't reply, but looked down at the menu again. I wanted to say something encouraging, but I wasn't sure what.

Geraint, Morgan, and Ellis sauntered over with Suzie and Michelle, the two dental nurses, and we went back into the snug to eat. After a while. when a few people had got up to go to the bar, Joe leaned over the table, and said, 'So, how about it? Shall we go and surprise Helen with a song?'

'And it was going so well,' I said, trying to sound light. 'No.'

'Look, can I let you into a secret? People really aren't taking as much notice of you as you think,' said Joe. 'This is London. You could get up there in a PVC catsuit and no one would even stop drinking. And so what if they are looking at you? You'll never see them again. Whereas Helen's your best mate, and she will remember tonight for the rest of your lives. Do it for her.'

I stared at his irritating, earnest face and bit back a retort. In the back of my head, a little voice was telling me that he was right. Annoyingly.

'And even if you don't want to do it,' he went on, keeping his eyes fixed on mine and his voice low so no one else could hear, 'when you've got through the three mortifying minutes – ooh, all *three* of them – think how it'll feel to have surprised yourself. Don't you like surprising yourself?'

'No,' I said.

'Oh, come on. Everyone likes to surprise themselves now and again. Don't you ever wonder why I've got some of those shirts?' The ghost of a smile flickered around the corner of Joe's mouth.

Something stirred in the pit of my stomach. I wasn't sure if it was the way Joe was looking at me, or the atmosphere, or the nice supper, or what. But I felt a silvery flutter of excitement – maybe it was at the idea of surprising myself.

'Okay, then what if we all sang together?' He gestured over to Wynn's mates, who were, I had to admit, much more fun than I'd assumed dentists would be. 'We could do that other song from *Grease*, the one with the girls and the boys. I'm sure you'd be up for it, wouldn't you?' he added to them.

'Yeah!' they all said at once.

And from that point, I didn't really have a choice.

I think the rest of the pub found it amusing when twelve people of very different shapes and sizes crammed themselves onto the tiny stage and starting singing 'Summer Nights' around four microphones.

Wynn and Helen took the main parts, obviously, but we took

it in turns to do the others, and by the time it was my turn – the unimpressed Rizzo bit, obviously – I was actually enjoying it enough not to care if people were looking at us.

Okay, maybe *enjoying* is a bit strong. But the nervous adrenaline mixed with that giddy sense of team spirit (not something I normally went for, to be honest) made it far more fun than I'd imagined it could be, and when Joe insisted that he and I do a duet, I was too revved up to say no.

I recognized the oom-pah-pah introduction to 'I Got You Babe' immediately, and groaned, but Joe was already swinging along, a blissed-out expression on his face. I felt a bit sick. I didn't know how high this song went. My armpits tingled with sweat.

Then Joe turned to me and sang the opening lines in a solemn hippie voice, and I had to stop myself laughing out loud. He raised his eyebrows, prompting my line, and somehow the words came out, half-spoken, half-sung, but enough for him to carry on.

My singing was a bit uptight, but after a verse suddenly I got what Joe was doing. We weren't supposed to be amazing like Wynn and Helen, or even in tune like Wynn's mates. He was being clownish so no one would laugh at me. So *I* wouldn't be the one everyone was staring at.

Then he opened his eyes, faded blue like old jeans, with those long sandy lashes, and gave me a conspiratorial wink, and for a moment I forgot how irritating he was in real life.

We'd sung nearly the whole song, and Helen and Wynn were smiling up at me, their arms round each other, and I was beginning to think that actually Joe might have been right, when the whole evening stopped being fun, like a needle jerking across a record, when the second nasty surprise of the evening exploded on me.

Dominic walked into the restaurant, with a New Betty on his arm.

I saw his familiar bearded shape appear through the crowd while my mouth was still forming the climactic 'I got yoooooooooo,' and my brain froze. My knuckles went white on the microphone.

It took Joe a second to work out that something was wrong, because he was striking a pose, but when he realized my 'yooooooooooo' was going all wobbly, he looked where I was looking, swore under his breath, and without saying anything put his arm around me and started making me sway from side to side with him.

'I got you, babe!' Joe sang for both of us, and made the audience sing along, too. I heard Helen's voice, Wynn's voice, Geraint's. Not mine. My throat had gone dry. And then my voice came back.

I don't know how I managed to get the lyrics on the screen to come out of my mouth, because my brain was sending the words *He's here to review it with her, who is she, is that the Swedish one, is it a new one, what is he thinking?* across my brain like frantic subtitles. My stomach lurched, but somehow, with Joe's rigid arm moving me like a puppet, I got through to the final 'I got you'.

And then, without warning, Joe bundled me up in a huge bear hug and lifted me up off the floor and turned my whole body so there was absolutely no way I could see Dominic even if I'd wanted to.

Everyone clapped, Helen did her special wolf whistle, I could hear the Welsh boys bellowing; but most of all, I could hear my own heart thudding in my ears, pressed against Joe's warm neck.

Dominic's going to think we're a couple, I thought, and a funny sensation rippled through me.

When Joe put me down, again with my back to the crowd, he whispered, 'Did you surprise yourself?'

I didn't say anything. I couldn't say anything.

I had.

CHAPTER TWENTY-ONE

Everyone at the Bonneville loved Valentine's Day, and the week or so that led up to it. Everyone apart from me. And possibly Delphine, who claimed that making heart-shaped pastel macaroons was a sacrilegious waste of her Parisian pâtisserie training.

Dino loved it, because the hotel bar was packed full of flirty couples ordering recklessly from his selection of classic cocktails and then leaving for dinner, so the next round of flirty post-dinner couples could sweep in and take their places for the nightcap menu.

Helen loved it, because the restaurant was fully booked by the same flirty couples willing to splash out on a meal, and also married couples who wanted to go somewhere treaty and not talk to each other.

Laurence loved it, because sometimes the flirty couples or married couples who could afford babysitters booked rooms after the meal and stayed for our Valentine's breakfast.

I suppose I half-loved it, because there was always someone who wanted to get married on Valentine's Day; but I also half-hated it, because, on a personal level, it was always a crushing anticlimax. The adult equivalent of praying Santa will bring you a Sindy horse and carriage set, only to unwrap a *Blue Peter* annual and a tangerine. And then discovering all your friends not only got the Sindy horse, but the stables too.

This year, I'd managed my expectations. Right at the start of February, I told Gemma and Joe I was doing the petty cash to keep them well away from my office, then poured myself a coffee and made a list of reasons my singleton Valentine's Day would actually be better than those I'd spent with Dom.

First, I had a wedding booked in for noon (second time round, small guest list, afternoon tea, then everyone leaving by five, on account of childcare logistics). In the days before Valentine's Day, I'd be very busy finalizing arrangements, and then, on the day, ensuring that the bride's sister didn't try to steal her limelight by going into labour, as the bride feared might happen.

Second, I wouldn't have to waste time finding a witty but not overly romantic card to send to Dominic. It was impossible to find something that summed up our relationship in a non-passive-aggressive, non-overdoing-it way.

I chewed my pen morosely. I should have seen the writing on the wall when all my Valentine's Day cards to him featured *New Yorker* cartoons.

Third, I wouldn't have to drive myself to an ulcer watching the post and chasing every floral delivery in the hotel in case it was for me when it never was. Also, I wouldn't run the risk of last year's embarrassing moment when I snatched a bunch of flowers from Jean, head of housekeeping, thinking I saw Rosie on the card when it fact it just said *Roses*.

Fourth . . .

I got stuck at four. But three was enough. The main one was that I was already pretty miserable, and at least Dominic couldn't make me more so, by giving me a meat tenderizer and a bar of Dairy Milk. I hadn't seen him, or heard from him since the night in the pub, but I still hadn't quite broken the habit of checking my phone for texts of wee-small-hours-regret first thing in the morning. None, of course, had ever come.

One less welcome side effect of Helen's sudden conversion to easy relationships was that she'd developed an evangelical attitude to pairing the rest of us up. In the space of what felt like a few weeks, our secret coffee breaks on the fire escape had gone from mutual support sessions to remote speed-dating, especially now I'd met most of the contenders.

'You and Geraint were getting on like a house on fire the other night!' she told me, stopping just short of getting her phone out to show me his Facebook page. 'He's really funny. And he loves the theatre.'

I gave her a scornful look. 'Loving the theatre' was something people only ever claimed to do on internet dating profiles, and even then only in London, I'd noticed. You never met anyone in, say, Ross-on-Wye who claimed to love the theatre, and yet they probably went as often as the average Londoner.

'What's that got to do with the price of fish? I *don't* love the theatre,' I reminded her. 'I saw *The Lion King* once, and that was only because Sam got too many tickets from that agency and Laurence made us all go, so as not to waste them.'

'The theatre's a brilliant place to go for a date,' she said. 'It's somewhere new, you don't have to talk, you can discuss it after – it's good to get out of your comfort zone.'

'What is so wrong with having a comfort zone? The clue's in the name. Anyway, I'd rather take up hill-walking. And you know how I feel about that.'

'But Geraint's a great—'

'Helen, it's really sweet that you're trying to pair me up, but can you stop doing it, please?' I broke some heart-shaped shortbread in half and grimaced at the symbolism. 'I'm fine as I am. I don't need a boyfriend. I'm focusing on work.'

'No, but there are men out there who need the joy of your company.'

'At least keep your cheesy compliments credible.'

'What are you doing on Valentine's Day?' she asked.

'Why?' I could see the awkward shape of a double date looming into view.

'I was thinking Wynn and I could arrange another get-together at the pub and invite a load of single people, so it would be a nice low-pressure way of mingling. Not just romantically,' she added, 'it's always good to broaden your horizons. You know how hard it is to meet new people in our line of work – anyone you meet's already spoken for, by definition. And it's a numbers game. Mr Right could be a friend of a friend of a friend.'

'How do you know I don't already have a date?'

Obviously, I didn't. I just didn't like the assumption that I was at such a loose end that I'd be grateful for dinner with a man who liked the theatre, or a singles night in a pub.

'Do you?' Helen seemed surprised. Then she peered more curiously at me. 'Do you?'

'I might,' I said airily. 'I might be at that delicate stage of a relationship where I want to keep things very much under my hat.'

She looked at me a second longer, then reached for a second biscuit. 'You're not, though. You're going to be working.'

'How do you know that? Have you seen the rota?'

'I don't need to. You always are. Even more so now you're living over the shop and Laurence is paying you overtime to camp downstairs at the reception desk.'

I could hardly deny that, but Helen wouldn't give up, even when I collected the mugs and climbed off the fire escape back into the plusher environs of the fourth floor. She was still extolling the joys of 'singing with friends and letting yourself go!' when the lift pinged and let us out into the hotel foyer. We could have gone down into the *bowels of the earth* and she'd still have been going on about it.

'. . . need to recalibrate your expectations about men,' she finished. Finally.

'You're done?'

She nodded, and before she could start again, I said, 'Helen. Please don't make me spend Valentine's Day singing Tom Jones classics with the Clapham Leek-Fancying Association.'

'Sounds fun,' said Joe, wandering past with an armful of tablecloths. 'Open to anyone?'

'Joe!' Helen seized on him with a bold look at me. 'Have you got plans for Saturday night?'

'Er, Saturday night?'

'It's Valentine's Day,' I reminded him. 'Isn't it marked in your calendar?'

'Oh, *Valentine's Day*,' he said with an unusual amount of wariness.

Joe, like me, had had a lot of enforced dating attention from Helen over the past few weeks. In an unguarded moment over the kettle one evening, he'd confided that he was starting to understand how the pandas in London Zoo felt, but without the privacy of a cave to hide in.

'Because if you're not doing anything,' Helen went on, with the determination of a zookeeper armed with a bag of aphrodisiac-laced bamboo, 'my sister's flatmate Kate has got a spare ticket to *Hamlet* at the Barbican that she's trying to get rid of—'

'So Kate's very keen on the theatre, too?' I asked. 'I had no idea you moved in such thespian circles.'

Helen ignored me. '—and maybe you'd like to go? She's very nice.'

'I'm sure she's very nice,' said Joe. 'But even if I wasn't doing anything, which I am, *Hamlet*'s not my thing.'

'I know. It's not exactly a date-night play,' I pointed out. 'Family feuding, ill-advised second marriages, two of the unfunniest funny men in the whole of English literature. And the bride goes mad and drowns herself.'

Joe gave me a funny look. 'I am familiar with the play, thank you. Anyway, why would I want to go to the theatre when I can watch all that happen in the comfort of my own home?'

'Oh, you two,' said Helen with a playful swipe; then she

turned serious again. 'But have you got a date for Saturday, Joe? Because I was thinking of having a party . . .'

He gave me a quick sideways look, and I said, 'Don't look at me, I'm going out.' I don't know why I said that. I ignored the slight intake of breath from Helen. 'I booked the night off ages ago.'

Joe paused for a second, then said, 'Good for you. Me too.'

Helen looked intrigued. 'Who's the lucky girl?'

'Yes, who?' I realized I was staring, and coughed.

'Sorry, I thought I just had to book the night off with Dad, not with the romance committee,' said Joe. 'Now, if you'll excuse me, I've got to talk Flora out of releasing a hundred London pigeons as she and Milo say their vows.'

'And how are you going to do that?' I asked.

'I'm going to agree with her that it's a brilliant visual spectacle, then ask how many umbrellas she thinks she'll need to protect her fashionable guests from stray pigeon poo. It's very lucky,' he added. 'Pigeon poo.'

I nodded. 'You should probably feed them beforehand to ensure it's a very lucky wedding. Maybe you could suggest that? Then, as a back-up plan, obviously, suggest white rose petals scattered from the windows above the courtyard. Easier to clean away and they smell less of old chips.'

Joe pointed at me – an annoying habit months of effort hadn't yet broken (though he was now wearing a more normal, if brightly coloured, shirt instead of his surfer ones) – and grinned. 'What a team. I'll let you know what she says.'

Helen and I stared after him as he loped down the corridor

towards the lounge bar where most of his meetings with Flora took place. She was finding it particularly hard to decide on her signature cocktail for the exclusive after-party, and kept making appointments to try new ones.

'I wonder who Joe's got a date with?' Helen mused. 'Not . . . Flora?'

'I doubt it,' I said. If Joe was seeing someone, he'd been doing it very quietly. We didn't exactly live in each other's pockets upstairs, but I certainly hadn't noticed him making any calls or texting anyone. He hadn't mentioned seeing anyone. Should he have? We talked about quite a lot of other things.

I realized I did feel a bit . . . funny about it, actually.

Helen grabbed my arm as if she'd just thought of something. 'Oh! Rosie! Do you think it's someone from America? A girl?'

'Caroline says there wasn't a girl in America,' I said at once.

Although there had been that moment at New Year's when clearly something was going unsaid at the mention of that one perfect person . . .

The burning sensation in my chest increased. What if he had met someone? And he brought her back? The bedroom walls were, as I may have mentioned, very thin.

If even Joe found someone . . .

'Then it must be someone new.' Helen's eyes widened. 'Maybe someone he's met at a wedding? Or one of Flora's bridesmaids? There's a whole string of them turning up with Flora to try cocktails with him in the bar . . .'

'I really don't think so!' I said, and my voice was so high Helen gave me a strange look.

I didn't have time to think about stuff like this. I had weddings to sort out. Registrars with flu to check up on. Extra chairs to order. 'Sorry, I mean I don't know. And, no, before you ask, I'm not going to hang around the flat waiting to see who turns up.'

'Of course not,' said Helen. 'You'll be on your date, won't you?'

I didn't know what I could politely say to that, so I smiled tightly and marched off to deal with the reported broken headboard in the honeymoon suite.

Obviously, I didn't have a date for Valentine's night but there was no way I was going to let Joe know that, or Helen.

Instead, once my bride and groom had been safely waved off in their taxi to Heathrow, and their few remaining guests discreetly handed over to the clutches of Dino and his cocktail cart of delights, I'd planned a date night *with myself*. I'd be able to relax properly in the flat for the first time: Joe was going to be out on his mystery date, and Laurence was due for his regular monthly night out 'with his bridge friends' at their club in Mayfair.

Part of my New Year, New Me resolution included a full overhaul of my beauty regime. I'd splurged on various treatments brides had told me about over the years, including a hair treatment that the girls in the spa downstairs insisted would turn my hair into a gigantic mane to rival Flora's, and a facemask made with Swiss mud. While it was all working, I'd got a box set of a Danish crime drama I hadn't had time to see when everyone else in the country was watching it.

And then I planned to have an early night. I hadn't had one of those in *months*.

Joe was already in the bathroom when I let myself into the flat after handing over to the night manager. I could hear him splashing around, making his usual mess. I could also smell him applying liberal amounts of aftershave and deodorant, which only made me feel grumpier and weirder.

I didn't want to see him come out of the bathroom in his towel, all fresh and hopeful, while I was the Last Singleton in London, so I went straight to my room, got changed, and waited until the flat door slammed shut. Once the whistling had died away, I dashed into the bathroom, slapped on the face mask, combed the conditioner through my hair, got my DVD and a bottle of wine, and settled into the old leather sofa.

This was actually *nicer* than going on a date, I thought, flicking through the opening credits. I wasn't stuck in an overpriced restaurant, being forced to make conversation while trying not to make eye contact with all the other couples. I didn't have to eat any squid, or think of anything amusing to say about the menu.

Best of all, I could now watch the whole of *The Killing* without Dominic complaining about the errors in the translation even though he didn't speak Danish, or making sarky comments about the plot.

That alone, I thought, happily topping up my glass, was worth the price of the box set.

*

The problem with Danish crime dramas, it turned out, is that you really have to concentrate on the subtitles. After two episodes, I was so focused on the subtitles that I wasn't prepared for the unexpected movement in the very outer corner of my eye-line, exactly like a Danish murderer sneaking up on an unsuspecting victim.

'Aaaargh!' I squeaked involuntarily

My heart gave an almighty thud and I jumped off the sofa as if it were on fire, while the remaining wine in my glass arced up, and then down in a perfect curve over the carpet.

'What the hell is going on?' yelled a familiar voice. 'Urgh! I am covered in – Jesus, what have you done to your hair? And Jesus Christ! Your face! Are you all right?'

I stared, panting, at Joe. He was wearing his running clothes.

'I didn't hear you come in. I thought you were on a date,' I said accusingly.

'No, I said I was going out. I've been out, for a run, now I'm back. *You* were the one on a date.'

I could feel myself going red under the face mask. 'Did I say that?'

'Yes.' He glared at me. 'You did.'

'But . . . I heard you in the bathroom.'

'Well, we're not the only people who live here.'

I felt a bit ill. I'd just sat and listened to my boss, singing in the bath and applying deodorant.

There was an excruciating pause, and then a wry smile twitched the corner of Joe's mouth. 'I guess you've been out and come back too?'

'That's right.' I lifted my chin and a few flakes of dried mud peeled off. 'It was . . . a cocktail date. Finished early.'

'Fair enough,' said Joe. 'So, what are you watching?' He picked up the DVD box. 'Oh, is this that Scandinavian murdering thing everyone's been talking about? I've been meaning to watch that. Mind if I join you?'

I realized, belatedly, that having dismissed Helen's offers of *Hamlet*, we were, in fact, settling in to watch Danes killing each other, and wondered if Joe had noticed too.

He didn't show it if he did. 'Brilliant . . . Want me to ring the kitchen and see if they'll do some room service?'

'Why not? It's only their busiest night of the year.' Joe really had weird blind spots about the hotel business.

'Brilliant.' He rubbed his hands, then said, 'Don't take this personally, but do you think you could go and wash whatever you've got on your face off? I don't want to feel like I'm watching it *with* the murder victim.'

I narrowed my eyes at him. Comments like that were probably a good thing. They reminded me that, despite the more frequent flashes of sensitivity, he was still the same fundamentally irritating Joe underneath.

I'd got up and was heading towards the bathroom to rinse my hair and chip away the remains of the facemask when I heard him call, 'Rosie?'

'What?' I braced myself for some comment about my 'skin condition'.

Joe gazed at me from where he was standing beside the wall-mounted phone. He looked embarrassed and conspiratorial at the same time. 'We won't tell Helen, will we? About the . . . dates?'

I paused. 'Well, technically . . .' I stopped.

'What?'

Should I say it? I heard my own voice in the flat. 'Technically, we are on a date. Of sorts. I just can't tell her who with. And neither can you.'

There was a pause; then a slow smile broke over Joe's face.

'Secret date,' he said, and pointed at me. 'I like your thinking.'

My stomach did an unexpected loop, but then I was *very* hungry.

Kevin sent up a pizza with parma ham, mozzarella and extra sarcasm half an hour later, and Joe and I polished off a bottle of wine and four episodes of *The Killing*. He was a much better co-watcher than Dominic.

'Sorry you're having such a crap Valentine's Day,' he said, when the fourth episode ended. 'Pizza and DVDs with your annoying intern.'

'Oh, I don't know.' The wine and the pizza had made me mellow. 'It's better than last year. Anglo-Afghan fusion in Old Street, and an argument with the chef about whether calling cocktails after weaponry was in bad taste. We left in a taxi, but I remember feeling relieved at the time that it wasn't a police car.'

'Ha.' I liked Joe's laugh. It was more of a snort than a giggle.

'How does this rate on your Valentine's Day scale?' I asked.

'Hmm. This time last year I was drinking mimosas and playing pool with the most—' He stopped, and looked at his empty glass. Then he filled it up again.

My chest felt hollow. I hadn't expected him to say that. I'd expected him to say something about parachuting naked across the Grand Canyon for the fun of it. So there had been a girl. Of *course* there had.

'Go on,' I said. 'With the most . . .?'

Joe stared at his wineglass.

'I won't tell Helen,' I added. 'I'm pretty good at keeping secrets. You have to be round here. Who were you playing pool with?'

Joe hesitated a few seconds, then said, 'With the most beautiful girl I've ever met. We met at a party on the beach. It sounds cheesy, but I remember thinking she was just like a mermaid. She had the most amazing hair . . .' Joe mimed long, wavy hair, a lost expression on his face. 'I remember thinking it was just like the bonfire, red in some lights but blonde and darker as well. Damp where she'd been swimming in the sea. Everyone out there's tanned, but she was pale, with freckles on her arms. She was the only girl at the party who wasn't wearing a tiny bikini, but no one was looking at them, just at her, in her long white dress . . .'

Something tugged inside me – I wasn't sure what it was. Jealousy? It was the way he was talking about her. As if he could see her right now, in here, with us. Not jealousy of her and Joe, just of the impression she'd made on him. I longed for someone to talk about me like that.

'And did you talk to her?' I half-joked.

'Of course I talked to her.' Joe was miles away, on the beach. 'She was funny. And she had the most incredible eyes. Green eyes.'

'And what happened?'

'She told me she'd never been surfing, so I offered to teach her. We went surfing, we went hiking, we did everything together.'

'And then?'

There was a longer pause. 'And then she finished with me.'

'Why?'

He shrugged. 'I don't know. It was all going really well, we were spending loads of time together, every day, and then suddenly – *prttph.*' He made a flat gesture. 'I'd been planning a trip, we were going to go surfing, and she just . . . said she couldn't do it. Never saw her again. Blocked my calls, everything. No idea why.'

I wanted to ask her name, but Joe looked so hurt that I didn't feel I could.

'I'm sorry,' I said instead. 'But it sounds incredible. Better to have loved like that for however long it lasted than never to have experienced it at all.'

He glanced over. 'Thanks.'

'Does it help to say next time it'll be easier?'

'No,' he said, shortly. 'You don't get over something like that.'

'Oh, you do.'

He tipped his head to one side and regarded me cynically. 'Don't take this the wrong way, Rosie, but the fact that it only took you a few weeks of extreme to-do listing to get over Dominic suggests that he didn't have quite the same impact. This was life-changing.'

'Dominic isn't the only person who's broken my heart.' I lifted my chin.

Joe sat up straighter.

'I've been jilted,' I said. The wine was making me honest, and I didn't like the implication that I hadn't known Real Love. 'Right at the altar. In front of nearly everyone I knew, and I got over that. So I reckon you can get over a beach romance.'

Joe had started to argue back as he topped up my glass but at the word *jilted* his hand wobbled, and he turned back to look at me in surprise.

'What? You were jilted? How? Who? I never knew that. Were my mum and dad there?'

'Of course they were there. Everyone was there. That's generally how weddings operate. Vows in front of everyone you know.'

Joe handed my glass back to me with a different expression on his face. He looked curious but sympathetic. 'Want to tell me what happened?'

I shrugged. 'The usual. College boyfriend. Proposed at twenty-four. Local church. Fiancé decided at the last minute that he couldn't go through with it.'

'And?'

'And my dad had to stand up and tell everyone it was off, and that they should go to the reception and eat all the food because it was paid for.' I paused. 'When we got to the reception, I'm afraid I told everyone to hit the bar hard, because Ant was paying for that, and they'd got his credit card details.'

'Oh.'

I managed a wonky smile. 'I've never seen my mum that wrecked before. She kept saying, "I'm doing this for you, darling", and throwing back another cherry brandy. We had to drag her off the dance floor in the end.'

'There was a *disco*? At your non-wedding?'

'Why not? The DJ had already set up his gear. Did it for nothing in the end, as a goodwill gesture, because everyone was roaring drunk and up for a good time.'

Joe looked impressed. 'Good for you.'

'Well, what else was I going to do?' I fell silent, remembering. When it hit me the next day, the blankness was like nothing I'd ever felt before. I couldn't breathe. Mum nearly called an ambulance.' I pressed my lips together. 'Every day it hurt a tiny bit less until now . . . now I just think, thank God I didn't marry a man who didn't want to marry me. Because that'd be worse.'

I was staring at the fireplace but I wasn't seeing the four-bar electric fire. I was seeing Anthony. His dark hair, his wire-rimmed glasses, his familiar tall shape in a crowd. Every wedding I'd arranged had pushed the memory, and him, a bit further away. I realized with a shock that I couldn't remember exactly what colour his eyes were. I knew they were blue. Ish. Bluish-grey, but I couldn't picture them. Not like Joe could obviously still see this woman's eyes.

I was going to ask him her name when he suddenly reached over and gave my hand a quick squeeze.

'Sorry if I sounded flippant just then. I didn't know. It's amazing that you've got over that.'

'What else could I do?' I turned to look at him so he could see how true that was. 'Everyone knew. And they all knew I planned weddings for work, too. Ho-ho.'

'So you didn't become a wedding planner to work through your issues?'

'I was, and still am, an events manager,' I pointed out. 'So enough with the armchair psychology, thanks. The point is, you get over it. You move on. You're a slightly different person, but that's fine.'

Joe sighed. 'I think you only get to meet one person who affects you like that. One big wham in the heart.'

'But, Joe—' I started, feeling oddly affronted.

He looked me straight in the eye. 'What?'

God, he was handsome. Especially with this new vulnerability in his blue eyes. Really blue, with tiny golden flecks around the iris, and those long lashes that . . .

We both heard the front door at the same time, and I jumped so hard I nearly spilled my wine.

Laurence strolled in, looking very pleased with himself indeed. When he saw me and Joe on the sofa, his expression immediately changed to that of a guilty schoolboy.

'I thought you two were going out,' he said. 'Separately, of course . . .'

'Of course,' I said. 'And now we're back.'

'What time do you call this?' Joe asked, tapping his watch.

'Bit early for the disreputable bridge sharks to throw you out, isn't it? If, of course, that's where you were? Eh?'

I thought Laurence looked shady – and much as I'd have liked to continue the conversation with Joe, that seemed like a good cue for me to excuse myself.

'I'm off to bed,' I announced. 'Good night, one and all.'

No one, but no one, needs to hear the post-mortem of their boss's Valentine's Day.

CHAPTER TWENTY-TWO

'So, what do you think?' I asked. 'Move the bank of seating to position A, under the cherry tree, like *this*, or B, nearer to the fountain? Like *that*?'

'A,' said Joe. 'If you put older guests too near a water feature, it might have unfortunate consequences. Weak bladders and all that.'

I hadn't even considered that. Typical that it was Joe's first thought. 'Hmm. You don't think there's a risk of petals falling on people, or birds in the trees . . . you know?'

'I know what I'd rather have, given the choice between some petals in my hair and Auntie Doris having to go *now*.' He raised his eyebrows.

'Thanks for that image,' I said, and moved the seating back under the tree.

I had to squeeze an extra forty guests into Marianne Trelawnay's wedding at the end of the month, thanks to almost her entire social circle assuming their invite meant 'plus one' and her being too wet to tell them otherwise. I'd made a model of the courtyard out of an old shoebox to try to visualize it better, something Joe had laughed at until he realized I was deadly serious.

'And I don't know what we're going to do about the meal,' I said, staring at my second model, this time of the restaurant. 'I can't put forty people on their own in the private room. It'll look like she's making a point about their eating habits.'

He raised his eyebrows. 'Or you could have a cup of tea, call Marianne, and tell her that she might have to do her reception as a buffet. She won't mind. People mingle more when they're standing up. Unclench, Rosie.'

'Unclench? What does that even *mean*?' I asked irritably.

'It means, stop with the control freakery. Do you want me to call Marianne?'

Since he'd talked Flora down from twenty-six bridesmaids to a more manageable eighteen, Joe seemed to think his negotiating skills were on a par with the UN.

'It's all under control. Isn't it about time you went to meet Jean for your bed-making master class?' I enquired. 'As I remember, your hospital corners could do with some one-on-one instruction.'

'Eleven o'clock, she said.' Joe checked his watch. 'I've got another ten minutes. Anything else you'd like some help with? Or should I just leave you here to chillax?'

I glared at him. He knew I was busy. He only said *chillax* because he knew I hated the word almost as much as I hated *unclench*.

There was a brief knock on the door, and Gemma appeared round it.

'Ah, just in time!' I said. 'You can have the casting vote. Would you rather sit under a tree or next to a fountain?'

'Or would you rather stand, with a glass of champagne to take your mind off your shoes?' Joe added.

'Ignore option C,' I said.

But Gemma didn't come steaming into my office as usual, even though there was a glass cake stand of Delphine's smallest cupcakes on the table, ready for Sadie Hunter's cake testing later on. Instead, she hovered by the door, and seemed to be hopping from foot to foot.

I frowned. 'Gemma, come in, there's a draught.'

'And we need to know urgently about these seats,' added Joe. 'Or else Rosie's going to call Marianne and make her sack some guests.'

Gemma twisted her face up, then blurted out, 'Something's happened that I think you should know about but I don't really want to be the one to tell you, but I don't want you to find out from anyone else so I guess I've got to tell you but I *really* don't want to.'

'Here we go,' said Joe. 'Someone's asked to have "Angels" by Robbie Williams as their first dance. Rosie's going to have a meltdown, because it's not on her approved list, and then stage an intervention.'

I gave him a withering look.

'Oh you two, you *love* a good panic,' he said. 'I've noticed. No wedding's complete for Rosie McDonald unless something goes a bit wrong so you can swoop in and make it all perfect.'

'Do I look as if I'm panicking? The silver lining of my constant clenching is—'

'Buttocks you could bounce a pound coin off?'

'No, it's that I am across all problems before they happen. And I'm very calm about it.' I turned back to Gemma.

To be honest, I wasn't that calm. I just wanted to prove a point to Joe. I was already mentally rifling through my messy cupboard of secret panics.

Buttocks you could bounce a pound coin off? I felt a delayed-reaction blush spread across my face.

'Rosie, it's . . .' Gemma glanced at Joe. 'It's about Flora.'

Joe leaned back in his chair, hands folded behind his head. 'Oh, well, then it's fine. I know what it's about – which social media platform to launch the wedding countdown on. I've dealt with that. Hashtag NoSweat. Hashtag WellDoneJoe.'

Gemma didn't reply. Instead, she looked slowly between both of us. 'You haven't seen the papers yet?'

Laurence was the only member of the staff who had the luxury of perusing a fresh copy of the *Daily Mail* with his morning coffee, while the rest of us sprinted round like headless chickens running his hotel. 'Of course not. I haven't had time.'

Gemma slowly passed me Laurence's copy of the paper.

'"*House Prices to Rise in Central London,*"' I read off the main headline. '"*Duchess Kate's Bikini Body*" – do I have to read this entire rag? I've got things to do.'

'Let me see about Duchess Kate's bikini body?' said Joe, but before he could grab the paper, Gemma took it back and began flicking through the pages. She didn't have to go far before she folded the paper and handed it back.

My eye travelled down the page – it was the gossip column

bit in the middle, the part with all the non-stories about people being spotted in a new (free) car, or 'sharing a joke' with someone (represented by the same agent) at a party thrown by a PR company.

'I can't see what – oh, it's Flora.'

A familiar dazed smile beamed up at me, surrounded by a very familiar mane of tousled blonde hair. It was Flora, in a skinny white trouser suit and no shirt, clutching a glass of champagne in one hand and the fiancé in the other. Milo was wearing a bright blue suit, thankfully with a shirt, and a very smug grin. Even smugger than normal.

'Oh, is this about that new contract she's got with M&S?' I said. 'I heard about that. That's a really nice suit she's wearing, very Bianca Jagger—'

'Er, no,' said Gemma. 'Read the article?'

'I know, I saw the headline. "*Wedding Bells for Model Bride Flora*" . . .' I read. 'I told her to mention her wedding whenever she could. "*Lingerie model Flora has been engaged to millionaire art dealer Milo McKnight for nine months,*" yadda yadda, "*Plans for a glittering celebration in a top London hotel,*" very good, well done, Flora! Although you could have got our name in. Yadda yadda . . .' My eye continued skimming, then stopped.

Oh.

'Yadda?' suggested Joe.

You could have heard a pin drop in the office. I could actually hear Gemma trying not to breathe too loudly.

I carried on reading, on autopilot. '"*So friends and relatives were taken by surprise when the leggy beauty announced that . . . she and Milo had tied the knot in Manhattan's exclusive Tribeca Rooftop. . . ."'*

I closed my eyes, but when I opened them, the paper was still there, and when I looked closely, so was Flora's enormous wedding ring.

Black spots appeared in front of my eyes and I felt faint. Flora had got married. All our plans, all my spreadsheets . . . The Bonneville's wedding of the year wasn't going to happen. Nope. I couldn't process it. It was too big.

I probed the problem. My totals, the cancellations, the abrupt loss of all the useful publicity tumbling in our direction . . .

Yes, there it was. It hit me all at once.

Oh, my God, Flora has cancelled her wedding.

I made a choking noise and Gemma flinched.

'Bloody hell!' I roared. 'I knew Flora would be a handful from that first meeting, but I never thought she'd do this. I thought she'd just wear the wrong dress, or sack her bridesmaids and get her dog to walk her down the aisle, or something bloody *kooky* but this . . .'

'Calm down, Rosie,' said Gemma automatically, then looked as if she regretted it.

I spun round to face her. 'How can I calm down? This is my entire year's work going down the drain here.'

'*Your* work? What about *my* work?' Joe swung his feet off the desk. That was how cross he was. 'I was the one who had to explain that we couldn't put an ice rink in the ballroom, or get Nelson Mandela to conduct the ceremony because he was dead.'

I stared at Joe, surprised by the venom in his voice. I'd

expected the 'calm down' thing from him, too, but instead, I have to admit it gave me a flicker of pleasure to see the corner of his mouth twitching.

Good. *Good*. Now he knew how I felt most of the time.

'Does this mean they're not getting married here then?' Gemma asked anxiously. 'Didn't we sign contracts?'

'We did sign contracts, but all that means is that we keep the deposit,' I said clearly – not that I was trying to see what it would take to make Joe crack. Not at all. 'It's four months in advance, so she's not liable for much. We can't make them get married here.'

'But they could have a, what do you call it? A celebration of the vows here, for their London friends?'

Gemma really was feeding me the lines beautifully. 'I don't think so,' I said, enjoying the sound of Joe doing 'woman in labour' breaths through his nose in a yoga-ish way some guru had probably taught him on a beach. 'I'm sure Flora will want to celebrate with her friends much sooner than that.'

'Oh no.' Her eyes were perfectly round. 'Are we going to lose loads of money?'

'Yup. She had two whole floors of the hotel booked. And four parties.'

'Two of them fancy dress,' moaned Joe, almost inaudibly. 'And a stag night.'

'But the thing is, Gem,' I went on sadomasochistically, 'it's not just about the money, it's about the press coverage. And the hours and hours of planning and hassle, and the fact that we now have a vacancy on *the* prime wedding date that I could have sold about a hundred times over – but which no one in their right mind is going to take because it's far too short notice to plan an expensive wedding *now*.'

We looked at Joe. He was struggling manfully with himself, his broad forehead creased with the effort of trying to think positive and be forgiving and stay in the moment and all the other guff he liked to spout to me when I really didn't need to be told to keep calm.

Gemma opened her mouth to speak, but I raised a silent finger.

After about thirty seconds, he couldn't stand it any longer.

'Argh!' Joe buried his head in his hands. 'All the time I was sourcing bloody snowdrops to bloom in bloody June at the exact moment she walked into the reception room, she was getting hitched on a New York bloody – bloody *rooftop*. In a horrible suit with no bra!'

The fashion thing surprised me. I didn't know he cared about things like that. I pushed the glass bonbon jar on my desk towards him. 'The big ones are mint imperials, and the little ones are ibuprofen.'

'Hit me up.' Joe stretched out a hand, and I put two of each into it.

'But it's not that bad, listen, she does mention us,' Gemma said, reading from the paper. "'*I've loved planning my wedding at a top London hotel, but Milo said he couldn't stand another four months of talking about table plans with my mum, so he swept me off my feet while we were here in New York!*" said Flora, the new face of Queen & Country lingerie.'

Gemma looked up. 'Oooh, no. Her mum's not going to like that.'

'That's her new son-in-law's problem,' I said, just as my phone started ringing. 'We don't do aftercare. Although I'm starting to think we should. Let me get this.'

I reached into my bag for my phone: **Julia Thornbury mobile**. Brilliant. I wondered if she'd called Laurence first and he'd passed her on to me.

'It's Julia,' I groaned. 'I wonder if she's been waiting until this morning to tell me the news?'

'Nope.' Joe leaned over and dropped the call for me. 'If I know Flora, Julia's just opened the paper herself. In which case it might be wise to let her leave a message, and get back to her when we've all had a chance to work out what we think.'

I raised an eyebrow. He sounded much more businesslike and determined than normal. Quite masterful, in fact. 'What? Not call her back at once and give her some peace and love?'

'No,' said Joe flatly. 'Not on this occasion.'

I met his gaze. I wondered if I should feel thrilled or guilty that I'd finally beaten Joe down to my way of thinking.

'Ten minutes,' he said, reading my face. 'And then I'll give her some peace and love, if you can't face it.'

'So what are we going to do?' asked Gemma.

'There's not a lot we can do. We can't force Flora to get married here,' I said again. I got up and walked over to my Bridelizer, and yanked the photograph of Flora off the 20 June spot. She was the only one of my brides to have a professional picture, and it had encroached on poor Jessie Callum (May) and

Violet Hartley (July). They both instantly looked a lot prettier without Flora's million-dollar face next to them.

'There you go,' I said, passing it to Joe. 'You can draw a moustache on it.'

He started to say he didn't want to, then changed his mind and got a black marker out of my pen-holder with unseemly relish.

I turned back to the chart and sighed. Flora's gap, marked with a trace of Blu-tack, seemed enormous. I was never going to fill that space now. Anyone planning to get married on 20 June would have booked it months and months ago. Last year I'd had loads of enquiries for June, all with a hopeful 'I expect you're already full' note, and I'd had to turn them down. No one had asked about June since September.

'Oh . . .' I said.

It still hadn't fully sunk in. It probably wouldn't for a few hours. Like when you stub your toe and your brain generously gives you ten seconds' thinking time to consider exactly how hideous the pain's going to be when it arrives.

Maybe it was the novelty of Joe's reaction that had distracted me, I thought. It was actually quite cheering to see him pissed off. It showed he cared about the hotel. I felt a gratifying warmth inside.

We all sat in silence for about two minutes; then Gemma gasped.

'Oh, wait! I've had a genius idea!' she exclaimed, clapping her hands together like a small child. 'We could make it a prize! On the radio! We can offer the booking to someone who's about to propose to their boyfriend – or girlfriend! – as long as they get married on that date in June!' Her eyes shone. 'It'd be brilliant publicity for the hotel! And it would be so romantic.'

I thought about it. 'That's actually not a bad idea . . .'

'It'd make it pretty obvious we've had a cancellation.' Joe looked up from his furious defacing of Flora's photo.

'People call off weddings,' Gemma pointed out. 'Everyone knows some flaky friend who's bailed out at the last minute. I mean, like Stephanie Miller! Remember? The bride Joe talked to, and she called it off? It happens. It's not the *hotel's* fault people get cold feet.'

I looked at my feet. Joe looked uncomfortable.

I swallowed and said, as if I'd never experienced a jilting myself, 'Stephanie and Richard have postponed. I'm sure that at some point they'll—'

'Yeah, postponed.' Gemma rolled her eyes. 'Saved them both a bullet there. I'm amazed it hasn't happened to us before now. But really, the night *before*? Surely you know if you don't want to marry someone? It's not like it suddenly dawns on you . . .'

Ouch. This time I flinched, and though I pretended to check something in my day planner, I caught Joe looking at me. When our eyes met, he glanced away, but not before I'd seen some sympathy in his eyes.

My cheeks burned. There was a very good reason I hadn't confided my secret in many people.

'I'll put that on the strategy list, Gemma,' I said briskly. 'Good thinking. If you have any more brainwaves, let me know.'

'Maybe she could have a party here?' Gemma was on a roll now. 'Ooh. What about a baby shower? Maybe she got married quickly because she's up the duff.'

I held up the newspaper: Flora beamed out at us in her skinny white jacket. 'If that oven has a bun in it, it's a petit four.'

'That's enough,' said Joe, pushing himself off his seat. 'You two have finally driven me to a master class in bed-making. It's that bad.'

'If you have any brilliant ideas while you're doing it, let me know,' I said as he left.

'Wow,' said Gemma thoughtfully when he'd gone. 'Joe's taken that personally.'

I gave her a close look. 'How do you work that out?'

She nodded at the cake stand, temptingly placed between my desk and the door. It held the samples for Sadie Hunter's afternoon tea cake tasting; and it remained full, and untouched. 'He didn't try to nick a cake on his way out.'

She was right.

In the end I was on the phone to Julia Thornbury for over an hour, and said about twenty words in total, in the ninety seconds when she wasn't screeching, wailing, or telling me what Flora's father intended to do to Milo McBloodyKnight when he got hold of him.

(I heard a voice that sounded a lot like unwilling chief bridesmaid/younger sister Abigail's shout, 'Shake him by the hand and wish him luck' at that point.)

As Joe had guessed, Julia had found out about the same time

we had, having been away with friends all weekend, and she wasn't best pleased, to put it mildly.

'Of course I blame Flora,' she assured me. 'You've been nothing but efficiency itself throughout and I'm extremely sorry for the inconvenience she's put you to. And Joe,' she added, with a sigh. 'Please apologize to dear Laurence for me. He's been so helpful.'

'I'm sure he'll be as disappointed as we are. Maybe . . .' I had a belated flash of efficiency. 'Maybe he could take you out for lunch to see if there isn't something we can do for Flora – you might throw her a little party perhaps?'

'Oh, what a sweet idea. Maybe you could put me through to his PA so we can arrange a time?'

Fine, I thought, when I finally hung up. At least I could tell Caroline I'd got Laurence a lunch date out of all this.

I spent the rest of the day on the phone to the suppliers and – because I hated to see a job done badly – making a list of people who'd already saved the date for Flora, so she could get onto the stationers and commission a special 'oops, we've already done it' card. At least that might get me a sympathy mention in the gossip columns.

By five o'clock, I was thoroughly depressed, and called it a day.

Laurence had gone out for dinner with his osteopath, possibly in preparation for his lunch with Julia Thornbury, and Joe hadn't been released from the iron grip of housekeeping, so at least I had the flat to myself when I let myself in. It was funny, but I barely noticed the décor now; it was soothing, like going back home to your mum's house. It even *smelled* of someone's mum's house, I thought: biscuits and carpets and comforting blankets. No wonder it had resisted Ellie's attempts to redecorate.

I changed out of my work suit, then opened the French door in the kitchen that led onto the balcony, to look out over the roofs of Piccadilly. The London skyline never failed to cheer me up, and the view from Laurence's kitchen was special, especially after dark, when the panorama lit up like a movie-set version of London town.

It only just qualified as a balcony, being half fire-escape, and littered with the skeletons of Christmas trees 'left to recycle naturally' according to Laurence, but there was a solid rail to lean on and it felt like being on the prow of a ship, high above the city. I loved this secret side of the hotel: the plain windows dotting the rear walls, lit up yellow or darkened depending on whether the curtains were drawn, as well as the various roofs and flat spaces of the surrounding buildings. The streets were pure Regency elegance from the ground level, yet plain and unmade-up from here, angular and darkened like the underside of a car, all function and purpose.

I watched the red tail-lights move in stops and starts down the Mall, and reminded myself that Flora's cancellation was just a hitch. That I could get round it. That something would turn up. But I still felt flat.

I was disappointed for Joe, too. He'd put in so much work, not just office hours but in the long personal conversations he'd had with Flora, trying to unravel what she actually wanted. I felt bad for being pleased at seeing him lose his cool. Lately I'd found myself trying to copy his approach, and annoyingly, sometimes it had helped.

I heard the door open inside, then the radio go on. I hoped Joe would leave me to my thoughts for a bit, but after a few minutes the balcony door opened, and then I felt something warm pressing into my upper arm.

Not just warm. Hot. Ow. Boiling hot, in fact.

I jumped and rubbed the burning sensation. It was a mug of . . . something.

'Cocoa,' said Joe. 'It is cocoa you drink, isn't it? Something from the nineteenth century, anyway.'

It didn't smell like any cocoa I'd ever made. I didn't know what Joe had poured boiling water onto, but it seemed chocolatey, and I took it, more to warm my hands than anything else.

He joined me, leaning over the railing. 'We used to love sneaking out here as kids. Mum banned us when Alec tried to Spiderman down the side one summer. Got as far as the rooms below before he ran out of sheets.'

'How high up was that? God. That must have given your parents a shock.'

'Not as much as it shocked the guests in the room below.'

I laughed, and gazed out at the city. 'I love it up here,' I said. 'All those windows. You get a real picture of just how many different lives there are going on under this one roof. Every room with a different guest, a different reason to be here, a different life . . .'

'Little did the guests know,' he said in a movie trailer voice, 'that the deputy duty manager was watching their every move . . .'

'I'm not,' I said. 'I'm just weighing up how long we could stow Flora's body out here before anyone noticed.'

Joe laughed. 'I got a text this morning – of her wedding ring, would you believe? She says she'll pop in to show you herself when she's next in town. I honestly don't think she gets how much chaos she's caused.'

'I'm sorry. You worked really hard. It's not fair. But it happens.'

Joe leaned his chin on the rail. 'I guess so. It's probably karma, getting me back for lecturing you about letting clients be romantic and follow their hearts, not their heads.'

'That's a very generous way of looking at it.'

'Something will turn up,' he said, turning his head to look at me. 'You've got to put your faith in the universe.'

'Ha! I don't think so. That's the one thing I don't put any faith in.' I sipped suspiciously at the cocoa. It had a funny tang of curry powder. 'In my experience, the universe specializes in doing exactly what you don't need, at the exact moment when you haven't time to deal with it.'

'So it's all down to you?'

'It's all down to me.'

'Maybe you should leave a bit more space for the universe.'

Before I could even think of a reply sarcastic enough, Joe reached out and pointed to something moving over the skyline.

'Look! Quick, there!'

'Where?'

He waved his finger. 'Shooting star. Quick, wish on that.'

'That's not a shooting star,' I scoffed. 'That's an *air ambulance*.'

'No, it's a shooting star,' Joe insisted. 'Make a wish.'

I started to tell him what a ridiculous idea that was – especially when the shooting star had a red flashing light – but something in Joe's expression stopped me. Mingled with the earnestness I'd come to tolerate over the past few months was a flash of self-deprecation, as if he was only acting like this because he thought I expected it.

'Don't make me say universe again,' he warned. 'Humour me here. Like I humour you about folding loo paper into shapes.'

I felt a funny twist in my stomach, and looked quickly up at the sky. The 'shooting star' was heading for St Mary's Hospital in Paddington, but who was I to argue?

'Wish outrageously,' said Joe. 'Don't hold back. Be greedy and ambitious, let your subconscious guide you, and—'

'Okay, okay,' I said. 'I'm going along with your ridiculous shooting-star thing, but I'm still British.'

I closed my eyes and wished for another high-profile, big-budget wedding to fill that prime June slot Flora had just abandoned. I wished for the hotel to be filled with happy laughter and well-dressed guests, the smells of perfume and wedding cake and rose-petal confetti in the foyer. I wished for cute flower-girl bridesmaids in ballet shoes, Rolls-Royces pulling up outside, the clink of glasses and the click of cameras, the hotel gleaming and sparkling, a buzzing after-party in the hotel bar, and, at the centre of it all, I pictured myself, keeping everything under calm control, ticking off every secret list.

Me and Joe.

I frowned. The image in my mind's eye was of me and Joe. I tried to move him offstage, but he wouldn't. He was there next to me, smiling at the guests, telling me to calm down and relax and all the other annoying things he came out with, just when I really didn't want to relax. But now I did feel relaxed. A comforting, positive feeling swept over me, as if things *would* be all right. Something *would* come along.

The Joe in my mind's eye slipped his arm around my waist and smiled at me, and I felt my mouth smiling back. My real mouth, in real life.

I snapped my eyes open in surprise.

The real Joe was an arm's length away, leaning next to me on the balcony, and he was watching my face. And the feeling was still there. The gauzy, cashmere-blanket feeling of comfort, wrapping me up lightly in its cosy embrace.

My cheeks burned; I wondered if he'd somehow been able to see what had just gone across my mind. I hadn't thought it on purpose. It was just like one of those random dreams, when you find yourself doing unspeakable things to your optician and then feel odd when you polish your glasses for reasons you don't want to think about.

'Did you wish for something nice?' Joe asked, and his voice sounded different.

I shivered, and it was nothing to do with the February air out on the balcony. 'Er, yes.'

He smiled slowly, and the edges of his eyes crinkled. 'I hope you didn't just run a series of budget proposals past that shooting star,' he said with a nod towards the sky.

I didn't know what to say. A fluttering had started in the pit of my stomach.

'Did *you* wish for something?' I asked instead. 'On the shooting ambulance?'

He looked at me, and his expression became slightly more solemn. The fluttering spread up towards my chest, making all the little hairs on the backs of my arms stand up.

'Yes,' he said. 'I did.'

We looked at each other, and I could feel the breath stop in my throat.

'Joe? Joe! Joe!' yelled a voice inside the flat.

It was Laurence. I recognized that note of panic.

'It's your dad,' I said.

'I know,' said Joe, without taking his eyes off me.

'He sounds a bit panicky.'

'I probably left the fridge open.' Joe bit his lip, as if he was trying to work out how to say something, and I shivered again at his lovely square white teeth and the way they pulled at the soft pillow of his lower lip. 'Rosie,' he began.

'What are you two doing out here?' Laurence appeared at the balcony windows. 'The fridge was wide open! I've got temperature-sensitive vitamins in there.'

'That wasn't what I wished for, by the way,' said Joe, still looking into my eyes.

Every hair on my skin tingled. He was even more handsome

in the half-light of London. And he was still in love with someone else. Something tore inside me, with regret and longing. Fate was showing me a man who knew how to fall in love with a woman – but I wasn't supposed to fall in love with him myself.

'I know,' I said, and went back in.

CHAPTER TWENTY-THREE

Obviously, I believed in the wish-granting potential of the universe about as much as I believed in the proposal-predicting power of a randomly chucked bouquet and the divorce-preventing properties of a blue garter and a sixpence in the shoe.

So I was really not expecting the call I got from Charlie Nevin, wedding photographer, on Friday morning.

I was actually making a to-do list for a new bride I'd signed up for a winter wedding in December, and had just reached 'Photographers: a selection' when Nevin's own face came up on my phone.

'Nevin!' I said with delight. 'Just the man.'

'Good,' he said. 'I think?'

Nevin was my favourite of the wedding photographers we used, and the one I recommended most often. He shared my belief in planning, to the point where he had fully thought-out strategies for thunderstorms, power cuts, light rain, heavy snow, and various key personnel not turning up. Part of his contract was that he be allowed to attend my early meetings to 'run through' (i.e. vet) the bride's requirements; he had the sort of polite but remorseless focus that cut through the dithering of more indecisive couples. If he was in the area and at a loose end, I sometimes asked him to drop in anyway, just to sit in meetings and firm up bridal decisions more quickly.

'I don't suppose you'd like to come in and have a chat with a delightful couple planning a December wedding, would you?' I asked.

'It would be my pleasure.' Nevin also had the mother-of-the-bride-friendly trait of sounding as if he'd wandered off the set of *Pride and Prejudice*. 'But I was calling because I've got a favour to ask of you.'

'If it's another wedding reshoot, that's a yes from me. We love the overtime and the chance to dress up here.'

'Ha! But no. This is rather cheeky,' he went on, 'but it's for a special client – long story short, she was booked into another hotel – full package, honeymoon there, full ceremony, no expense spared – but there's been some kind of mix-up, complete freak-out, and now she and her chap need to find somewhere else, asap. I don't suppose you've got any dates free in June, have you?'

'In June?' The busiest wedding month of the year? I started to say, 'You'll be lucky,' but then I realized I did. I had a plum date free. *The* date in June, in fact.

My heart beat loudly.

'They were booked in for June the twentieth' he went on, sounding even more hopeful. 'Save-the-dates have gone out, the dress and flowers are arranged, most things are in motion, so if there is any way on earth you happen to have that date free . . .'

'June the twelfth?'

'I think they'd be prepared to, um, make it worth your while if there was some magic you could perform. They're not exactly skimping on the budget.'

'Well, as it happens, I might be able to squeeze them in.' I highlighted 20 June on my laptop calendar and prepared to fill in some details.

'What, really?' He sounded amazed.

'For you, Nevin. Not for any old snapper.'

'Now, hang on. Are you bumping some other poor couple?' He was a photographer, but he did have some scruples.

'Ask no questions, Nevin, and I'll tell you no lies.'

'Marvellous. Too kind.' I could hear the astonishment in his voice. 'Well, I can tell you now,' he went on cheerfully. 'The groom's an actor, Benedict Quayle?'

I blinked. 'Benedict Quayle? From the *Dark Moon* series?' I'd only seen the first in the trilogy myself, but Gemma was a massive fan. The day she'd stood behind Lorenzo della Chiamo in Harrods food hall was a day none of us would ever forget. Mainly because Gemma liked to remind us of it once a month, or whenever she had a pasta salad ('Lorenzo' had had gluten-free fusilli, which apparently made him and Gemma soul mates).

'Yes! Him. And his fiancée's an actress too but she's not very famous yet, she's called Emily Sharpe. What's a bit sticky is that they're both currently working in America. He's filming . . . whatever the new *Dark Moon* film is.'

'*Return to the Light*.'

'Probably. And Emily's in that, and some play or other, I believe. Or a film. I'm not really up on these things.'

'So is that why they're getting the photographer to reorganize their wedding? Didn't they have a wedding planner?'

'No, they were using the wedding planner at the hotel. The best man and chief bridesmaid are apparently on hand to sort things out on the ground in London, but Emily asked me if I could recommend a venue. She's very stressed, as you might imagine, but I knew you'd be able to calm things down. If anyone can make sure she has an even better day than the one she's just lost, you can, Rosie.'

'Well, it's lovely that you thought of me. I'll do everything I can,' I reassured him.

I was so excited I could have done laps of my office with glee. Not just a wedding to fill the June twelfth slot, but a celebrity one! Featuring one and a half celebrities who outranked Flora in the first place!

A small voice at the back of my mind wondered what had happened to get someone that famous double-booked at a hotel in the first place, but I shoved it to one side.

'I always knew you were a miracle worker, but this is fantastic,' said Nevin. 'So may I give them your number? Probably don't need to say this, but you'll have to keep it under your hat. Can't have word getting out that Transylvania's most eligible vampire's getting married and all that.'

'He's a shapeshifter. From Venice,' I said automatically, thinking of all the security I'd had to block-book months in advance for Flora. Brilliant. I wouldn't have to cancel that. I hated cancelling security.

Anyway, I thought, putting the phone down with a silent *yes!*

I'd need at least two people to keep Gemma away from Benedict. Another good reason to keep this completely to myself.

Calls were made, emails were sent, and the first meeting with Benedict Quayle and Emily Sharpe's marital representatives in London was set up for later that week.

As I'd promised Nevin, I hadn't told anyone about the meeting. I had no idea what Gemma might do if she thought someone who knew Benedict Quayle's actual pasta salad preferences was in the building, but also if the booking didn't materialize, I'd never hear the end of it from Laurence. He was still on a series of herbal remedies to get over the loss of Flora's room bookings.

Part of me wanted to tell Joe, to prove his shooting-star guff had worked, but since Flora's cancellation he'd reverted to his old 'weddings are for snobby people who want to show off to their mates' attitude, and had turned his back on events to focus on making the Bonneville's laundry more eco-friendly, to Jean's despair. Besides, as he took great delight in reminding us while Gemma was reading *Heat* magazine's engagement special aloud to us, he had no idea who these people were anyway.

Besides, I wasn't allowed to tell anyone. I'd had to sign a confidentiality agreement emailed over by Benedict Quayle's agent. It went on for *pages*. Missy Hernandez wasn't going to be present at my planning meetings in person, but she'd managed to make herself very, *very* present in my email inbox.

On this particular Thursday morning, Missy's extensive list of security requirements was in the joint possession of Ben and

Emily's wedding proxies: chief bridesmaid Chloë, and best man Magnus. They were not together.

'We're not together, him and me,' Chloë informed me, gesturing with a finger between her and Magnus, before I'd got past 'Hello, and welcome to the Bonneville Hotel.'

'You should be so lucky, love,' said Magnus, before I'd had time to react to Chloë's statement.

'No, I think I'm lucky already.' Chloë was American, but she'd certainly got the hang of British sarcasm. 'And please don't call me love. I'm not your mom's cleaner.'

'Sorry,' said Magnus, then paused. Glimmer of a smile. I *knew* what was coming next.

So did Chloë. 'And don't say babe,' she shot back without dropping her smile to me.

'Forgive me. Darling?'

'Does it *look* like it's working, Magnus?'

The first grippy sensation of a stress headache began to press against my temples. I hadn't expected this. Not from a wedding whose flower budget suggested an extreme interest in peace and love.

'Would you like to come through to the Palm Court?' I asked.

Before I met them, I'd been quite glad Chloë and Magnus were coming as a pair, because, to all intents and purposes, anyone passing the Palm Court would assume *they* were the couple planning their wedding with me. The obvious tension between them made it even more authentic. It wasn't the sort of tension normally resolved by a bout of urgent snogging behind a convenient door. It was the tension of two people unable to decide where to kick off the argument proper, and what might get broken in the process. In other words, the sort of fury often engendered by weeks of discussing whose mother got to wear pistachio and whose mother got the bigger hat.

Still, I managed to get things back onto a cheerful front as I welcomed them to the Bonneville and commiserated about Emily and Benedict's 'disappointment' with their first booking.

'It's a blessing in disguise.' Chloë crossed her legs and looked scandalized. 'Oh, my God, can you imagine how badly things could have gone wrong on the day, if she's this disorganized now? I feel sorry for the clients who *got* the date. The woman is a liability. I can't imagine how it could have happened.'

I could. An assistant who hadn't saved a document. A lost booking from the previous year. Computers crashing. A really bad hangover and too much paperwork . . . My blood ran cold just thinking how easily it could have happened.

Magnus stirred two sugars into his tea and clattered the spoon round the china cup, causing Chloë to wince theatrically. 'Or someone more famous bunged them more cash. I can find out. I've got contacts in that game.'

She didn't even turn her head. 'Stay classy, Magnus. But it's critical that we regroup and focus. Especially as Emily can't be here to check things out herself, I think it's even more important to have absolute confidence in every detail going forward.'

Chloë, I soon discovered, was a solicitor, a junior partner in a firm specializing in family law. She was very friendly, but as I was pouring the coffee, she put her phone on the table with the clock app open, as if she would be billing me if we overran, and I decided not to make a joke about Emily and Benedict arranging their prenup with her.

Magnus, on the other hand, did something in property. He was good-looking in a raffish, public-school sort of way, but he wore yellow socks and reminded me a little bit of Dominic, specifically the way his eyes glittered at his own jokes and how he talked over Chloë and me. I was surprised by how wearing I found him. Maybe my tolerance had worn off in the weeks I hadn't been living with Dom.

'So, have you two known each other long?' I asked, to push away the Dominic thought.

'I've known Emily since boarding school,' said Chloë, answering the question she wanted to answer. 'My dad's English and I went to school here. Em and I shared a flat together in London. We're very close.'

'Although you haven't seen her for a while, have you?' Magnus toyed with the biscuits, touching all of them deliberately, and then settling on a Bourbon cream. Delphine made them herself, dementedly pricking individual marks into them to make them look like the mass-produced version.

'I've been busy with work, going back and forth,' Chloë explained to me. 'Obviously Emily's been out in the States for the past year or so. With Benedict.'

'Are we calling him Benedict now he's famous?' Magnus enquired. 'Even though he's been Benny for the twenty-five years I've known him?'

Chloë finally turned her head and gave him a withering look.

'I wouldn't know. I've only known him for the *seven years* he's been dating my best friend.'

'On and off,' said Magnus. 'Seven years, on and off.'

'Have you had a stopwatch running?'

I let out an inner groan and poured myself a cup of tea to disguise it. Seven years of these two squabbling like this? God almighty. No wonder Emily and Benedict had decided to give things a go in America. If they were in America. If it were me, I'd have moved to Glasgow and set my alarm to email at appropriately time-delayed times of the night if it meant getting away from this over dinner.

Come on, Rosie, I told myself. *Channel your inner Joe. Find the joy in these two. Enjoy their spark. Imagine them fighting their rising feelings over a big argument about what colour cravats the ushers should wear . . .*

'So anyway,' I said, hauling the meeting back on track. 'I can show you two around today and give you a sense of how our weddings work here, where we hold them, what sorts of party spaces are available. We can try to replicate what Emily and . . . um, Benedict? had planned originally, or we can create something completely fresh.'

'I think they should have something bespoke,' said Chloë, decisively.

'Bespoke? It's a wedding. Not a three-piece suit,' said Magnus. 'Now, thank God Benny got his *suit* ordered early. More to the point,' he added to me with a wink, 'the stag's still going ahead as it was. Track day, then paintballing, then we'll draw a discreet veil over the rest.'

'For the moment,' said Chloë darkly. 'I don't think you've seen Missy's official risk assessment of your track day, have you? Let alone the *veiled stuff*. Good luck getting that past Benedict's insurance.'

I looked at Chloë, then Magnus, and foresaw weeks of frozen smiles ahead of me. For the first time ever in my career, I was actually grateful I only had twelve weeks to plan a wedding.

'Do you know if Emily or Benedict has ever visited the Bonneville?' I asked. 'I'm thrilled that we've got the opportunity to host their wedding, but it would be nice if we could reference some personal memory they have?'

Chloë shook her head. 'I don't believe so. But Emily is happy to do FaceTime when she's available, and you can walk her around so she can get a feel for the place? I'm recording all our conversations too, obviously.'

I glanced at the phone. 'Really?'

'Well, edited highlights.'

'Good! Lovely!' I found myself leaning forwards towards the phone. 'Lovely!'

Oops. No. Awkward. I sat back and found myself wishing that Joe would walk past so I could lean on his charms to smooth these two down.

Then I remembered no one else could know about it. Bollocks.

'Em's hoping to be back next month.' Chloë's face lit up, and she looked excited for the first time. 'She's been reshooting a tiny part she had Benedict's film, so her schedule's up in the air, but fingers crossed she'll make it back. It'd be a shame for her to miss out on the fun bits like the cake tasting.' She held up her crossed fingers.

I held mine up too, and smiled.

Maybe the shooting helicopters only delivered half a wish. The rest you had to work on yourself.

CHAPTER TWENTY-FOUR

To everyone's surprise, but mainly mine, Helen and Wynn's wedding ceremony at the end of May wasn't going to take place in the hotel, even though Laurence offered to give them free venue hire, use of the honeymoon suite, and also the services of a top wedding planner (me) as his gift.

Instead Helen accepted the generous offer of the top wedding planner, but told me that they'd decided to get married in a hidden-away Welsh chapel in the City, 'where there will be decent singing,' according to Wynn, and beautiful backdrops for the photographs, according to Nevin, who was giving them a mates' rates package.

'It's sweet of Laurence,' Helen explained over our first official wedding planning lunch in a pub round the corner from the chapel, 'but I already feel as if I'm a bit married *to* the hotel as it is. I don't want to be married *in* the hotel. And Wynn's mum wants him to have a proper Welsh service. The whole family's coming on a bus. And there'll be a choir.'

Wynn nodded. He'd taken the morning off to choose wedding bands and already looked as if he'd reached the outer limits of his interest in the process. But being a good-natured bloke, he was hiding it by nodding a lot and (probably) thinking about his stag do, which Helen had agreed would be a rugby international match of his choice.

'And you'll be pleased to know,' he added to me, as our lunch arrived, 'that Helen's selected her retinue. No open auditions or weight testing required.'

'It's just going to be you and Joe,' Helen confirmed, tucking into her steak pie. 'And possibly Gemma, if she promises not to cry like she does at everyone else's weddings. I'm thinking *bridesmates*. I'm trendsetting here. What?' She looked up at me, fork poised over the shortcrust pastry.

'Nothing. You're just the first bride I've seen who eats *more* after the engagement,' I observed.

Helen snorted, and reached for the tomato sauce. 'It's been a long morning. I'm hungry. What's the point of going on a stupid diet just when I need the energy most? We're in March already, the wedding's in under ten weeks. I'm hardly going to lose much between now and then. I don't want to be like that girl you had to sew into her dress and force-feed baklava, only to have her pass out on the wedding cake.'

Wynn looked startled.

'Delphine was furious,' I explained. 'You can't easily repair a cake with a whole face imprint on the top layer.'

'Still, the French swearing brought her round quickly enough.'

'And I want to marry the beautiful woman I met in the first place,' said Wynn. 'Not some too-skinny, fake-tanned version.' He stopped smiling at Helen long enough to give me a stern look. 'Helen's been telling me about what happens to women when they get onto this wedding conveyor belt thing. It's your job as chief bridesmaid to stop her changing at all, please.'

'Aw, thanks, babe,' said Helen, and grabbed his big hand.

'Please stop,' I said faintly.

Wynn left us to head back to his surgery, and Helen and I caught a bus through the City. It was a lovely spring day, the sort of day when London feels fresh and positive, the pigeons gleam with reflected sunlight, and people smile as they barge each other off the pavement.

'You're in a good mood,' Helen observed when we alighted at Leicester Square and walked through the crowds of tourists towards Piccadilly and the hotel.

'Am I?'

'Yes, you are.' She scrutinized me. 'And I know why.'

'Why?' I smiled benevolently at a motionless Japanese tourist and didn't tell him that the first rule of walking in London is never ever stop walking ever, not even if it means going round in a giant circle.

'It's because you're over Dominic.'

The certainty in Helen's voice surprised me. I'd been expecting her to say, 'Because you're doing well at work,' or 'Because Tiffany Noakes's wedding was in the back of *Tatler*.' But actually . . . she was right. It was days since I'd read one of Dominic's columns, digging my nails into my palms whenever the word *Betty* appeared. I'd actually forgotten that today was one of his review days.

Blimey.

'See?' Helen pointed at me. 'I'm right, aren't I?'

'You might be,' I said, and realized that I was happy about it. Or rather, I didn't feel sad any more. It was like a scab had fallen off, to reveal perfectly smooth healed skin underneath.

How had that happened? How had that low ache of misery suddenly worn off . . . almost without me noticing? 'I thought it'd take longer than this,' I mused aloud. 'Huh.'

'I know why, too,' Helen went on.

We'd reached the pedestrian crossings at Piccadilly Circus, waiting for the lights to change so that the slow ribbon of black taxis and red buses would stop to let us cross, and we could be mown down by cycle couriers instead.

'And why's that?' I glanced across at her. 'Actually, don't tell me – I know. It's work. I've been too frantic with meetings to think about Dominic and his stupid reviews. But that's a good thing, for once, so don't give me the You Work Too Hard, Get a Life lecture.'

Helen gave me a withering look normally reserved for waiters who couldn't manage more than three plates at a time. 'What? No, of course it's not that.'

'It is.'

'Oh, for God's sake . . . of course it isn't.'

'Well, what is it then? Are you going to say it's because I didn't really love Dominic in the first place?'

So far, Helen hadn't sunk to the usual depths of most smug fiancées when it came to extolling the joys of finding The One, but there was always a first time.

She looked at me for a long moment; then the green man appeared above the crossing. 'If you don't know,' she said, 'I'm not going to tell you. You'll just have to work it out for yourself.'

'What? What's that supposed to mean?' I stared at the back of her immaculate French pleat as she strode across the zebra crossing, but when I caught up with her, Helen changed the subject and insisted on talking about birdcage veils and whether it would be a classy Grace Kelly move to learn her vows in Welsh to surprise Wynn.

And so as March turned into April, the flowerbeds in our paved wedding garden burst into life, and the hats got smaller and the shoes got strappier as we headed towards the peak weekends of May and June.

The eager women I'd first met in the autumn were now blooming into fully fledged nutjobs as their big days hove into view: Jessie Callum had taken my suggestion to choreograph a dance so seriously that she and her fiance were now doing ballroom classes, and Daisy Wallace had gone on such a radical diet/makeover since our first meeting that it was a good job I had a photo of her on the Bridelizer, or else I wouldn't have recognized her at the cake tasting. (I had to taste the cake for her and describe it.) Thanks to Ben and Emily's Hollywood budget, and a few last-minute parties I squeezed into the events diary, I was still on track to make my target, just. I'd started to look for studio flats I could afford when I had my bonus in my hand, but it was a little half-hearted. To be honest, I wasn't in a hurry to move out of the staff quarters.

Laurence, Joe and I had got into an easy flat-sharing routine, made even easier by Laurence's frequent evenings out at either his friends' clubs or his various medical treatments. I saw more of Joe, though his trips to the gym and my hours in the office meant that we tended to bump into each other quite late in the evenings, when he was working his way through seasons of various TV series that had passed him by while he was in the US. We piled the DVDs in a stack by the television, moving them up and down according to their rank in our Chart of Box Sets. I didn't mind watching television with him, explaining key cultural details he'd missed during his years out of the UK while we ate pizza on the sofa. He didn't seem to mind being around me either, and although we never mentioned my jilting or the Girl Who Broke His Heart again, the understanding between us grew, often when we both winced simultaneously at an on-screen dumping, or an awkward goodbye – and said nothing. Sometimes friendships are more about what you don't say than what you do.

In short, life just felt easier. I couldn't put my finger on why. It could have been the weather, which was mild for April and caused an outbreak of unseasonal shorts in Green Park. It could have been two different 2012 brides calling me to tell me they'd had babies and asking whether I could arrange christening parties at the Bonneville. (Of course I could! We offered discounts for that sort of thing.) It might even have been – and don't laugh – down to the fact that I now automatically wished for good things every time I saw an air ambulance shoot across the London skyline when I was standing at the kitchen sink washing up. And God knows there are always plenty of those, thanks to the rich tapestry of London nightlife.

Whatever was causing this streak of sunshine in my life, it peaked at the end of April, when three things happened unexpectedly.

The first thing was a strange call Gemma took for me, from a bride who called herself Janet.

'Janet?' I frowned. 'Really? I don't think we've ever had a Janet . . .'

'She sounded like she knew you, though,' said Gemma. 'Asked for you specially. She wants to meet you at the Wolseley, at a time that suits you tomorrow.'

'Not here? Not in the hotel?' This was weird.

'That's what she said. Call her back and arrange it.'

I did. But it turned out that Janet wasn't a bride. She wasn't even called Janet. She was called Mary Waters, and when I met her at a discreet corner table, I discovered she was the HR director of the hotel that had catastrophically double-booked Emily and Benedict's wedding.

'I know you're a busy woman so I'll get to the point, Ms McDonald,' she said briskly, ordering a large black coffee, no sugar, eggs Florentine, no muffin, sauce on the side, no butter, all without looking at the waiter. 'We've just had to say goodbye to our events manager, Loren Symons. Very sad, new pastures, fresh challenges, blah, blah.'

Sacked, in other words. Sacked from a great height. Plus, she actually said 'blah, blah.' That's how furious Mary Waters was about her hotel losing the high-profile Quayle/Sharpe wedding – or 'Benily', as Gemma's magazines referred to them.

'I'm pleased to say that I've been tasked with finding a candidate who can kick our event portfolio up a gear,' Mary went on, waving away the bread basket as if it contained used tissues. 'Someone with a strong vision and ambition for our international profile going forward. I've long admired what you've been able to achieve at the Bonneville with a – don't take this the wrong way – woefully limited resource set and second-division budget constraints. We'd be able to offer you a different class of hotel to play with, plus a larger dedicated hospitality team, a bigger salary, and, of course, a bonus incentive.'

I felt giddy with excitement. No one had ever headhunted me before. Also the coffee here was *much* stronger than at the Bonneville.

'Would I be overseeing the whole events programme?' I asked in a calm voice that didn't sound much like mine. My mind whirled with the possibilities: I'd been to a wedding at this hotel with Dominic, and it was an amazing location, for any kind of event. Three ceremony rooms, a fully equipped conference suite with cinema, capacity for several hundred guests, a whole dedicated nursery for the hotel's flower requirements, a Michelin-starred restaurant . . .

I saw Mary's face, and faltered. 'Or just weddings?'

'You do seem to have a knack for delivering a particular kind of wedding,' said Mary. 'It's all in the details. Obviously, we keep tabs on our competitors, and your details are absolutely *pin*-sharp. You really *run* events.' She gave me a conspiratorial nod. 'I've been talking to some of your very satisfied brides.'

'Really?' I just stopped myself asking, *Which ones?*

'Of course. They're the best referrers. I'm surprised your ears weren't burning. In fact, more than one said how you made it feel as if she didn't have to make a single decision.' She nodded approvingly. 'You've clearly got excellent client management skills. Nothing worse than a bride ruining a spectacular wedding by making emotional decisions.'

I smiled, but my buoyant mood was suddenly brought up short.

A bride ruining a spectacular wedding by making emotional decisions? What?

It sounded so controlling. And mean. And yet it was something I knew I'd said to Helen before now. I'd said it to Joe, too: it was better to guide the bride into the decision I could see was best for her, rather than have her make some sugar-deprived snap judgement. I'd been joking, obviously, but . . .

I started to feel a bit cold. Mary sounded so pleased with herself. Was that what I sounded like?

But Mary didn't seem bothered at all. Her food arrived, and she began to dispatch it efficiently, still talking. 'The directors would be very keen to have an informal chat with you about the possibility of your taking on this role within our organization,' she said. 'As you know, we have sister hotels in New York and Paris, so there's the possibility of travel.'

I shoved my misgivings to one side. For the time being. I'd changed my wedding style over the year. Well, not changed. Evolved.

'And could I bring any of my team with me?' I thought of Gemma and – yes – Helen and Joe, too. Even Delphine. They made the Bonneville weddings what they were. They understood my shorthand. They knew my discreet hand signals for 'drunk bridesmaid', 'lost usher', 'bridal loo emergency'.

I had a flashback to the hysterical bride in the huge crinoline who'd overdone the champagne but couldn't fit into the loo cubicle. Helen had had the brainwave of getting Ripley's old potty from Laurence's flat. The chief bridesmaid had volunteered to hold it in return for front-row positioning on the bouquet tossing. Thank God the bride had seen the funny side.

Mary's voice snapped me back to the moment. 'We do have specialists within the department,' she said, and I heard a no. I also heard, *hotel that probably wouldn't have a Teletubbies potty to hand*.

I sat back in my chair. 'It's a lot for me to take in,' I admitted. I couldn't be cool. This was too amazing. Headhunted!

'I don't expect a decision right now.' Mary smiled at me, as if even an old hand would struggle to assimilate the scale of the opportunity on offer. 'I just wanted to float it past you off the record. Have a think and get back to me. The opportunities are all here for you. As you know, openings like this don't come along very often, and it's vital for us that we get the right person. And I believe you, Rosie, are that person.'

'Thank you,' I said. I didn't know what else to say.

As I strolled down the sunny side of Piccadilly on my way back to the hotel, I allowed myself to imagine a life as executive events director. I pictured myself in an upgraded suit, more like Helen's stylish designer-wear than my normal high-street ones, constructing fabulous, big-budget weddings, delegating the tedious jobs like chair-counting and favour-positioning to assistants . . .

I frowned. Although, would I? In a funny way, those were the parts I enjoyed. Ticking off the details. And the budgets were never a factor; I liked to make every single penny work for my couples, no matter how much they had to spend – in fact, that was part of the challenge.

Mary Waters' offer was flattering, and I *was* tempted, but as I turned the corner and saw the Bonneville's elegant windows shining in the midday sun, the curving brass details glinting on the revolving door, Frank, our dignified doorman helping an elderly couple into a shiny black London taxi, I felt a tug of something more than just job satisfaction towards the old 'second-division' hotel.

I'd learned so much here. Everything, in fact. And now, finally, I was getting to a position where I might actually get the promotion I wanted, and I couldn't throw that in Laurence's face. If Mary Waters considered me management material, then surely Laurence could speed up his decision.

More than that, I didn't want to leave the Bonneville. Not now. Not even for the fanciest hotel job in London.

I'd only been back in the hotel for about ten minutes when the next surprising but nice thing happened.

Joe had interrupted my Stage 3: Red Alert check of Daisy

Wallace's RSVPs to bring me some new sponge cake Delphine was testing; for some reason, he was one of the few people she would allow to take samples out of the pâtisserie room.

'Come on,' he cajoled, when I tried to tell him I was busy. 'Take a break. You don't want to know what I had to do to get this. She said most of your *brides* don't even deserve her cakes, let alone the staff.'

Would I miss chilly Delphine and her hands of pastry genius? I thought, as Joe put his feet up on my desk and helped himself to pale-green genoise sponge, topped with ivory Italian buttercream, dropping crumbs on my interactive model of the courtyard.

Yes, I probably would, I thought.

'I tried to find you this morning,' Joe said through a mouthful of cake, 'but you weren't around. Where'd you get to? Were you refereeing that squabbling couple?'

'Most of our couples squabble. They're getting married. Narrow it down a bit for me.'

'The big guy with the yellow socks and the uptight dark-haired girl. I only saw them from a distance. The couple you won't let anyone talk to.' He squinted at me. 'I've been meaning to mention it, but I know I obviously messed things up with Flora, but—'

'What? No, you didn't! That wasn't your fault.'

He shrugged and looked cross with himself. 'Feels like I let you down somehow. I should have spotted it coming. But I feel like I was learning something, and I should get back on the horse.' He looked hopeful. 'Maybe I could help with this one?

I'm good with squabbling couples. We make a good tag-team with squabblers.'

I stopped chewing the cake. He meant Chloë and Magnus. Or, rather, Benedict and Emily. The one couple I couldn't let Joe – or anyone else – near, even though, to be honest, I could have used his help.

'Um . . . they're nearly done,' I floundered. I was touched Joe wanted to make up for Flora. I *did* want to work on a wedding with him . . . just not this one. 'Maybe, er, you could sit in on a meeting I've got this week, for December? They want a fifties Christmas theme.'

Joe gave me his X-ray specs look. The one that went right through me to whatever I was trying not to show.

'Don't you trust me?' he asked simply. 'I'm really trying.'

'I know.' I meant it. 'And you're great. And—'

My desk phone rang. I ignored it. 'And I want to . . . I really want you – oh, for God's sake.'

Joe lifted an eyebrow. 'Pick it up. It'll kill you not to.'

I did. It was Gemma, doing a shift in reception. 'I've got a couple of familiar faces here for you,' she said. 'Shall I send them through?'

Stephanie Miller and Richard Henderson had called in at the hotel to see me and, surprisingly, to see the reason for their unexpected and socially awkward wedding cancellation, Joe 'Don't you want to swim naked in the sea? If not, why not?' Bentley Douglas.

'I'm so glad we've caught you both,' Stephanie said, smiling at Joe, who had the grace to look a bit nervous.

'Me? Are you sure?' he said.

'Absolutely. If it hadn't been for that . . . lightbulb moment last year, I don't think Rich and I would ever have had the conversations we ended up having. It completely changed our relationship. For the better.' Stephanie touched Richard's arm as she spoke, and he smiled in quiet agreement.

I noted they weren't wearing matching golf sweaters any more, but there was a different sort of coordination about them. They seemed more relaxed. More in tune with each other.

She turned back to us, and her face glowed with contentment. 'We want to fix another date for the wedding. What do you have free in November?'

'You're actually going to get married? That's wonderful news!' Did that sound too effusive? I wondered. Too surprised? 'I mean, it's exactly what I hoped you'd – no, that I knew you'd—'

'Don't apologize!' Stephanie laughed. 'It's fine. We needed to step back. Things had gotten too intense; we were hung up on the little things and not talking about the big things. It mounted up, and we got overwhelmed.'

'When you've called off a wedding, there's nothing you can't talk about,' said Richard. 'So we got talking. Had some time off. Had a bit of a think. I realized Steph was the best thing in my life. Made some changes. Got back together. Here we are.'

That was literally the most I'd ever heard him say in one go.

Stephanie squeezed his hand, but looked at me and Joe. 'Thank you,' she said. 'You guys derailing our wedding was the best thing that ever happened to us.'

'In that case,' I said, feeling oddly pleased, 'the least we can do is make sure you have the best-ever day this time around.'

'And would you like to try some cake?' suggested Joe.

Laurence sent champagne, and we toasted their re-engagement, but as Stephanie and Richard left the hotel hand in hand, an unexpected melancholy descended on me. I wasn't proud of it, because it was selfish, but I couldn't help thinking, *They fixed things.* Things had gone as wrong for Stephanie and Richard as they could possibly go, but somehow they'd turned it around and talked, been honest, and now they could face anything.

A little voice inside me whispered, *What if . . .*

I pushed it away, but the thought clung to my brain. *What if . . . ?*

Not me and Dominic – that was done. I knew why we'd finished; it was because we'd never really started. Me and Anthony. My own wedding that never happened. Could that have been saved?

'What's that frown for?' Joe asked. 'Are you worried you've double-booked them?'

I shook my head and set off down the corridor towards my office, where I could make some lists and not think about this.

But Joe followed me, still bouncy from the meeting. 'You are going to let me work on this wedding, aren't you? I feel like I owe it to them. Or maybe it's a service we could offer? A rigorous road-testing before the wedding!'

'No!' I stopped in front of an alcove filled with a tumbling arrangement of spring flowers. There were no fake flowers in the hotel, one of Caroline's rules.

'Tell me what you're thinking,' said Joe quietly, after a moment's pause, and I knew he knew exactly what was going through my mind. He was one of the very few people in the world who did.

I didn't turn around because I didn't want him or anyone else to see my miserable expression. I pretended to be checking the flowers, and as I moved, Joe turned slightly so he was shielding me from anyone passing. It made me feel safe, just for a second.

'Don't bottle it up,' he said. 'Get it out.'

I swallowed hard. I didn't want to cry but now I'd started thinking about all this stuff, after bottling it up for so long, it was making me weirdly tearful.

'I was thinking, what if someone like you had made me and Anthony talk, before he decided to jilt me,' I said in a rush. 'Could we have worked things out like Stephanie and Richard did, if someone had had the guts to make him admit something was wrong?' I stared at the waxy orange blossoms in the arrangement. I couldn't imagine any of Anthony's friends having the bollocks – or the imagination – to do what Joe had done. And we'd broken up so abruptly and completely that I couldn't imagine even speaking to them now, let alone asking if they'd spoken to him before. But . . . 'Maybe I could have made things right.'

'Maybe,' said Joe. 'Or you might both have wasted another two years trying and trying to be something you weren't, until he met someone else and left. And you wouldn't have had your great story, and your drunken disco. And knowing how great your mum and dad would be in a crisis.'

'But I'll never know what I did wrong.' Tears stung my eyes, hot tears that felt more angry than sad. I didn't expect to feel them at all, not now, but suddenly I felt close to the younger me, stuck in that limbo of not knowing. I'd blocked all this out with Dominic, and work, but now . . .

'Why do you need to know?' he asked gently.

I looked at him. Joe made me question all this stuff. No one else ever really had. 'Because my life could have been different.'

He rolled his eyes. 'Right. You could be stuck in a marriage with a man who doesn't really talk to you, feeling dissatisfied but not quite knowing why, talking even less now you've somehow got a baby . . . instead of which you're the best events manager in London, you've got the world in front of you, and you're not even thirty.'

'I'm thirty-one.'

'Well, you don't look a day over twenty-nine.'

'Thanks.'

Joe sighed and ran a hand through his hair, then looked at me. 'Bit of honesty coming up,' he said. 'Are you braced?'

I nodded. At least he warned people these days.

'Maybe Anthony just realized he didn't love you enough, and because he's English and he's a guy, he didn't know how to put it in a way that wouldn't destroy your confidence forever. It happens. He just chose to humiliate you in public instead. *He* looked like the knob. Not you. But people change,' he said. 'Thank God, we change, we grow, and we leave things behind.

It's one of the redeeming features of being human. Otherwise we'd be stuck trying to find the first person we ever fell in love with, for the rest of our lives. Can you imagine? Being forty, and desperately searching for that teenager you had a crush on at school?'

I managed a watery smile.

'If Anthony came back now, you probably wouldn't even give him a second glance, because thanks to the way you pulled yourself out of that crappy situation, you're a better, braver, wiser person than the one he left,' said Joe. 'Don't deny it. You're strong, you're independent, you're *so* smart. Way too good for someone who can't be honest with you. Or see what sort of woman you are.'

I was about to mumble 'Thanks,' or something equally eloquent, when he held my upper arms and looked straight at me. The intensity of Joe's gaze took me by surprise; it felt as if he wanted to burn what he was thinking directly into my mind. I wobbled on my heels.

'All I can tell you,' he said slowly, 'is that if Anthony didn't appreciate what he was losing, then he can't possibly have been good enough for you. You should thank every lucky star in the sky that you're free, so someone else can feel like the luckiest man alive when he gets the chance to start a life with you.'

My lips parted to speak, but no words came out. Instead I just kept looking into Joe's blue eyes, at his handsome, honest face. At the unselfconscious warmth and positivity that seemed to surround him. At his simultaneous familiarity and his tingly otherness.

He didn't speak either. He just gazed at me.

And then the third amazing thing happened.

I realized with the sudden clarity of a curtain lifting in my head that I'd fallen in love with Joe Bentley Douglas.

The trouble was, I'd now spent enough time experiencing Joe's peace-and-love beliefs to know without a shadow of a doubt that he would have said exactly the same thing to Gemma, to Helen, to any of the brides who walked into our hotel, as he'd just said to me, and have meant it just as much.

'Thanks,' I said. My voice cracked. 'I've never . . . I've never talked about this with anyone before. I'm sorry if it's a bit . . .'

'Don't. No need to say it.' He looked at me for another few, long seconds, then said, 'I mean what I said.'

And then, just as my heart was looping a slow somersault around my chest, Gemma arrived with the pink phone of pre-wedding panic, and I was right back to sacking another bridesmaid.

CHAPTER TWENTY-FIVE

Chloë and Magnus (or Tweedledee and Tweedle-Shut-Up-I'm-Talking, as Helen called them), came in twice more during early May to check over the arrangements for Benily's June celebrity wedding.

They really didn't need to; I had the spreadsheet to end all spreadsheets covering every possible circumstance. And I really didn't *want* them to, because every time they started squabbling I had to fight the urge to send them to Joe to be lovingly psychoanalyzed into a dinner date, but I couldn't risk *any* details of the Benily wedding getting out till the last minute.

But Chloë and Magnus came anyway, probably because, like me, they were copied in on the constant emails arriving from Missy the agent, whose latest request was for Nevin to outline all potential photo angles to her, in order to ensure there'd be no potential eating/drinking shots. Plus I think Chloë felt she had a responsibility to make sure there wasn't going to be a beer fountain at the reception.

Maybe she was as sick of them as I was, but in the middle of May, Emily asked if she could call me while she was in her trailer between takes, so I could 'show' her the preparations via the video-calling function on my phone.

'*I so wish I was there!!!*' she emailed. '*It feels so weird getting other people to organize my wedding!!! It's kind of like being in a film! If you know what I mean!!!*'

Even without all Emily's exclamation marks, I was nervous before our scheduled call. Flora Thornbury – I can't even tell you what Helen called *her* since her elopement and subsequent *total silence* – was famous-ish in London, but she wasn't that different from the other posh brides I dealt with, being skinny, welded to her phone and blissfully ignorant of the price of a pint of milk. Emily, on the other hand, was a proper star. In the last few weeks I'd started to notice her heart-shaped face popping up in the celeb pages of magazines, as the publicity for her even-more-famous fiancé's new *Dark Moon* film began to build, and on the morning of her call I got up an hour early so I could blow-dry my hair.

The plan was to 'walk her around' the courtyard by walking about with my phone, then chat about the details I'd arranged for the cake and flowers and the fun things that all brides liked to discuss, even Hollywood ones.

I'd been lurking around the hall between the hotel and the gardens, waiting for her to ring, and ducking into the alcove whenever Gemma or Laurence wandered past, when Joe appeared. He had his 'looking for something' expression on, and when he saw me, his eyes lit up as if he'd just found it.

'Hey!' he said, and waved.

My stomach flipped. Since my moment of realization, my

stomach flipped every time I saw Joe, but since I honestly didn't know what to do about my crush – work colleague, flatmate, boss's son, how many bad ideas did you need? – I was learning to live with it, the same way you get used to having a sprained knee or a wheat allergy.

When he got nearer, he said, 'I've been looking for you,' (my stomach did a double flip), and pointed at me.

I realized he was pointing at the folder I was clutching, and it unflipped.

'Is that Helen's reception folder?' he went on. 'She asked me to have a look at the drinks menu. I've had some ideas for a personalized cocktail. Does Wales have a national spirit?'

'Leek brandy?'

'Very good!' He peered at me more closely. 'You look different this morning. More . . . coloured in?'

'I'm wearing lipstick.'

'You look nice.' Joe smiled approvingly, then raised an eyebrow. 'Are you going somewhere?'

'No! I mean, no? I just like to look nice for work.'

Before he could reply, my phone rang and I fumbled it out of my pocket, trying not to let the caller show. 'Um, I should get this.'

'I'll wait,' said Joe. 'I need to ask you about something else.'

'I might be a while,' I said with an unconvincing casualness. 'I'll come and find you later?'

Immediately he was intrigued (although not as intrigued as Helen or Gemma would have been), and hovered by a painting of his great-great-grandmother, pretending to check his own phone.

Awkward.

I walked out into the garden, but Joe followed, and I had to shoo him away.

He looked at me strangely and mouthed something with a questioning expression.

Was it *Dominic?* I couldn't tell. Maybe *Who is it?* I shook my head, and walked to the far side of the gardens, and when I looked back, he'd gone.

I took a deep breath and picked up the video call, and the shock I got when the face appeared at the other end nearly made me drop the phone.

This wasn't the Emily I'd seen on Google. This face had red eyes, a long black wig that reached down to her waist, and a small pair of horns at the outer edges of her forehead.

'Hi!' it said, and waved. 'LA calling!'

I must have looked a bit startled, because she squinted and said, 'Oh, God, sorry, I've still got the lenses in! Sorry! I'm supposed to be in a shapeshifting state! It's how they tell! Just ignore them! As much as you can!'

Emily's exclamation marks weren't limited to her emails.

'It's lovely to talk to you,' I said. 'Thanks so much for making time.'

'I know!' She broke out a dazzling but friendly smile. 'Although I feel like I already know you through your emails! They're so funny! And thoughtful! I love that you're really thinking of everything, and giving me the easy stuff to decide!' The exclamation marks dropped for a second. 'I have to tell you straight off, Rosie, I am so grateful for all the effort you're making for us, when we landed this on you at such short notice. It could have been a train wreck, but it's sort of fun. I mean, the emails I get from Chloë . . . I should let you read them one day.'

I couldn't place Emily's accent. It was a smooth mid-Atlantic blend, although the longer she talked to me, the more English she sounded.

We – well, I – walked around the garden where the wedding would happen (under our special canopy if wet); then I took her through the Palm Court, into the pretty orangery, and – after sending Dino down to the cellar for a hastily invented wine request – a whistle-stop tour of the hotel lounge, which I'd booked for their post-wedding celebrations.

Emily didn't speak for a moment or two, and when I checked the phone, a smear of red make-up gave away the sneaky tear she was wiping away.

'Sorry, sorry, Ben always says I get over-emotional,' she gasped. 'It's so perfect! It's like I was meant to get married here all along? Like we were meant to go through all that stress with the other place! It's weird how things turn out. Thank you so, so much.'

'You're welcome,' I said. I honestly hadn't expected Emily to be so nice. She was a whole lot easier to deal with than most of the everyday brides I had to handle.

I heard a knock at her end; she turned and spoke to someone offscreen, then leaned forwards to me.

'I have to go. That's my call. Listen, I'm stuck here with a crazy reshoot schedule that seems to change every day, but if there's any way I can fly back early and maybe call in to see things for real, can I do that?'

'Of course,' I said, mentally flicking through the weddings I had booked in between now and then. 'If you give me some notice so I can arrange security . . .'

'Oh, there's no need for that.' She looked sheepish. 'Missy's done one of her lists? I guessed she would. She's got a job to do but . . . You can smuggle me in as a waitress or something. I've done enough waitressing to pass myself off as one.'

'No problem,' I said. 'Just let me know.'

'Sure! Thanks again! I'm going to be recommending the Face-Time wedding planner to anyone who asks me out here!' Emily smiled, popped her fangs back in, and she was gone.

I stared at the phone, still buzzing with adrenaline, and grinned to myself.

If I'd needed a sign that I was right to turn down Mary Waters' Big Job Offer, that was it.

Emily's crazy schedule meant she didn't manage to fly over in time to see Sadie Hunter and Jamie Thomas's vintage wedding the following week, or Jessie Callum and the Honorable Walter Fitzgerald's *My-Fair-Lady* wedding the week after.

I was sorry she missed those, because they had gorgeous sunshine, a harpist and an Irish piper respectively, and some of the best flowers I'd ever seen. Having said that, I wasn't sorry she missed the sight of me accidentally catching Jessie Callum's bouquet, then immediately throwing it back in the air as if it were on fire, only for *Joe* to catch it. Joe then lobbed it in the air in a panic, and Gemma half-dived underneath it as if she were playing beach volleyball and ended up spiking it to the intended recipient, Jessie's best friend and chief bridesmaid.

I was mortified, but it made for some funny photos, according to Nevin. I checked his memory card afterwards and sneakily deleted the picture he'd got of me. The expression on my face – and the way my eyes had slid sideways to fix on Joe – was a bit of a giveaway.

Needless to say, I hadn't done or said anything about my messy feelings for Joe, which were not wearing off as I'd hoped, but which were instead intensifying with every tag-team wedding meeting or cosy pizza night in with catch-up box sets at the flat.

I still hadn't moved out. I couldn't afford to, not having reached my bonus-triggering target yet, but more than that, I didn't want to. And neither Laurence nor Joe seemed to be in any hurry to evict me.

Helen, of course, had noticed immediately. She claimed she'd noticed months ago.

'You've *got* to say something,' she told me for the millionth time. 'Or else I will. And you realize that today I can do almost anything I like and no one will stop me?' she added, with more glee than was really befitting someone being laced into a wedding dress.

We were perched on stools in her tiny flat, while the make-up artist and hairdresser finished turning Helen into the perfect bride. They'd managed to smooth my hair into a mini up-do and given me immaculate fifties cat-eyes flicks; I wasn't unaware that this was the prettiest I'd ever looked, and I'd be spending most of the day standing next to Joe, doing the 'bridesmate' duties of handing out orders of service and explaining which loo was the gents to the non-Welsh speakers.

'I don't understand why you can't just *say something*,' she said, also for the millionth time. 'It's not the nineteenth century. And he likes you. It's so obvious.'

'But Joe likes everyone, it's his Sagittarian thing, man,' I groaned. 'And there are so many things that could go wrong. Work. My living situation. What people might think if I got promoted afterwards—'

'Shut up, Rosie,' said Helen. 'Listen to me. If I've learned one thing this year, it's that if you're constantly looking ahead to what's about to go wrong, you really stand to miss what's already going right.'

'I bet that sounded better on the original fortune cookie.'

She ignored me. 'Joe's not going to be working here forever. Laurence can hardly give him the job you're already doing, can he? And what happened to his six-month stay? He's only still *here* because he likes 'doing weddings' . . . with you. Plus, even if things didn't work out, you said so yourself – he's a world traveller, man. He'll insist on you staying friends and move on.'

'Well . . .'

Helen tilted her head so the hairdresser could pin the chic birdcage veil onto her signature French pleat, and gazed at me through it. 'Can't you just let yourself be happy for once? Take a chance. I am going to throw the bouquet at you this afternoon, and by the time Wynn and I leave for Paris tonight, I want *you* to tell *me* you've seized the moment with Joe.'

'But how?' I tingled at the thought of seizing the moment. I'd seen couples 'seizing the moment' most weekends for the past five years – weddings were like a cocktail shaker for hormones.

'You'll think of something,' said Helen, and stood up, smoothing her satin gown, ready for her Rolls-Royce downstairs. 'You usually do. And if you don't, there's always champagne.'

Wynn and Helen's wedding was beautiful, even though I didn't understand half of it. In fact, it was the bits I didn't understand that made me cry most. That and the singing. We all cried at the singing. The Welsh could have guarded the border with England just by singing at them and then stealing their weapons while they blubbed uncontrollably.

Afterwards, the new Mr and Mrs Davies emerged blinking into the sunlight outside the chapel in a shower of confetti and rose petals, started by me and Joe. Our fingers touched as we both reached into the basket of petals at the same time, and an electric shock tingled up my bare arm.

Say something, I told myself, but I couldn't think of anything. I just smiled dopily, and he smiled back, and everything about the world suddenly felt absolutely right. I really didn't want to ruin that moment, so I didn't.

Nevin ran through the photographs in double-quick time, and then Geraint and the ushers loaded us onto the red London bus hired to take us back to the hotel for the reception. It had a white ribbon on the front, and disposable cameras and mini bottles of champagne on the original checked seats. Once Joe and I had clattered up to the top deck like excitable schoolkids, we discovered that Helen had reserved the front seat for us. The ride back through the oldest streets of the City in the Routemaster, sipping champagne like ghost tourists, was magical. Another moment I didn't want to spoil.

I'll definitely say something after the reception, I told myself as Joe took a selfie of us both, our heads squeezed together with St Paul's Cathedral in the background. Then the Strand. Then Piccadilly Circus. Lots of selfies, in fact. A whole camera full. My eyes were shut in most of them: I'd closed my eyes to imprint the smell of him, and the feel of the side of his face against mine.

The speeches were very sweet, and quite short, and thankfully in English; then Helen and Wynn cut the cake, which Delphine had covered in tiny fondant daffodils, and we all went out into the courtyard gardens to chat and enjoy the late afternoon sunshine.

'That was the nicest wedding I've been to,' Joe said, chasing the pigeons off the wrought-iron garden seat so we could sit down.

'Wasn't it? They really fit together. And yet,' I was feeling quite indiscreet by now, 'Wynn is so not the kind of guy I expected Helen to marry.'

'No?'

I shook my head. 'This time last year, if you'd told me she'd give up dangerous, strung-out chefs to marry a Welsh dentist just a tiny bit shorter than her, who likes walking outside for no good reason . . .'

We watched the new Mr and Mrs Davies doing the rounds of Wynn's family. The aunties and cousins were hugging Helen, and she was laughing and blushing. Loved, I thought. She looked *loved*. That's what she and Wynn had in common; they loved each other. And, different or not, their lives would grow together around that.

'It's like I said, people change,' said Joe. 'Doesn't mean you weren't right then, just that we grow. It's natural. Move on. Don't cling to what suited you in the past, focus on who you are now. It's obviously working for Helen.'

I studied my glass because I was terrified that if I opened my mouth, *I am in love with you* would come streaming out.

'If you mean Dominic, I'm well over him,' I said instead.

'Good,' said Joe. He looked at me, eyes crinkled against the sun. *Sunlight is his natural background*, I thought. *Sun and blue skies.* 'Good.'

I thought he was going to say something else, and my heart was up in my chest, when Amy, one of the weekend receptionists, approached us, looking apologetic.

'Sorry to interrupt, Rosie, but there's one of your brides to see you? She says you're not expecting her, but could she have a quick word? She's been trying to call you today, and left a couple of messages.'

'Oh. I didn't get any.' I turned my phone back on, and it started bleeping.

'What? Did you turn your phone off for Helen's wedding?' Joe pretended to look shocked. 'The ultimate compliment!'

'Of course I turned my phone off.' I looked up at Amy; I had missed calls from about seven different brides. 'Who is it? Did she give you her name?' I mentally flipped through the brides it could be: most of them lived in London – it might be Cressida Connor. She'd been on the phone most of this week, wanting me to sack the bridesmaid refusing to get her hair cut to match the other three.

'No, she wouldn't give a name at all.' Amy paused. 'She was wearing big shades. Like she didn't want me to recognize her.'

At that I knew immediately who it was. Emily. My pulse skipped. Brilliant! This was the best possible wedding for her to see – I could slip her in, show her round, and maybe introduce her to Helen and Wynn. Helen would love that.

'Where is she now?' I asked.

'I took her to your office,' said Amy. 'With a cup of tea.'

'Great! Oh . . .' I panicked. Had I turned the Bridelizer round before I left? And, more to the point, had I taken the photos of Flora Thornbury with devil horns and a moustache off the filing cabinet?

No. I hadn't. Joe had been throwing Otto's sponge darts at her yesterday.

I shoved my glass at Joe. 'I'll be two seconds.'

'Don't worry,' he said, 'I won't let Helen toss the bouquet without you!'

I dashed back into the hotel, down the corridor, and burst into the office, wishing I'd tidied up last night.

'Hello!' I opened the door and saw a woman standing by . . . the Bridelizer.

'Oh, my God, this gave me a shock!' hooted Emily. 'I saw Magnus and Chloë and I thought, what didn't they tell me?'

I laughed manically – I'd had to put a decoy photo up, which had taken ten minutes to take, thanks to their squabbling about whether Magnus needed to put his arm around Chloë – while taking in Emily's very, very different appearance. The long black wig she'd worn in all our FaceTime conversations was gone; her real hair was a chestnutty crop that brought out the perfect heart shape of her pretty face, and her skin was porcelain-smooth, if not as pasty as it had been under make-up. She was dressed in a simple green sundress and little make-up beyond some peachy lip gloss, but she had a special aura about her, that Hollywood specialness that I guessed made her glow onscreen.

It was a bit surreal seeing Emily Sharpe in my office, sounding all normal, which is probably why I said the very stupid thing I did. 'I'm sorry, I didn't recognize you without your horns.'

Emily laughed and clapped a hand to her forehead. 'And the wig! Don't forget the wig! I feel so weird without it now. Like half my head's missing! Listen, is it all right? Me dropping in like this?'

'You've picked a great time,' I assured her, gesturing towards the door. 'We're actually in the middle of a function right now. My best friend's having her reception in the courtyard gardens.'

'Your best friend!' Emily looked aghast. 'Sorry! Am I taking you away from it?'

'Not at all. Helen's our restaurant manager, she'd love to meet you.' I led her down the corridor, talking as we went, and Emily slipped on her big shades, so as not to attract too much attention to herself. 'She's having an afternoon tea in the palm court, then a private party in the hotel cocktail bar, which we've also arranged for your guests.'

'With the bespoke cocktails? I love that idea! Missy was all, "Oh, you have to make sure they're non-alcoholic," but Ben and I were like, "Are you kidding? At that hotel where Ava Gardner tied one on with Frank Sinatra in secret? Gin us up, baby!" Oh, wow, this is so *Great Gatsby*! Or *High Society*!'

We paused at the long doors that led from the shady arched hall into the gardens, so Emily could enjoy the full impact of the scene playing out: the white-clothed tables of glasses and silver cake trays, the string quartet playing in a bandstand by the rose garden, Helen moving gracefully among her guests in her ivory column dress, all the grannies enjoying tea from proper china cups.

I felt very proud of the Bonneville at that moment.

I caught Helen's eye as she stopped to talk to Joe, and beckoned her over.

'This is Helen who sent the tasting menu?' Emily said excitedly. 'The one that made Chloë break her Paleo diet? Don't tell Chloë I told you that, by the way! I am so excited to meet her!'

Helen was walking over with Joe, and he was staring at us. I widened my eyes at him to stop staring – I didn't want him to draw attention to Emily.

But he carried on staring, which was really unlike him. Even on the rare occasions that he recognized a celebrity at a wedding, he made a point of pretending he didn't know who they were.

'Congratulations!' Emily held out her hand to shake.

'Is this . . .?' Helen looked at me, then at Emily, and seemed confused.

'Helen, this is Emily,' I said proudly. 'She and her fiancé will be getting married here on June the twelfth.'

'What? Not Tweedledum and Tweedle-Shut-Up – oh, sorry, hello!'

'Hello! Oh, sorry, this is so rude of me, one second.' Emily lifted her sunglasses to shake Helen's hand, and then I really noticed her eyes for the first time. Even without any make-up, they were incredible: the deep green of wine bottles, or forest leaves. Eyes that could break a heart with one glance and stay with you forever.

Wow, I thought, dazzled. Proper film-star eyes, like Liz Taylor or Sophia Loren.

Something brushed past me, and I realized it was Joe. Even as Helen and Emily were shaking hands and exchanging pleasantries about the shrimp dip, Joe's face had set into the grimmest expression I'd ever seen, and he marched off without even saying hello.

'Joe?' said Helen, but he was gone, his linen suit vanishing into the depths of the hotel.

CHAPTER TWENTY-SIX

I think, deep down, I knew why Joe stormed off the second Emily slipped off her sunglasses, but part of me hoped there was another reason. A really good one, maybe something to do with a forgotten taxi or . . . or . . .

I was struggling.

'Helen, I've got to pop back into the hotel for some paperwork,' I improvised quickly as my heart pounded in my chest. Not in a good way this time. 'Would you mind showing Emily your gorgeous cake?'

Helen read my face instantly. 'I'd love to!' She smiled. 'Emily, would you make my husband's year and come and say hello? He is such a fan of the *Dark Moon* series. . . .'

I let Helen lead Emily towards the cake table, then I scurried into the hotel. It was very quiet, and I could hear my pulse beating in my ears as I peered in room after room, trying to find Joe.

I eventually tracked him down in the empty lounge bar, knocking back a large whiskey in one of the heavy crystal glasses. He was leaning on the polished oak counter, his head in his hands, and with his rumpled suit and even more rumpled expression, I couldn't help thinking Joe had a sort of old Holly-wood air about him, too.

Oh, God, I was *so* out of my league with these beautiful people, and their beautiful, dramatic, stupid lives.

'Are you all right?' I started, as calmly as I could. 'It's just that that lady out there is the most high-profile client I will probably ever have, and you've just barged past her as if you're on *Dynasty*.'

Joe didn't turn around, but refilled his glass instead. It was as well Dino wasn't around to stop him going for the best scotch.

'Of course I'm not all right. You know exactly who that is,' he said. 'I can't believe you could do that to me. Either of you.'

I gaped in confusion. I was getting a strong feeling of déjà vu here. Between my outrage and Joe's furious man-sulk, we'd gone back to the bridal suite where we'd met. I didn't want to see that Joe again, angry and defensive, and a stranger to me.

'As far as I know, that's Emily Sharpe, the actress. What else should I know?'

Joe's face was ashen. 'That's the girl I told you about. The one I was in love with, who I thought was in love with me, and who dumped me and vanished. And she's decided to get married in my family's hotel, as if I needed my nose rubbed in it any more, and you've been arranging her wedding behind my back.'

'How the hell was I supposed to know that?' I protested. 'You never even told me her name!'

'I did!'

'You *didn't*!' I was hurt and outraged to think he could think

I'd be cruel. 'And I think I'd have remembered if you'd included the small detail of her being a Hollywood actress!'

'Everyone in LA is a Hollywood actress. You stop believing it after a while.' Joe slammed his glass back on the counter and reached for the bottle again, but I grabbed his arm.

'Please, you can't honestly think I'd do that to you,' I started, but he didn't want to listen.

He shook my hand away. 'Whatever. You know now. You arrange Emily's wedding and have a lovely time with her. The whole lot of you can just fuck off.'

I stared at him, hurt and surprised and with disapointment surging through me, then I turned and went back to Emily, and my best friend's wedding.

Arranging weddings prepares you for some awkward moments – I've never known a bride who didn't throw at least one totally irrational fit about something completely random, like spoons – but having to pretend Joe had just 'had an urgent phone call' threw me so much that I struggled to get through the next hour with Emily Sharpe.

Half of my brain was focused on giving this VIP bride a magical tour of the place she'd chosen to get married in. Emily wanted to hear *all* the romantic old stories, and kept asking more and more questions about the famous guests, the secret tunnels, the renovations. She even made me promise I'd smuggle her and Benedict in for the Farewell to the Year, if they flew back in time.

Meanwhile the other half of my brain was going round and round in circles, trying to work out whether Joe was right and I *should* have worked this out ages ago.

I'd have had to be a mind reader. I'd assumed Joe's girl was some Californian beach bunny, but why would she be? He knew lots of expats out there, they all hung out together and ate Walkers crisps, he'd told me so. I hadn't spotted her reddish-brown hair under the wig she'd worn for all our calls, and the Google photos I'd seen of her showed her with every kind of hair for various different small parts she'd had.

But it was Emily's beautiful eyes that were the giveaway, I thought, as she swept around the marble bathroom, gasping in delight at the original fittings. Normally I'd have been thrilled to see someone adore the hotel as much as I did, but I could only think about Joe. My heart lurched when I remembered his face as he'd described her on Valentine's Day. I could see what he'd seen reflected in all the mirrors: thickly lashed green eyes that you would remember all your life, eyes that would make you look a million miles away when you told someone about them years later. Because they weren't just beautiful; they were kind and intelligent and funny.

That, I decided, as she finally jumped into her taxi with a folder of my notes, was the kicker. Emily Sharpe wasn't just major league beautiful, the sort of girl you could never compete with; she was also genuinely nice.

I went back to Helen's reception and struggled to hide the other thoughts beginning to worm their way through my gloom. Emily *was* nice, yet she'd blanked Joe when she'd met him just now. And, like he'd said, she'd arranged her wedding in his family's hotel. Could you do that, if you'd really loved someone? But that was accidental, I reminded myself. Or was it?

My head was a swirling mess of arguing voices, and I was so distracted by them that I totally forgot to catch Helen's bouquet.

'Rosie!' I blinked, and saw Helen standing in front of me, the bouquet back in her hands, and Wynn's cousin Seren behind her, looking annoyed as if she'd recently been divested of a hard-won bouquet. 'You weren't ready,' she said, pointedly. 'I'm throwing it again, okay?'

Worse than that, when she forced me back into the centre of the line-up, and virtually shoved the flowers at me, I realized I didn't even want it anymore.

It's amazing how quiet a flat above a busy hotel can be when there's just one miserable person in it.

Laurence was away for the weekend, and Joe didn't come back that night. I couldn't tell Helen what had happened because she was now on her honeymoon, and I certainly wasn't going to tell Gemma, who didn't even know about Emily and Ben in the first place. My mum wasn't brilliant at relationship advice – she blamed herself for not guessing Anthony was planning to stand me up, and had refused to give any opinions on any romantic situation ever again, in case she called it wrong too. As for Dad, well. Where would you start?

The one person I wanted to talk to was, of course, the one person who wasn't there.

I was sitting on the ancient leather sofa, not really watching the last of the *Broadchurch* box set Joe and I had started, when it dawned on me how much I'd come to depend on his company over the past months. The shorthand chats we'd had in the evenings about Laurence's current ailments or the milk levels in the fridge. The in-jokes about our Chart of Box Sets, stacked up the side of the fireplace according to our ratings. He knew how I liked my coffee; I'd pulled his clothes out of the washing machine after three days to stop them getting mildew. We'd been *living* together. I knew more about Joe – not the facts of his life, but his quirks and moods – than I'd ever worked out about Dominic in the years we'd shared a flat. Some of it was irritating. Some of it was surprising. But every scrap of new detail made me want to know more about him.

One cup of tea after another went cold next to me as I hugged my knees and explored the aching hollowness pushing out from my chest to my whole body. I had to face it: this was the worst possible outcome. Not only had our friendship snapped, but he thought I'd gone behind his back to arrange Emily's wedding, *and* he was still in love with her.

It stung, but I forced myself to hear it. Of course Joe was still in love with Emily. How could he not be?

I finally heard the door to the flat open on Sunday morning, while I was forcing myself to eat some toast in the kitchen. Inexpressible relief filled me. I jumped to my feet and tried to get all my thoughts in a coherent line; then Joe walked in, unshaven and bleary but sexily so, and the thoughts scattered like pigeons.

'I've come to get a bag,' he said shortly, before I could get a word out. 'I'm going to spend some time at Mum's. She's running a conference, and she says she could do with a hand.'

'Joe, please don't be like this,' I said. 'Can't we talk about it?'

'What's to talk about? It's just work, isn't it? I'm going to be working at Wragley Hall for a while. Forward any mail, you know where I am.'

'You'd rather be with Alec and his homemade explosives than here?'

'Yup.'

I followed him into his bedroom. Well, not into it. I hovered at the door as he shoved T-shirts into his leather holdall.

'I honestly didn't know,' I insisted. 'It was random – they were booked in at another hotel. It was Nevin who recommended us. Emily never mentioned you.'

He winced and I felt terrible, but in quite a complicated way.

'I know you didn't know,' he said gruffly.

'I'm sorry. Do you want me to cancel her?' I asked. Even as I said it, I knew we couldn't, not at this stage, but it was all I had.

'Of course not, that would be totally unreasonable.'

'I could get another planner in?' I said, scrabbling for gestures I could actually make. 'I could tell Emily I was handing over to Gemma because of a prior commitment? Leave all my notes and let someone else handle it.'

He stopped packing and looked at me. His clear-eyed gaze raked my face and I wobbled inside, yet I still couldn't say the things going through my mind.

'You can't do that,' he said. 'It's a big break for you. You're going to give Emily the perfect wedding, she'll tell all her friends, you'll meet your target and Dad'll promote you. Happy ever after.'

A small voice in the back of my head pointed out that Joe would be the first person to call someone else on melodrama but I let it go. One more comment like that, though . . .

'I'd do it, if it'd convince you that I didn't take it on knowingly.'

Joe seemed to struggle with himself, then shoved a handful of boxer shorts into the bag. 'Look, I know you didn't know. I just can't . . .' He frowned. 'I just can't.'

Neither of us needed to spell it out: what Joe was really tormented by was Emily and her strange lack of acknowledgement. I didn't come into the picture at all, I thought unhappily.

I don't know what made me say it, but I heard my voice in the room.

'This maybe isn't the best moment to say it,' said the voice that sounded like mine, 'but all those things you said to me about growing up and moving on from Anthony were so true. I can see that now. I know it probably doesn't feel like it now, but you and Emily met at the right time for who you were then. You had that wonderful experience, but perhaps it was only ever supposed to be intense and of that moment—'

'It's *nothing* like you and Anthony,' he said, outraged.

'How is it not like me and Anthony?' I demanded. He'd had a holiday romance; I'd been jilted. 'My experience is worse! I was left in the actual church. But I've let all that go, because it's not who I am now. You're not that same Joe now. This year, you've changed a lot.'

'Yes, but you . . . Rosie, you and me, we're very different people. I believe in love, and you believe in . . . lists.'

This time, it was as if he'd slapped me across the face. My mouth fell open, and I took a step back. Joe seemed to regret it almost before the words were out of his mouth, but it was too late. It hung there between us, echoing in our heads.

He rubbed his face with his hand. 'Oh, bollocks. I didn't mean it like . . . I . . . Rosie?' His eyes were apologetic, but I didn't want to see that. My own vision was blurring with hot tears.

'Fine,' I said. 'Suit yourself. Give my love to Caroline. Come back when you've stopped sulking.'

And I went off to someone else's old bedroom, shut the door, and cried.

Of course, the irony was that while Joe got to nurse his wounded pride in a five-star luxury country-house hotel, I had to get on with organizing the big-budget wedding that was causing all the trouble.

I was still under strict instructions not to leak details, so Helen and Laurence were the only people who knew who was really getting married in our courtyard. Helen was off-radar for the first time in years, enjoying her honeymoon in Paris, and Laurence only had to be shown Missy the agent's ever-growing list of clauses and conditions for him to turn white and sit down with a wheatgrass shake.

Security details piled up on top of the florists, on top of the dietary requirements for the star guests, on top of the complicated room bookings. I had to field calls from Emily's dress designer about flying the dress over for fittings, sneaky calls from journalists fishing for scoops, and, for light relief, a few more personal appearances from Tweedledum and Tweedle-Don't-Even-Look-at-Me-You-Pig, who were even less cordial following 'incidents' on the hen/stag weekend in Las Vegas that neither of them could bring themselves to talk about.

Caroline, obviously, was the only other person who knew, because, as co-owner of the hotel, she was a co-signatory on the various confidentiality agreements Missy had made the hotel sign.

'It sounds like a nightmare,' she said cheerfully. 'Are you utterly at your wits' end? I bet the bookings are through the roof for next year.'

'No one knows,' I said. 'I've been keeping a very tight lid on things.'

'But it'll be worth it,' she reassured me. 'Puts those B-list Thornburys in the shade, doesn't it? Still no word of apology from the bolting clotheshorse?'

'Not from Flora,' I said. 'Julia's been out for a few lunches with Laurence.' I paused. 'The first few were apology lunches, apparently, but I don't know what the excuses for the others were. She's very keen on herbal medicines, apparently. And they go to the same osteopath in Highgate, so that's good.'

I waited for Caroline's cackle of approval, but instead, just heard a thoughtful *hmm*.

Should I ask if I'm still fixing up your ex-husband? I wondered crossly. No one at the Bonneville seemed to give me actual instructions for anything any more, while at the same time expecting me to have done things by telepathy.

Fortunately Caroline then changed the subject to the only thing I really wanted to talk about but couldn't ask about, for obvious reasons.

'You must be delighted to have got Joe out of your hair at last,' she said. 'I must say, it's nice having him home. Even if he is a bit . . . glum.'

'Glum?'

'Mmm. Keeps wandering about with this glum thinking face on. Going for long walks. I've been making him take the guests' dogs with him, but that's not what I brought him back to Wragley Hall for. What do you think it is, Rosie? Was there some girl trouble in London?'

'I don't know what's going on with Joe,' I said, which was the truth.

'Well, he won't talk to me about it, that's for sure,' she sighed. 'I suppose he'll just have to walk it out, whoever she is.'

And that wasn't what I wanted to hear at all, so I didn't ask any further.

At least planning the wedding with Emily was fun. I did wonder whether Emily Sharpe was such an amazing actress that she was hiding a reptilian dark side beneath the sunny transatlantic exterior, but eventually I came to the reluctant conclusion that she would have been just as nice if she'd stayed in London and I were organizing her wedding to an architect, rather than to the undead, half-wolverine seducer of Renaissance Venice.

She came back the week before the wedding to help sort out final details, but there wasn't much left to do. I had to invent an entirely unnecessary cake testing, so she wouldn't feel she'd missed out.

Emily and I were sitting in my office on Wednesday morning, sampling tiny squares of pastel genoise sponge (yes, she was so nice she was even actually *eating* the cake before her wedding) when she hesitated a couple of times, then said, 'Rosie. I've been meaning to ask you for ages. Who was that blond guy I met at Helen's wedding? The one who blanked me?'

'Joe?' My heart bumped in my chest, but I tried to make it sound casual. 'That was Joe Bentley Douglas. The owner's son.'

'Joe.' Emily groaned, and she covered her mouth. 'Oh, my God, it *was* him. I thought it was, then I thought, no that's just too weird, and then he left before I could ask . . .' She lifted her eyes to me, and I could see she was genuinely mortified. 'I thought my films had some freaky coincidences in them, but this is just too much.'

'You know him then?' I asked, twisting the knife in myself, more than in Emily.

She nodded, then winced. 'I do. What did he say?'

'It's not really any of my . . .'

Emily put her hand on mine. She was very good at theatrical gestures, I noticed.

Oh, stop it, I told myself. *She's just a friendly, tactile person. Like Joe.*

'He said you two dated in America,' I confessed. 'And you dumped him and never returned his calls.'

'Is that what he said?' Her beautiful eyes drooped.

'More or less.'

Emily chewed her lip, and then covered her face and made a muffled 'aarrrggghhh' noise.

'Rosie, this might be TMI,' she said through her fingers. 'But do you ever do shitty things you're not proud of, and hope they'll never come back to bite you – and they do?'

'They always do,' I said. 'Yet the noble stuff vanishes without a trace.'

She pummelled her own head, groaning, then looked up at me. 'I'm going to tell you this because I feel like maybe you can get Joe to forgive me? It's just so weird and coincidental. It has to be the universe pushing me to do it.'

'Joe's very big on the universe,' I said drily. 'He'd back you up on that.'

She sighed, and looked at me. I tried to keep my face neutral, even though my heart rate had just doubled.

'Okay, so, I met Joe while Ben and I were on a break.' Emily did guilty air hooks to show she knew it was a cliché. 'Ben had gone off to do a film in Canada; I'd just got down to the last two for a few projects and lost them. It's not always easy being an actor, dating an actor. Anyway, my American friend Amber was desperate to go to this beach party in Santa Cruz. I didn't want to go, but I did, to be her wingman, and I met Joe. And he was . . . well, you know him, right? He's lovely.'

I nodded. He was so much more than just lovely.

Emily gazed at the Bridelizer but she wasn't seeing it. 'It was one of those perfect holiday romances. Right place, right time. He taught me to surf, I taught him to make pancakes, we spent all day together, and all night, if you know what I mean. But it was intense, it wasn't going to last. It couldn't have. Even if Ben hadn't come back from Canada and proposed, which he did . . .' She looked genuinely guilty.

'Is that why you didn't return Joe's calls?'

'Yeah. I know. I'm not proud of that. Ben had to fly back to Europe to do some location filming, and I'd got a part this time, so I went with him. I didn't know how to handle it. I just thought it would be easier to put Joe and what we had in a box and leave it in California.'

'He didn't find it particularly easy.'

She pulled the layer of marzipan off her cake. 'No. I realize that. I don't think I'll ever forgive myself for that look on his face when he saw me here.'

'And you really had no idea this was his family's hotel?'

'Of course not! You think I'd have come here if I did?' Emily looked horrified. 'He never told me his parents had a hotel. He didn't even tell me he had a fancy surname – he was just Joe Bentley. I got the impression there was some sort of family business he wasn't interested in taking over, which was why he'd come out to the States, to do his own thing.'

And instead he'd ended up coming back, I thought. Back to the hotel he didn't really want to work in, to be bossed around by me, and then to find Emily there. No wonder he'd flipped out.

'Poor Joe,' I said aloud.

'Well, he's kind of an idealist.' Emily looked honestly at me. 'I guess you know him better than I do, but I never expected to find he was a *wedding coordinator*. He was so down on marriage. He used to say it was meaningless, but at the same time he'd be insanely idealistic about the perfect woman.'

'That's you.'

She shook her head. 'No. It's not me. His perfect woman's a lot more down-to-earth. He needs someone to balance him out. And, come on, I work in films. We all know there's no such thing as perfect. Even I don't look like Emily Sharpe half the time.'

We picked at our cakes in silence; then Emily said, 'Can you tell him all that? Can you explain?'

I felt my face go red. 'I don't think I'm the right person, to be honest. I think he needs to hear it from you.'

'Okay.' She wrinkled her nose, more at herself than anything else, I guessed. 'It's just . . . I feel so bad about this. I feel like I can't marry Ben knowing I've . . . knowing I've maybe broken Joe's heart. But he was so lovely . . .' She pulled herself together. 'What if I wrote a letter? Would that be enough?'

'I think that might help,' I said. 'But . . .' I hesitated. 'Be kind. I know it's hard, but your relationship meant a lot to him. If you could explain what he meant to you, not underselling it or giving him false hope. Just . . . recognizing it was the right thing at the right time. A part of who you both are now.'

'I like that,' said Emily. 'I'm going to do that. Thanks, Rosie.'

'Pleasure,' I said. It wasn't.

CHAPTER TWENTY-SEVEN

With Joe gone, and my desk full, I focused my energy on all the positive, happy, wonderful things going on in my life. Because for once, I had a lot of blessings to count. June was pleasantly warm; Emily wasn't a diva; I got an amazing discount on champagne flutes because I didn't care about negotiating like a hard-arse; but the truth was that without Joe around, for the first time my fourteen-hour days at the Bonneville were beginning to feel *too* long.

To my annoyance, Laurence didn't seem to appreciate the effort I was putting into being his deputy manager as well as everything else. He'd gone very vague again, and was spending quite a bit of time away from the hotel, not answering his phone. I knew I should be worried in case he'd had some new health scare, but frankly, I didn't have the energy. What little I had left after running round the hotel covering for Joe, Laurence and Helen was going into feeling unspecifically cross whenever I didn't have to deal with the public.

Worse – and this had *never* really happened before – I found myself feeling jealous of the brides who floated in, starry-eyed and drunk with love, to talk about their big days. Where was

I going to find that, wiring emergency buttonholes at two in the morning, or putting out two hundred gold chairs because everyone else had gone home?

Even the hotel seemed to be closing itself off to me. It had never felt so much like someone else's business as when I was letting myself into its empty heart, at the top of the building, behind the fire door.

The final straw came when the second Mrs Bentley Douglas arrived three days before the Benily wedding, just as my stress was reaching maximum velocity, and dropped Otto and Ripley off in my office, which was stacked with handmade name cards, crystal table settings and other fragile and expensive things.

'Only for a day. Or two. I'd have left them with Laurence, but he's nowhere to be found, as per usual,' she said, as Ripley tapped her way over to the window and started lisping 'All That Jazz' out of it as if it were a television screen.

'He's here,' I said. 'Did you check under his desk?'

'Of course I did,' she said over the tapping. 'And in that little room next to his office. I know all the tricks, Rosie, I used to help him hide from Caroline.'

'Then can I give you the number for our emergency nanny?' I was probably a bit spikier than I should be. 'Because much as I love spending time with Otto and Ripley,' I gave Otto a quick smile; he was sitting on my spare chair like a constipated owl, 'I'm about to go and deal with a lot of glass, and it would be awful if something happened.'

The door opened and Gemma bounced in. 'Rosie, I've got the – oh.' She tried to reverse her way out, but it was too late.

'Mummy, why is that lady so fat?' asked Otto, pointing at Gemma.

Gemma made a choking noise, but I was past caring.

'My assistant will take you two down to the restaurant and get you both an ice cream!' I announced. 'Won't you, Gemma? You will! Wonderful. Off you tap.'

When I'd shoved the three of them out of the office and closed the door, Ellie wrinkled her eyebrows sympathetically. Well, as much as they still could wrinkle. 'Rosie, can I give you some advice?'

I bit back the retort that since she'd worked in the hotel industry for about three years and I'd been here, on and off, since I was sixteen, I wasn't sure what that would be. But I was tired.

'Go on,' I said. 'Everyone else does.'

'You're working too hard.'

'No, no, it's fine, I—'

'You're not getting any younger,' she said brutally. 'And you've got to think about yourself. Laurence wants to hand this place on to his kids – it's all he's ever wanted. If he had his way, Otto and Ripley would be sent off to catering college now. Joe's being lined up as the manager, and even if you stay you'll never be in charge. Laurence will take advantage of you, just like he took me for granted, *and* Caroline. It's what he does.'

I thought this was pretty rich, coming from someone who was about to leave both her children with a woman who couldn't even keep a 'Thank you for arranging our wedding!' orchid alive beyond the honeymoon, but I said nothing.

She fixed me with a piercing look. 'You must have been head-hunted by now, yes?'

'Um . . .'

Ellie was sharp; she caught the brief flicker on my face. 'Well, don't be stupid, if someone's offered you a better job, for crying out loud, take it. Leave and come back if you have to. But don't end up like Caroline. Pouring your heart and soul into your new hotel because you let your old hotel screw up your family. There's more to life than folding other people's bloody towels into swans, Rosie.'

And suddenly, I saw the truth of what she was saying. Something clicked inside me. I couldn't stay here, regretting what hadn't happened with Joe. I had to do my own thing. Open myself up to new chances. Let the universe—

Oh, for God's sake.

'You can always come back,' said Ellie, then added over her shoulder, 'though I have no idea why you'd want to, seriously. The spa here is woeful these days.'

Caroline and Laurence were very surprised when I asked if I could have a meeting with them both in Laurence's office, the day before the biggest wedding of the year.

Caroline had come in specially from Oxfordshire, and Laurence had cancelled a morning's extended dental check-up to make the only time I had free, in between emailing confirmations of canapé calorie counts to Missy Hernandez and arranging nail technicians. I was secretly relieved I didn't have time to think too hard about what I was going to say, because my heart was flip-flopping back and forwards on the decision every quarter hour. But I had to do it. I *had* to.

'If this is about your bonus . . .' Laurence began nervously.

'. . . you've picked a punchy time to negotiate it,' Caroline finished for him. 'I can't say I'm not impressed, though. Have you been on another management course?'

'It's not that.' I fidgeted with my watch. I'd made notes and gone over and over my reasons, but now Caroline and Laurence were sitting behind the desk, the way I remembered them from my very first interview, surrounded by black-and-white photos of film stars and memorabilia of the hotel's glamorous past. They'd given me my first chance. They'd supported me and encouraged me. But at the same time, I could see that they'd let the hotel dictate their lives and ruin their marriage, and much as I respected them, I couldn't let it happen to me. I had to be bigger than my job. I had to have a life outside it.

'I don't know how to put this,' I said, 'but I've been offered a promotion, with another hotel. I've decided to take it. I'm giving you my notice, starting from Monday. I'll get this big wedding out of the way first, and obviously I'll work with my replacement to make the handover as smooth as possible.'

My confidence wobbled when I saw the shock on Laurence's face, and the disappointment on Caroline's.

'But we were going to promote you!' said Laurence.

I did feel a twinge of guilt about that; but at the same time

I knew the goal posts would have shifted again, come deadline time. They always did, with Laurence.

'You keep promising me promotions but the goal posts always move,' I said. 'This job is on the table. With no strings.'

'Oh, Rosie,' said Caroline. 'What can we offer you to make you stay?' She spun round to eyeball her ex-husband, who quailed in his chair. 'Did you negotiate the bonus for her target? I hope you weren't mean with it.' She turned back to me. 'We'll double whatever it was. What if we formally offer you the position of manager right now? Because it's yours.'

'It's not that,' I said. This was agony. 'I just think . . . maybe it's time I set myself a new challenge. I love working here, but . . .' I swallowed. I was on the verge of tears. 'I need to feel appreciated for what I know I can do.'

Laurence coughed. 'You've had a hard year, and I know we don't show our appreciation enough. But, Rosie, you understand this hotel. You bring so much of yourself to your job.'

'Maybe that's the problem. I feel, Laurence . . .' It was all too late. 'I feel as if you take it for granted that everyone loves this hotel so much that they'll sacrifice everything for it. Social life, relationships, free time, promotion . . .'

I glanced at Caroline. Laurence had lost the one woman who properly understood him because he'd made her put his stupid hotel first, instead of their marriage. And I'd started to turn into an automaton too, telling brides what kind of weddings they should have, to fit the hotel's demands. Joe had shown me that.

'The Bonneville's a wonderful place,' I said, 'but it shouldn't be more important than people. Nothing should.'

Caroline looked taken aback, but then her expression melted into a sad one. Laurence just looked taken aback.

'I understand what you're saying,' she said gently. 'There's nothing we can say to make you stay?'

You can make your son come back, I thought. *And wave a magic wand. And fill the sky with magic wishing helicopters.*

I didn't say that, obviously. I shook my head and tried to look like the slick business professional I didn't feel like inside.

And then there was a brief knock on the door, and to everyone's surprise, Joe barged in. When he saw the three of us – particularly me – he stopped but, to his credit, didn't back out. He stood in the doorway, filling it with his off-duty checked shirt and jeans.

'Oh, *here* he is,' said Caroline sarcastically. 'They seek him here, they seek him there. They seek Joe Bentley everywhere. Where did you get to? There are five dogs back at Wragley Hall missing their walker.'

Joe shoved his hand into his messy blond hair. It had grown since I'd seen him last; it was falling into his eyes. 'Yeah, sorry, Mum, I just needed some space.'

'Your mother's been very worried,' said Laurence.

'And very understaffed,' she added. 'I had to let Alec show that couple round. They're not getting married at Wragley Hall now, you won't be surprised to hear. Although the groom is coming back for an extreme survival stag weekend.'

'Yeah, well, that's why I'm here,' said Joe. He looked directly at me, and I felt a shiver run across my skin. 'I know Rosie's understaffed for the wedding at the weekend, since I – since I walked out, so I'm back to help with that.'

'You don't have to,' I said at once, feeling my face turn red and hot. 'It's all under control.'

'No, that's a *good* idea,' said Caroline. 'You need to pick up as much from Rosie as you can, Joe, while she's still here.'

'While she's still here?' Joe glanced up, surprised 'Why? Where's she going? Have you poached her, Mum?'

'If only.' Caroline seemed genuinely sorrowful. 'I'm sorry to say Rosie's working out her notice and leaving us.'

Joe turned to me, and I couldn't read his expression; it was guarded, but his eyes moved quickly over me, as if he wanted to say more but didn't know how. 'I'm sorry to hear that,' he said stiffly. 'I hope it's nothing . . . we've done.'

'No.' I shook my head. 'Just an offer I couldn't refuse.'

An awkward, sad silence descended on the room, and I tried to think what Ellie or Helen would say now. Or Emily. Emily would have some charming way of diffusing tension. I wished I could be more like Emily.

'So . . .' Laurence opened the globe-shaped cocktail cabinet. 'Anyone fancy some wheatgrass? I know I do.'

'If it's okay with everyone else, I've got to make some calls,' I said, and excused myself.

I heard the door open, and the rustling sound of footsteps following me down the carpeted corridor.

'Rosie? Wait.'

I stopped without turning, then felt Joe touch my arm. The

skin tingled where he touched it. Maybe he felt it, because he drew his hand away almost at once.

'It's nothing to do with me, is it?' he asked. 'Please don't leave on my account. I'm thinking of going back to the States, in any case.'

'Are you?' A cold breeze went through me. I made myself look at him, a forced cheerful expression on my face.

He nodded, and bit his lip. 'It's one option.'

I knew I should say something, but I didn't know what. He seemed to be struggling with the right words, and my own track record in that department was so woeful that I'd only make it worse.

'You don't have to help tomorrow,' I said. 'I meant it about everything being under control. I can see it'd be painful to be—'

'I'm not going to try to stop the wedding, if that's what you're thinking,' he said.

'I didn't think you were,' I lied.

Had Emily written that letter to him? I'd forwarded some mail on to him at Wragley Hall, but nothing that looked like a life-changing, heart-breaking love letter.

'I want to be there to help you.' Joe held my gaze for a long moment, then said, 'I'll pick up the schedule for tomorrow from Gemma.'

Then he turned and walked off. No apology, no explanation, nothing.

Charming.

You're doing the right thing, I told myself. *The right thing.*

*

I know I said that I liked a few tiny details in a wedding to go wrong so I could fix them, but I'd ironed out every possible snag in Emily Sharpe's wedding so firmly that when the day finally dawned, there were no tiny details that *could* go wrong.

No. Just whacking great enormous ones.

The day got off to a brilliant start when I checked with Helen and Dino that the wines for the evening meal had been set aside – and we discovered that the suppliers had delivered ten cases of hazelnut liqueur, not the exquisite Tokay Benedict had requested to go with the pudding. Dino went into a very Italian meltdown, Helen had to re-source the wine, which, it turned out, was quite rare, and – I'm cutting this short, you understand – the upshot was that Wynn and his trusty Volvo were dispatched to a warehouse in Wembley to collect it.

That was the first cock-up, all before I'd had the special bridal breakfast of fresh croissants and coffee in silver pots sent up to Emily and her attendants, getting ready in fits of giggles and tears in the bridal suite. I took the trays up myself on a cart, partly to wish them well for the day, but also to check that there wasn't anything I needed to nip in the bud there.

(Apart from a minor outbreak of stress rash on Emily's sister and a missing pair of shoes, it was all fine. I'd banned mobile phones in the bridal suite, which also helped the stress levels.)

For the rest of the morning I whizzed around, getting Nevin in place for the pre-wedding photos, ushering the hair and make-up team around, and keeping the peace between Tam and the hired-in security guys, and I thought I'd had my only cock-up when the next one reared its ugly head.

I was on my way back up to Emily's suite with more coffee when I heard two voices coming from nowhere. *Fuuuuuurious* voices. It was as if the hotel were being haunted by the Ghosts of Acrimonious Divorces Past, or the worst Hogwarts portraits ever.

'Hello? Hello?' bellowed a fruity British male voice. 'Nope, it's stopped. I think it's broken.'

'Well, duh! That's what happens when you press all the buttons at once, you complete . . . you complete . . . !'

'Don't tell me you've run out of words?'

'Polite ones, yes.'

I stopped, entranced despite myself.

'Where's your phone, Magnus?'

'In my pocket.'

'I'm not going into your pocket, if that's what you want. Just give it to me! We need to call someone.'

'If you'd let me finish . . . it's in my pocket of *my morning coat*, which is in my room.'

'It's not a coat, it's a jacket.'

'We call it a coat. Don't you go to any weddings with proper etiquette? Anyway, where's your phone?'

'Does this dress look like it's got room for a phone?'

'You want me to look?'

I decided to put Chloë out of her misery. 'Hello?' I called at the lift doors. 'It's Rosie. I'm so sorry, I don't know what's happened, but we'll get you out of there in no time. Just keep calm, and don't . . .'

I'd just told two people to keep calm. The two people, after me, least likely to respond well to that suggestion.

'Um, take deep breaths and I'll be right back,' I said.

Tempting as it was to leave them there for a while, I dashed off to find someone who could release them before they either throttled each other or made up so violently the lift was broken forever. And yes, I did wish Joe was with me to deal with it. He could have turned a crisis into an anecdote before you could say hashtag awkward.

I was downstairs waiting on hold at the reception desk for the lift engineer – out fixing a lift round the corner – when Gemma appeared looking shell-shocked. When she deliberately waited until Emily's hair and make-up team had gone past in a cloud of Elnett and shrieking, I knew whatever had shocked her must be bad.

I laid my head briefly on the mahogany counter. *I give up,* I thought. *This wedding isn't going to be perfect. It's going to be a complete disaster.*

But what had Joe said? That it was the little things that made each wedding special to the couple? That something would always go wrong, and that's what made the most precious memories of the day, not all the things that went perfectly that no one noticed?

As I thought that a funny calm spread over me, the same calm you get at the end of the day when you take a very tight pair of shoes off.

This wedding was not going to be perfect. It already wasn't. And how many people knew that? Not many.

'Rosie?' came Gemma's tentative voice.

I raised my head, steeled myself, and got my pen out to add to the growing list of things I needed to do before the afternoon. 'Go on, what is it?'

'Flora Thornbury,' she whispered. 'She's here.'

'What?' The pen fell from my fingers and I scrabbled to pick it up. We hadn't heard from Flora in months, and *now* she turned up, wanting VIP treatment on the day she'd blown off? 'What's she doing here? She's not on the guest list.'

'No, she's in the bar.'

'Why?' It had only just gone ten. 'Has she forgotten she's not getting married? Is it still in her diary and the silly mare's just trotted along here anyway?'

'I don't know. Milo's not with her. She keeps asking for Joe.' Gemma dropped her voice. 'I think she might be a bit . . . T-I-P-S-Y.'

'Oh, great,' I said. The last thing I needed with actual, real international celebrities turning up any moment was a pissed minor British model falling around the place. Then I said, 'Oh, *great*,' with more enthusiasm. Someone with as little body fat as Flora had to pass out quickly. 'Give her two more drinks, Dino's strongest, then put her in a taxi. With Joe, if you have to. Kill two birds with one stone.'

As I said it, out of habit, I suddenly wasn't sure if I *wanted* Joe out of action. I needed him around, where he could help me out with his cool head and refusal to be wound up. A pang bloomed in my stomach. I needed Joe here, but I could never ever tell him.

Pull yourself together, Rosie, I told myself.

'Are you sure there's no room for her? She was saying something about getting some publicity for the hotel?' Gemma looked hopeful. 'I recognized a couple of the friends she's got with her . . .'

'Think about it, Gemma.' I gave her a *Seriously?* look. 'A drunk supermodel crashing a Hollywood A-lister's wedding – is that the sort of publicity we want?'

'No.'

'No. So get rid of her. No, wait. Get Tam to keep an eye on her, so Emily's security people don't chuck her out, *then* get rid of her.' I turned back to the phone, discovered that the lift engineer was going to be 'at least another two hours', then I hung up. 'Wait, before you do that, does Tam still have a contact number for his mate who was in the SAS? They're good at getting people out of small spaces, aren't they?'

I thought that was it. Once I'd got Magnus and Chloë released from the lift – looking rather pink, I noticed, and rumpled, although I didn't want to know any more than that – I went through all my checklists determined to find *anything* that could go wrong. I hadn't seen much of Joe that morning, besides catching sight of him moving chairs or helping with wine; Emily hadn't mentioned him either, but when I'd brought her bouquet and floral headdress in, she'd given me a private smile and a squeeze of the hand. I know, I was hoping she'd throw a tiny diva strop, just so I could see one in action, but she didn't. Not even when Missy texted her to remind her to do the same forehead-to-forehead pose she'd done with Benedict in the famous *Dark Moon* wedding scene.

The ceremony was due to start at three o'clock sharp, and at half past two I went downstairs to check in with the two registrars conducting the ceremony. They normally arrived at least an hour in advance to get everything ready, and also to scoff the complimentary refreshments we laid on. I'd delegated the job of looking after them to Gemma, who was much better at making small talk about non-religious but still spiritual music options than I was.

I was waylaid en route by a couple of guests needing directions, and then by Laurence, who claimed not to be feeling very well, so by the time I found Gemma hovering in the hallway between the main hotel and the gardens, it was nearly twenty to three.

'Where are the registrars?' I asked, checking my clipboard. Guests were already taking their seats outside and the string quartet was playing classical versions of rom-com themes. 'I need to run through some things with them.'

'They're not here yet.'

A tingly sensation spread through my bones. 'What? Why didn't you tell me before now? Have you rung them?'

'Of course I have,' said Gemma. 'I've been ringing since two. I didn't tell you before now because I knew you'd flip.'

I gripped my head. 'They can't *both* be held up! Aren't they supposed to travel separately, so this doesn't happen? Like the royal family?'

'They do. Freda's stuck on a bus, and I can't get hold of Jan. She's probably on the Underground. Calm down, Rosie—'

That was the final straw, I'm sorry to say.

'Calming down is not an option!' I roared. 'I've just got two people out of a lift using secret and possibly illegal SAS methods, and seven thousand pounds' worth of dessert wine crossing Mayfair in Wynn's Volvo! I will not be defeated by the London bloody transport system!'

Gemma's eyes widened as two guests walked past behind me.

'Sorry, I'm sorry,' I muttered. 'It's . . . I think they put something extra in the coffee.'

Helen suddenly materialized from behind a seven-foot arrangement of lilies and roses, phone in one hand, the wine receipt in the other.

'Wynn's unloading the booze with Dino, and I've got Freda on the phone.' She stuck one finger in her ear and clamped her mobile to the other, as if she was breaking a story on BBC News 24. 'Where are you now, Freda? She's getting off the number nineteen and she's walking down . . . she's nearly at Shaftesbury Avenue!'

'Brilliant!' said Gemma.

'Shaftesbury Avenue's twenty minutes away!' It was now quarter to three. Sweat prickled under my armpits.

'Freda, what kind of shoes are you wearing?' Helen asked urgently. 'Sensible ones. Of course you are. Can you run in them? Well, can you . . . trot?'

We all stared at her, twitchy with nerves.

'Can you walk a bit quicker?' said Helen in a very coaxing voice. 'I know, plantar fasciitis is awful. Poor you. It's just that we have about fourteen Hollywood stars here, and three of them have got helicopters on a parking meter at City airport and . . . Oh, lovely. Well, we'll get some ice in a big bowl ready for afterwards. Good girl!'

She snapped the phone down. 'She's on her way.'

I checked my watch and glanced up to the fountain, where Benedict and Magnus were already in their seats, along with family, friends and several high-profile shapeshifters.

I had to get back upstairs fast. Emily would be almost ready to leave now. In fact, if she was following the checklist, she would be getting into the lift.

Helen grabbed my arm. 'Stop,' she said. 'Breathe. It'll be fine. If someone needs to do a song and dance to distract the crowd for a while, you've got professionals here. You can't control everything.'

I gazed up at her, crisp and elegant in her special pale-blue events suit. When I'd told Helen I'd given in my notice, we'd had a cry. In fact, that was the only moment I'd wondered if I'd made a mistake. I would miss working with my best mate, in so many ways. But she'd told me I needed to go, and had given me another version of her 'let life happen to you' speech.

'I want this to be my best wedding,' I said. 'I want to go out on a high.'

'I know.' She gripped my hand. 'But that won't happen if you have cardiac arrest, will it? The registrars will be here when they're here. These things happen. It's not like the bride and groom haven't turned up, is it?'

I flinched. Then I took a deep breath. She was right.

'We'll just have to delay Emily somehow,' I said, but as I did, I heard Gemma squeak, and I knew what had happened.

Slowly the three of us turned, and there, partially hidden inside the door to the hotel foyer on her father's morning-suited arm, was Emily in her cream ballerina-length wedding dress, a thick circlet of blood-red roses balanced on her head like a crown, and a euphoric expression lighting up her heart-shaped face. The funny thing was, most regular brides looked like film stars when the make-up artist had finished. Emily the film star looked like the most beautiful girl-next-door in the world. Albeit in a ten-thousand-pound Vivienne Westwood dress.

Chloë stood behind her, still doing deep yoga breaths through alternate nostrils, and casting death looks down the aisle to Magnus; the two flower girls were fidgeting with their baskets of petals; and behind the group was Nevin, taking photographs.

I hurried over as nonchalantly as I could, so as not to give anything away to the guests. Five minutes late, fine. Ten minutes, muttering. Fifteen minutes and Twitter would be alive, even though Gemma had personally organized the phone amnesty in reception, on Missy's specific instructions.

'Emily, you look like an angel,' I said. How had I ever imagined Joe could get over this? She was a once-in-a-lifetime girl.

She beamed. 'Sorry! I know I'm early! I just couldn't wait! I had to come down!'

'I'm more nervous than she is,' admitted her father. He was from Birmingham. 'That photographer! And someone's powdered my head. I don't know how she does it, all these folk watching. My heart's racing.'

'In that case, let's not rush.' *Thank you, universe.* 'Why don't you . . .' I steered them firmly back towards the calm green anteroom '. . . have a quick glass of champagne in here to steady your nerves? We've got five minutes. The harpist is still playing.'

Emily glanced out at the garden.

'Don't worry, Ben's there! Everything's fine!' I signalled to the waiters to bring champagne and the tiniest, least greasy canapés. 'You take a second, relax, be in the moment, I'll be right back . . .'

I marched back out again, but even Helen was looking anxious. 'Still nothing.'

'Where's Joe?'

'I don't know.'

Why did that make me feel so panicky? I realized, with a sinking sensation, that I needed Joe here. I needed him to say something calming, something sensible, something . . . really irritating so at least I'd know what to do.

Helen touched my arm, 'Rosie, you'll have to say something. Tell them there's a short delay because of the registrars.'

'I can't! It's not my hotel. Where's Laurence?'

'Being sick.'

We spun around. Joe had appeared from nowhere. He'd changed into a linen suit, which made him look just as much of a movie star as the real ones. More so. My heart thudded in my chest. A lot more so. His blond hair, darker than when he'd arrived straight from the beach last year, was brushed back, and his white shirt was open at the neck, revealing the soft hollow at the base of his throat. He looked more London now, and yet even further out of my league.

He and Emily – I could see it now. I could see exactly why they'd had that wonderful romance. They were both so beautiful.

I swallowed, and tried to focus on the moment. 'Oh dear. Is he all right?'

Joe pulled a face. 'Not really. Well, come on – it has to be bad if he's not out here hobnobbing with Meryl Streep.'

'It's not Meryl Streep,' said Gemma. 'It's—'

'Gemma, you know I don't care who these people are,' he said.

'Joe, there's a problem, the registrars are late. You'll have to say something,' said Helen. 'You're second in command, after Laurence.'

Second in command? What did that make me? *Third?* After all the work I'd done?

That did it.

'No, if anyone's second in command, it's me,' I said, and marched towards the front. I thought I heard Helen mutter something about that being the way to spring me into action, but I didn't care. I wasn't going to risk Joe getting up there and . . . I put the thought out of my mind, and concentrated on walking without falling over in my new higher-heeled shoes.

That was all well and good until I got to the front, and about the first five faces I saw I recognized from the sides of buses and *Heat* magazine. Forget what they say about celebs being airbrushed and styled. They look like that in real life, too. It's *really* unnerving.

'Ladies and gentlemen,' I began in a croaky voice, then cleared my throat. 'Sorry, ladies and gentlemen, I'm afraid we have a slight delay in proceedings, due to a technical problem with . . .'

I saw several people slip their phones out of their pockets. My heart sank. I'd told Gemma to persuade people to put their phones in the special baskets. Emily didn't want back-of-row-12 photos appearing on the internet.

'A technical problem with . . .'

Someone took a photo of me, and I flinched. Funny how my worst wedding nightmare had always been the one where Anthony didn't turn up. It had just been overtaken – by a country mile – by this one, where I was centre of attention all over again.

My throat went dry, and my tongue stuck to the roof of my mouth as every face in the crowd turned my way, expectantly. Oh God. My whole head had gone blank. All I could hear was a buzzing in my ears that had nothing to do with my fascinator.

To my horror, Joe was walking up the aisle. But he was walking in a completely different way: loose-limbed, professional, in charge. Towards me.

He smiled as he joined me at the front, and then I felt a hand on my arm. A hand that patted me, then firmly moved me bodily to one side.

'Ladies and gentlemen,' said Joe, with the same confidence that both Caroline and Laurence had at their fingertips. 'I know it's traditional for the bride to keep everyone waiting at cere-monies of this sort, but today I have to apologize profusely on behalf of the hotel. We're currently missing a pair of registrars. What can I say? I'm sure you've all seen enough Richard Curtis films to know that London transport likes to play a part in Hollywood weddings!'

I slid my eyes sideways in horror. Ironically, very much the same way that Emily had slid her eyes sideways in the big mirror when Contessa Vittoria shapeshifted up behind her in the last film.

'So, anyway, while we're waiting.' He'd actually started to sound like Hugh Grant now. Or Colin Firth. I looked around the assembled guests, now openly staring at the pair of us, as if we were about to break into a song and dance version of 'Love and Marriage'. 'There's something I would like to say – to the bride and groom.'

And then I knew that this day could not get any more out of my control, so I gave up.

CHAPTER TWENTY-EIGHT

The entire congregation fell silent, and unexpectedly, I suddenly felt very light, as if I was observing all this from three rows back in the congregation. I could almost see my own horrified face.

This was it. Not only was Joe Bentley Douglas about to torpedo my chic and sophisticated wedding ceremony with some half-baked universe-based guff, he was probably going to tell beautiful, famous Emily that he was still in love with her. Maybe not on purpose, but it would be so obvious to everyone from his body language that he might as well strip off and throw himself at her feet.

Some higher instinct seized me. St Ramada, goddess of the hospitality industry, maybe. I had to stop him. I just had to stall until Freda arrived.

'Um, no, it's fine.' I coughed. 'I've, er, I've thought of what I was going to say.'

I looked up, and at the back of the garden, Helen covered her face with her hands, unable to watch. So I stared at the windows of the hotel out of everyone's sightline. 'Before we begin, I wanted to say a few words about love.'

Joe looked at me sideways. 'So did I.'

'Well, my . . . thing about love is . . . better!'

I would tell you I was dying inside, but the weird force seemed to be holding me up. The congregation tittered. It probably looked as if we'd been practicing this tedious stand-up routine on purpose, just to give Emily and Ben's wedding a 'worst Oscars ever' touch.

Joe was opening his mouth to argue; I had to get on with it. With luck the registrars would arrive before I had to get too far into anything more complicated than 'Marriage is like a packet of Hobnobs,' or whatever it was that vicars normally came out with before the main event.

But what to say? What was marriage like? Apart from Hobnobs.

I gripped my clipboard, and had a sudden brainwave.

'I'm a wedding planner,' I began, 'and I've got a checklist of everything I need to do to make the wedding perfect. The seating plan, the RSVPs. The groom's here – check. Rings here – check. And, er, the bride *is* here, by the way, just in case anyone was wondering . . .'

There was a murmur of amusement, which I gratefully acknowledged while I glanced at the door. Still no sign of Freda and/or Jan.

'I might have hit a snag on *my* checklist with the registrars,' I said desperately, 'but Emily and Benedict have ticked every box on theirs. Emily was telling me only yesterday that her wedding gift from Benedict was a season ticket to Lord's Cricket Ground. Now, if a woman's prepared to sit through an entire five-day test, she's obviously ticking patience, understanding and the very highest form of love!'

It was corny, but the congregation laughed. I was going to move on to something about bowling maidens over when I felt Joe shift me to one side.

'However,' he said, 'the point *I* was going to make is that despite Rosie's laudable efforts to make everything perfect for Emily and Ben, today isn't perfect, and that's a good thing.'

'I – what?'

'I've met a lot of brides in my short but colourful career as a wedding planner,' he informed the crowd, conversationally, 'and they're all dead-set on one thing – having the perfect day. Much to my colleague's horror, I've tried to talk them out of that, with varied success. Because, being a bloke, I've always been a big believer in human *im*perfection. It makes us interesting, and it makes us open to growth.'

I closed my eyes and tried to stay calm, while racking my brain for something funny to say. We were two breaths away from the universe and/or some terrible John Lennon quote, but at least this didn't sound like an attempted coup on the groom. So far.

'I definitely didn't think the perfect woman existed,' he went on. 'But then, like Benedict, I met a woman who is everything I'd ever imagined a woman could be, and it blew me away. Funny, clever, thoughtful, smart, and movie-star beautiful.' As he said it, I wanted to crawl away and die. But I couldn't. I was trapped on a stage in front of two hundred people, and I had to keep smiling like a demented newsreader while Joe described

Emily again, with that hypnotized expression I remembered from Valentine's Day. The *she's perfect* one.

No one had ever said that about me.

'She's not perfect in a *boring* way,' Joe explained, as if anyone cared. 'She's got her hang-ups and bad habits. She drinks way too much coffee, for a start. And she won't surf because she thinks she might get slammed in the face with the board and lose all her teeth.'

The congregation laughed. I didn't. I thought that was totally reasonable. Sensible, even, for a movie star. It was why *I'd* never surfed, and I only needed my teeth for eating, not flashing in *Vogue* shoots. Emily and I had so much in common. We could have been friends if we'd met at school.

'If anything, this incredible, intelligent, *indescribable* woman is so obsessed with everything being perfect that she completely misses how great she is already, imperfections and all. The only thing that could make her even more amazing than she is now would be if she'd only let someone into her life to mess it up a bit.' Joe ruffled his hair sheepishly, and despite the leadenness of my heart, I felt a lurch of desire. I would miss him.

'Apparently that's what boyfriends are for,' he added, and everyone laughed. 'Husbands, even more so.'

Joe was really winning the crowd over, I thought, looking around. Some couples had slipped their hand into each other's; a few were leaning their heads on their husbands' shoulders, fancy hats permitting.

I'd never felt so single in my life.

He coughed, and I guessed he was getting to the point at last.

'So when I look at Emily and Ben today, even though they're famous and successful, and from the outside everyone will imagine their life is perfect, I hope that they'll each have the little imperfections that, when put together, will make their relationship last a lifetime. Like the lumps on jigsaw pieces, or the patterns on tyres that help them stay on the road. Imperfections are what help us stick together. To give us room to breathe, to heat up and cool down. To grow.'

He stopped and looked at me, and I glared back, thinking, *Why are you looking at me with that dozy expression like I'm supposed to say, yes, go for it, run off with her like in* The Graduate.

'I just hope this perfect woman I know will let someone in to do the same for her,' he said.

Someone in the crowd went, 'Aaaah.' And then a few more did.

Joe smiled tentatively, and did a sort of prompting nod, as if he'd expected a reaction from me by now.

'What?' I hissed, a bit ungraciously, I will admit.

'I mean you,' he muttered under his breath. 'You daft cow.'

He meant me. Joe was talking about me.

I opened my mouth, but nothing came out. (Thank God.)

Joe nodded gently, his gaze never leaving my face. 'Definitely you.'

And my heart filled with a sudden rush of happiness, then seemed to burst out of me, rising into the air like a helium balloon, or a Chinese lantern, or a white dove. Up, and up, and up, past the tree, past the windows, up past the honeymoon suite balcony. I felt so light, looking into Joe's eyes, that I could have floated right away.

I felt I'd come home.

The registrars arrived at the moment he took my hands and led me off the little platform, but apparently no one even noticed.

'That was very bad form,' I said, once the service was under way and the crowd was listening to a top soprano from the Royal Opera House sing 'My Heart Will Go On'. It was awful, but I didn't mind. It was Emily's mother's favourite song. 'Hijacking someone else's wedding like that.'

Joe didn't seem unduly bothered. 'Oh, they love it, actor types,' he said. 'Bit of drama. Someone will be commissioning a screenplay about it, just watch.'

'I hope they get someone glamorous to play me,' I said.

'No, they'll get a sitcom actress doing her first film,' said Joe affectionately, picking a stray petal off my hair. 'One that scrubs up well, though.'

We were sitting under the tree, in a corner of the garden where no one could see us but where I could keep an eye on any major disaster that might unfold. Not that I cared about that either. I didn't care about anything, apart from Joe's hand holding mine. He'd been holding it for ten minutes now, and our skin was getting a bit clammy, but again, it didn't even register. A happy serenity had come over me.

'I should probably have told you I was going to say something,' he went on thoughtfully, 'but I didn't plan it. It just seemed like the right thing to do at the time.'

'You don't think Emily minded you stealing the limelight at her wedding?'

'To be honest . . .' Joe screwed up his face. 'It's her own fault. I got this letter from her while I was at Mum's – she basically said everything you'd said—'

'Which was everything you'd said to me.'

'But she said it in a kinder way? That everyone needs a fling like the one we had in their past, to show them how incredible a strong everyday love is.' He reached into his pocket, as if he was going to show me the letter, and I made *no no no no* gestures. 'What she actually said was that having a Ferrari for a fortnight on set made her appreciate how much she liked driving her regular car that always started and fit her real life.'

'And you were like the Ferrari?' Emily was so nice.

More to the point, she'd described her film star husband as a regular car? I'd have to tell Gemma that. Or maybe not.

'I was. Well, I can see the comparison. But . . .' Joe turned my face to his, with his finger under my chin, and gazed at me with a glint in his eye. 'I got the letter, and it was exciting for about ten minutes, then I suddenly realized that I wanted to tell you about it. And you weren't there. And then I *really* had a moment.'

'I know,' I said softly. 'I think I had the same one.'

'Wragley Hall seemed pointless without you there. The countryside, pointless. Hotels, pointless. Meals, pointless. I wanted you to be there, telling me how it could all be better, or different, or whatever.'

'Nagging.'

'Not nagging. Sharing. Living.' His lips parted slightly as his eyes locked with mine, and I felt a shiver run through my whole body.

My heart was really thumping now, making me feel vivid and alive and aware of every single breath I was taking.

'I've been stupid,' said Joe. 'But I'm learning. Can you put up with my many imperfections in the meantime?'

'Your useless hospital corners? Your messy eating habits?' I reached my hand out and touched his ear, the tanned skin of his chin. It was thrilling to have unspoken permission to touch him at last. I had to force myself not to trace his cheekbones, his long nose, his wide mouth. Those tattoos on the base of his spine. Those long, golden-haired legs with the lean muscles. 'I think so. The rest is pretty fine.'

Joe took my hand and pulled me nearer to him, sliding his arm around my waist. 'I didn't want to do this up there,' he said. 'I mean, I don't hold with all your ridiculous wedding etiquette but I do know *this* is bad form.'

With each word he'd leaned a little closer until now our noses were almost touching. A tiny gap of air was all that separated our bodies, and it fizzed and sparked with electricity. I could feel his warm breath on my face, and my heart was beating so hard in my chest I was surprised I couldn't see it.

'What's bad form?' I breathed.

'For two people to kiss at a wedding before the bride and groom,' he whispered, and slowly he bent his head to mine, closing his eyes and touching his lips against my surprised mouth. His lips were warm and soft, but then more insistent, and I let myself sink into a kiss that felt both familiar and strange, as the nearness of his body, the heat of his skin through the fine linen shirt, overwhelmed all my senses at once. He was delicious. Perfect and delicious.

'Flora Thornbury's in the pool,' said someone about a million miles away. Gemma, I think.

'What? In the pool here?' said another unfamiliar voice.

'Yes, completely naked!'

I should really do something about that, I thought. *Send Tam down with security, or call Missy, or Laurence. Or someone.*

Then I thought, *No. I've got better things to do.* And I tangled my hands in Joe's thick blond hair and pulled him closer, so I could kiss him again.

THE END

(Roll romantic credits; top opera singer to sing song)

LONDON WEDDINGS

Details supplied by Rosie McDonald, wedding consultant, Bonneville Hotel.

Caroline Bentley Douglas, owner of Wragley Hall, Little Oaks, Oxon, and Laurence Bentley Douglas, owner of the Bonneville Hotel, London W1

How they met: At the British Hospitality Awards dinner in 1984, when the bride's quick thinking saved the groom from an allergic reaction to a prawn *vol au vent*. The couple married soon after, raising two sons, Joseph and Alec, and co-managed the family hotel, but separated in 2007. However, recent events brought the pair back together, only for them to find that, rather like the recently renovated hotel itself, some romances just improve with age.

Proposal: the groom originally planned to surprise the bride during a private chef's table dinner in the award-winning hotel restaurant, Daffodil, but instead, thanks to a surprise London rain shower, popped the question under a tree in nearby Green Park.

Venue: The wedding took place in the rose garden of the Bonneville Hotel, now managed by the couple's elder son, Joseph, and his fiancée, Rosie McDonald.

Bride's outfit: The bride wore a knee-length oyster satin dress with matching embroidered coat, and a Philip Treacy feather headpiece. Her 'something old' was the groom, her 'something new', their plans for a health spa/luxury hotel in Scotland; the 'something borrowed' and 'something blue' was the pen provided by the wedding organiser to sign the register at the last minute.

Groomsmen: Best man was Joseph Bentley Douglas, assisted by Alec Bentley Douglas.

Bridesmaids: There were no bridesmaids. The bride was attended by her two Labradors, Winston and Horatio, and was given away by her father, Sir Devonald Craig-Lockart.

Vows: The couple wrote their own vows for the ceremony.

In addition to their promise to love and cherish each other properly this time, the groom also vowed to listen to the end of every sentence, and to leave tea to brew properly, while the bride promised not to interrupt, and to take a daily multivitamin.

Witnesses: Model Flora Thornbury and Hollywood actors Benedict and Emily Quayle were witnesses to the wedding, as all three had played a special role in bringing the happy couple back together.

Flowers: The bride's bouquet was made up of forget-me-nots, lilies of the valley to symbolise 'returned love', and ivy to symbolise fidelity and friendship, and the couple married under an arch of cream roses entwined with myrtle. The reception was decorated to match the Art Deco theme.

Jewellery: The bride wore a string of pearls from the groom's grandmother, Maude Bentley Douglas, founder of the hotel's famous 'Farewell to the Year'.

Reception: An evening reception for three hundred people was held in the ballroom after the earlier wedding ceremony for close family and friends. Music was provided by the Jack Tempest Swing Orchestra, a late supper of oysters, champagne and bacon sandwiches was served, and a fleet of black taxis ferried guests home in style at three a.m.

First dance: 'The Second Time Around' by Frank Sinatra. Followed by a flashmob dance of 'Oops I Did It Again', led by Joe Bentley Douglas and Ripley Bentley Douglas Perkins.

Honeymoon: After a night as first guests in the Bonneville's newly renovated honeymoon suite, the bride and groom spent three days in a luxury health spa, followed by ten days touring the vineyards of California in a vintage sports car.

Photographer: Charles Nevin.

Videographer: There was no videographer. The best memories are the ones in your heart (which also has a very kind filter after a toast or two).

Acknowledgements

Tucked in the back of Rosie McDonald's *Advice to Brides* pack is a list of etiquette musts, and top of that list is *Write Your Thank You Notes*. *Prompt, heartfelt and handwritten*, she bosses. These aren't handwritten (or particularly prompt, sorry), but they're very heartfelt.

Thank you to my brilliant, patient, and very funny editor, Kathryn Taussig at Quercus Books, and to Jo Dickinson, a tremendous support and inspiration over the past year; and also to the whole team at Quercus for their amazing enthusiasm. No (wedding) party is a party without the magnificent maid of honour, Lizzy Kremer, ably assisted in bouquet-tossing and hankie-passing by Harriet Moore, and everyone at David Higham Associates.

And finally, thank you to the friends who've invited me to their weddings over the years, beautiful brides every one. I'm sorry for line-outing the bouquet on a few occasions, very sorry for some of the after-hours dancing, and please believe me when I say that none of these brides are based on you.